SHIVER

Tiffinie Helmer

ISBN-10: 061585754X
ISBN-13: 978-0615857541

Cover Designs by Kelli Ann Morgan with Inspire Creative Services
Interior book design by Bob Houston eBook Formatting

Publishing History: First Edition
Published by The Story Vault

ACKNOWLEDGEMENTS

First, to my grandmother, Afton Blanc, for sharing with me your love of legends, passion for Alaskan Native Arts, and breeding and training your own sled dog team. You never let anyone stop you from doing whatever you wanted to do. What an amazing example you were to a impressionable young girl. You are still, and have always been, my hero. I miss you every day.

To Paige Woodson for all the medical help in how to treat a bear trap injury and the resulting deep puncture wounds. Any mistakes made are mine and not of the sweetest, most caring RN I know, the exact opposite of my demon nurse Eva.

To Mrs. Young, my Lathrop High School art teacher, for imparting in me a love for throwing pottery that is still with me today. I entered your art class thinking of how I could skip out since I had no talent for drawing. You put a lump of clay in my hand and a potter was born.

To Janet Juengling-Snell for falling in love with the Wild Men of Alaska and offering to spearhead my street team, Tiff's Wild Readers. Meeting you in Anchorage was one of the highlights of my summer. In fact, it has been so much fun working with you that it doesn't seem like work at all.

To the Wild Readers. You are one wild bunch. Your support and willingness to help get the word out about my books warms my heart. Here's to more Wild Wednesdays!

Thank you.

DEDICATION

To my youngest son, Montgomery Helmer, a hero in the making. For your love of superheroes and fanciful creatures. Never stop believing. Love you, Mom.

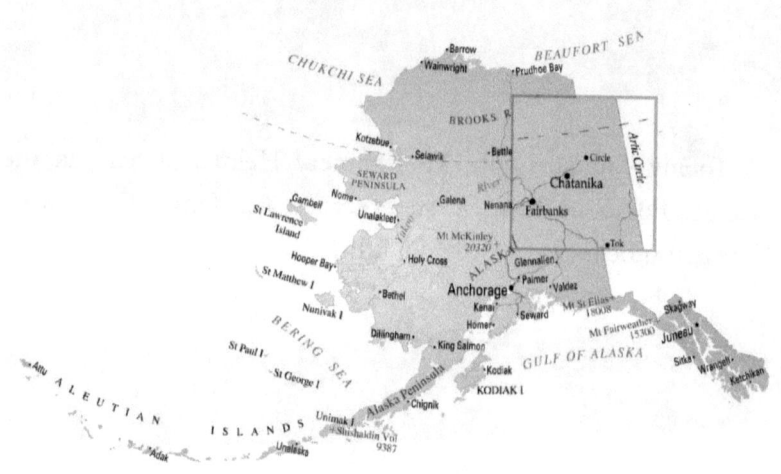

CHAPTER ONE

Aidan Harte stepped out of his rented SUV and right into Hell. Chatanika, Alaska to be exact, where it was so cold it burned. He'd been born in this forgotten gold-mining town, lost in the interior of the state, north of Fairbanks by about thirty desolate miles.

"Well, Dad, you finally got me back here." And it hadn't been over *his* dead body but that of his father's. Aidan slammed the door shut on the SUV. He was here to exorcise ghosts, while he closed out his father's life. The faster he saw Chatanika in his rearview mirror the better.

Not much had changed in the—what, eleven, twelve years?— since he'd last been here. It was midafternoon and the sun was already headed to bed, it being November. Snow and ice smothered the landscape into a state of unconsciousness, stunting spruce trees, and stripping birch branches until they resembled fragile bones.

Aidan pulled the collar of his coat up around his neck and wished he'd stopped in Fairbanks and bought a parka. His winter coat, which was perfectly adequate for Seattle, might as well have been a windbreaker in this hostile environment.

The outside thermometer on the Tahoe had said two. Now with the sun setting, the temperature would drop fast. Predicted temp for tonight was negative fifteen.

Aidan picked his way toward the family homestead, his feet crunching through the ice-crusted snow. The cabin's roof hung precariously over the rotted porch. The porch had been rotting when he'd last been here the summer he'd turned eighteen. He'd clearly remembered falling through and cutting up his leg. And the kiss he'd received from Raven Maiski. She'd had the power to drive more than pain away with her kisses.

It was eerily quiet. Spooky. The kind of night where you could hear yourself breathe and shadows took on a life of their own. He approached the makeshift fence made of twisted chain link and sharp, rusted barbwire. A chain and corroded padlock secured the front gate as well as a screaming red 'No Trespassing' sign. He should have figured this. Earl Harte had always been under the delusion everyone was out to get him. Many probably were, or had been. It no longer mattered now that the bastard was dead.

Aidan studied the gate. He could climb it and probably get cut from the barbwire or attempt to knock it down. It probably wasn't any better built than the rotting front porch. Problem was, his dad was notorious for booby-traps.

He checked around the gate, looking for wires or sharp instruments, and then gave it a solid kick. The gate swung open.

Well, that seemed anticlimactic.

Puffs of air steamed in front of his face. His breathing increased as he struggled through the snow toward the cabin. He didn't want to go in there. Nobody had been living in the dump for four months. Who knew what could have crawled in and died? For that matter, who knew what kind of condition Earl had left it in? His dad had never been the best about picking up after himself.

Aidan took a moment to rethink staying in the cabin while he went through what remained of his father's life. He could get a room at the Chatanika Lodge instead. But then he was sure to run into people—people he didn't want to see. Or, more precisely, people who didn't want to see him.

Maybe he could risk catching a glimpse of Raven.

Nope, the faster he could clean up and clear out the better. No one wanted anymore to do with him than they had his father. No one would miss Earl Harte.

Not even him.

Aidan kept an eye out for anything that looked suspicious. Earl would have a trap or tripwire set on the front entrance that would release something sharp and nasty for anyone stupid enough to bother him. He rounded the corner of the cabin heading toward the back door, hunching his shoulders against the cold and slapping his thin-gloved hands together in an attempt to warm them. The snow was deeper around the side of the cabin. Nothing looked like it had been disturbed. Not even animal prints cut the icy crust of the snow.

Suddenly, he skidded, his arms flailing wide. He regained his balance and looked at what he'd slipped on. A piece of tin. He glanced up and saw where it had fallen off the roof at some point. The place was falling apart. He shook his head and stepped carefully.

A bear trap sprung, steel teeth spearing into the flesh of his lower leg.

"Son of a bitch!" He screamed as pain stabbed through his leg.

He clawed at where the teeth of the rusty trap punctured through his jeans, through his boots, and into the tender flesh of his leg. Dropping in the snow, he cried out again as pain seared like fire through his leg, causing him to shake. He moaned through gritted teeth, struggling with the jaws of the trap. Sweat dripped down his face.

He quickly looked around, for anyone—anything—that would help free him from the snare.

Silence.

The only sound was his own choppy breathing, his pounding heart, and his useless moaning. He was alone. He was freezing.

He was seriously fucked.

What kind of sick son of bitch laid traps next to the back door of his own home?

Aidan clenched his teeth, grabbed the edges of the steel-teeth trap, and tried to pry the jaws apart. He roared and strained with everything he had. The effort was wasted. Blood soaked through his jeans and dribbled like syrup, staining the snow.

The sun dipped and shadows grew long and menacing.

Cold seeped in like death.

Aidan's heart grew heavy in his chest. He sat in the snow, spent, the heat of his body causing the snow to melt through his jeans and freeze next to his skin.

Think Harte, think.

Damn, but it was hard to think when his body was racked with pain. Maybe, he could crawl to the SUV with the trap and drive for help. He scratched around in the snow until he found the chain attached to the anchor of the trap. He heaved until his muscles drained.

No use. The anchor was encased in ice, frozen into the earth.

Come up with something else quick, or you're a dead man.

He patted his pockets, and pulled out his keys. Nothing on the key ring that could help him. He pocketed them and felt around for more. A Jolly Rancher. He snorted out a laugh. Not much of a last meal. Then he found his cell phone.

"Yes!" He flipped it open and dialed 911. No bars. "What the—"

He shook the phone as if that would miraculously gain him coverage. Nothing. He moved the phone around him, over his head, searching for reception. "Come on," he prayed. "*Come on.*" Again, nothing.

It started to snow.

Big, quiet, heavy flakes that smothered the earth. Despair began to settle in, becoming partners with the throbbing pain. He was going to die here. Born and died in the same place. It was kind of funny. Or ironic.

He wondered when his body would be found and by whom. Would it be spring? Or would an animal find him and have *him* for a last meal? He unwrapped the Jolly Rancher and popped it in his mouth. Grape. He grimaced. It tasted like cough medicine.

Chances were good no one would know what became of him. His therapist had encouraged him to return to Alaska, to make peace with his father, and his past. What a laugh.

His editor might be the one to make some noise but not until his deadline was closer on his next graphic novel. He didn't have any close friends. For family, his uncle Roland was hiding from the law, and his cousin Lana was back in college. She'd miss him, but she'd get over it soon. The only thing they had in common besides their summer commercial fishing operation was that both their fathers were assholes.

The only people who'd really wonder what became of him would be the IRS. What did that say about his life?

He heard a howl. Then another. And another.

Wolves.

God, he prayed they waited until he was dead to feast on his carcass. He laughed, the sound bitter. He'd been born under the sign of the wolf. Conceived under the Northern Lights and born in a blizzard. His Athabascan mother, before the booze had drowned all the love and warmth from her, had strung him tales about the power of the wolf he was supposed to possess.

Guess that had been a load of shit too.

He heard the wolves grow closer. He knew what they'd do. They'd circle him. Enclose him in a death ring. That is, if they were brave enough to venture onto Earl Harte's property. But with a warm meal staked out for them like a buffet, they'd come. They'd surround him, enclosing the circle closer and closer. Yellow beady eyes shining with greed and hunger, gleaming, sharp teeth dripping with saliva, until one of them—the alpha male— would lunge for his throat. At least when that happened, he'd die quickly. He wouldn't feel them tear into his stomach and feast on his organs, shred the meat off his bones. At least, he hoped.

They were closer now. He could hear them breathe.

"Hey, Mr. Harte, nice wheels. Fishing must've been good. About time you got...home." A young, gangly teenage boy, dressed in a fur-rimmed parka and mukluks, skidded to a stop when he saw Aidan. "You're not Mr. Harte."

Aidan had never been so glad to see anyone in his life. "I need help. And we better hurry. I hear wolves."

"Wolves?" The boy scowled in confusion and then smiled. "Those aren't wolves. They're my sled dogs." He ventured closer and saw the trap. "Don't know much about Mr. Harte, do you?"

"More than I wish I did." Aidan gestured to the trap. "Help me out here?"

"I can try." He knelt down in front of Aidan and looked him in the eyes. "You're stuck pretty good. Must hurt bad."

"You could say that." Aidan clenched his teeth. He was also freezing to death. He struggled to his knee for added leverage and grabbed the jaws of the trap.

The boy put his hands next to Aidan's. "Ready?" he asked.

Aidan nodded, and as cold as he was, he began to sweat. They pulled, heaved with all their might, but the springs wouldn't budge. Aidan felt the teeth move but not enough to release his leg.

"All right, break." He moaned. Any minute now he was going to cry like a baby. "What's your name?" Aidan asked, trying to concentrate on anything that could help distract him from the pain. This kid might be the last to see him alive.

"Fox. My name's Fox." Fox tilted his head to the side. "Are you related to Mr. Harte?"

"Yeah," Aidan scoffed. "You could say that."

"Well…are you?" he asked as though the answer meant something. "Either you are or you aren't. What is it?"

"Earl Harte is…was my father."

Fox fell back on his haunches. "You're Mr. Harte's son? The graphic novelist, Aidan Harte?"

A fan? Clear out here? "Yeah." He nodded and wiped sweat off his forehead.

"Whoa." Fox stared at him. Really stared. As though he were looking for something. "What do you mean Mr. Harte *was* your father?" Fox swallowed.

Could the kid have liked Earl? Nobody had liked Earl.

"He was ki—died this summer. I'm here to take care of his effects."

Fox's eyes fell to the ground, and he gave a heavy sigh. "I was afraid something like that had happened when he didn't come back. Seeing the SUV outside his place...well, I thought he'd finally made it home."

"Were you and him...close?" Earl hated kids.

"Kinda. It was a weird relationship." Fox took a deep breath and seemed to collect himself. "You ready to try again?"

"What the hell." They braced themselves and pulled on the jaws of the trap. They heaved and strained until Aidan couldn't help the holler of pain. "Stop. *Shit.*" He couldn't take any more of this. Just kill him and get it over with. It wasn't like he had a lot to live for anyway.

"We need help," Fox said. "I'm strong for my age, but this is bigger than me." Fox leapt to his feet. "I'll be right back." He turned toward the back of the cabin, walking in a zigzagging line to the back door. The kid obviously knew where the booby-traps were placed.

Fox entered the cabin and returned with a fur-lined hat and blankets. "Here." He gave the hat to Aidan, who immediately put it on, the flaps big and floppy over his ears, and then Fox carefully wrapped Aidan's legs with the blanket, adding another one around his shoulders.

Aidan fished out the keys in his pocket. "Take the SUV."

Fox shook his head. "My mom would kill me for driving. Besides, it's snowing too hard. I'd probably put it in the ditch. My dogs will get to help faster in weather like this. You hang in there. I'll be back as soon as I can."

"If I'm..." He didn't want to say dead, but that's where he was headed.

"Don't worry. I'll be back before you know it. Think warm."

Aidan heard excited barks and yips as Fox turned the corner and was out of sight. The kid was gone, and Aidan was once again alone in the arctic night.

He tried to disassociate from the pain throbbing in his leg where the metal teeth were clamped around it. It was becoming easier to do as he lost feeling, either from blood loss or the cutting off of circulation.

He lay down on the hard, frozen ground. Snow fell so thick he couldn't see more than a few feet above him. Sticking out his tongue, he caught the flakes and swallowed as they melted. He used to love doing that when he was younger. Snow had always been magical. Blanketing everything in white. Softening the edges of the harsh landscape. Glowing blue and green in the dark winters when the Northern Lights would dance like spirits in the sky above.

Would Fox be able to make it back in this?

He no longer felt the cold, either because the kid had wrapped him up or because shock had set in. Snow began to cover him, adding another welcomed layer of insulation. He pulled the hood of the hat over his face and closed his eyes.

He didn't know how long he'd stayed like that. Maybe he slept. But suddenly he heard a truck's brakes squealing as it came to a fast stop, then voices and the sound of footsteps crunching through the snow.

"Harte!"

Aidan tried to lift his arm to pull back the hood, but someone beat him to it, dusting off snow that was attempting to camouflage him. He opened his eyes and stared into Lynx Maiski's hard unforgiving face.

Shit. He was hoping not to run into his former childhood comrade.

"I can't believe it," Lynx said. "I thought the boy was suffering from exposure when he told me you were here." Air puffed from his angry mouth. "Didn't think I'd ever see you again."

"Can we get me out of this trap before you lay into me?"

Lynx looked him over. "You're not much competition at the moment." He lifted a brow and indicated Fox behind him. "If the kid wasn't so concerned about you, I'd be tempted to leave you."

And he'd be justified.

"If you're going to leave me, shoot me first."

Lynx laughed. "Don't tempt me. Fox, hand me those clamps." He looked at Aidan. "This is going to hurt."

"Worse than stepping into the damn thing?"

"Wait until the blood gets flowing again." Lynx smiled as though enjoying the picture he painted.

Aidan rose into a sitting position. Fox kept quiet, glancing worriedly at Aidan every few seconds. The kid actually seemed to care. Aidan studied him. Was he Lynx's son? There seemed to be a resemblance of sorts.

Lynx tightened down a C-clamp to the front spring and then attached another to the back. "Fox, you tighten this clasp, and I'll do the other. Harte, get ready to pull your leg out. These traps are ancient. It could spring back at any moment. I'm surprised you even attempted to come here, knowing Earl like you do."

"Didn't Fox tell you? Earl's dead."

Lynx paused then continued twisting the clap. "Couldn't have happened to a nicer guy. I hope it was painful."

A bullet to the chest. "Yeah. He felt pain."

"Glad to hear it."

The compression on his leg started to lessen. He reached out to help pull it out of the trap, as he'd lost most of the feeling in it. The pressure decreased but he couldn't get his leg out. The teeth were caught in the leather of his boots.

"Come on, Harte. *Pull.*" Lynx tightened his jaw. "Who knows how old this trap is. It could go off again at any moment. I don't want the kid hurt."

"Don't worry about me," Fox said. "I'm quick. Let's just get him out."

The kid was wise. Listen to the kid. Finally, the jaws released enough of their hold and he scraped his leg out of the trap. As soon as he was free, the trap sprung, snapping into the air.

"Shit," Lynx said, jumping back. "Your fucking father should have been shot for laying traps like that around here!"

Aidan grabbed his lower leg as feeling began pumping through his veins like hot oil.

"Do you think it's broken?" Lynx asked.

"Don't know. Hurts too bad to tell."

"Fox, bring that sled over here."

Fox positioned a sled next to Aidan and they both helped him into it.

"Let's get out of here. This place always gave me the creeps." Lynx pointed at Fox. "You and I are going to have a talk later on how you know where the booby-traps are hidden."

Fox gulped and looked away.

"Lead us out of here, Fox." Lynx grabbed the rope tied to the sled and pulled, following Fox's trail. They reached a crew-cab 4x4 pick-up with the National Wildlife Refuge seal painted on the side.

Aidan stood with Fox and Lynx's help, using the door of the truck as a crutch. He climbed in, clamping his mouth shut as he bumped his leg.

"Working for the State?" Aidan asked when they were under way. The snow came at them so hard there was no visibility.

"Yep," Lynx answered, concentrating on keeping the truck on the road. How he could tell where it was, Aidan hadn't a clue.

Aidan turned around to Fox, sitting quietly in the backseat studying Aidan. "Thanks, Fox. I owe you my life."

"You're welcome," he said, giving Aidan a hesitant smile.

They pulled into the heart of Chatanika. An old gold mining dredge sat like a metal monster to the left, the main tourist attraction. The old lodge cabin squatted across the street on the right. A few outlying cabins dotted, circling the center of town, vague shadows in the rapidly falling snow.

"We won't be able to get you to Fairbanks in this weather," Lynx said, parking the truck and switching off the engine. He turned to Fox. "Run and get Eva. I'll get him into the lodge."

Fox jumped out of the truck and took off.

Aidan wanted to insist they drive him to Fairbanks. He didn't want to meet any more people from Chatanika. At least he didn't recognize anyone by the name of Eva. She must be new. But if he went into the lodge, memories where going to swamp him. "Who's Eva?"

"My wife. And, lucky for you, an NP. She's the best thing we got in medical care out here." Lynx stepped out of the truck and walked around the front.

Aidan opened the door and gritted his teeth. Getting into the lodge was going to be the easy part. Seeing the occupants was going to hurt.

"Ready for this?" Lynx asked.

Aidan didn't know if he was asking about his physical well-being or the emotional havoc to come. "Not much choice in the matter," he mumbled.

Lynx put his arm around Aidan's back. Aidan swung an arm around his shoulder and they hobbled to the front door of the lodge.

The door opened and Fiona, Lynx's mother, stood there, looking the same as Aidan remembered. Round and happy—well, more concerned at the moment—she'd always seemed to make the best out of what life handed her, and it didn't seem as though that had changed.

"Aidan Harte! I thought I'd seen a ghost when you pulled up." She quickly looked him over. "Always coming to my place injured in one form or another, aren't you?" She motioned for them to follow her. "Come on. Let's get you patched up. Can't wait to hear the story on this escapade."

A lump lodged in his throat as he looked around the lodge. The walls of its rough homespun interior were decorated with vintage mining materials and snow shoes, while over-sized furniture sat in intimate corners and soft old leather couches flanked the stone fireplace.

Fiona was the closest thing to a mother he'd had growing up, since his own mother had checked out most of the time. Fiona had fed him cookies, washed his scraped knees, and scolded him within an inch of his life when he stepped out of line. Damn, he didn't want to deal with these old feelings.

God, he hoped Raven was no longer living here.

Please, he prayed, let Raven be happily married and living in the Midwest somewhere. Far away from Chatanika.

"Bring him in here." Fiona opened the door to one of the guest rooms. The room was decorated simply, with an old quilt on the bed, a wooden rocking chair in the corner, and an old thrift store dresser. Criss-crossed skis hung above the queen size bed, and diamond willow lamps sat on birch nightstands. Nostalgia hit him like a snowplow. The lump in his throat grew.

Lynx threw him down on the bed, and Aidan landed with a bounce. He held up his leg to keep blood from getting on the spread and gave Lynx a dirty look. He didn't care that Lynx hated him, but he needed to take better care with Fiona's things.

"Lynx," Fiona scolded. "That's no way to treat an injured man." She'd grabbed towels from the bathroom, and folded back the quilt, laying the towels down. "All right, Aidan, you can set your leg down now." She gave him a once over. "Whatever did you do to yourself?"

"He got himself caught in one of his father's bear traps," Lynx said with a sneer.

"No." Fiona gasped. "Oh, you poor thing."

Next she was going to be kissing his forehead and smoothing back his hair like she used to do. He wondered if she still had blueberry shortbread cookies in the cookie jar.

"What is Earl thinking?" Fiona tsked.

"Apparently, he's no longer thinking or doing much of anything." Lynx gave a cat-like grin. "Earl's dead."

Fiona sighed. "Well…"

There was no, 'Isn't that a shame.' Or, 'I'm so sorry for your loss.' Nobody in the room would shed a tear for Earl Harte.

"I take it you sent for Eva?" Fiona asked Lynx, who nodded. "Good. I'll go and grab some medicinal beverage. Aidan, I'm sure you could use a drink."

Oh yes, he could. "Thanks, Fiona. For everything."

"You're welcome. It's good to see you, son." She walked over to the bed and smoothed the hair back on his forehead. "You always did have the best manners around." She left the room. The lump that had been forming in his throat clogged it closed.

"Suck up," Lynx said. "I'll never understand why she doesn't hate you like the rest us."

He had to clear his throat to speak. "She doesn't blame me for the sins of my father."

"Acorn doesn't fall far from the tree."

"Have you ever seen an acorn tree growing in Alaska?" He tightened his jaw. "And I'm not my father."

Lynx snorted, but looked away like maybe Aidan had touched a nerve.

A woman entered, who Aidan thankfully didn't know. A little thing except for her very pregnant belly, with blond hair cut short and spiked around her pixie face. She reached up and gave Lynx a kiss. Interesting. She also carried a black bag. Must be the nurse practitioner.

"Harte this is Eva, my wife. Eva, this sorry excuse for a man, is Aidan Harte."

"Nice to meet you." She glanced at Lynx when he snorted again. "Are you going to be helpful?"

Aidan couldn't help the chuckle.

"What?" Lynx demanded.

"Just interesting to see who wears the pants in your relationship. Really nice to meet you, Eva." He gave her a full smile.

She smiled back and set the bag on the side of the bed, next to him. "Let's take a look at you. Fox said you were caught in a trap?"

Aidan nodded.

She opened her bag, yanked on a pair of latex gloves, and pulled out scissors. She started at the hem of his jeans and carefully cut up the sides of one leg and then started on the other. "Your pants aren't going to survive. Let's see if we can save the rest of you." She gave him a twinkling smile. "Lynx bring me over that trash can." She indicated the one in the corner. Lynx begrudgingly brought it over. Eva stopped and straightened, looking Lynx in the eye. "If you're going to be like that, send someone else in here to help me." She discarded the ruined jeans in the trash can.

"Fine." Lynx made a face, the same one he used to make when they were kids and Fiona would make him do something he didn't want to.

"Good." Eva turned back to Aidan, and threw a crocheted blanket over his lower half, covering his batman boxers.

He was going to like this woman. Lynx had grown into a bear of a man. His Athabascan and Tlingit heritage shone through like muscle. His black hair, dark eyes, and tanned skin contrasted with Eva's short blond, blue-eyed, ivory-skinned, fairy looks.

Eva surveyed Aidan's leg. "Lucky you were wearing boots."

Yeah, one thing he had to be grateful for tonight, while so many other things had gone straight to hell.

Fiona entered the room with a bottle of whiskey and no glass. "Better drink up, my boy, before Eva goes any further. She's cute, but wicked." Fiona handed him a bottle and stuffed pillows behind his back when he sat up to drink. He took a long swallow, and relished the burn as it flowed down into his gut. His eyes watered, and he did everything he could not to cough. Not in front of Lynx, who was waiting to insult him. He took another swallow and then handed the bottle back to Fiona, who sat it within easy reach on the nightstand.

"All right, what can I do to help?" Fiona asked.

"Get him to drink more," Eva said, going for the boot laces on his good foot first. "You're going to need a new pair of boots."

"Beats a new leg."

Eva chuckled. "I like a man who can keep a sense of humor at times like this. Unlike someone else I know."

Lynx folded his arms and rolled his eyes.

"I like a woman who's capable and pretty to look at." Aidan flirted back and smiled when Lynx gave him the evil eye. He grabbed the bottle and took another swig. It barely burned at all this time. He swallowed some more, loving how it warmed his blood as it swam through his body.

Eva started on the chewed up boot, cutting through the laces with her sharp scissors. A hush settled over the room, and Lynx and Fiona leaned in. "Step back and give me room to work." She glanced at Aidan. "Why don't you take another drink?"

"Sounds like a dandy idear," he slurred. He wasn't much of a drinker. Since his mother had been a lush, he'd stayed away from it. The alcohol hit him hard and fast, like a moose during rutting season. He downed another long swallow. It was too much effort to get the bottle back onto the nightstand, so he cradled it in the crook of his arm. He was feeling no pain.

Until Eva—the evil fairy from hell—pulled on his boot.

"Ahhh!" He screamed like a baby. He'd tried to keep it in. Even bit his tongue, but with the booze, the holler had escaped.

"Damn, I hope you didn't break this," Eva scolded him like it was his fault he was hurt. "No way we can get you to Fairbanks with that storm out there." She surveyed the situation. "We need to get that boot off. If he broke it we'd better leave it on until we can get him to a hospital. But then what kind of infection has already taken up residence from the trap?"

Aidan quirked a brow. "Are you expecting an answer from me?"

"She likes to talk out her problems," Lynx said, scowling. "Leave her alone."

Aidan took another swig of the whiskey, really getting into the numbing effects.

"How's he doing?" Fox asked, rushing into the room, his eyes wide as he viewed Aidan's leg. "Ooh, that doesn't look good."

Aidan hadn't looked. In fact, he'd looked at everyone and everything in the room, avoiding the sight of his mangled leg.

"Fox, you shouldn't be in here," Lynx said, walking over to him and laying a hand on his shoulder. "Don't you have dogs to feed?"

"That's what I was doing. They're all bedded down for the night." He looked at Aidan, worry shining in his eyes. "Is he going to be all right?"

"He's going to be just fine." Fiona walked around the bed and reached for Fox. "Come with me. I need your help getting him something to eat." Fiona steered him out of the room, giving Aidan a backward glance with a wink.

"Let's get the boot off," Eva announced, tightening her lips. "I think that's the best course of action." She went right to work. Before Aidan could down any more of the bottle, she had his boot off in one quick excruciating yank.

"*Shit. Fuck. Son of a bitch!*" He gasped—had trouble getting his breath back—and started to shake.

"Sorry about that," the demon nurse from hell said. "Guess I could have warned you, but I prefer the rip-off-the-bandage method. Why prolong the pain? Now let's take a look."

The edge of his vision started to blur. God, he hoped he passed out.

Then she walked in.

Raven.

The woman who had haunted him all his life. From his dreams to his fantasies. The woman who had broken his heart.

"So it's true," she said, glaring at him from the doorway, her hands planted on her hips. Her voice was deeper, huskier. It vibrated through him like a stone thrown into a pool of water. She slowly stalked toward the bed. "I can't believe you had the nerve to come back here."

He gazed up into her dark, bewitching eyes. How he had loved to gaze into her eyes for hours as he stroked her soft, honeyed skin. "Why aren't you in the Midwest?" he asked. And he thought dying was the worst thing that could happen to him tonight.

"Midwest?" She frowned and glanced at Eva and Lynx. "Did he hit his head too?"

"Nope," Lynx answered. "But he's had a *lot* to drink." He indicated the half empty bottle of whiskey snuggled in the crook of Aidan's arm.

He took another swig. *Man, that went down nice.*

"Where's Fox?" Raven asked.

"In the kitchen with Mom," Lynx said. "He found Aidan, saved his sorry ass. He also knew how to navigate Earl's booby-traps. It would be interesting to know *how* he knew that."

"Yes, it would. In the meantime, what are we going to do with *him?*" She pointed at Aidan as though he was something rotten that needed to be disposed of.

He wasn't worried. Hell, he was feeling fine. Aidan took another drink and some of the liquid dribbled down his chin. If they were going to kill him, they would have left him to die in the trap. With the temperature dropping to well below zero, he wouldn't have made it through the night.

Eva wiped the blood, rust, and dirt from his leg, while Aidan lost himself in gazing at Raven.

She'd changed since he'd last seen her. At eighteen she'd been a skinny thing, all limbs and sharp angles. She'd gained weight and it had settled in all the right places. She was curvy. The kind of curvy a man could spend hours navigating, losing himself. He remembered the night they'd given each other their virginity. How they'd fumbled, laughed, and spoke of forever. How would it be to lie with her now?

"Ouch." He jerked as Eva poked him. "That hurts."

"Well, yeah." Eva snorted. "You got your leg caught in a trap." Weren't nurses supposed to be compassionate?

"Lynx, hand me that syringe." She held her hand out. "Yes, that one." She glanced at Aidan. "You've got a lot of crap in these wounds." She glared at him like it was his fault. "I'm going to flush them out with saline and hope we wash out all the debris."

Aidan dropped his head back on the pillow as Eva went to work on him, snapping orders at Lynx for more towels.

"What are you doing back here, Aidan?" Raven asked, her lips flattened into a line. She had such nice full lips that could stretch into a wide, welcoming smile. Why couldn't she have smiled at him when she saw him instead of the scowl that wrinkled her forehead and made him feel like scum? Didn't she have any fond memories of him that she revisited?

"Earl's dead," Lynx answered for him.

"Well." Raven folded her arms under her breasts—breasts that were considerably larger than they had been at eighteen. "It couldn't have happened to a nicer guy."

"I need those tweezers." Eva pointed to a sterile package in her bag, snapping her fingers for Lynx to speed it up. For such a little thing, she had a Napoleon attitude. She tore into the packaging and pulled out wickedly sharp, stainless steel tweezers. "I didn't get all the debris with the wash. I'm going to have to dig some of it out with the tweezers. Raven, hold his shoulders down. Lynx, you hold his leg immobile. And I mean don't *even* let it twitch." She flicked a glance at Aidan. "You aren't going to like this."

"Surprise," he said. "I haven't liked any of it so far."

She smiled at him as though she approved and then narrowed a look at Raven. "Hold him down."

Raven took a deep breath, her eyes slanting. She didn't want to touch him. But then he didn't want her touching him either, for different reasons all together.

She sat on the edge of the bed and placed her hands on his shoulders. Her scent drifted to him. In all these years she still smelled the same. Earthy. Berries, ferns, exotic underbrush. He vaguely felt Eva poking at him. The real pain came from having Raven so close and discovering he still had unresolved feelings for her hidden in the depths of his mangled heart.

And she still hated him.

"All right, I hope I got it all," Eva said. "That trap must have been decades old and reverting back to nature for the amount of rust I washed out of the wounds. When was the last time you had a tetanus? Earl Harte should be shot for leaving things like that around his place."

Aidan laughed, though the sound was more sardonic than happy. Earl had been shot all right.

"Aidan?" Eva hollered at him. "Tetanus shot? When did you last have one?"

"Can't remember," he mumbled.

"Are you allergic to any antibiotics?"

"Nope."

"Are you all right?" Raven asked, looking suddenly concerned.

"Do you care?"

She tightened her lips, released him and scooted off the edge of the bed. "No."

"Then don't bother asking." He shut his eyes. Man, he was tired. It had been a hell of a day. It had been a hell of a few months. Who was he kidding? His life had always been hell. He'd be better off dead then he wouldn't have to feel. Darkness closed in on him. Not comforting, but numbing.

Whatever. He'd take it.

CHAPTER TWO

Raven grabbed the bottle sliding out of Aidan's grip right before it would have fallen off the edge of the bed. "He's out." Thank the lord, she thought.

"Good," Eva said. "I hate patients who complain."

"I didn't hear him complain," Raven said, wrinkling her brow.

"I know." Eva reached for packing strips. "I can't sew him up. The puncture wounds are too deep. They'll need to heal from the inside out." She glanced at Raven and then Lynx. "We'll need to care for him. Change his packing, bandages."

"The hell we will," Lynx said, crossing his arms over his chest. "It would have been better for everyone if Fox hadn't found him." He glanced at Raven. "You need to have a talk with your son about picking up strays. Some things are better off left to die."

"Lynx," Eva scolded. Just the tone of her voice had Lynx standing down.

"Fine," he grumbled and pointed to Aidan prone on the bed. "But I don't want *him* here any longer than he has to be."

"He'll have to stay a few days," Eva said. "I don't believe his leg is broken, but he isn't going to be driving out of here on it. He's going to need his bandages changed, his wounds repacked, and I'm worried about infection. We'll have to take turns caring for him."

"Hell no," Lynx said, arms back across his chest. "You're asking too much, woman."

Eva narrowed her eyes. "If that's the way you're going to be, it'll be hard on me, with the pregnancy *so* close to term and all." She sighed. "But *I'm* not going to let the man die."

She was good, Raven thought. Her brother had married his match and then some.

"Well, shit," he muttered.

Eva turned to Raven and quirked a brow.

"Fine," Raven said. "But I don't want Fox in here."

"Good luck keeping him out," Lynx scoffed. "You know the boy. Finders keepers."

"We'll have to keep him busy." Raven stared at both of them. "I don't want him anywhere around Aidan."

"We'll do our best," Eva agreed, but Raven knew she was going to be hounded with questions later over why. Eva turned back to her patient. "I still need to pack his wounds." She sighed. "I hope he sleeps through it."

"He drank enough whiskey to put him into a coma," Lynx said.

"You would have done the same in his situation," Eva said. "Make yourself useful and hand me those packing strips."

Raven watched as Eva doctored the punctured wounds the teeth of the trap had made. There were six in all around Aidan's calf. She couldn't imagine how much it had hurt him. A pang of something unwanted and uncomfortable intruded. She stamped it down. She no longer cared for Aidan. That was long over and had been a mistake from the get go. But being with Aidan had resulted in Raven's greatest joy.

Fox.

She had to make sure her inquisitive son didn't get attached to Aidan. Fox had no way of knowing Aidan was his father, and Raven would make sure he never acquainted himself with that part of his gene pool.

"Okay, that's done." Eva placed gauze pads over the packed wounds and then wrapped his leg in an ace bandage. The skin was bruised black and blue from the force of the trap clamping down around it and already swelling. "I'm going to place a soft splint around this in case he did break it. I don't think so, but he could have a hairline fracture. If he hadn't been wearing his boots, the bone definitely would have snapped. When the snow stops we'll take him to Fairbanks for an x-ray."

Raven and Lynx looked at each other.

Eva stood and placed her hands on her lower back and glared at both of them. "Yes, one of you is going to take him. You can fight it out between the two of you because I'm not doing it." She pointed to her protruding belly. "I have a good excuse."

"Fine," they muttered.

"Okay, I need to give him a couple of shots. An antibiotic in the ass and a tetanus in the arm. Which one of you is going to volunteer to stay with him tonight?" She glared at them. "Don't give me any flack. He needs to be watched. I don't want him trying to get out of bed, and we need to keep an eye on his temperature. Plus, I want to ice his leg. We need to keep the swelling down. I don't want any chance of blood clots forming."

"What about Mom?" Raven suggested.

"Oh, come on." Eva looked at her with annoyance. "She's already got three guests to watch out for. You want her up all night taking care of a patient too?"

Raven felt low being scolded like a kid. She glanced at Lynx, but the jerk wasn't volunteering. "Fine, I'll stay." Aidan would probably sleep the whole night through from all the whiskey he'd drunk. "But Fox will have to bunk down at your place." She pointed at Lynx. "And you have to drive Aidan into Fairbanks when the roads are clear."

"Lynx?" Eva prompted when he didn't quickly agree.

"All right."

"Wow, you guys are acting like selfish brats," Eva said. "I know Earl Harte was an asshole, but what did Aidan ever do to you?"

Raven looked down at the sleeping man she used to love and had always thought she'd spend her life with. "Because of Aidan our father is dead."

Aidan awoke and ran his tongue over his hairy teeth. What had crawled into his mouth and died? And he badly needed to pee.

He looked around the darkened room. A light had been left on in the bathroom leaving a soft amber glow to illuminate the bedroom. Where was he? A timber wolf pelt hung like a trophy on the wall, and a pair of handcrafted fur-trimmed Eskimo masks flanked a mirror over an old dresser where a woven basket with an Inuit design sat on the surface.

The bear trap.

He was at the Chatanika Lodge. *And he'd seen Raven.* Over the years, he'd wondered many times what she looked like now. How her beauty had matured. Well, now he knew and wished to God he didn't.

He sat up and looked at his leg propped up on pillows and wrapped in a splint of sorts. The pain was down to a welcoming throb. Getting to the bathroom was going to hurt like hell. His head pounded. He shouldn't have drunk so much of the whiskey. He never could hold his liquor. There was movement in the corner of the room from the rocking chair.

"You're awake." Raven's voice was low and husky, reminding him of dark nights like this when they'd snuck away to be together.

"You're here?" Surprise didn't even begin to explain the jumpstart of his pulse. She'd undone her braid and her thick, blue-black hair hung straight down to her lap. Beautiful hair. Soft and silky and flowing.

"Eva made one of us volunteer."

"*You* volunteered to watch over me?"

"It was the lesser chore. Lynx has to take you to the hospital when the roads are cleared."

"So one night, which I'd probably sleep the most of, instead of hours in a car and then what? Wasting time at the hospital?"

"Yep."

"You always were the smart one."

"Except you're now awake." She frowned. "Go back to sleep so my plan works for me."

"I...can't." He glanced longingly at the bathroom. He really had to pee.

She followed his gaze. "You've got to be kidding."

"'Fraid not." He shook his head. "Too much whiskey."

"Or not enough," she grumbled, throwing back the afghan she'd curled up under in the rocking chair. "Let's get this over with."

"I'd rather not do it with you."

"Good. If you did, I'd think you really were sick." She reached for a pair of crutches. "Eva already considered this. She had Lynx drop these back by. She doesn't want you putting weight on your leg until it's been x-rayed." Raven brought the crutches over to the bed. "Don't think of crossing her. She's very pregnant and very moody."

"You forgot to mention she's also very scary."

Raven laughed, and it looked as though it surprised her. She was quick to smother it. "She also told me I'm supposed to take your temperature if you woke."

"Bathroom first." He didn't want to embarrass himself in front of her. It was hard enough breathing the same air when he never thought he'd see her again. He swung his legs over the side of the bed, being careful of his injured one. Someone—probably Lynx—had removed his flannel shirt, leaving him in an undershirt and boxers. His leg throbbed but felt a hell of lot better than earlier. He reached for the crutches and noticed how careful Raven was to not let their hands touch. It said a lot about a person when they could care for you and still hate everything about you. No wonder he'd always worshipped her. She reminded him of his ex-girlfriend, Sonya. Or had Sonya reminded him of Raven all these years? It would explain why he'd latched onto the idea of him and Sonya being together.

But then he'd fucked that up too.

He stood, balanced on one leg, and put the crutches under his armpits. He was shaky but holding his own. Manning up, he swung on the crutches toward the bathroom and shut the door behind him. He didn't want Raven's help in this department any more than she wanted to give it.

He finished, flushed, and hopped to the sink, leaning the crutches against the counter. Thankfully, he found a new toothbrush and paste laying on the vanity, which he used to scrub the nasty taste off his teeth and tongue. Then he splashed water on his face and stared at his reflection in the mirror.

He looked like shit. But then again, he felt like shit.

He didn't want to go back out there. Raven had looked at him like he was trash. And he was. He'd never been worthy of the Maiskis. Not worthy to be Raven's lover or Lynx's friend. He should leave. But how the hell was he going to do that? He was stuck by a snowstorm, a chewed up leg, and he still needed to do what he'd come here to do. Then he could be done with this place for good. Never to return. Never to have his heart ripped out of his chest, his love thrown back in his face. Never disappoint those he cared about again.

He returned to the bedroom and headed to the bed. Raven was gone. Guess he hadn't needed to delay his time in the bathroom avoiding her.

Carefully he sat on the edge of the bed, breathing a sigh of relief he'd made it under his own steam. History had taught him that relying on others was always an exercise in disappointment. He swung his leg over and repositioned himself on the bed, pulled the blankets up to his chin, and tried to get back to sleep. But his head pounded and he was thirsty.

Sure, one minute you have to pee, and the next you want something to drink. Suffer. He wasn't getting back up again.

The door squeaked open, and Raven entered carrying a glass full of water like an angel, or dark angel. Had she poisoned the water? But then that wasn't like her. If she wanted him dead she'd had plenty of opportunity while he'd slept. Besides she wouldn't have chosen poison.

She'd gut him.

"Here. Eva said to take two aspirin if you woke." She handed him the pills and the glass of water.

"Thanks." Gratefully he took the items she held out, again making sure they didn't touch.

"Don't thank me. Just following orders."

"Got anything stronger than aspirin? My head is killing me."

"The aspirins are supposed to help prevent any blood clots from forming. Oh, I was also supposed to give you some Ibuprofen." She scratched her head. "But I wonder if you should be taking them together." She shrugged. "It's your choice. I'm not waking Eva to ask her."

"Give me."

She dumped two pills in his hand. He motioned for more. She dropped two more into his palm. "That's all. You can overdose on your own time."

He tossed back the pills and swallowed them down with another long drink of water. He set the glass on the nightstand and laid back down, his head propped up on pillows. Raven presented a thermometer.

"I don't have a temperature," he said.

"Orders. Open up."

He opened his mouth, and Raven placed the thermometer under his tongue. They waited. Raven refused to look at him. She gazed off into the room. As it was dark, with just the glow from the bathroom, he didn't know what she saw, but it must have been preferable to looking at him.

When a sufficient amount of time had passed, she reached for the thermometer, turning on the diamond willow lamp to read the number. Her brows rose. "Don't have a temperature, huh?" She held the thermometer out for him to read.

"That hardly counts." It was barely a hundred.

She harrumphed and shook down the thermometer and then set it on the nightstand. "Let's see how you react to the pills you just took." She turned off the light and walked around the bed to the corner rocking chair, curling into it and wrapping the crocheted afghan tight around her shoulders.

"You don't have to stay," Aidan said.

She scowled at him. "I promised Eva, and I don't mess with that chick."

"How long have she and Lynx been married?"

"Three years." She fidgeted in the hard chair, trying to get comfortable.

"You don't have to sleep in the chair." He felt the heat of her glare burning him from across the room.

"I'm not sharing your bed. It's hard enough being in the same room."

"Don't be an idiot. I'm in no condition to try anything, besides you'd kill me." She snorted in agreement. "The bed's plenty big if you stay on your side."

"Like I'd cozy up to you."

"Fine. Be uncomfortable if it makes you feel superior."

She swore and stood, trailing the afghan behind her. Looked as though Raven still fell for the idiot ploy. She dropped to the bed, obviously not caring if she jostled him, but being extremely careful not to touch him.

A brick wall might as well have been between them as they lay next to each other. Aidan was in no condition physically or emotionally to try scaling it. But he also couldn't sleep. And he could smell her. Definitely needed a distraction.

"How did Lynx and Eva meet?"

She turned her head on the pillow and looked at him. "We aren't going to share, are we?"

"Listen, I can't sleep. I was curious."

"Fine." She sighed and turned back to facing the ceiling. "You know how Lynx has always rescued animals." She didn't wait for Aidan to nod. "Well, a moose he befriended took a liking to Eva right after she arrived, and chased her into the woods and up a tree. To make a long story short, Lynx was hooked."

"What does she do?"

"She runs the medical clinic in town."

"The town's really grown."

"Yeah." She snorted. "We even have a volunteer fire station."

"What about a school?"

"A group of us got together and converted old Wilkerson's place when he died. We take turns with lessons for the handful of kids around. It's a step-up from homeschooling. We got the borough to agree to send a bus halfway up the Steese to pick up the few high schoolers." She yawned. "Every year, it seems, we become more civilized. Still no Starbucks though." He heard the frown in her voice.

"What have you been up to?" he couldn't help asking.

She didn't move, but he felt her stiffen. "Same old stuff."

He laughed. "Right. Still planning on playing guitar for Bon Jovi? Wait a minute, you had a full scholarship to Berkeley to become an architect. What became of that?"

"None of your business," she snapped. "Now go to sleep."

He'd obviously touched a nerve, pushed far enough. Silence settled over the room. Unfortunately Aidan wasn't tired, and without conversation he started to feel the throbbing in his leg, the aching in his head, and the hunger in his stomach. He hadn't eaten since he'd picked up the rental car and stopped at the Food Factory in Fairbanks for a steak sandwich before heading to Chatanika. Man, that sandwich had been good. One thing Seattle didn't have was the Food Factory. Guess there were some things he'd actually missed about living here.

His stomach growled.

"Can't you be quiet over there and just go to sleep?" Raven asked, her voice muffled as she'd turned her face into the pillow.

"I'm hungry."

She raised her head and looked at him. "You've *got* to be kidding."

"I haven't eaten since lunch. And that was around one. What time is it now?"

"Time to sleep." She tossed the pillow over her head. "Ignore it. It'll go away."

His stomach growled again.

"Oh, for heaven's sake." Raven slapped the pillow aside and got out of bed. She stomped to the door. "You were supposed to stay in a drunken stupor." With that she left the room.

He hoped she was coming back. But he assumed the worst. After all the worst was what he usually got.

"I can't believe I'm getting food for that man," Raven muttered under her breath, her head inside the refrigerator looking for leftovers. No way in hell was she cooking for him.

"To the right on the third shelf there's some roast left over from dinner," Fiona said.

Raven lifted her head over the door of the refrigerator to find her mother leaning against the counter, her arms folded across her chest. "Why aren't you sleeping?" Somebody should be getting some shuteye. Raven pulled out the container her mother had indicated and closed the door to the refrigerator.

"I heard someone roaming around in my kitchen." Fiona raised a brow. "You really ought to work on your muttering. Never know when someone might hear something you don't want them to."

"Why? You hear something tonight?"

"Aidan isn't the bad man you think he is."

"I don't want to get into it, Mom." Raven grabbed a plate and filled it with roast and potatoes that were also in the container.

"Both you and Lynx have blamed him for far too much over the years."

"Yeah, and you haven't blamed him enough." She didn't want to hash over this. Not again.

"You need to keep an open mind, my daughter. You're too young to be this cynical. People make mistakes. It's what makes them human."

"So, I'm what? Supposed to forgive him of murder?"

"He didn't murder your father."

"He might as well have." She returned the container and slammed the door to the fridge. "I gotta go. *Mr. Harte* is hungry."

"Raven, I didn't raise you to hate like this." Fiona pursed her lips and then hit Raven with words that had the power to twist guilt like a screw in her gut. "I'm disappointed."

There was nothing worse than having Fiona Maiski disappointed in you. She loved everyone, thought the best of everyone. Case in point, Aidan Harte resting comfortably in her place about to eat her home-cooked food.

"I'm not willing to forget, and I won't forgive. I can't."

"If you don't soften your heart, I fear for your happiness, daughter." Another final look and Fiona turned and left the kitchen.

Hell. Aidan was back and she was fighting with her mother. The one person who truly had her back. Those qualities she'd listed earlier were the qualities that Raven counted on herself. She needed her mother to love her unconditionally, to be proud of her. Because she was a bitch to love. She knew it, and so did everyone else. And she had no intention of changing. Especially for a man. She lived perfectly fine without one. Had all these years. The only man she needed in her life was her son. And she was raising him to be a fine man, one who could handle a woman like her. Not that she wanted Fox saddled with someone like her. But if he fell in love with one, he'd know what he was in for and be able to handle it.

Raven grabbed a fork, stabbed it into the roast, and picked up the plate of food she'd gathered for Aidan and headed out of the room, snagging the plate of brownies her mother had set on the counter as she left. She didn't need the sweets, but she was up late and having to deal with the one person she'd hoped never to see again. A few brownies didn't even come close to making this night bearable.

Raven entered the bedroom and handed Aidan the food, keeping the plate of brownies for herself. "Here. Don't choke on it." Then she turned and walked around to her side of the bed and climbed in.

"I didn't think you were coming back."

"Scared of Eva, remember? Now eat, and shut up." She bit into a brownie. Oh, man, her mother sure could cook. Raven felt bad for the way she'd talked to her. She'd have to apologize tomorrow. Another thing to throw at Aidan's feet.

"Oh, wow, this is great." Aidan chewed and swallowed. "Moose?"

"Hmm," she agreed around the brownie in her mouth.

"I haven't had this in years. Even cold, it's great."

What? He expected her to warm it up for him? He was lucky she actually fed him anything.

"Thanks, Raven. I appreciate it."

Hell. "You're welcome." Now she was feeling guilty for the way she'd treated him? What was up with her? Her time of the month? No, at least she didn't think so. She'd never been that great about keeping track. Look at Fox. That should have taught her, but then Fox was the greatest blessing she had in her life. He was the reason she got up in the morning. "Here." She held out the plate of brownies. "Want one?"

"Yeah, thanks." Aidan took one off the plate and bit into it, making an appreciative noise. She remembered that sound. Just like that she was eighteen again and Aidan had his hands on her.

He had magical hands. Knew right where to touch. How hard, how soft. When to push, and when to let her fly. She hadn't been with a man since who could make her respond the way he had.

She was older. Surely, sex with him now would pale in comparison. Teenage love was always built up to be more than it was. That had to be it. Nostalgic times when life had been easy, simple, happy.

When her father had still been alive.

She set the plate of brownies on the nightstand, no longer hungry. She scooted down on the bed and pulled the covers up over her head and tried with everything in her to put Aidan Harte out of her mind.

She did a fair job of it until she fell asleep. Then her subconscious took over, the part of her who liked to dream of Aidan. It had been dreaming of him for the last twelve years and was damn good at it.

CHAPTER THREE

Aidan woke to find a pair of brown eyes regarding him from an inquisitive face.

Fox.

"Hey," Aidan greeted, glancing to the other side of the bed. A lump was curled under the covers. In fact, the lump had stolen *all* the covers. Aidan cleared his throat and looked at Fox again.

"Feeling better?" Fox studied him as though he were dissecting an insect not previously found. "You look bad."

"Okay." Aidan rubbed his raspy jaw. A shower would do him good. A cold shower. Maybe Raven hadn't stolen the covers. He probably kicked them off. It was hot in here. "Could you open a window?"

"It's like ten below outside." Fox gave him a look, questioning his intelligence.

"Sounds perfect," he muttered. His head hurt and he needed water and the bathroom again. He sat up and the room spun before it settled back into place. He felt funky.

"You look really bad," Fox repeated. But Aidan didn't hold it against him as the kid handed him a glass of water.

"Thanks." He drank the whole thing down and wished he had more. His mouth and throat felt like he'd swallowed a beach full of sand.

"So, why does everybody hate you?" Fox sat on the edge of the bed, hiking one knee up.

"You'll have to ask them." Aidan closed his eyes for a minute, hoping that would help his head. It didn't. The door was open to the hallway so between the light out there and the one still on in the bathroom, there was enough to illuminate but not enough to hurt. He knew it was morning even though it was still dark outside. The sun didn't rise this time of year until around nine-thirty or ten. And the darkness increased every day until the shortest day of the year. The winter solstice.

"You don't know why they hate you?" Fox lifted a brow. "I might be a kid, but I'm not stupid."

"I don't think you're stupid. Far from it. In fact, if it wasn't for you, I'd be dead right now." He didn't know if he should thank Fox for that or not.

"You know in some cultures, when you save a life, that life belongs to you."

"Son, you seriously don't want to own my life." He sure as hell had never wanted it.

Fox seemed to pale.

"But I do owe you," Aidan continued. Dying from exposure, while snared in a trap, or being ripped apart by wild animals would have been a horrible way to die. There were many others much more pleasant. "Thank you, Fox."

"You're welcome." Fox looked away, his gaze resting on the lump that had started to stir on the other side of the bed.

Raven tossed back the blankets and poked her head out. She yawned and looked around, her eyes widening when she saw Fox.

"Fox." She scrambled out of the bed, tugging her shirt down over her pants. "What are you doing in here?"

She actually blushed, like she'd been caught doing something she shouldn't have been. Sleeping with him, for instance. Aidan smiled. She looked adorable, outraged, and embarrassed, her hair mussed up and trailing down her backside in a ruffled black curtain. He'd never forget how soft and long her hair was. He was really glad she hadn't cut it. The length became her. Gave her that wild, sexy look he'd loved.

"Mom? Did you...*sleep*...with Mr. Harte?"

"*Mom?*" Aidan asked. Fox was *her* son? "I thought Fox was Lynx's son."

Raven glared at him and dismissed him just as quickly. "Fox, we weren't sleeping together. I stayed here last night to make sure *he* was going to be all right." She glanced back at Aidan as though laying blame for this situation. He was too stunned from learning that Fox was her son to help her out. Besides, she was cute when she bungled.

"But you were in the same bed." Fox looked to Aidan and stared as though seeing something Aidan couldn't.

"It was uncomfortable in the rocking chair, so I moved to the bed." She shrugged and tried to laugh. "It was no big deal. Have you had breakfast?"

"Yep."

"Are you ready for school?"

"Yep."

Raven fidgeted as though thinking hard of some other reason Fox would need to leave. Aidan finally decided to take pity on her. Besides, he needed to use the bathroom. And some more pain pills wouldn't be out of the question. His leg throbbed to the beat of his heart.

"Guys, I need to use the facilities, if you don't mind."

Fox and Raven looked at him and then began moving at once. Fox handed Aidan the crutches and Raven made sure nothing was in the pathway to the bathroom and that the door was fully open.

"Do you need any help?" Fox asked, looking him over and frowning.

Man, he really must look bad. "No, I got it. Thanks." He swung his leg over the side and reached for the crutches. When he stood, the room tipped.

"Mom!" Fox hollered. She must have been watching because she was there to help catch him as he fell.

"Whoa," he said. His head pounded and the room spun. How much had he drunk last night? This didn't feel like a normal hangover. He'd only been drunk a few times, not counting last night.

"You're burning up." Raven gave him an accusing look. "Back on the bed." She tried to push him, but with Fox on his other side, Aidan had his balance.

"Not before I go to the bathroom."

"Why you stubborn son of a—" She stopped her tirade and glanced at Fox.

"Don't worry, Fox. She's called me worse." He thought that was really funny and began to laugh, which made his head hurt worse.

"Let's get you to the bathroom and then right back into bed," Raven said.

"Said like that, how am I to resist?" he said suggestively.

Raven blushed and looked away. Hmm. What did that mean? Could she still feel something for him besides hate? They said there was a fine line between love and hate. But whoever had said that, probably didn't hate the way Raven did.

They helped him to the bathroom. Raven stood there with him next to the toilet. He raised a brow at her. "I can't pee with you watching."

"I don't want you falling to the floor."

"Just think, if I do, I might hit my head hard enough that I'd no longer be your problem."

She pursed her lips. "Fine. Come on, Fox. Let's give him some privacy."

Fox looked at Aidan and then his mother. "No." He shook his head. "I'll stay with him."

"I can do this on my own." In fact, he'd be doing it in his boxers if they didn't get out of here.

"Your life is mine, remember?" Fox continued. "I saved you. I won't let you die now over something stupid."

How did you argue with a kid who spoke with such wisdom? "Fine." He looked at Raven. Seriously, she needed to leave.

"All right," she muttered and left the room, closing the door with a snap behind her.

Fox shrugged. "Women."

Aidan cracked a laugh. "Yeah, women."

He emptied his bladder, flushed, and then moved to the sink to wash up. He caught his reflection in the mirror. Wow, he *did* look bad. His skin was red and blotchy and had a yellowish cast. His eyes were sunken with dark bags under them.

"See, I told you, you looked bad," Fox said. "We'd better get you back to bed, before you pass out."

"Good idea. Let me brush my teeth first."

"What's taking you guys so long?" Raven's muffled voice came through the door.

"Just a second, Mom."

Aidan grabbed for the toothbrush he'd used last night. And the room swam. He made a reach for the vanity counter.

Fox was there at his elbow, holding him steady. "I think you'd better brush you teeth sitting down."

"I think that's a good idea." What was wrong with him? He sat on the turned-down toilet seat, the crutches falling to the floor. His head became too heavy to hold, and he had to rest it in his hands. There was a buzzing in his ears.

Suddenly, Raven was there, peering into his eyes, feeling his forehead with her soothing cool hand, and cussing like a broke prospector. "Fox, go and get Eva. Hurry."

Fox scurried from the room.

"Back to bed for you." Raven helped him to his feet. "Lean on me." She held him up and cursed again when he fell against her.

He yelped in pain as he came down on his leg. She took his weight and somehow had the crutches under his arms.

"I can't do this without your help, Aidan. Come on, I'll steady you, but you're going to have to do most of the work."

Some part of his brain heard the worry in her voice, another heard the anger. Once again he was making her life hard. She should leave him. "Get out," he said. He was tired of her seeing the worst of him. Believing the worst of him.

"Yeah, you'd like that, wouldn't you?" She nudged him. "Move."

She pushed and pulled and finally he was sinking back onto the bed. Bad breath didn't seem as important right now as slipping back into nothingness.

Raven stood back, breathing hard. Holy shit, Eva was going to kill her. The heat coming off Aidan felt like a stoked wood stove. She grabbed the thermometer from the nightstand, shook it and placed it under his arm. He'd had a slight fever during the night, but that was to be expected after the trauma he'd been through. But this…this was more. This meant there was something really wrong. She glanced out the window. It was still dark…and still snowing. No heading into Fairbanks.

She should have watched him closer. Regardless of how she felt about him, she should have kept a better eye on him.

"What's wrong?" Fiona asked rushing into the room. "Fox hollered something as he rushed out."

"Aidan's got a fever. He can't even stay on his feet." She shared a worried look with her mother.

Aidan's head tossed back and forth on the pillow. "Fine," he said, his voice weak. "I'll be fine."

"Right." Raven wanted to smack him. "Why didn't you say you weren't feeling well?"

"Doesn't matter," he mumbled, his eyes closed. "Nothing matters anymore."

"Oh, my." Fiona reached down and placed her forearm on his forehead. "A hundred and three. We need to get him cooled down right away. I'll get some ice." She rushed out of the room.

A hundred and three? Come on. Raven grabbed the thermometer from under Aidan's arm. *A hundred and three.* How did she *do* that?

"Tell me," Eva demanded, blowing into the room, shedding her coat and hat, snowflakes falling to the floor in her wake.

Raven passed over the thermometer.

"Hmm," Eva said as she read it. "Bummer." She sighed. "I must have left something in there."

Fox entered. "Is he going to be all right?"

Raven's heart clenched. When she'd awoken and seen her son talking with his father it had thrown her. Why couldn't life have turned out that way? Waking to see her men having a conversation. She buried the thought. It would do no good to wish for what might have been. She needed to deal with what was. And right now her son was worried that the man he'd saved from death was journeying toward it again.

"Do you think a patient of mine would dare not get better?" Eva asked. When Fox shook his head and released a breath, Eva smiled and mussed his hair. "Right. Now, I need you to go to school. No." She shook her head when he went to interrupt. "The best thing you can do for me is to go to school. Aidan needs rest. He'll be better when you get home. Okay?"

"Promise?" Fox asked, worrying his lower lip.

"I'll do my best. No way will Aidan disappoint the both of us. Got it?"

Fox took a deep breath. "Okay." He turned to Aidan who was out cold on the bed. He leaned over and whispered something in his ear that Raven couldn't hear. Then her son turned and faced her, his young eyes serious. "Take care of him, Mom. He needs us."

She felt like she'd just taken an arrow to the heart. When had her young boy become so wise? He'd always been smart, but there was a difference between smart and wise. She wrapped her arms around him, his head already even with hers. Another year and he'd be taller than her. He'd gotten those genes from his father. "I love you, Fox." She kissed his cheek. "Now, don't worry. Eva's right. Aidan wouldn't dare disobey her."

Fox gave each woman a solemn look before leaving the room.

"He's gotten attached to his stray," Eva said.

Raven nodded. Fox was notorious for bringing home wounded animals.

"All right, Eva. What do we do?"

"What?" She raised a brow. "Volunteering?"

"No. Just…no."

Eva laughed. "That was well said."

"Listen. I just want him out of here. And that won't happen if he's not better. You know Mom, she'll insist he stay."

"Let me get this straight." Eva opened her bag and took out supplies to change Aidan's bandages. "You and Lynx hate him for his part in your dad's death, but Fiona doesn't?"

"She doesn't have it in her to hate anyone."

"She hated Earl Harte."

Raven frowned. "Yeah, but…everyone hated Earl."

"Fiona wouldn't hate someone because everyone else did." Eva soaked a gauze pad with alcohol and lowered Aidan's boxer short past his hips. "What's this? I don't remember seeing it last night."

"What's wrong?"

"This tattoo. Look." She pointed to the tattoo of a sun on Aidan's hip.

Raven caught her breath. She had a corresponding tat in the same area. She and Aidan had gotten them together when they were young and stupid, twelve years ago. She took another arrow to the heart at seeing the sun on his hip.

"Pretty," Eva said. "Not your usual sun. It has a Native Alaskan design. Interesting." She tore a syringe from a plastic covering and injected the antibiotic into Aidan's behind.

He tossed his head on the pillow and opened his eyes. "What's going on?"

"You have a very high fever, idiot," Raven said. "Why didn't you say something?"

"You had your head buried under the covers. And you'd told me to shut up." He closed his eyes again.

"You slept with him?" Eva asked.

Raven rolled her eyes. "I slept in the bed after getting cramped in the rocking chair."

"Lynx told me you had been sweet on him. Sure there aren't any unresolved feelings between you?"

"Let's just concentrate on getting him better and getting him out of here."

"Humph," Eva said, turning to the work at hand. She arranged items on the bed and then barked at Raven to hand over whatever she needed as she once again flushed the angry wounds in Aidan's leg. The sight of them made Raven's stomach twist. She couldn't imagine the pain the trap had caused him. She glanced at Aidan. He was out cold. Not seeming to care what Eva was doing to him. Raven knew from experience that Eva didn't have the softest touch. Eva was more than qualified, but she was no Mother Teresa.

Aidan lay there. It was like he didn't care if he lived or died. Lines etched his face, a face more ruggedly handsome after all these years. His soft brown eyes had been sad. Like his soul was dying. She shouldn't care. He deserved whatever he got. Just like that bastard father of his.

"Ah-ha!" Eva suddenly exclaimed, raising her tweezers with a piece of rusted metal clamped in the tines. "How did I miss this? Still, he shouldn't be having a fever that high from this yet. What aren't you telling me?"

"Me?" Raven asked.

"No." She pointed to Aidan. "Him. There has to be more going on for him to become sick so fast." She looked down at the swollen, bruised, and battered leg. "I really don't think it's broken. But I've been known to be wrong." She sat back and rubbed a hand over her stomach. "There's nothing we can do about getting him to medical care with the storm outside. So let's concentrate on what we can do. First, the fever has got to come down." She looked to Raven. "I'm going to need your help."

Raven went to interrupt, but Eva put her hand up. "Don't even. Fiona has her hands full with the guests. Lynx is off doing who knows what in that blizzard. And I'm eight months pregnant." She looked down her nose at Raven. "You know what they say about bad weather and labor, don't you?"

Raven paled. Eva was right, she could go into labor. And with the blizzard it would fall to Raven to help deliver. She'd rather not. "But I have orders to fill."

"They'll have to wait." Eva shrugged. "Sorry, but that is the way it is." She didn't seem sorry.

Raven sighed. "What do I have to do?"

Eva smiled as though she was going to enjoy this next part. "Sponge bath. We need to get his temp down, and that will be the quickest most efficient way."

You have got to be kidding me. "You want me to give Aidan a sponge bath."

"Yep. Repeated sponge baths until his temp is down under a hundred." She rubbed her belly again. "I couldn't reach enough of him with this beach ball in my way. You're the next best person for the job."

"What did I ever do to make you hate me like this?"

"Nothing, I just get off on making people do things they'd rather not. Call it a personality flaw. Besides, I need some entertainment. And the snow has knocked out my satellite dish."

"You're sadistic."

"Uh-huh," Eva agreed, giving Raven a bottle of pills. "Here. Give him one every eight hours, with food. And call me if he gets worse. Until then—" she rubbed her belly again, "—I'm going to go downstairs, have a huge stack of your mom's sourdough pancakes and then take a mid-morning nap." Eva stood and waddled her way out of the room.

Raven turned to Aidan.

Sponge bath?

CHAPTER FOUR

Raven gathered items for Aidan's sponge bath and approached the bed.

"Aidan?" she called. No response. He lay there, not doing much more than showing a pulse. She set the pan of tepid water on the nightstand. A washcloth floated under the surface.

Where to start?

He rested fitfully in his shirt and boxers. Batman boxers. He obviously still loved his superheroes. She was *not* taking them off, but guessed the shirt would have to go. She slipped the fabric up his stomach, watching as she dragged the material over his abs, his ribs, waiting for any change in Aidan's reaction. Any awareness. There wasn't. He was sleeping like the dead. It seemed extreme that if she didn't give him sponge baths he might actually end up taking a dirt nap. It was just a fever. Granted a high one. So he'd lose some brain cells. They were all going to grow old and senile anyway. He'd get there faster.

She grumbled under her breath as she pulled the shirt up and over his head. "Oh, my." She gulped catching full sight of him without his shirt. He'd kept himself in shape. Carved muscles were hot under her hands. Hot with fever. Her gaze jerked back at his face. Nothing. She turned back to his chest. Her eyes took in the smooth burnished skin, the dark nipples, the washboard abs, traveling lower to the groin muscles before his boxers covered the rest.

Maybe she should take off his boxers.

No. Absolutely not.

On a huff of disgusted breath, she grabbed the cloth and wrung the excess water out of it. She laid the washcloth on the side of his face, gasping in surprise when he moaned and turned his face into the cold material. She held her breath as she moved the cloth over his cheek. Rewetting the cloth, she ran it along his chiseled jaw, over his collarbone, slowly dipping into the hollow of his throat. He moaned again. She stopped and waited, breathing easier when he didn't do anything else. She dragged the washcloth over his chest, around his erect nipples.

She'd made love to this body. Worshipped it. They'd both been young. He'd grown into a man since then. He'd had a lanky body before. Thin, wiry, made of long lean muscle. Now he was a man with a man's body. His chest had spread, filled out, his shoulders and arms were muscled and thick. The body of a man who knew how to work. She'd heard he'd continued to commercial fish in Bristol Bay every summer with Earl. She ran her hands over his biceps. Obviously that was how he'd built these guns. She found herself licking her lips, and feeling a bit hot herself. She tossed the washrag into the pan of water and stood, running her hands through her hair. Absently, she started to braid the long length of it as she walked toward the window, in a vain attempt to cool off.

The snow was beautiful. White, pure, peacefully blanketing the earth in soft big flakes. She loved days like this, usually. There was nothing to do but wait the weather out. Snow days gave her the opportunity to lose herself in her pottery studio. She didn't have to drive anywhere. Errands were put on hold. She usually would throw something in the Crockpot and settle in front of her wheel and mold one creation after the other. But not today. Today she was stuck being a nursemaid. She glanced back to Aidan. And she shouldn't like it as much as she was.

After braiding her hair, she retrieved the tie she'd put in her pocket last night when she'd released it. A quick twist and it was secured and out of her way. She opened the window and let the cold air into the room and turned down the thermostat so the heat wouldn't kick on. She wasn't spending the next few hours sponge bathing Aidan's body to bring down his temp. Outside forces would have to help.

Raven returned to the bed and took a deep breath, picking up the rag and starting where she'd left off. Cooling down the room would hopefully cool her down too.

She ran the cloth down his ribs, over one side then the other. Reaching his six, no, eight pack of abdomen muscles, she rewetted the cloth. She traced each muscle. Admiring his form, the beauty of a well-conditioned male body. That was all. She could appreciate the beauty of his body even if she didn't appreciate the soul of the man inside of it.

She dragged the rag across his belly button, dipping inside then trailing to the waistband of his boxers. She noticed that something was awake. Very awake. Her eyes flew to Aidan's face, where he regarded her with his lids at half-mast.

How long had he been conscious? How long had she spent tracing each muscle on his abdomen?

She felt herself blush. His hands reached up and grasped her shoulders.

Oh, crap.

She read the intent in his slumberous, heated gaze just as he dragged her up his body. She should stop him. But then she was face to face with him, chest to chest, groin to groin, and he angled his head toward hers.

Her eyes widened, her heartbeat increased, and her lips parted just as his mouth took hers.

Suddenly her world stopped turning and then began spinning as fast as her pottery wheel. And like that clay, he molded her to him.

Oh, God, she'd missed him. No, not him. She'd missed *this*. Kissing. It had been a long time since she'd been in the company of another man. Months. Get real, it's been years. And no one had ever kissed her like Aidan Harte had, *was*. He made her shiver. He made her *want*. His body had changed, matured, and so had his kissing.

She was in trouble.

He flipped her onto her back and settled his weight against hers in all the right places. His body burned against hers, the cold room causing a delicious contrast. He yanked at the knit top she wore, freeing it, leaving her wearing her plain bra, sweatpants, and socks. His hands found her breasts, and he groaned. Tearing his mouth free from hers, his fevered eyes met hers as his hands kneaded her breasts.

"So soft." He reclaimed her mouth and rubbed his hard length against her. It was her turn to groan as his leg spread her thighs, making room for him to settle himself deeper against her.

How could she want this so badly when she hated him so much? He'd been gone without a word for twelve years. He'd never called, no letter, not even a freaking email. Yeah, she'd told him to never contact her again, but did he have to do exactly that?

His hand cupped her bottom and he lifted her against him. *Oh God, that felt good.* She hadn't had an orgasm in…in…well…in a damn long time. Couldn't she just let him—

No. Stop this now, before it goes any further.

His hand snaked under the waistband of her sweats right to her center. *Oh, yes, like that.*

Too far, too far. Put a stop to this, now.

Almost far enough—

His fingers entered her. Oh God, *yes.*

Her body bucked against him. She grabbed the sides of his hips. Her hand covering the tattoo they'd gotten together. His of the sun. Hers, the raven who carried the sun, bringing light and heat to the north. When their bodies were in this position, it looked as though her raven carried his sun on its back just like the Athabascan legend had foretold.

It was erotic. Especially after they'd gotten the tats and Aidan would come up and just place his hand on her hip, right over his raven. They'd share a look and know what the other was thinking. She'd missed that. She'd missed this.

She'd missed *him.*

What was she doing? She shouldn't be under him. Shouldn't be letting him touch her like this. Shouldn't be caring for him all over again. A sob escaped her. She pushed at his shoulders. No response, just his lips traveling to her neck, his stubble strapping her skin.

"No," she moaned, pushing at him again. This time her foot connected with his injured leg. He gave a yelp of pain and released her.

She scurried out from under him and stood next to the bed, breathing hard. Her chest rose and fell with the effort, her body mourning the heat of his hands.

He lifted his head and looked at her, his eyes sad and beseeching. "Why did you stop loving me, Raven?"

She opened her mouth to answer him but couldn't find the words. He closed his eyes and let out a breath as though his spirit was in pain and dropped his head to the bed. His shoulders slumped, and she knew he was out again.

The door opened and in walked her mother. "Raven?" She frowned. "I thought you were giving Aidan a sponge bath? Not yourself?"

"What?"

Fiona indicated Raven standing there in her bra.

She grabbed her shirt that was half under Aidan, yanked it free, and put it on.

"What's been going on here?"

Heat burned her cheeks. "Nothing, I just needed to change my shirt."

"Into what? You didn't bring any clothes with you." Fiona gave her a calculating look but let her off the hook with her next question. "How's your patient?"

"He isn't my anything."

"Right. Want to go over why you were only wearing a bra again?"

"No." She cleared her throat. "I don't know how he's doing." She didn't even know if he'd been fully conscious when they'd kissed. She had the feeling she really didn't know anything at all anymore. Especially about herself.

"I made lunch and thought I'd check to see if he wanted anything to eat." Fiona glanced down at Aidan. "By the looks of him, he isn't up to eating food, yet."

Had her mother put an emphasis on that 'food?'

"I'm hungry. I didn't get breakfast."

"I'll bring you up a plate then." Fiona went to leave the room but turned back when she was at the door. "It's really too bad you two didn't stay together. I always thought you and he were soul mates."

Fiona softly closed the door behind her after delivering that sucker punch.

Soul mates?

Raven looked at Aidan. Maybe at one time they might have been destined. But no longer. People made choices that affected everything. Things too big to overcome. She couldn't be with Aidan.

Not with the glacier that had formed between them.

Chapter Five

Aidan groaned. His body shook, shivered with cold. Was he back in the trap? No, he felt the pillow under his head. Well, if he had a pillow, he had to be lying on a bed. Where the hell were the blankets?

Right, Raven had stolen them. She'd always stolen things from him. Gum he'd carried in his pocket, dessert left on his plate. His heart.

But she'd given that back, broken and bruised.

He cracked open an eye. The sun had risen but didn't give him any idea of the time of day. It brightened the dreary view outside the windows. Snow continued to fall. He reached out a hand, feeling for the bedcovers and felt only sheets. He glanced around and found himself naked, except for his plaid boxers. Okay. That was new. He didn't remember stripping down.

What else had he missed?

"You're awake," Raven said, entering the room from the bathroom carrying a towel over her arm and a large bowl of water. "How do you feel?"

"Cold." He eyed the bowl of water. A memory teased the corners of his mind. Had they—no of course, they hadn't. Raven wouldn't allow him to touch her. She definitely wouldn't have willingly touched him.

"You're cold?" She rushed to the side of the bed, as quick as the pan of water in her hands would allow without spilling. Setting it down, she grabbed the thermometer. "Open up."

"I'd rather have a few blankets."

"Not yet. You've had a fever. Under the tongue, or I'll stick it somewhere else."

He opened his mouth. She stuck the thermometer under his tongue. They waited while he froze, goose bumps prickling over his skin. Was the window opened? The room was freezing. She pulled the thermometer out of his mouth and checked it.

She sighed. He couldn't tell if it was from relief or frustration.

"Am I going to live?"

She actually smiled as though she cared.

His heart skipped.

"Looks like." She held up the thermometer. "You're normal."

He cracked a laugh, his voice rusty. "Nobody's actually called me normal before."

"I meant, your temperature is normal. We thought we might lose you there for a while."

He frowned. "A while?"

"You've been in and out of it for two days."

"Two days?" He ran a hand over his eyes. *Two days.* Had Raven nursed him for two days? He was about to ask her when the door opened and Fox peeked his head around the edge.

"How's he doing?"

Raven gestured to Aidan with a smile. "See for yourself."

His eyes lit when he saw Aidan. "He's awake."

"His fever's broken too."

"'Bout time." Fox walked toward the bed. "We've been really worried about you."

"You have?" He glanced at Raven.

Raven placed her hand on Fox's shoulder. "Apparently he owns your soul now since he saved you from dying."

Aidan smiled at the kid. He wasn't in the mood to tell Fox that he wouldn't want any part of his soul. Not when it was black and rotten. He shivered. "Any chance of getting a blanket now that my fever's gone? I'm going to die from exposure in this room."

Raven tossed a blanket over him. It felt heavenly. "Thanks." She also went to the window and shut out the cold seeping through it. The cold room explained Raven's hoodie and knit cap she wore. She looked adorable. What he wouldn't give to—

"I'm sure you're hungry, since you haven't eaten in two days." Raven turned to Fox. "Will you run down to the kitchen and see what you can rustle up?"

"You bet." He looked back to Aidan. "Be right back." Then he scampered from the room.

Raven busied her hands with straightening the items on the nightstand, her eyes downcast. "Who's Sonya?"

The question hit him like a punch to the chest. "How do you know about her?"

"I don't. You just said her name a few times while you were out."

"What else did I say?" Had he confessed that he was a murderer?

"That's all I could make out. Are you married?"

"No. Are you?"

She lifted her head and met his gaze. If she were going to ask pointed questions, then so was he. "Uh, no."

"Fox's father?"

She glanced away. "We…uh…weren't suited."

It didn't look as though she was going to say any more on the subject. "I asked Sonya to marry me."

Raven looked at him again. "She's your fiancée then?"

"No. She didn't want to marry me. She's in love with another man."

"But you're still in love with her?"

Was he? Being back here and seeing Raven had tipped his world. He'd tried for the last twelve years to forget her and her family, transferring a lot of what he felt for them to Sonya and her family—his fish camp neighbors in the summertime when he commercial fished in Bristol Bay.

"Don't answer that," Raven said, standing, and smoothing her hands down her jeans.

He reached out and grabbed her arm. "I thought I loved her. But it wasn't a strong love." She tried to pull away from him, but he didn't let go. For some reason it was too important that she know. "I wanted the kind of love that *we* had with her, but it didn't work." He paused, then added quietly, "She wasn't you."

Her eyes flicked away from his, and she wetted her lips. "I need to go and see what's keeping Fox. You must be starved."

He released her, and she ran from the room.

Why had he said that? He had no chance with her.

Not when his father had killed hers.

She wasn't you.

Raven ran from Aidan's room, gasping. She couldn't breathe. Her heart pounded and her palms sweated.

She wasn't you.

Did he still care for her? After all these years? After all she'd done? What was she thinking? There was no room for Aidan in her life. Not with the past between them. She couldn't allow there to be. Fox had to be considered. She'd been very careful with him, raised her son to be different than his genetics. The part of him that had come from Aidan, and Aidan's parents, Earl and Marjorie Harte. There was also Roland Harte—Earl's brother—to be considered, who liked to visit during the winter, trailing mischief and mayhem in his tracks. Roland had also done jail time, hadn't he? How many Hartes had spent time in jail? Earl was a murderer. Dangerous, mean, and cunning. She'd seen that same kind of cunning in Fox. She didn't want any of the Hartes' unsavory qualities to negatively influence her son. She'd made life-altering decisions based on that reasoning.

Raven entered the kitchen and found Fox and Fiona along with her grandmother, Coho, who sat at the table beading an intricate Athabascan design into a leather band while Fiona helped Fox put together a tray of food.

"Hey, Gran," Raven greeted, dropping into a seat across from her grandmother.

"*Camai*, birdie. A few exciting days you've had." Coho frowned over her bifocals. "I had to hear these things from others, you understand."

"I'm sorry, Gran, but I have been busy taking care of *that* man."

"And how is Aidan doing? I have missed him over the years. Such an interesting boy. So unlike his black-hearted father and weak-minded mother." She sighed and threaded beads onto her needle. "It's nice to know he didn't follow in his parents' footsteps."

"What do you mean?" Raven asked. How would Coho know what Aidan had done with his life? *She* didn't even know.

"I thought you knew? Fox has known for years."

"Grandma Great," Fox rushed over. "You weren't—"

"Oh, that's right." She laughed. "I wasn't supposed to tell. Oops." She smiled, acting forgetful, but Raven knew she was anything but. Coho's mind was as sharp as the needle she pierced through the leather band.

"What weren't you supposed to tell?" Raven looked to her grandmother and then to her son, who glanced at his feet. "What's going on?"

"Better come clean, grandson," Coho said out of the corner of her month as she continued to sew beads into the leather strip.

Fox fidgeted but glanced at Raven when he spoke. "I know who Aidan Harte is."

Raven's breath caught. Her son knew Aidan was his father? How? Nobody knew. *She'd never told a living soul.*

Fox went over to his backpack and pulled out a book, laying it on the table in front of her. "Mr. Harte is a famous graphic novelist. See, he writes a series of novels that feature the powers of the totem."

"*This* is what you didn't want me to know?" Raven frowned. So Fox didn't know Aidan was his father? The light in the room seemed to dim as Raven's heart tried to regain its normal rhythm.

"Uh, you probably wouldn't consider them appropriate reading material." Fox hesitated to begin. "But they *so* are," he rushed on. "He writes about the battle between good and evil and good always wins, though sometimes it looks like there is no way they can, but he always makes it happen."

"Where did you get these?" She caught the look shared between Fiona and Fox.

"I ordered them off the Internet," he mumbled.

"With whose help?" Raven shot a look at her mother.

"With mine," Fiona answered, raising her chin. "I didn't see the harm in it, and besides, I've read them and they are quite good. It's nice to know that Aidan has made such a success of himself."

Raven picked up the glossy book and thumbed through it, a little smaller than the size of a magazine but bound like a novel. The pages were full of vibrant colors, the words captured in bubbles. Kind of like the old-time comic books, but in a much more elegant, sophisticated style. She immediately recognized the level of talent it would have taken to draw the characters and settings. She glanced at the front where Aidan's name was prominently featured in bold letters. "Can I read this?"

Fox looked worried. Appropriate content? Right.

"Sure, but keep an open mind, Mom. See the whole story, not just a few of the scenes. Okay?"

Raven raised a brow but nodded.

"Who is taking a lunch tray to Aidan?" Fiona asked. "Fox or you?"

She raised her hand. "I will." She didn't want her son getting more attached to Aidan than he already was.

"But, Mom," Fox objected. "I wanted to."

"Is your homework done?" She nailed him with a look. "Chores?"

"No, and no," he muttered.

"Get them done then. Besides, Mr. Harte needs a lot of rest so that he can recover quickly." And get the hell out of their lives before he really messed them up more than he already had.

CHAPTER SIX

Raven walked into Aidan's bedroom, balancing the tray on one hand. The bed was empty. Could she be so lucky? She heard colorful words coming from the bathroom. Guess not. She set down the tray on the nightstand and followed the cursing. Aidan was sprawled out on the floor, one of his crutches completely out of his reach by the linen closet. "What *are* you doing?"

"Trying to take care of myself," he growled like a wounded bear.

"You've been in bed with a fever for two days. I won't even bring up the trap. You have no business getting out of bed. You want a relapse?"

"I need a shower." He looked at her with that same look Fox developed when he decided he had to do something right this minute and was going to be stubborn about it.

"And you thought you could accomplish that by yourself?" He was just like any other man. Stupid.

"You want to give me a hand?" he asked. "Help me undress, soap me up, dry me off?" He raised that brow of his, suggestive and sardonic at the same time. How did he do that with one look?

"No, I don't want to help you." She stuck her hands on her hips. "I've been giving you sponge baths for two days. Believe me, you are clean. You don't need a shower."

"So…" He cocked his head to the side. "I *didn't* dream that?"

The sponge bath or the kiss followed by the almost sex? She felt heat rise in her cheeks. Just what did he remember? "Dream what?"

"You. Us. On the bed. Together. My fingers inside—"

"Dreaming!" she interrupted. "You definitely were dreaming *that*."

He gave her a look that said he wasn't buying it, but he let the subject drop. "You going to help me up, or leave me here on the floor?"

She would have loved to leave him on the floor, but she was never one for tormenting someone. Unless it resulted in pleasure for them both. Like that time she had—

What was she doing? Remembering their sexual escapades wouldn't do either of them any good. She walked over to the crutch that had skidded across the floor and picked it up. "How did you end up in this position anyway?"

"Reached to turn on the shower. Lost my balance and came down on my bad leg. It gave out, and I went down."

She pursed her lips. "Do you think it's broken then?"

"I don't know. but it hurts a hell of a lot."

"It's supposed to stop snowing sometime this afternoon. They'll get the plows out here hopefully tomorrow or the next day." Until then, it looked as though she was stuck playing nursemaid.

Why didn't the reality of that upset her as much as it had earlier?

Aidan sighed with relief once he was back in the bed. The trip to the bathroom and then the literal trip *in* the bathroom had taken what strength he'd had. The fever had zapped him of everything it seemed. He was shaky, tired, and his head pounded like an Inuit drummer calling for the sun. He watched through narrowed lids as Raven tended to him. Her actions were fast and choppy like she was nervous.

He hadn't dreamt that he'd had his hands on her, his lips. That she had moaned his name, kissed him, grabbed his hips. She still desired him. He smiled inwardly. He hadn't felt good about himself for a long time. Life had sucked for a long time.

Whether Raven wanted to admit it or not, she still cared. Her body's response didn't lie like the words coming out of her mouth. The same mouth that had kissed him, bit him.

She propped a pillow under his leg and covered him with a light blanket. He was still only wearing boxers. She kept stealing glances at his bare chest so he folded the blanket down, letting it rest over his hips as he leaned against the headboard. She set the tray across his lap and then moved back.

"Thank you," he said. "I can't remember a time when I've been so hungry." He looked over Raven's body until she blushed. Satisfaction rose inside him, warming him. He glanced at the tray of food wishing he could take a taste of her instead. A bowl of hearty stew with a side of crusty bread, lathered in butter, and canned peaches filled the plate. "Let Fiona know how much I appreciate her."

"You'll be able to tell her yourself, later."

He tried the stew. Full-favored with chunks of moose meat. Must be leftovers from the roast the other day.

Raven busied herself straightening up the room while he spooned in the stew. There wasn't much to clean so she soon didn't have anything to do. She took a seat in the rocker and curled her feet up under her. A yawn surprised her. He wondered how much sleep she'd gotten while caring for him the last few days.

She caught him watching her. "Eva should be here to check on you soon."

He grimaced. "The demon nurse from hell?"

She cracked a laugh. "You called that right. But she does know her stuff." Raven leaned her head back against the chair.

"Why don't you get some sleep?"

"I'm fine." She yawned again.

"No, you're not." He spooned more of the stew into his mouth and chewed.

"Don't worry about me." She scowled at him.

He set the spoon down. "Does it bother you that I think about you? That I've thought about you many times over the years?" His voice lowered. "Wondered how you were?"

"Don't do that." She stiffened. "If you thought about me like you say, why didn't you ever call?" She clamped her mouth shut, lips tightening into a line, as though she couldn't believe she'd just asked that.

"You told me to never contact you again. Made me promise, remember?" He looked down at his stew, his appetite waning. "After your dad died, you had every right to hate me. I thought I was doing what you wanted."

"You were. You did." She sighed and rubbed her temples. "It was what I wanted."

"Is it still?"

Her eyes met his, large and dark, and swimming with secrets. Would she be honest with him? She *had* missed him, he knew it.

The way she'd responded to him told the tale, but was it enough with what lay between them? She opened her mouth to answer and then promptly closed it. The demon nurse from hell entered the room looking sweet in pink. What he wouldn't give to know what Raven had been about to say at that moment.

"Hey, you're awake," Eva said as she sailed into the room, tossing her coat over the end of the bed and a bag on the floor. "And it looks as though the fever has gone." She turned to Raven. "Good job, told you sponge baths would do the trick." She regarded Aidan. "About time you started to cooperate."

Like this had been his fault. He set aside the meal, finding himself full after only eating half of what was on the tray. Eva took his vitals, checked his blood pressure, and removed his bandages, all in the space of a few minutes. The little Napoleonite didn't waste time. She was efficient, if not compassionate, in her ministrations.

"Hmm," she hummed, while regarding his leg.

"What?" he asked, trying to see what she did.

"The swelling has gone down. I still want an x-ray as soon as we can get you to Fairbanks." She narrowed a look at him. "Don't go thinking you can get up and do cartwheels now."

He hadn't been thinking cartwheels, but getting out of this room was at the top of his list. Cabin fever had already started to wander in. The last few days, he'd only seen Eva, Raven, Fiona, and a little of Fox. He hadn't seen anything of Lynx, who was obviously avoiding him. The coward. Aidan had hoped to sneak into town, clean up his dad's messy life, and sneak right back out. Avoiding everyone.

So much for that.

Now he needed to make the best of it, and maybe in the process, make some amends. He looked at Raven, and smiled.

She'd fallen asleep curled up in the rocking chair. She looked so innocent, her hair tied back into a lose braid, wisps falling around her face. Her smooth skin was stained with dark crescents under darker lashes, highlighted by sharp cheekbones. She'd been beautiful as a child and a young woman. Now she was breathtaking.

"So what's the story between you two?" Eva asked as she rewrapped his bandages.

"She hasn't told you?"

"Would I be asking if she'd given me anything to go on? And before you tell me that it's none of my business, remember who your pain pill supplier is."

"We were really good friends once."

"Right. If I were to guess, I'd say you guys were high school sweethearts. I wouldn't be surprised if you two hooked up. Am I right?"

Aidan shrugged. Not agreeing or disagreeing. Not that it did any good as Eva continued.

"Of course, I'm right. I've watched you moon over her the last few days. Now, Raven, she plays things close to the chest. A lot like her brother, that one. But there has been more spark in her since you've returned."

"She's probably thinking of scenarios to get rid of me."

"Oh, I'm sure of it. But at least she's showing some fire." Eva finished and gathered her supplies. "I'll be back to check on you tomorrow unless you have a setback." She pointed a sharp finger at him. "Don't do that, got it? I want a good night's sleep." She rubbed her belly. "This little tyke does enough kicking to keep me up. I don't need you adding to it. Understand?"

"Yes, ma'am."

"Good." She turned to leave.

"Before you go, could you cover Raven up with a blanket?"

Eva's smile turned soft. She grabbed the afghan that was folded on the other side of the bed and covered Raven with it. "Doubt she'll get a lot of rest in that position." She shrugged, turned to Aidan and pointed again. "No cartwheels."

"Wouldn't think of it."

"Good patient." Eva indicated the bag she'd dropped next to the side of the bed when she'd entered. "There are some clothes in there that ought to fit you. I assumed your clothes are stuck out at your father's place. Can't have you running around naked, though I'm sure some wouldn't mind." She gave his bare chest a long glance, and then she was gone, closing the door behind her.

Aidan lay on the bed, weak but aching to do something besides sleep. He picked up a notepad next to the phone on the nightstand and rooted around in the top drawer until he found a pencil. He hadn't been able to write or draw since his dad's death. His therapist had told him that he needed to work through it. Like he didn't know that. He was paying her a hundred and fifty dollars an hour for 'work through it.' Many times he'd tried. Many times he'd tried. The exercise had ended in frustration, a few broken pencils and one smashed drawing board. For months now, he hadn't even bothered to pick up a pencil.

But this afternoon, with the weak light coming through the window, the snow softly falling outside and Raven slightly snoring, he began to draw.

Raven woke cramped, her legs and back aching. She straightened in the hard, wooden chair, her bones creaking in the silent room. Sleeping like this had to stop. She glanced over at the soft bed with longing. But sleeping with Aidan couldn't happen again. She stood and stretched, yawning as she studied him. He was fast asleep. Dark lashes created deep shadows, making the smudges under his eyes even darker. He looked…strained. As if his body was going through motions needed to function, and that was all.

The clock on the bedside said five. But was it evening or morning? There was no telling with the sun hibernating.

She needed to see to Fox. It seemed like she hadn't spent any quality time with her son in days, not with Aidan taking up all her time. She walked over to the bed and lightly laid her hand against his forehead and breathed a sigh of relief. No fever. She made sure his covers were tucked around him, then grabbed the leftover tray from his lunch and quietly left the room.

A soft light at the end of the hallway guided her to the main living space. She nodded to the few guests sitting around visiting. Must be five in the evening. Fiona would probably get a few extra reservations from this snow storm for the weekend. The snow machine trails in and around Chatanika were legendary.

She made her way into the kitchen and found her younger sister, Chickadee. She hadn't seen her in days, either. Hadn't even thought of her. Showed where her head had been. She'd neglected her son and forgotten her baby sister. Aidan definitely had to leave. She needed to get back to her life.

"Hey, Dee. What've you been up to?" she asked.

"I've been buried in mountains of snow at Shawnee's place. Her dad finally dug us out and brought me home." She flipped her black straight-as-rain hair, like a shampoo model, over her shoulder. "I thought *I* was having fun, but I heard you're the one having all the excitement."

Raven set the tray on the counter and took a seat at the table. "Excitement that I could have happily done without."

"Is he as hot as Mom says?"

Raven arched her brows. "Mom thinks Aidan's hot?"

"Okay." She rolled her eyes. "Mom said dashing, but I interpreted that to mean hot." She leaned forward. "So, is he hot?"

"It doesn't matter, because he's my age and *you* are only fifteen."

"Yeah, but there aren't any men around here. I'm bored." She pouted.

"Don't let Mom hear you say that."

Chickadee looked around, fear flashing for a moment in her dark eyes. The kid ought to be scared. 'Bored' was a dirty word around these parts. If Fiona heard any of her children utter the word, it was bound to get them saddled with cleaning toilets, or worse.

Fiona breezed into the kitchen. "There's my girls. Just who I needed to see."

Raven and Chickadee looked at each other. Chickadee's expression clearly wondering if the word 'bored' had brought her mother like a homing pigeon.

Fiona narrowed her eyes, planted her hands on her hips, and addressed Chickadee. "What's going on?"

"You're going to want us to do something," Chickadee made the mistake of saying. Fiona looked to Raven who kept her mouth zipped.

"Well, in this case, you're right. Bree called in snowbound, and I need a waitress for tonight. Who's going to put on an apron?"

Raven refrained from commenting, though she did grin when Chickadee looked at her and batted her eyelashes as in, "Please, Raven, I'm too young and cute to waitress." Raven shook her head. "I'm playing nursemaid. You get to be the waitress."

"This sucks."

"Chickadee," Fiona scolded. "That's a dollar you owe the swear jar. Better make it up in tips tonight."

Raven bit her lips to keep from grinning. There had been many times when she had funded the swear jar herself. Now she was more discrete when she let lose one of the five 's' words. At least around her mother.

Fiona turned to Raven. "Aidan's fever still down?"

"Uh…" If she admitted Aidan was doing better, Fiona would rope her into waitressing too. "Eva said he still needs to be watched. Have you seen Fox anywhere?"

"He's in the restaurant. Pike's got him peeling potatoes. All this snow makes people hungry." She frowned. "Aidan ought to get up and move around some. Lying about in bed isn't going to do him any good."

Aidan chose that moment to bump his way into the kitchen on crutches, wearing green and blue striped Bermuda shorts that Raven recognized as Lynx's and a blue t-shirt that had 'Alaska Grown' written across the front.

Raven jumped to her feet. "What are you doing out of bed?"

"Going stir crazy," he huffed. She helped guide him to one of the chairs at the kitchen table. He sat and gathered the crutches in one hand. "I must be out of shape."

"It couldn't be fighting a fever for the last two days." The body she'd sponge bathed was not out of shape. Raven took the crutches and leaned them against the wall. "If you wanted to get up, why didn't you wait until I returned? You could have fallen again."

The look on his face said he didn't like her informing the room he'd had trouble earlier. "I didn't know if you were going to return. I woke up alone," he said, his tone almost a whine. He behaved a lot like Fox did when he was sick. Raven didn't like seeing the similarities. She retook her seat.

"Well, I'm glad to see you feeling better, Aidan." Fiona came over and patted him on the shoulder. "Let me reintroduce you to my baby."

"M-o-m," Chickadee moaned. Poor thing hated being called the baby. She'd been a big surprise to her parents as there were thirteen years between her and the youngest of the other Maiski offspring. And she still constantly surprised everyone.

"Last time you saw her, she was only three. This is Chickadee, or Dee as she likes to be called now that she's older."

"Wow, am I feeling old." Aidan studied her. "You look a lot like Raven did at your age." His voice turned soft, reminiscing.

Raven got up from the table and made her way to the sink to make a pot of tea. She didn't need to think about how she'd looked when she was younger. Or how she'd acted.

Chickadee smiled. "As long as I don't look like Lynx."

Aidan laughed. "Nope, nothing like Lynx."

Raven put the kettle on to boil and turned around. Aidan was looking directly at her.

"What about Tern?" he asked, not taking his eyes off Raven. "Is she still around, causing trouble somewhere?"

"Tern moved to Fairbanks and opened an art gallery type gift shop called The Arctic Tern," Fiona said. "She's doing very well. I've given up hope of any of my girls settling down." Fiona arrowed a look at Raven.

"What?"

"Nothing." Fiona moved to the fridge and opened it, pulling out sandwich makings. "Still a fan of my Reubens, Aidan?"

His mouth dropped open. "Yes, ma'am."

Fiona smiled. She loved a man who appreciated her cooking, but this time she set all the ingredients out on the counter and turned to Raven. "Here you go, Raven. Make him a sandwich. Come on, Chickadee." She motioned with her hand. "Let's go help out in the dining room." Chickadee grumbled but followed Fiona out of the kitchen, leaving Raven to wait on Aidan.

The lodge had a private kitchen for the family, and then an industrial version, with her Uncle Pike running the stoves, adjacent to a large dining room and restaurant for guests and anyone else after a hot, home cooked, Alaskan meal.

The tea kettle whistled. Raven turned off the heat and prepped her mug with a tea bag, pouring hot water into it, adding in milk. "You want a cup of tea?"

"Yeah, that sounds great."

She placed a mug in front of him, along with the cream. "There's sugar if you want it." She indicated the pottery bowl squatting in the middle of the table.

"Thanks." He reached for the cream and stirred, leaving out the sugar. He ran his finger down the side of the cup. "Great mug, love the colors how they bleed from blue to green."

"Thanks." She turned back toward the sandwich makings. "I made them."

"You made this?" He looked closer at the mug. "It's nice. Great form, stylish yet functional handle." He glanced around the kitchen, noticing other pottery pieces. He picked up the bowl in the middle of the table that her mother used for fruit. "Did you make this too?"

"Yes."

"You're very talented. How did you get into pottery?"

"Long story." One she didn't want to go into right now as it was one of those choices made as a result of her teenage pregnancy. "You still want that Reuben?" She needed to get his mind on food and off her.

"Can you make a Reuben like your mom?" Aidan put the bowl down and looked at her skeptically. "If I remember right, you weren't too handy in the kitchen."

She scowled at him, set aside her tea, and grabbed the corned beef. "One little fire and nobody will let you live it down."

"It wasn't so little."

"You want to eat or not?"

"All right. Shutting up."

"Careful, that's one of the 's' words."

He laughed. "Fiona's still doing that? Is the cost still a quarter?"

"Of course she's still doing it. With inflation the fee has now risen to a dollar."

"Ouch. I'll have to put in an IOU until I can get to my things." He glanced out the dark window at the snow-blanketed wilderness. "Have any idea when that might be?"

"Tomorrow, hopefully." She sliced thin pieces of corned beef and heated them in a skillet. Toasting thick slices of rye, she spread on her mother's secret sauce, and then transferred the heated pieces of meat to the bread.

"Man, that smells good," Aidan said. She glanced up and caught him watching her, and raised a brow. He smiled. "Seems you've found your way around the kitchen, after all."

Fox came busting in, carrying a plate of French fries, a smile splitting across his face, the dimple on his left cheek winking. "Look what I made."

Raven grinned with pleasure at seeing her son. His face was alight with accomplishment and pride.

"Uncle Pike told me what to do, but he let me do it all by myself. I even handled the deep fryer myself." He held out the plate. "Taste 'em. They're great."

Raven grabbed a fry and bit into it, the taste exploding in her mouth, spicy and tangy with the perfect amount of salt. "Fox, these are wonderful. What did you put on them?"

He gave her a clever smile. "It's my secret recipe." He glanced over at Aidan, and his face brightened even more.

A twinge of uneasiness embedded itself in Raven's heart.

Fox brought the plate over to Aidan. "How are you feeling, Mr. Harte?"

"Much better, thanks. And call me Aidan."

Fox beamed. "Sure, Aidan." He offered up the plate. "Try one of my fries."

Aidan took a fry and bit into it, his eyes widening. "These are amazing."

"Uncle Pike's going to put them on the menu and call 'em Fox's Fabulous French Fries." He set the plate on the table and claimed a chair.

Raven placed the Reuben in front of Aidan, along with a napkin and silverware. "Thanks." He glanced up at her with gratitude. "This looks great."

"You're making Reubens?" Fox asked. "Can I have one?" He turned to Aidan. "Aren't they the best sandwiches ever?"

Aidan laughed. "I've always thought so." He took a bite and closed his eyes. "Nobody makes a Reuben like Fiona. At least that's what I've always thought, until now." He gazed at Raven. "Very good."

Raven felt herself blush and turned away, a lump rising in her throat at the domestic scene. This was the way things should have been. She started another sandwich and listened to Fox fill them both in on the great day he'd had. Once school had gotten out, he'd trumped his friend Grand in a snowball fight, taken care of his dogs—all eight of them—then filled Aidan in on his plans to run his dogs in the Fur Rendezvous and then the Yukon Quest just as soon as he was old enough. And then, once he'd gotten a few wins under his belt, he planned to race in the Iditarod.

Raven added ketchup and mustard to the table and the kettle in case Aidan wanted to refill his cup. Once Fox's sandwich was done, she cut it diagonally and placed it in front of her son.

"Aren't you going to eat?" Aidan asked her.

She was too melancholy to eat. She went to shake her head, but Fox added, "Come on, Mom."

Aidan, she could turn down, but not Fox and his sweet smile. She picked up a plate and took a seat, grabbing a fry. She wasn't hungry, but they were good. She could get down a few.

"Here," Aidan placed half of his sandwich on her plate. "I'm hungry, but my stomach doesn't want to hold much after going without the last few days."

She looked down at the sandwich, and tears filled her eyes. She rapidly blinked them back and took a deep breath. Why did he have to be kind to her? She didn't want him to be kind. She wanted him to leave.

Raven had made choices that had left her a single parent. Those choices were based on good reasons. Reasons she still believed in. She picked up the sandwich and bit into it, even though she didn't want it. She chewed and swallowed, went through the motions as her son continued to entertain them with his antics.

She prayed the roads would be clear tomorrow and they could move Aidan out. She didn't want any more interactions between Fox and Aidan. Didn't want them to become close.

Aidan would break her son's heart too.

CHAPTER SEVEN

"All right, time for bed, young man," Raven said, standing from the table. It was past time to call this 'family dinner' over. She bent down and kissed Fox on the forehead.

"M-o-m." He gave her the look that said he wasn't a little boy anymore, and please don't kiss him in front of the man he was trying to impress.

Raven knew all of this, even understood it, but she was his mother and if she wanted to kiss her son on the forehead when he was sixty, she'd do it. "Come on. You have school in the morning."

"Thirty minutes more?" he pleaded, his large dark eyes framed with long fluttering lashes appealing to her to give in. He must have picked that look up from Chickadee.

"Nope. Besides, it's time for Mr. Harte to go to bed too." She stared at Aidan and he wisely nodded.

"Okay." Fox got to his feet and shuffled toward the back door, grabbing his parka off the hook where it hung among the others. "Am I spending the night with Uncle Lynx or at our place?" He slipped into the coat but failed to zip it up.

Poor guy had been batted around from relative to relative while his mother had been saddled with taking care of Aidan. "Our place. I'll be there as soon as I get Mr. Harte settled. Remember to brush your teeth," she hollered as he opened the door and walked through it, biting back the words to zip up his coat as the cold air flooded into the room.

"I'm almost twelve," he hollered back. "I can remember to brush my own teeth." He let the door slam behind him. She wondered, briefly, how long it took for kids to learn to shut a door instead of slamming one.

She turned and regarded Aidan, who was much too handsome in the soft, intimate light around the kitchen table. "You ready?"

"Where's your place?" Aidan asked, getting awkwardly to his feet, and reaching for the crutches leaning against the wall next to him. The room seemed to get smaller as he stood.

She'd always loved his height and broad shoulders. Even when he was a thin and wiry teenager. Now that he was more filled out, she liked it even more. He made her feel protected, and delicate standing next to him, even though she knew she could lose a few pounds. She needed to keep her mind on his body. *Off his body.* Jeez. She was in more trouble here than she thought if her subconscious couldn't even keep up. "We built a cabin a few years ago, just behind the lodge, through the trees overlooking the river."

He stilled his movements, his eyes heating as he looked at her. "Fool's Cove?"

Why hadn't she just said her place was behind the lodge and left it at that? "Uh...yeah. Come on. Let's get you to bed so I can get some sleep myself." She reached for his arm to help him, but he stopped her.

"You built a cabin at Fool's Cove? Where we first—"

"It had nothing to do with that." Like she was so heartsick she'd built her home on the spot where they'd first—and many times after—had snuck away to make love. Get real. "The spot has an amazing view and access to the river, close to the lodge without being too close, and I got it for a song when old man Tack died." He'd willed it to her as he had a soft spot for the young lovers he'd interrupted that summer. She'd always suspected he knew Aidan was Fox's father. But he'd never said anything, which she was supremely grateful for.

"Old Tack died? How?"

"Run-in with a bear."

"Oh, that's great. He always wanted to go out with a bang like that." Aidan smiled. "Remember that time he caught us making love and proceeded to lecture us on birth control and family planning?" He laughed.

"Yeah." *Real funny.* They should have paid more attention to what old Tack had told them. But then she wouldn't have Fox in her life now. She urged Aidan out of the kitchen and down the hallway. The trek was slow.

No way was she staying the night again. She'd make sure he had everything he needed, tuck him into bed and be done. He was doing better, able to move around on his own with the help of crutches. If not graceful, at least he was mobile. He'd be fine on his own.

Following Aidan into the bedroom, she straightened his bedding while he brushed his teeth and used the bathroom on his own. He'd brought up the subject of a shower again, but the look she'd given him had shot it down.

He reentered the room, and she stepped back from the bed as he approached. "I have a glass of water here." She pointed to the nightstand. "Your bottle of antibiotics and anti-inflammatories. Is there anything else you need?"

"Yeah." He leaned the crutches against the bed and stood in front of her. "Who is Fox's father?"

"What?" Her heart stopped. She stepped back, but Aidan grabbed her shoulders and kept her in place.

"All the talk about old Tack and Fool's Cove got me thinking what I should have been thinking before." He flexed his jaw. "Who is Fox's father?"

Panic crawled up her spine. "None of your business."

"I don't believe that. I did the math. Fox said he was almost twelve when you reminded him to brush his teeth." His hands tightened on her shoulders. "Is he my son?"

She swallowed hard and shook her head. *This couldn't be happening.*

He looked deep into her eyes. "We like the same kind of sandwich."

"A lot of people like Reubens. That doesn't mean they're related," she scoffed, while inside she was screaming.

He stared deep into her eyes, searching. "Are you sure?"

She glanced away. She'd never lied to Aidan before. They'd promised to always tell each other the truth. Always. It had been a huge thing with Aidan as his parents had lied constantly to each other and to him. But she'd made that promise when they'd been young and stupid. Adults sometimes lied to protect those they cared about. That was all she was doing. Protecting Fox. "When you left, I slept with a man I met in a bar. Call it a rebound." She studied her feet. "I never saw him again."

He shook her once, making her look at him. "Is *that* what you've told Fox? That his dad was a one-night-stand and you didn't have the sense to get his name and number after you fucked him?"

She caught her breath and pushed out of his grip. He fell onto the bed, off balance. "Why do you care?" she demanded.

He stood back up. *"Why do I care?* You were everything to me, Raven. I loved you. There wasn't anything I wouldn't do for you. And you knew it. Why else would I have left you when it was the last thing in the world I ever wanted to do?"

It hurt to breathe. Her heart raced, and the room seemed to be closing in on her. "I gotta go."

"Damn it, Raven." Aidan grabbed her again and yanked her into this arms. His eyes—hurt and troubled—stared into hers.

She knew he wanted to say something else, but then his tortured gaze fell to her lips. He groaned and crushed his mouth to hers. She whimpered, a little with fear, a little with excitement, and a lot with need. His arms came around her, squeezing her to his chest like he was afraid she'd slip away. She tasted desperation but didn't know if was his or hers, and the sweet, sweet taste of memories of what could have been. Her arms stretched of their own accord. Her body began doing things she didn't want it to do. Like rubbing against him, arching into his erection, cradling it with her heat. He groaned and swiveled on his one good leg until the back of her legs were against the bed. Then he lowered her down to the mattress.

His hot hands tunneled under her shirt, right to her aching breasts. Her nipples hardened making them ache even more. He tore his mouth from hers and his eyes bored into the depths of hers. "God, I've missed you."

He kissed her again, his fingers undoing the clasp of her bra, freeing her breasts to his searching hands. She hadn't been touched like this in so long. There had been a few fumbles since

Aidan, but none of them had been him. He'd spoiled her for any other man. The way he'd worshipped her body, made her feel like she was everything. Tears leaked from her closed lids. She wanted him. Oh, how she wanted him.

Aidan pushed his leg between hers, spreading them wide for him to settle his erection at the heart of her, rubbing against her, making her moan, arch, and writhe under him. His hand reached between them, releasing the button to her jeans. She sucked in her stomach as his fingers trailed down. She needed to stop him. Needed to stop herself. Somehow he'd lost his shirt, and her hands kneaded the hard, strong muscles there.

His fingers trailed fire as they caressed her tattoo. "Raven, let me make you fly."

A sob hit her at his words. "No." She pushed at his immovable chest. His broad shoulders blocked out the light, keeping her cocooned within the power of his arms. What she wouldn't give to stay here within their promised protection. Life alone was hard and lonely. But she couldn't betray her father's memory by loving the son of his murderer. She pushed against his chest again, harder. "No, Aidan."

He stopped, his hands on her hips, fingers digging in, ready to strip her of the remainder of her clothing. His breathing was hard, like the rest of him. She wanted what his dark, smoldering eyes promised. Wanted him to send her flying. She'd flown solo all these years. And solo was a lonely flight.

"You want me, Raven," he said, his voice strained.

"Yes, but I can't have you."

Raven entered the kitchen on shaky legs and headed toward the back door. She reached for her coat but didn't put it on. The cold would do her good. Maybe she'd even take a minute to lie in the snow and snuff out the flames licking her body.

"Are you going home?"

Raven yelped and swung toward her mother's voice. With all that was in her head and the unfulfilled yearning in her body, she hadn't noticed anyone in the kitchen. Fiona sat at the table going over a list—she was famous for her list making—while nursing a cup of tea.

"Yes. Aidan will be fine on his own tonight." If he felt well enough to engage in the type of activity that they had been engaging in, he was well enough to take care of himself.

"Do you think that's wise?" Fiona lifted a brow.

Very wise. "He doesn't have a fever, he's mobile and he's an adult. And besides, I'm not his keeper." Why was Fiona giving her that look? The one that said she was in trouble. Did her mother know what she and Aidan had been doing? Was it painted on her face? Fiona always seemed to know whatever her kids had been up to. She would have caught on sooner with what Aidan and Raven had been up to twelve years ago if she and her dad hadn't been fighting a land claim with Earl Harte. "Is there something wrong, Mom?"

"Actually, yes. Have a seat, daughter. I need to talk with you."

Raven sat. Her mother sounded serious. Had something else happened?

Fiona flexed her hands around her mug. "I know who Fox's father is. I've always known."

Raven gasped.

Fiona continued, "I've been content not to say anything while Earl was alive. But he's dead. It's no longer an issue to keep Fox's parentage a secret. I understand why you did what you did, but

Aidan deserves to know he has a son. He should have known all along."

"How…" Raven tried to swallow past the lump in her throat. *Her mother knew? Had always known?*

"I can do the math. I know you said you'd met a man at party, but it didn't add up. You were already pregnant before you started college. The only man you ever had stars in your eyes for has been Aidan Harte. You and he were thick as willow branches that summer your dad died. I understand why you lied, and at the time I agreed. If Earl had found out he had a grandchild, who knows how this would have all turned out. But that's the past. You need to make things right."

"I can't let Aidan know." She shook her head. "And what will Fox say? He'll hate me."

"No, he won't. That boy loves you. He might be angry, but he'll come around."

"Aidan could take Fox away, have you thought of that?"

"Yes. But I don't think he would do that. I think Fox will benefit the most with having two parents."

"I don't want Fox having anything to do with Aidan or the people he comes from."

"You raised him to be a fine young man. Have faith, my daughter." She drank from her tea and set the empty cup down. "Besides, the longer Aidan stays here, the better chance the truth will come out. I am not the only one who will see the resemblance."

"What resemblance? Just because they each have dark hair and eyes doesn't make them look alike."

"Watch them smile. They each have the same dimple in their left cheek." Fiona gave her a measuring look. "I won't be the only who will notice."

Reuben sandwiches and now dimples. What else?

"It's the right thing to do, Raven." Fiona stood and laid her hand on Raven's shoulder, giving it a squeeze. "Put it right in your mind. You were never one to act rashly. But don't take too long. I'd hate to have someone else spill the news to Aidan."

CHAPTER EIGHT

Aidan woke the next morning after a fitful night. His leg felt better, but the rest of him didn't. One place in particular ached like a son of a bitch. He could still smell Raven in his room, feel her with his eyes closed. He'd never hoped where she was concerned before. But last night had changed all that. Raven still cared about him. Still desired him. Those were things he could work with. Use them to get her to see past what his father had done to hers. Somehow he needed to make it right. He had no clue where to start, but lying in bed wasn't going to get him anywhere.

It was dark, though his internal clock told him it was morning. He reached for his crutches, already looking forward to throwing them away. He stood, and with the crutches under his arms, gradually applied weight onto his bad leg. It was painful but not excruciating.

"What the hell are you doing?" Eva asked.

Aidan had been concentrating so hard, he hadn't heard anyone come into the room.

"Don't be standing on that leg until it's been x-rayed." Eva walked over to him and swatted him on the arm. "Don't mess with my orders. I'm very pregnant, very moody, and very capable of carrying out my threats. We understand each other?"

"Yes, ma'am." The little powerhouse scared the shit out of him. How did Lynx live with her? Lynx had always been easygoing, willing to try anything no matter how dangerous or stupid it sounded. If there was fun to be had, you'd find Lynx in the middle of it.

"Sit down. Let me check your vitals." Eva pushed him onto the edge of the bed. A blood pressure cuff was strapped to his arm and she pumped up the pressure. The woman was efficient. She had his blood pressure read, his temp jotted down, and the dressing changed on his leg before he'd worked up the nerve to ask her a question.

"Have you seen Raven this morning?"

"She's arguing with Lynx." Eva finished with the bandages, straightened, and rubbed the small of her back. "They're fighting over who has to take you Fairbanks. The roads have been cleared."

He frowned. "I thought that was already decided. Wasn't Lynx saddled with the chore?"

"Yep, that's Raven's argument. But Lynx has been called out on an injured eagle run."

"Injured eagle?" Sounded like a wild goose chase to him.

"Apparently there was an incident involving beer, snow machines, and jumps. An eagle got in the way."

"Well, I'll get ready to go with whoever loses. You got anything else for me to wear besides Lynx's Bermuda shorts?"

"Yes. You should find what you need in that bag." She indicated a duffel by the dresser. "I'll need to find you something to put over your foot, too. I don't think you should try putting your foot into a shoe until the swelling has gone down. You'll be grateful to know that I saved your boots."

He was, since they were expensive, the kind of boots he only needed to buy once a decade or so. "Thanks, I'm appreciative. And for more than saving my boots."

She tilted her head and looked at him. "I think you can be a real sweetie when you want to be. No wonder Raven seems nervous."

He smiled. He could learn to like this little dynamo.

"I'll let the battling siblings know you're on your way."

"Thanks, Eva." He hobbled toward the bathroom. As soon as he heard the door close, he tried putting weight on his injured foot again. It took it, screamed while it did, but it was bearable in small doses. He quickly washed his face, sponged bathed what he could, dressed in Lynx's jeans and t-shirt, and strapped on his own boot. At least one foot was covered. The weather outside was clear, which meant beautiful and wicked cold. He made his way down the hall to the main meeting room. His heart pumped faster at the prospect of seeing Raven.

"There's something's more than *fowl* about this whole thing, Lynx," Raven hollered as Lynx finger-waved while escaping out the door. Raven stomped her foot, obviously losing the argument over driving him to Fairbanks.

"Morning, Raven," Aidan greeted, smiling when she jumped and swiveled around. Her cheeks flushed.

Was she blushing because he'd caught her stomping her foot, or because she was nervous over seeing him after the position they'd been in last night? If she hadn't called a halt to their activity, they would have woken up together. And if he'd done his job well, she'd be more than happy to take him to Fairbanks.

"If I have to go to Fairbanks, then I'm killing two birds with one stone."

"Okay?" He didn't know what she meant, but okay. All he knew was that he was getting to spend the day with her, alone. Granted in a car, and not a bed, but alone. "Let's get going, then. Early bird catches the worm."

"What?" She narrowed her eyes.

He shrugged. "There seemed to be a lot of bird analogies flying about. Thought I'd add another."

Her lips twitched. It wasn't quite a smile, but he'd take it. "This whole situation *is* for the birds."

That's the girl he remembered.

Fiona stuck her head into the room from the kitchen. "You two aren't going anywhere until that man gets something to eat. Come on, I've made breakfast."

"But, Mom," Raven objected. "I've got to hurry and get back."

"You have time for breakfast." She motioned for them to enter the kitchen. Fiona was a stronger force, and besides, he was starving.

Eva sat at the table already eating a plate piled high with home-style hash browns, covered with eggs, grated cheese, chopped green peppers, and bits of ham. His mouth watered. He hobbled to the table and took a seat, ready to dive in.

"I've already eaten," Raven said, walking to the back door, grabbing her coat off the hook. "Since I've got to head to Fairbanks—your husband's a deadbeat, Eva—I'm taking a load with me. Mom, if there's anything you need me to pick up, get it written down."

"I already have a list." Fiona held up a piece of paper.

"Of course you do," Raven said. "Aidan, I'll be back by the time you're done eating."

"Need any help?" he asked.

"Yes, but you're in no shape." Raven left, shutting the door behind her.

"What kind of load?"

"Pottery," Fiona said. "Tern sells Raven's pottery. Don't worry about Raven. She's taken care of herself for years. She just likes to make noise." Fiona took a seat and served him up a plate.

"But what if she really needs help? Pottery is heavy."

"If she can't do it herself, she'll give her Uncle Pike a call."

Eva tossed a ski mask across the table at Aidan. "Put this over your foot. It's the best I could think of to keep your toes from getting frostbitten. I also called the doctor and got you an appointment. Here are the particulars." She handed him a piece of paper.

"Thanks, Eva."

She grunted around another mouthful. How did someone so small eat so much? He watched her polish off a full plate and then fill it up with a huge cinnamon roll. Was she only eating for two?

"Did you sleep all right, Aidan?" Fiona asked.

"Fine, thanks. The lodge is very comfortable."

"What are your plans?"

"I need to go through Earl's things and—according to his will—spread his ashes over the gold claim."

"It'll be hard getting to Trapper's Creek this time of year. You'll need a snow machine and good weather to make it safely through the pass. Promise me you won't attempt it alone."

Who was he going to get to accompany him? No one in this town would want to attend the sprinkling of Earl Harte's ashes. But he nodded. He ate and then covered his foot with the ski mask Eva had found and was waiting in the main room for Raven when she pulled up in a big black Suburban. A mean, tough-looking gas hog.

He wished he could drive it.

Aidan met her on the wooden covered porch. The sun had started to rise, a faint peach blush in the east, casting the hills in dark shadows. The snow had blanketed everything in big white puffy shapes. Limbs drooped, heavy with snow. It looked like a fairytale Christmas card. The sky was a dark blue that would lighten with the sun until the combination of white-covered landscape and bright blue sky hurt the eyes to look at it. His sunglasses were in his rental. He'd had his wallet in the pocket of his coat. Eva had saved it from his jean pocket before tossing out the pants she'd cut off of him.

He knew he looked a sight, one leg in a hiking boot, the other covered in a ski mask. But this being Alaska, nobody would look twice at his crazy get-up. He hobbled to the end of the porch, looking at the slick ice and snow gleaming over the parking lot. While he'd put pressure on his bad leg, he didn't want to slip and come down hard on it.

Raven jumped out of the Suburban, jogged around to the passenger door and opened it. She parked so that he wouldn't have to walk far. But it was still ten feet or more. She approached and took his arm to help steady him on the ice-covered ground.

"Just take it slow. We aren't in any hurry."

He raised a brow. "What about you saying you had to get back early? That you had a lot to do?"

"I always have more to do than I can get done. Doesn't mean that you have to hurry. Chances are if you push it, we'll both end up on our butts, and this will take longer."

She had a point. They reached the Suburban. "Nice rig," he said admiring the leather seats.

"I like it." She held his crutches while he grabbed the handle above his head and stepped on the running boards to propel himself onto the seat. The seat was heated. And she had turned it on for him. Heaven.

Raven opened the back door. He glanced behind him to see the seats down and the back of the Suburban filled with boxes. She placed the crutches to the side, shut the door, and walked around to the driver's side, and got in. She clicked her seatbelt in place and looked at him. "Ready to fly this coop?"

He smiled. "As the crow flies, or should I say raven?" That must have hit too close to what he'd said last night, because her expression shut down. She turned her attention to the road as she put the SUV in gear, the four-wheel drive already engaged.

"I think we've exhausted the bird clichés." She turned onto the Steese Highway, which would take them past Fox, another gold mining town, and then into Fairbanks. Though the trek was only thirty miles, it would take them at least an hour or more with the road conditions. The Steese wasn't known for a smooth, pleasant drive. The road was plagued with frost heaves that changed yearly due to the freeze and thaw of the permafrost under the asphalt. The posted speed limit was fifty, but you were crazy to travel at such high speeds in the winter. Those who did usually ended up in the ditch, crashed into a tree, or plowing into a wayward moose.

Raven put in a Jon Bon Jovi CD. He admired the way she handled the big rig, her hands lightly placed on the wheel, confident in her ability.

"Quit it," she said, her attention on the road. "Quit looking at me."

"I can't help it." He wanted her. Always had. He knew now that what he had tried to feel for Sonya was based on her similarities to Raven. Both were capable, confident women. Both came from well-adjusted families, unlike his severely dysfunctional one. "You've grown into a strikingly, beautiful woman, Raven."

She glanced at him, her eyes quickly returning to the road. "Don't flatter me. It won't work. I'm not sleeping with you."

"You think that's all I'm after? Your body?" He scoffed. "Don't sell yourself short. You have so much more to offer."

Her hands tightened on the wheel, the only outward sign of his words affecting her.

The sun rose over the hills, turning everything a brilliant white. Clean, pure, yet brutal in its beauty.

"Tell me what you have in those boxes back there." He needed to get her to talk to him. They used to be able to talk about everything.

"Pottery."

"Come on. It's a long drive. Talk to me. How did you get into pottery? Are we talking molds, wheel-thrown items? Hand-building?"

She slid him a glance. He registered her surprise before she once again turned back to the road. "We could just enjoy the quiet and scenery."

"I'd rather get to know who you are now."

"Why? You'll be leaving soon. Getting back to your life."

He didn't really have a life. Other than his pretend one. And he could pretend anywhere. "Humor me. What will it hurt?"

"Fine." She sighed. "When I found out I was pregnant, I had to give up the scholarship to Berkeley. I enrolled at the University of Alaska Fairbanks instead. On a whim I took a pottery class. As it turned out, I had a knack."

"Did you graduate?"

"What, because I was pregnant you assume that I never finished my education?"

"No. That isn't it. But since you found your knack, I wanted to know if you took it further? That's all."

"Sorry. I'm a little touchy on the subject since so many people pressured me to quit and get a real job to support the both of us." She shrugged as though it wasn't a big deal now, but he knew better.

"Who pressured you?"

"Everyone, except Tern and Grandma Coho."

"Fiona?"

"She was the toughest. She wanted me to stay and work at the lodge. That way I could be with Fox every day."

"How did you do it?"

"My teacher, Mrs. Bailey." She smiled now, and it caused his heart to jump. "She believed in me so much she rented me the apartment over her garage for next to nothing and helped me with scholarships that supported us until I graduated with an arts degree. For repayment, she calls me in as a guest teacher a few times a semester, and I also do a summer class, where students come out to the lodge and we do Raku firings and the like."

"You really enjoy it, don't you?" When she looked at him in confusion he expanded, "I hear it in your voice, see it in your face, the love you have for your craft."

"Yes. I do love it." She gestured with her hands, lifting them off the wheel for a moment before returning them. "It's hard to explain, and most people don't understand, but to create something from the earth, something that is art yet has form and function, a simple casserole dish that has been molded, fired twice at extreme temperatures and comes through it stronger, more resilient, able to last centuries, thousands of years. It's amazing." She stopped and blushed. "I can get carried away."

"Don't apologize. We should all feel that way about what we do."

"Do you?" She looked at him. "Do you feel that way?"

He took a moment to gather his thoughts. She'd been honest in her answers and it had shown as bright and pure as the sunlight hitting the snow around them. "I love it, yet, hate it too." He laughed when she looked at him funny. "I know it doesn't make sense. When everything is going right, it's a rush, like a drug. But when it's going bad, it can be very bad."

"How bad?"

"Like bashing your head into a wall every day. Fighting with words that won't form the way you want them to. Characters who refuse to cooperate. But the worst is the silence. When nobody wants to talk. When that happens, life seems like it's over." His voice had turned quiet at the end. He hadn't meant to reveal so much.

"Is that the way it's been lately?" she asked softly.

He'd known she'd see more than he wanted her to. He took a deep breath. "Yeah, lately it's been tough."

"Because of Earl's death?"

Time for a change of subject. Maybe her idea of quiet and enjoying the scenery had more merit than he'd first given it credit. He didn't want to bring Earl into their conversation. Anything to do with his father would ruin their day and any progress he might have made with Raven. "That and other things. I've had some life-altering experiences lately." He laughed, knowing the sound came out sarcastic but he couldn't help himself. "Stepping into a bear trap being one of them. Nothing like facing your own mortality to help you reevaluate your life."

"So what have you learned?"

"I'll let you know when I figure it out." He wasn't ready to share what he'd come up with so far. And he knew without a doubt she wasn't ready to hear it. He noticed they were getting closer to Fairbanks, coming up on Hagelbarger. "Do you think we could pull in for a minute?"

"Sure." She slowed and hit her blinker.

"I was in a hurry when I landed at the airport. I only made one stop before heading to Chatanika."

"Food Factory?"

He laughed. "You do know me well." The words, while said in jest, seemed to sober her.

She turned onto Hagelbarger's scenic overlook, one of Fairbanks' prime make out places. Hills sat protective as Fairbanks nestled contently in the valley. In the winter, the Hagelbarger Lookout was the perfect place to watch the splay of Northern Lights dance across the sky. During the day, Fairbanks sparkled like a winter jewel. The University of Alaska stood on the hill to the east, the airport to the west, and the Chena River like a frozen ribbon meandering sleepily through town.

"You've missed it, haven't you?" Raven asked.

He nodded. A lump in his throat. "I never thought I would. Hell, a few days ago this is the last place I ever wanted to be again." He turned from the view and looked at her. "I've found there are things here that I've missed more than I realized."

She couldn't hold his gaze and glanced away, put the Suburban in gear, and merged back onto the Steese. They traveled in silence, Aidan taking in the sights, an ache in his chest.

Raven turned onto Airport Way, stopping at every stoplight on the way to the doctor's office. Pulling into the Physician's Plaza, she turned off the engine, jumped out of the SUV, and grabbed his crutches from the back.

He'd obviously said the wrong thing when they'd been overlooking the city. He'd pushed too hard, too fast. Just as he had last night. He'd done the same things with Sonya, and look how that had turned out. Time to learn from his mistakes. He opened his door as she came around with the crutches. The cold slapped him. With the sun shining so brightly, reflecting on the snow, it seemed warmer than it was. While they were in town, he needed to shop for a better winter coat.

"Thanks." He took the crutches from her. She held the door open until he made his way clear, then she rushed to open the doctor's door.

He stopped and looked down at her before entering. "I'm sorry if what I said upset you. But it was the truth."

She tightened her lips but didn't respond. He waited a heartbeat then entered the doctor's office. Raven took control of the doctor visit, going up to the counter and signing him in. It didn't take long before a nurse called his name. He stood, while Raven stayed seated.

"Are you coming?" he asked.

"No." She looked up at him, her eyes hard. "I'm not your friend, your family or your wife. I'll wait out here."

The words stabbed at him repeatedly. Repetitive, like a bad record inside his head, each run-through tearing fibers from his heart. She was right. She was none of those things.

And he wished she were all of them.

CHAPTER NINE

Raven thumbed through a magazine. Her vision blurred as she blinked back tears. The hurt on Aidan's face when she'd thrown those hurtful words at him, cut her deep. Why had she done it? Because he'd said he'd missed her?

She closed her eyes and laid her head back against the waiting room wall. What if he needed her in the exam room? To hold his crutches? Hold his hand if the leg was broken and had to be reset? By now the bone would have tried to heal, built a bridge that would have to be broken in order for the leg to heal right. They'd give him a shot to help with the pain, but...

No more buts. She'd needed to reestablish boundaries. Since she'd done such a great job of busting them down last night when she'd been moaning under him and grabbing his tight backside. She mentally groaned. She was going to kill Lynx for making her drive Aidan to town. They'd had a deal. She didn't care about some damn injured eagle. Well, she did, but why did it have to be injured on the day the roads were finally cleared to travel to town? Was it fate? Was fate against her now too?

The door to the inner exam rooms opened and out hobbled Aidan, carrying the crutches. His leg was strapped in a walking medical boot, his face pinched with pain.

"What did the doctor say?" she asked, getting to her feet.

He reached in his pocket for his wallet, and without answering, headed to the counter and took care of the bill. She waited patiently, arms folded across her chest.

Aidan finished and, giving Raven only a glance, walked toward the exit. She followed. He stopped outside the back doors of the Suburban. She unlocked it and kept her lips buttoned shut. Obviously he wasn't going to tell her what the doctor had said. Payback for not going into the exam room with him or because her thoughtless, spiteful words had hurt him? She didn't like the idea that she had hurt him. She wasn't a mean person. Just a scared one. Scared over what Aidan was making her feel. Memories that he'd resurrected.

She climbed into the Suburban and started it up, waiting for the idle to kick down before putting it in gear. She glanced at him. He stared out the windshield into the frozen trees. "I'm sorry," she said. There was no response from him, other than the flexing of his jaw. "I didn't mean to say those things."

He turned to her, his eyes devoid of emotion. "Yes, you did. And you were right."

Being right didn't feel very good. "Are you going to be okay?" She didn't know if she was asking about his leg or his feelings.

"I'll be fine." He turned back to the view out of the frosty window.

Not knowing what else to say, and afraid that whatever she said would make the situation worse, she put the vehicle in reverse and backed out of the parking lot. Since he'd walked out of the doctor's office without using his crutches, she could only assume his leg wasn't broken. But the medical boot was a concern. What did that mean? She'd also noticed the pain lines bracketing his mouth. Whatever had happened in that exam room hadn't been comfortable for Aidan.

She turned back onto Airport Way and headed toward the Arctic Tern located in a cute, rustic log cabin near Pioneer Park.

"What happened to Alaskaland?" Aidan frowned looking at the large sign designating the entrance to one of the town's main tourist attractions.

"A few years ago the city overhauled the park and changed the name."

"What was wrong with the old name?"

"We'd all like to know that." She pulled into the Arctic Tern's well-cleared and well-kept parking lot and turned off the engine. It was only ten below, and as she didn't plan to stay long, she didn't bother plugging the SUV into the electrical outlets in front of each parking space.

Her sister ran a tight and profitable business. A wide-covered porch with benches graced the entrance. In summer, Tern would fill the area with overflowing flower pots, both hanging and squatting. Now, being November, Christmas decorations were already in place. Artificial Christmas trees strung with bright white lights stood as sentries at the doors, while glowing wired reindeer moved their heads to a timer. Soft holiday music piped through the speakers.

Raven opened the back of the Suburban and grabbed the first box. She turned and bumped into Aidan, almost dropping the heavy pottery. Pieces rattled as the box jostled.

"Sorry." He took the box out of her hands, preventing her from dropping it to the icy ground. "Let me help."

"I don't want to take the chance of breaking anything." She scowled, mentally going through what she had in this box and hoping she hadn't already done just that. Handles on mugs and pitchers were very breakable, and she had many of those in this delivery. "What about your leg?"

"It'll be fine. Don't worry, I won't break anything." He muscled past her with the box.

She didn't have much choice except to let him carry the box. She'd done that last night, and look at what had almost happened. "Fine. But you break it, you've bought it." She grabbed another box and led the way.

He followed her up the wooden steps to the glass-etched door. Tern must have seen them, for she was there at the door opening it for them.

"I didn't think I was going to see you until the end of the week," she said, when Raven entered.

"I had to come into town," Raven huffed out. She needed to put the box down before she dropped it herself. She also needed to pack them lighter. "Didn't see the reason to waste a trip." She went around the sales counter and through the door to the storeroom, setting the box on the large table in the center of the small room. Aidan did the same. She took one look at him and noticed the sweat on his forehead, the pain lines deeper around his mouth.

Sure he could handle it. Idiot.

"Take a seat before you fall down." She pulled out a folding chair. Aidan fell into it. "I told you they were heavy."

"I didn't think they were that heavy. How did you carry that?"

"I've been doing it for years, and I didn't just step into a bear trap and break a fever," she snapped back.

Tern entered the room, sucking in her breath when she recognized Aidan. "You have a lot of balls showing up here." She swiveled toward Raven and demanded, "What the hell are you doing with *him*?"

"Didn't Mom call you?" She really didn't want to go into explanations.

"Yeah, but it was busy so I let her call go to voicemail."

"Great." Raven sighed. "Earl's dead. Aidan returned to take care of his things, stepped into a bear trap, Fox saved his life, we're here seeing the doctor."

"Hey ya, Tern. It's really good to see you too." Aidan pointed to Tern's hair. "I like the red. Very becoming."

Tern frowned and looked from Aidan to Raven. "Can I talk to you please? Alone." Tern grabbed Raven's arm and pulled her out of the storeroom, across the sales floor, and right out of the building to the parking lot. She must have been steaming, because she marched to the back of the Suburban without stopping for a coat. her only protection against the cold was a thin silk teal blouse. A very good color for her, which complemented her plum skirt and black killer knee-high boots.

"What are *you* doing with him?" she asked, grabbing one of the boxes.

"*Your* brother's fault." Raven picked up another box, explaining how she'd come to town with Aidan in tow, as they returned to the storeroom.

Aidan was still sitting where she'd left him, but he was holding a tea pot in his hand. "This is beautiful, Raven. You made this?"

"Of course she did," Tern said. "She's an artist." Tern went to grab it from his hands, but Aidan pulled back, holding the tea pot next to his chest.

"No, I want this."

"What?" Raven asked.

"I want to buy it."

"You can't buy it."

"Why not? Isn't it for sale? Aren't these all for sale?"

"Y-yes," she sputtered. But she didn't want Aidan buying her tea pot. She loved to make tea pots, but they were labor intensive. A lot of time and energy, thought and love went into each one. This particular one was a favorite. The glaze had turned out exceptionally well, running into greens and purples over a midnight blue base. To her it was like the dancing of the Northern Lights.

"Then I want to buy it." He leaned over, looking through the items in the box. "Do you have any mugs that go with it?"

She did, but didn't want to say so. The thought of Aidan drinking out of one of her mugs, making tea in her tea pot when he left here and returned home, disturbed her.

Tern, always willing to make a sale, rummaged through the box and produced the four matching mugs.

"I just need the one. There's only me."

"Sorry, they come as a set," Tern said. "If you want one, you'll have to buy all four."

That wasn't true. Each mug was individually priced, and Raven bet Aidan knew it.

"Done." He pulled out his wallet. "Can you wrap them up for me?"

"Of course." Tern took his credit card and the tea pot. "Want to grab those mugs for me, Raven?" While it was a question, Tern wasn't excepting an answer.

Raven gave Aidan a confused look before she gathered up the mugs and followed her sister to the counter to wrap them up.

"At least you got a great sale out of taking him to the doctor." Tern nudged her with an elbow. "More than covered your time and gas money."

Raven didn't like it when she saw the total Tern had rung up. "Give him the friends and family discount for buying the set."

"Really?" Tern cocked a perfectly shaped brow. "You didn't want to sell them to him in the first place."

"Make it right."

Tern sighed. "Fine. I really hate that good-girl streak of yours." She prepared a new sales slip for Aidan. "Happy with that?"

No. She wasn't. She still had a problem with Aidan drinking tea from something she'd made. His mouth sipping from the rim she'd carefully molded, taking care to make sure it was smooth and comfortable against the lips.

The bell on the door dinged as a customer entered the store. "Here—" Tern handed her the sales slip, "—get him to sign this, and I'll finish wrapping his items."

Raven took Aidan's credit card and the sales slip into the backroom. In her absence, he had proceeded to unpack the rest of the boxes. Her pottery was all lined up on the table. Pitchers, pie plates, casserole dishes, bowls, platters, mugs, and another tea pot. "What are you doing?"

"You made all of these?" He looked at her, amazement reflected in his eyes.

"Yes," she slowly answered.

"I'm impressed." He raked a hand through his hair. Her eyes were caught on how the light reflected in the dark depths, highlighting a bit of red. He needed a haircut. "You are an amazing artist." He glanced at her again. "Can I see your studio?"

She caught her breath. Her studio was private. Yes, she gave lessons there, had students and family running through there all the time, but Aidan would see more than the others did. It would be like inviting him inside part of her soul.

Tern bumped into Raven, saw the pottery unpacked on the table. "Oh, good. You brought the pie plates for Mrs. Norwick. She just came in, and she brought a friend." Tern grabbed the pottery and returned to the sales floor, anticipating another sale.

Raven heard oohs and ahhs from the other room, but the storeroom seemed to be closing in on her. Suddenly she was too hot. Yeah, she hadn't taken off her coat, and it was warm in here, but that wasn't why. It was Aidan. He was getting too close, asking too much, seeing too much.

"I…uh…I'm going to get that last box." She turned and rushed out of the room, through the gift shop, not stopping until she was outside at the back of the Suburban, where no one could see her. She fell against the door and unzipped her coat, letting the cold air slap her heated skin.

But nothing seemed to slow the rapid beating of her heart.

Aidan stood to follow Raven, but Tern entered the room.

"You broke Raven's heart when you left the last time." Tern blocked the exit and planted her hands on her hips. "Are you going to do it again?"

What? "She's the one who told *me* to get lost." He shook his head. "She broke *my* heart."

Tern advanced into the room. "She was hurting. You should have waited, given her time. You should have known better."

"Staying wouldn't have helped anyone."

"She needed you, Aidan."

"I was the last person she needed or wanted to see then." He raked a hand through his hair. "Your dad had been killed. She blamed me for it."

"She was hurting, she lashed out. People do that. They hurt the ones they love the most because those are the people who are supposed to stay and be able to take it. If you aren't here to make amends, then make your trip short. Don't let her care for you again. It almost killed her the last time."

Were they talking about the same woman? "She looks like she's done just fine without me." There were no signs that Raven had suffered. She had a loving family around her. A business that was thriving. She seemed happy.

"Maybe outwardly it seems that way. But she doesn't date. Ever. She works too hard, never vacations, never cuts loose like she used to. She's different. A shell of who she once was."

"She's matured."

Tern shook her head, her long hair flowing around her shoulders. "This is different. She's old. Not mature. Grandma Coho acts younger than Raven." She sighed and looked away for a second before stabbing him with her huntress stare. "If you hurt her again, I will come after you this time. I will make you suffer like no one has made you suffer before. Got that?"

"Tern, the situation between us is really none of your business."

"Have you met my family? Of course it's my business. That's the way we work. You hurt her, you hurt all of us. And we defend those who would think to harm us."

"You done?" Raven demanded standing in the doorframe. Aidan wondered how long she had been listening. How much she'd heard. "Time to go, Aidan. I need to get back, and I still need to stop and get the things on Mom's list."

Tern had buttoned up as soon as Raven had announced her presence, but the look she gave Aidan spoke volumes. "I plan on coming out for Sunday dinner," she said.

Aidan knew it was for his benefit. He'd been warned.

"Fine," Raven said. "I'll let Mom know." She turned and left the room. Tern and Aidan followed. "I left the other box on the counter since you and Aidan were in deep discussion over my life."

"Raven—"

"You know, Tern, Aidan's right. What's between us needs to stay between us." She tightened her lips and then continued, "I don't need a keeper."

"I was just trying—"

"I know what you were doing, but I don't need my younger sister fighting my battles. I can do that myself just fine." She glanced fleetingly at Aidan before returning her attention to Tern. "I love you, sis. But enabling me doesn't do me any favors."

"Okay. But I don't like it." She directed that statement toward Aidan.

"See you Sunday." Raven left the shop.

Aidan lagged behind her due to the damn boot strapped to his leg, and being careful of the package of teapot and mugs Tern silently handed him. "It was good to see you, Tern. I like your shop."

Then he left and hobbled toward the waiting Suburban. Raven already had the engine running. He got in, set down his purchase, and buckled his seatbelt. Raven was quiet as she backed up the rig and left the Arctic Tern.

"Don't do that again," she said, her voice hard and tight.

He didn't pretend he didn't know what she was talking about. "Tern's quite your protector."

"I know."

"Why does she see herself that way?"

Raven sighed and rubbed the back of her neck. "I had some rough years. She stepped in and straightened me out. Now she thinks she's responsible for me, I guess."

"What kind of rough years?" Had he really broken her heart? Even though she'd been the one who demanded he left. Was Tern right? Had it been Raven lashing out because of the pain she felt over her father's death? Maybe she didn't blame him completely.

"I don't want to talk about it."

"One thing I've learned is that you don't heal without talking about it."

She pulled into the parking lot of Fred Meyer's, put the vehicle in park, killed the engine, and turned to look at him. Disbelief in her expression. "A man who wants to talk? Get real. I'm going to go and get what's on Mom's list. You stay here."

"I don't want to stay here."

"Too bad. I want to hurry." She glanced at his leg in the boot. "And you will slow me down." She handed him the keys. "In case you get cold." She opened the door and stepped onto the running board. "Don't go anywhere."

She slammed the door and left. He watched her walk into the entrance of the grocery store. He didn't like having to stay in the car. He wasn't a kid, or a dog. It was boring in the car. He looked around the parking lot. Mountains made of plowed snow were in the corners of the lot. Before break up, dump trucks would come and carry it all away to the river, far outside of town to help prevent flooding. For now, they were great places to climb and slide down, when the lot was empty. He remembered when he was young, coming to town and seeing kids do that. Not that he ever had. Earl hated town. Aidan hadn't gotten here often as a child, unless his mother needed a booze run and he conned his way into going along.

He rubbed his hands together, blew on his fingers, and noticed a Starbucks sign outside the building. Fred Meyer's had a Starbucks? He didn't have to think. He got out of the Suburban and made his way inside. He'd be back before Raven could get the many items on Fiona's list. He'd get her a cup too. Maybe that would sweeten her up.

Ever since he'd mentioned wanting to see her studio, she had shut down on him. No, that's wrong. It went back to when he'd told her he'd missed her when they'd been at the overlook on Hagelbarger. He walked into the building, enveloped by a blast of heat. Starbucks was off to the right. The smell of ambrosia, and suddenly he missed Seattle. He ordered a Americano with double espresso and a Carmel Macchiato for Raven.

He paid for the drinks, took a sip of his, almost burning his tongue in his haste, and savored the bold, rich espresso as it warmed him all the way down to his toes. Now this was more like it. He bought a bag of house blend to take with him. Who knew what he'd find at Earl's place? Earl had been a fan of canned coffee. Bitter and lifeless. Much like the man.

Aidan limped his way back to the Suburban and found Raven, her feathers ruffled, waiting outside with a cart.

"I told you not to go anywhere."

He held up the coffee cups. "Starbucks." He handed her the keys so that she could unlock the rig while he put the coffee in the cup holders and then went to help her unload. "You were faster than I thought you'd be."

"I told you I was in a hurry."

"Who would have suspected you could get a list of groceries faster than I could get a cup of coffee?" He helped load the last of the bags.

Her lips twisted. "What did you get me?"

"You? I got me two cups. It's Starbucks. It isn't like I can get my favorite cup of Joe in Chatanika."

"One of those cups had better be for me, or you're going to have a long walk back to Chatanika."

He smiled. "I always thought you were the Caramel Macchiato with a pump of chocolate type. Is that okay?"

She didn't quite smile, but it was better than the frown she'd been sporting. "Sounds good." She looked at him from under her lashes. "Thanks."

They climbed into the Suburban and headed back down Airport Way, past Lathrop High School where he and Raven had graduated. "Did you make the ten year reunion?" he asked.

"Yeah, you didn't miss much." She glanced at him. "Same people doing the same stuff, just ten years older. You could have made it. They held it at the end of July. Isn't fishing season over by then?"

"You were glad I didn't attend."

She was silent for a moment. "I was relieved, but I really didn't think you would've made the effort."

He'd wanted to. If things had been different. He'd been wishing for different all his life. He changed the subject. "Could we swing into Big Ray's? I need a warmer coat."

"As long as we make it fast." She made the left hand turn on Cushman.

"Why do you need to hurry?" He glanced at his watch. It was just after eleven. "Fox isn't out of school for another three or four hours, right? Or is it because you don't want to spend any more time with me than you have to?"

She tightened her lips. "I have things to do."

What did she have to do? Pottery? Work at the lodge? Just how busy was her life? He wanted to know. "Like what?"

She sent him an evil look. He threw his hands up. "I was just asking. Making conversation."

"You know that for the last three days I have done nothing but play nursemaid. My life has been on hold. I need to get back to it."

He gave up on conversation and looked out the window as they traveled down Cushman. She turned onto 2nd Avenue and pulled into Big Ray's. He was glad to see it was still in business and that a big chain from the lower forty-eight hadn't taken it over. "I'll make this quick." He opened the door and got out.

She opened hers. "I should get a new pair of gloves for Fox."

They walked into the store together, but separated. He headed toward the large array of parkas, while Raven viewed the gloves and hats on the opposite side of the store.

"Aidan Harte! As I live and breathe, I never thought to see you again." A big bear of a man slapped him on the back, knocking the air out of him.

Aidan looked up at him in confusion. "Uh…"

"You don't remember? I've grown a bit since the last time you saw me." The man spread his skillet size hands. "Remember junior year, you saved my sorry ass from getting pummeled by Sam Sagoonick."

"Tiny Tom?" His brows rose in surprise. No way this…giant was Tiny.

"Yup." Tiny shrugged as though a little embarrassed. "I got a growth spurt after high school. People call me Thomas now." He reached out a hand for Aidan to shake. "Good to see you, man."

"Yeah." Aidan shook Thomas' hand, his disappearing. "So, whatever happened to 'Slay 'em Sam Sagoonick?"

"I married her." He grinned. "We've got three rug rats, girls, just as tough and beautiful as their mother."

"You married Sam?" Aidan didn't know if he should pity him or respect him?

"Yup." Thomas grinned. "Never a dull moment with her around." His smile turned grim. "Hey, man, I was sorry to hear about your old man. My condolences."

Aidan frowned. "Who told you about my dad?" Nobody in Chatanika had known Earl was dead, until he'd arrived. How had Tiny Tom known?

"I'm not sure." He scratched his head. "I was hanging with the boys the other night at the Lonely Lady. Someone was talking about it."

"Who?"

"Sorry, man. I had a few too many." He elbowed Aidan. "You know what I mean? I have no clue who told me."

"That's all right." Though it wasn't. Who in Fairbanks would be talking about Earl?

"What about you?" Thomas asked, obviously trying to change the subject. "Married? Kids?"

"No and no."

"Too bad. A woman tempers a man. Makes life more enjoyable. You know what I mean?"

He wished he did.

"What'd you do to the leg? Break it skiing?"

Raven came up to them, a pair of gloves in her hand. "Ready? Hi, Thomas."

"Hey, Raven. Wow, seeing the two of you together is like old times." Thomas nodded. "How's your boy?"

Raven glanced from Aidan to Thomas and swallowed. "Good."

"He like those footpads for the dogs? They working out?"

"Haven't heard any complaints."

"Good. Good." Thomas cocked his head to the side. "Hey, why don't the two of you join me and Sam for dinner? It would be real great to catch up."

Raven's skin blanched. Obviously, she didn't like the idea.

"Thanks, Thomas. We have to get back. Maybe some other time." He grabbed a parka off the rack that was his size and looked at Raven. "Ready?"

She nodded.

"Well, let's get you two checked out then." Thomas stomped to the desk. A man that big didn't merely walk.

He rang them up. Aidan grabbed the gloves and put them on his ticket.

"Hey," Raven tried to object.

"You drove me here, it's the least I can do." He could tell she wanted to argue but she kept her mouth shut in front of Thomas.

"Seriously, man, it was great to see you." Thomas handed Aidan a bag with the items. "You staying long?"

Aidan glanced at Raven and then back to Thomas. "Not sure yet, but I'll stop in before I leave and catch up."

"You do that." Thomas winked at them. "You two take care, now."

Raven turned and beat a trail out of Big Ray's. Aidan hobbled behind her as fast as he could. His leg pulsed with pain as he reached the Suburban, Raven behind the wheel with the engine already running. He got in and before he had his seatbelt clicked, she was in reverse and backing out of the parking lot.

"What's up?" he asked, as she cut through town toward the Steese.

"Nothing."

"Want to elaborate?"

"No."

This wasn't getting them anywhere. He decided not to push. He'd already done enough pushing today, and it was tiring. His head pounded in time to the pulsing in his leg. He needed to elevate it. Take it easy. The doc had been impressed with Eva's skills. The x-rays had shown a hair-line fracture. And due to the type of wounds the teeth of the trap had made, a cast was out of the question. A boot was the next best option. And since it was only a stress fracture, the doctor had agreed to allow him to walk on it, but made Aidan promise to listen to the pain. If it got too bad, he should use the crutches. If that didn't help, he was supposed to return. Right now, Aidan wanted to lay his seat back and elevate his leg on the dash. One of the pain pills the doc had given him wouldn't be out of order either. But instead he sat there in a silent car, with a fuming woman, and a long drive over nasty roads. Once that was over, he got to look forward to moving into Earl's. He couldn't put out Fiona and Raven any longer.

He must have dozed, because the next thing he knew, Raven was shaking him awake. He sat up in his seat and looked around. They were right outside the lodge.

"Sorry." He rubbed his face.

"Where do you want me to take you? Earl's? Or do you want to stay at the lodge tonight?" Raven didn't seem as angry with him now as she had before.

"Earl's, if you don't mind."

"You sure?"

What was this? Just a little while ago she'd wanted to see the last of him. "The faster I get done what I came here to do the better for everyone."

"Okay." She turned right and headed toward Earl's. Chatanika wasn't a big town, and it didn't take her long to pull behind the SUV he'd rented. She parked and turned off the engine and pocketed her keys.

He raised a brow.

"What? You think I was going to just drop you off without seeing if this place is even livable?" She scoffed. "I'm not that heartless, and I don't want to come out here in a few days and find you dead."

There were worse things than being dead. He kept his mouth shut and climbed out of the rig. Grabbing the parka, he left the bag with the gloves for Fox in the car. "I'll need the crutches," he said.

Raven went around the back and retrieved them. "Probably a good idea. You aren't walking too steady."

And here he thought he was doing really well. He took one of the crutches from her and used them more as a cane than crutch. They walked through the gate, to the side of the house, and Aidan stopped. "We're going to need Fox. The snow covered up the path he had made to the back door. I don't know where the booby traps are."

"Fox actually knew how to get to Earl's back door?"

"Yeah. Walked in like he'd done it many times before."

Furrows appeared on her brow. "I need to have a talk with him. We could use the crutches as walking sticks. Set off any traps before we step."

He rolled his lips and shook his head. "Nope. I don't want to take any chance that you might get caught in a trap." He swore. "I will personally get rid of any booby traps Earl set. The bastard."

"No arguments here. All right, let's head back. I wonder what Mom fixed for lunch."

His stomach growled. "Let me grab a change of clothes from the rental."

They walked back to the road and dug out the snow-buried vehicle. Aidan went to open the SUV, but found it already unlocked. Had he been so out of it the night he'd arrived he'd failed to lock the door? That wasn't like him. Even though he'd grown up in an area that didn't have a crime rate, other than what his own family had added to the community, he was careful. He'd lived in the big city of Seattle long enough to make locking his doors a habit.

He opened the door to find his clothes thrown all over the back of the vehicle. His suitcase lay gutted along with his carry-on bag.

"Do you always travel with such a mess?"

"Someone's been through my things." Who would ransack his car way out here? And what the hell were they looking for?

CHAPTER TEN

Aidan pushed his plate aside.

"I need to borrow a gun."

"Do you really think a gun is necessary?" Raven asked. She didn't care for guns, even though she knew how to handle one. They'd returned from Earl's, and had grabbed something to eat in Fiona's kitchen. Well, at least, she had eaten. Aidan had picked at his tuna fish sandwich. She could tell he was shaken up over his stuff being ransacked. "It was probably some kids causing mischief. You know what it's like in the winter with nothing to do. You find something to do. Legal or not just to kill the time."

Aidan held her gaze, his eyes dark with secrets. "I need a gun. Whether you think it's necessary or not, I'd rather be prepared."

"What aren't you telling me?" She placed her hands on the table when he didn't answer her. "I'm not taking my son back to that hellhole without knowing what you know."

He pursed his lips. "My Uncle Roland is wanted for questioning."

"Questioning in what?"

"Murder."

She rolled her eyes and twisted her lips. "Birds of a feather."

124

"Yeah, I've heard it before."

"Fine. So you think he might be here?" She remembered Roland Harte well from when he visited his brother. He was a crafty bastard who had enjoyed the misfortunes of others. "Why would he be here?"

"I don't know." He raked a hand through his hair. "All right, this is what I need. I want Fox to draw me a map. I don't want him anywhere near Earl's place—"

"No arguments there."

"—and I need a gun."

"I don't have a gun."

It was his turn to roll his eyes. "This is Alaska. Everyone has a gun."

She couldn't argue that.

"When will Lynx be back?"

"I have no idea. He's on an eagle rescue, remember?"

"Pike. He won't have any problem loaning me one of his."

"You aren't going to get Packin' Pike involved in this. When Dad was killed, he put us all into lockdown. He was so afraid something would happen to us that he went overboard. It took years to get him back on track."

"Yet you still managed to get knocked up with a guy you met in a bar."

She sucked in her breath feeling as though he'd sucker punched her.

"God. Raven, I'm sorry." He threw his hand up and shook his head. "I shouldn't have said that."

"I'm sure you haven't been the perfect Boy Scout in all these years."

He scoffed and looked down at his feet. "No. That I haven't. I really am sorry, Raven."

The door slammed, and in trotted Fox. Raven stiffened. Fiona had noticed the dimple and it was only a matter of time before someone else did. What if that someone else was Aidan? Then what would she do? She didn't want to find out.

"Hey, guys." Fox smiled, happy to see them. "Whatcha ya doing?" Fox hung up his coat and scurried over, dragging his backpack.

"Nothing." Raven reached out and gave him a hug, which he barely tolerated. "How was school?"

"Stupid." Fox took a seat. Raven and Aidan sat across from each other, now Fox sat between them. Raven saw the irony in the situation. If Aidan found out who Fox's father was, the poor kid would always be caught in the middle.

"Why stupid?" Aidan cocked his head much the way Fox always did.

"I don't like math."

"Now, Fox."

"What, Mom? Math sucks."

"You owe the swear jar a dollar, young man."

Fox slouched in his chair. "Man, this day bites." He looked at Aidan under his lashes. "Sorry."

"Don't apologize to me," Aidan said. "This day does bite."

"Why? What happened with you? Are you okay?"

"Yeah. Just a stupid trip to the doctor's."

Raven was glad Aidan stopped there and didn't reveal that someone had gone through his things at Earl's place.

"Yeah, that su—*bites* as bad as math," Fox said with a quick look at Raven to see if she'd caught his 's' word slip-up. She let it pass.

"What's the matter with math?" she asked. He usually did well in the subject.

"I don't get how anyone can find a value of x." Fox looked at both of them. "Two plus two equals four. I get that. But 5x minus 2 equals 0? Give me a break. How does someone wrap their mind around that?"

Aidan chuckled. Raven shot him a "be quiet" look. He shrugged his shoulders and smiled.

"I'll help you with your homework later," she said. "You'd better get on your chores before it gets any darker. It's supposed to drop to twenty below tonight. Might want to give the dogs extra bedding."

"All right." Fox eyed Aidan's leftover sandwich. "Are you going to finish that?"

"Help yourself." Aidan pushed the plate toward him.

Fox picked up the sandwich and took a large bite. "Yum." He opened the sandwich to see what was in it. "I like this mustard. Spicy," he said around the food in his mouth. He swallowed. "What is it?"

"Dijon. Your grandmother had some in the fridge."

"I like it."

Great. First Reubens and now Dijon mustard. Dimples weren't going to be her only problem.

Fox swallowed another bite and glanced at Aidan. "You wanta see my dogs?"

Raven cleared her throat, trying to get Aidan's attention, but he ignored her.

"Yes, I'd like that," he said. "I used to have a sled dog when I was a few years younger than you." He looked off to the side, his expression sobered. "She was my best friend."

Raven remembered. Earl had shot Aidan's dog one night in a fit of rage. Right in front of him.

"What was her name?" Fox asked, his tone reverent as he picked up on Aidan's sorrow. Her kid was a sharp one. Another reason she needed to keep him and Aidan apart. What if Fox guessed the truth? She'd explained to him, when he was younger, that circumstances prevented his father from being a part of his life. He'd been four and hadn't brought up the subject again until he was seven. Then he'd suddenly stopped asking her questions and seemed to have accepted that he didn't have a father in his life. The dogs, she figured were a huge part of that. She'd gotten him a husky around that time, hoping to take his mind off the subject. It had seemed to work because she hadn't been plagued with questions since.

"Her name was Nugget," Aidan said. "She was a golden Malamute with the deepest blue eyes I've ever seen."

"She sounds beautiful."

"Yeah, she was." Aidan straightened his shoulders and collected himself. "You want to show me your dogs now?"

"No," Raven said a little too loud. Both of them turned and stared at her with surprise. "You can't. You need to put that leg up. Rest." Anything but spend time with her son.

"I'm fine. I took some of the pain pills the doc gave me." He studied her curiously. "Checking on dogs isn't going to do me in."

She wanted to object further but knew if she did it would only raise more questions. "I thought you wanted to head back to Earl's?"

Aidan turned to Fox. "That's another thing. Can you draw me a map on how to get past the booby traps? The snow covered up the tracks."

Fox's face brightened. "I'll go with you."

"No," Raven said, her tone hard. "I don't want you out there."

"Neither do I," Aidan agreed. "It's too dangerous. Until I can find all the traps around the place, I don't want anyone out there, but I do need you to draw me a map."

"But—"

"No buts, Fox," Raven said. "And I want to know how you knew where the booby traps were to begin with?"

Fox swallowed the last bite of his sandwich, looking from Raven to Aidan. "Uh…"

She waited. Fox glanced from both of them again, looking for an escape that wasn't coming.

"Fox?" she prompted with her no-nonsense mother's tone.

"Uh…I watched him…a couple of times." He looked down at his plate.

"Why were you watching him? I told you to stay away from him."

"I don't know." Fox shrugged his shoulders. "I guess I wanted to know why everyone thought he was dangerous."

"So you put yourself in danger to find out?" Obviously she'd allowed the boy too much freedom.

"She's right, Fox," Aidan said. "Earl was a loose cannon. Unpredictable."

Raven shot him a look that said she didn't need his help with *her* son. He must have gotten the message for Aidan leaned back in his chair, separating himself from the conversation.

"We'll talk about this later," Raven said. "Right now, get on your chores, okay?"

"Yes, Mom." Fox glanced at Aidan. "Still want to see my dogs?"

"Fox, that isn't a good idea," Raven said.

"Yes, I'd like to." Aidan stared at Raven, the look a challenge of sorts. "That is if it's all right with your mother."

Sure, make her the bad guy. Fox beseeched her with his large brown eyes. While letting Aidan and her son do anything together went against everything screaming inside of her, she couldn't see a way out of it. "Fine." She glared at Aidan. "I don't want to hear it if you hurt yourself."

He flashed her a smile, his dimple shining bright like a neon sign. "Thanks for worrying about me."

She scowled. "I'm not worrying about you. I want you healthy so you can move on."

"*Mom,*" Fox said, his tone chastising.

Crap. She needed to watch her tone. "Sorry," she gritted out. Aidan's smile got bigger. He was obviously enjoying the situation.

"Come on." Fox jumped to his feet. "One of my dogs has a golden coat too. You'll love her."

Aidan slowly stood, hobbled to the door, grabbed his new parka, and put it on.

"Don't overdo," Raven warned.

Aidan winked at her as he left. She should go with them, but didn't miss that her son hadn't invited her along. She understood he was of the age where he was looking for a father figure. He had Lynx and Pike. Why did he need another?

It was just a phase. Fox had saved Aidan's life so he felt connected to him. That would pass as soon as Aidan left.

The sooner he left the better.

For all of them.

Aidan followed Fox down the well-worn path from the lodge toward Fool's Cove. The beauty of the area slapped him as sharp as the cold. Scrawny Spruce trees, their pine needles heavy with snow bordered the trail, while branches of birch trees, were a drastic contrast with their white and black parchment bark. It was quiet here, the sound of their feet crunching in the snow and their breathing the only sound. No traffic, no horns, or the squeal of brakes. No people. Just him and Fox traipsing through the woods.

A chickadee sang a song to its mate, while a ptarmigan dressed in its white-feathered coat darted across their path, surprising Aidan. Fox took it in stride.

"So why haven't you come back home before now?" Fox asked.

"I promised never to return last time I was here."

"Why?"

Where did he start? He should have started with watching how he'd answered Fox's question in the first place. "If you haven't noticed, I'm not wanted around here."

"Yeah, I noticed. But nobody's told me why. I thought I'd develop my own opinion from the source. You."

Smart kid. "Bad things happened the last summer I was here." Some great things had happened, too. Lying with Raven. Loving Raven.

"Yeah, I know. My grandfather was killed. I'm named after him, you know."

Aidan smiled. "I figured that out."

Fox flashed him a smile in return. A dimple peeked for a moment and then was gone. Cute kid.

"I also know Mr. Harte was suspected to have some part in his death. But nobody tells me anything. Just that I needed to stay away from him."

Aidan tightened the gloves on his hands. How much should he tell young Fox? It wasn't his place. Actually it was, since his own father had caused the death of his grandfather, a great man. "Earl had everything to do with your grandfather's death."

"Why?"

Again with the whys. "There was a land dispute. Earl thought your grandfather's gold mine was his."

"Was it?"

"I think the word used by the property surveyor was 'undetermined.' But Earl was adamant that the mine belonged to him."

"Why?"

The more information he gave Fox, the more questions the kid came up with. "A lot of the land around here was homesteaded. Claims were laid on mines that sometimes had more than one claim attached. My mother's people and your grandfather's apparently were partners years back and laid claim to the Trapper's Creek mine. No gold was ever found, until about fifteen years ago. Your grandfather found the gold. And Earl found a deed to the claim. But there were questions, because the claim was in my mother's name, and she'd died by then."

"So, Mr. Harte could have had a rightful claim to the mine?"

"Whether he had a legal right to it or not, it didn't justify the means he used to get his hands on it. And all of it was for nothing."

"Because after the first strike my grandfather found, no other gold was recovered?"

Aidan had been right, this kid was one smart cookie. "Right. Greed always brings out the worst in people."

"That's what Mom always says too."

"She's right. You need to listen to her." They turned a corner on the path, and the trees opened up to reveal a home. A two story log cabin blended with the wilderness, adding rather than taking away. A smaller building was connected to the cabin by an enclosed walkway. He knew without being told that the building was Raven's studio. He wanted a peek. The workspace of an artist told so much about them. He wanted a chance to get to know this new side of Raven he never knew existed.

To the left was Fox's team. Six dogs sat or lay next to their own dog houses dotting the open land. Bales of straw were spread next to the houses, adding much needed insulation for the extreme winter temperatures. The huskies caught sight of Fox and leaped to their feet, their excited yips and howls echoing over the open area.

Fox beamed and ran to his dogs, ruffling the fur around their necks, allowing them to lick his face. It was clear that they loved him and vice versa. Aidan found a wide grin splitting his face as he watched the interaction. Every boy needed something like the unconditional love that these animals had for Fox.

Fox motioned him over. "Come meet my team."

Aidan limped into the writhing bodies of fur. The first dog— must be the alpha male—stuck out his nose, his nostrils flaring, his mismatched brown and blue eyes flickering. Aidan offered his hand, palm up. It was sniffed and then the husky rubbed his head against him. Aidan smiled, his heart swelling as he was accepted into the pack. No judgment to be found here. The others followed suit. They had no idea who he was. Who he came from. But judged and accepted him with their own insightful brand of measurement. Why couldn't it be that easy with people?

"Fox, you are the luckiest kid in the world." Aidan smiled. "I'd have loved this." He laughed as one of the dogs pushed him over and licked his face.

"Yeah, they're really cool." Joy lit Fox from within. "Wanta go for a ride with me? Not now, it's getting too late, and Mom will say no. But maybe Saturday?"

"You got it."

They shared a connection. Aidan didn't know how to explain it, but something at that moment connected him to Fox. To cover up the swelling he felt in his heart, he asked, "What are their names?"

Fox's face fell, and he suddenly looked uncomfortable. "Uh…I don't want to creep you out but…"

"Creep me out? How?"

Fox bit his lips and then in a rush pointed to each dog and named them. "Nanook, Kenai, Siku, Miki, Senyea, and my lead dog, Lucien."

Aidan was stunned and needed a moment to collect himself. He slowly got to his feet, his bad leg complaining—he'd obviously put it through too much today—and brushed the snow off his jeans. He looked at Fox who seemed apprehensive. "You named your dogs after the characters in my graphic novels?"

"I love the Spirit of the Totem series," Fox rushed on to explain. "I can't wait to see what's going to happen now that Lucien had to sacrifice Senyea. I really hope you bring her back. I loved her."

Aidan had no clue what was going to happen with Senyea. He had the novel halfway written but hadn't touched it since this summer. Since his dad's death, he'd lost the desire to write, to draw, to escape. He thought it was some kind of cosmic punishment. The gift of escapism he'd been given by a higher being to be able to deal with his father had been snuffed out with his father's death. Ironic in a twisted sort of way.

Raven pulled up in her Suburban along the plowed driveway. She climbed out of the vehicle, and as soon as Aidan saw her, his heart jumped. Her long hair blew away from her face with her fast gait. He just stared. This could have been his life. She could have been his wife—should have been—Fox his son, these dogs, this place. All of it. The pain in his chest flared.

"I thought you'd appreciate a ride back. Besides—" she looked at her son "—Fox needs to get his chores done and math homework started."

Aidan also heard the unspoken message. She didn't want her son spending too much time with him. Not that he blamed her. Though it was hard not to take personally. He laid his hand on Fox's shoulder. "Thank you for showing me your team. They're impressive."

Fox beamed up at him with admiration. Aidan stepped back. He couldn't remember a time someone had looked at him that way. The burning ache in his chest flamed hotter.

"Don't forget our ride," Fox said, keeping his voice low.

"I won't," Aidan answered, keeping his voice equally quiet. Raven would probably have objected. Case in point, her showing up to presumably give him a ride back to the lodge, when he knew it was to bring a stop to their time together.

He limped over to the Suburban and got in. Raven told Fox she'd be right back. Within minutes she had Aidan back at the lodge. She put the SUV in park and turned to him. "I thought about what you said. So I grabbed my dad's old gun. I'll have Fox draw me a map tonight, and I'll pick you up in the morning after he heads to school."

"Thank you, Raven." He wanted to reach out to her. Trail his fingers down her arm, caress her face, run his fingers through her raven hair.

She must have read what was in his expression, for she swallowed and looked away. "Better safe than sorry, right?"

135

Raven watched Aidan struggle on his way into the lodge and resisted the urge to jump out and help him. Instead, she put the Suburban in reverse and backed out, heading for home. She'd left Fox and Aidan alone as long as she'd dared. Long enough to hopefully not bring up any questions on why she was so overprotective, but short enough that no attachments would develop.

While she'd sat in her mother's kitchen and stewed, she'd also rethought the situation at Earl Harte's place. If Aidan was that freaked out about someone messing with his car, she shouldn't discount it simply because she didn't want to believe anything bad was happening in her small town. She'd discounted the situation between Earl and her father when she'd known something wasn't right. She'd caught Earl's evil glare. Had felt nothing good in the man. Knew he was capable of doing something bad if provoked. Any man who could shoot his son's dog in front of him was a man to be wary of. She'd known all this, and still, she hadn't acted on the instincts screaming at her during the land dispute, and because of that, her dad had died.

She'd never disregard those voices again. Not when the price was so steep.

CHAPTER ELEVEN

Raven walked into the lodge early the next morning. Ever since Aidan had returned, she hadn't had a restful night's sleep. She was plagued with memories of the past. The way he'd made her feel, the closeness she'd felt when he held her within his arms.

It was hard being a single parent, a self-employed artist always juggling with financial responsibilities. But that was the life she'd chosen. To dream of what could have been was a waste of time and energy. Instead of fighting the dreams, she'd forgone the sleep and spent the time in her studio. Unfortunately that left her tired and cranky. She wouldn't be able to sustain this schedule for long before she crashed. The faster she could get Aidan out to his father's homestead, the faster she might be able to get him off her mind and have a good night's sleep. The more time she spent with him, the more she wanted to touch him, have him touch her. Forget the past.

But she couldn't forget the past. She couldn't dishonor her father's memory that way.

She found Aidan in the lodge's restaurant, saddled up to the bar, a cup of coffee cradled in his hands, a half-finished plate of pancakes and sausages in front of him. His hair fell over his forehead and brushed the collar of his soft blue flannel shirt. The medical boot looked heavy and uncomfortable clamped to his jean-clad leg. She hoped he was feeling better. He'd never told her what the doctor had said. She should have handled that situation better when they'd been in town and not let her feelings sour her mood.

"Are you ready?" she asked, coming up alongside him.

"Morning," he greeted. He studied her and frowned. "Didn't you get any sleep?"

Now why did he have to seem so concerned? It weakened her resolve to keep her distance. "I'm fine."

"No, you're not. Sit, have a cup of coffee. Have you eaten?" He continued to regard her with a troubled, concerned look.

"Uh…"

"Pike," he hollered at her uncle. "Raven needs breakfast."

Pike gazed at her from the cutout in the kitchen. "What have I taught you, girl?"

"Most important meal of the day," she repeated the words her uncle had always stressed.

He grunted. "Pull up a stool."

"Not too much." She was too exhausted to be hungry.

"You'll eat what I cook you." Pike pointed at her with his spatula. He was a big man, tall and wide with thick salt-and-pepper hair. Her father would look similar to Pike if he'd lived.

"You're pretty brave, or really stupid," Raven said under her breath to Aidan. "Uncle Pike isn't the forgiving sort."

"I heard that," Pike hollered, arrowing a sharp look at Aidan. "If I was going to go after Aidan, it would have been twelve years ago and he wouldn't have seen me coming."

"Believe me, I'm completely aware of that fact." Aidan glanced at Raven and lowered his voice, "I'm still waiting to see if my food will stay down."

She gave him a smile. His eyes widened and focused on her lips. Unconsciously, she licked them and thought she heard him groan before he turned away, and picked up his coffee.

Pike came out of the kitchen and dropped a plate of scrambled eggs, bacon, and toast in front of her. "Eat."

"Thanks," she mumbled.

Pike poured a cup of coffee and set that in front of her too. Then he leaned over the counter and looked at her. "Why didn't you tell me what was going on at Earl's place?"

She turned to Aidan. "You told him?"

"He's head of the village council. Something happens here he needs to know."

"Listen to him, girlie."

Pike and Aidan on the same side? She really needed to get more sleep, either that or she was dreaming while awake. "It's probably nothing."

"I hope it is, but you should have let me in on it." He stood and grabbed the rag hanging over his shoulder and wiped down the spotless counter. "You let me know what you find out there."

"Yes, sir." She scooped up a bite of egg. They tasted like rubber. Her uncle was a great cook, so she knew the eggs tasted bad because of her poor appetite. Ever since Aidan had come to town, her world, her appetite, her ability to think were turned upside down.

"You got enough firepower?" Pike asked as though he'd just asked her what time it was.

"I grabbed Dad's old forty-five."

He raised a brow, reached under the counter, and handed Aidan his Magnum. "Here. Can't be too careful. You could have some squatters with that place empty all these months. Though I don't know who would be crazy enough to try and get into that dump. Look what happened to you. Your dad was one mean son of a bitch." He motioned to Aidan's leg.

"No arguments here," Aidan agreed.

"How'd he die?" Pike asked.

Aidan's cup froze half way to his lips. In fact, his whole body froze.

"Heart attack?" Pike asked. "No, he'd have to have a heart in order for that to be possible. Aneurism? Infection? Stroke? What finally did the old bastard in?"

Aidan swallowed. "He was shot."

Pike straightened. "No kidding. By who? I'd like to send the fellow a thank you card."

Aidan pushed his cup aside and stood. "I shot him." He threw some bills on the bar. "Thanks for breakfast, Pike. Raven, I'll wait for you outside."

He turned and hobbled out of the restaurant.

Pike looked at her. "Did he say what I thought he said? *He killed Earl?*"

"That's what I heard," she returned softly.

Pike shook his head. "Poor kid's even more messed up now than he was when he left here." Pike pointed at her. "You find out the whole story. I'm sure him killing Earl isn't the worst of it. Be careful out there today." He undid the ties to his apron. "In fact, I think I'll go with you."

"No." She held up her hand. "Let me feel him out. You're too strong of a personality, and I say that in a good way. He's not going to talk with you there."

"You're sure?"

She nodded, drank down her coffee. "Besides, if something is going on, I'd feel better if you were here watching things. Keep an eye out for any newcomers. Mom's got a lot of reservations for this weekend, due to the snow."

"Good point." He retied his apron strings and picked up his rag and once again wiped the already spotless counter. "Take care of that boy. I think he needs us."

Raven tightened her lips and nodded, afraid of what she'd say in response and followed Aidan out of the dining room. She found him sitting outside on one of the benches placed around the wide porch. He looked lost.

She walked up to him, wanting to reach out and touch him, but afraid to. Afraid of how he'd take the overture and afraid that if she opened herself to him where it would lead.

"Ready?" she asked.

He glanced up, and she had the feeling she'd dragged him back from a dark place. "Yeah."

He followed her to the Suburban, Uncle Pike's gun tucked into the waistband of his jeans. The gun he held brought new meaning knowing that he had shot someone. Killed someone. She swallowed and climbed into the SUV. They traveled to Earl's in silence, but once there, she couldn't take it anymore.

"Before we go any farther, I need to know what happened. How Earl died."

Aidan glanced at her and then faced forward, gazing at nothing through the windshield. "There was trouble this summer. Sonya." His voice broke on her name, but he cleared his throat and continued, "Sonya had decided to fish both types of gear, drifting *and* set netting, taking more of the season's catch. To make a long story short. Earl just…snapped, attacking Sonya and a fish cop who was protecting her. He was…crazed. Insane. He went to shoot Sonya, and I…I shot him instead." Aidan turned toward her, his eyes full of disbelief and pain. "Earl died in my arms. Just before he died, he looked at me with pride for the first time and said, 'Son, I didn't know you had the balls'."

Raven had so many questions, but one look at his face told her she wouldn't be getting any answers. So she sat and tried to digest what he'd said. "Is this the same Sonya you asked to marry you?"

He nodded but didn't add anything else. Almost like he had no more to give, that it had taken everything out of him to impart to her what he had.

"You had to stop him, or she would be dead."

"Yeah, too bad I hadn't stopped him from killing your father." Aidan got out of the Suburban and slammed the door.

She scrambled out after him. "Aidan, wait. Stop."

He halted just inside the broken gate. "I don't want to hear it, Raven. Let's just get this over with, and then I'll get out of your life."

She didn't know what she wanted to do. Leave him. Comfort him. Love him. No, she didn't want to love him. Couldn't. She wouldn't survive a second time.

"The map. Remember?" She reached into her pocket and pulled out the surprisingly detailed map her son had drawn for her last night.

Aidan turned back, his shoulders rigid, his dark eyes swimming with shadows. Right now he didn't care if getting into the cabin hurt him again or worse. She didn't want him hurt, and if there was a threat, they needed to know. She handed over the map. He took a couple of steps toward her until he could reach out and take it. The action, like coaxing a wounded animal, wasn't lost on her.

He glanced down at the map, his brows shooting up. "This is really good."

Crap. What was she thinking? Aidan was an artist, he drew characters. So did Fox. He'd drawn on everything as a little kid. From pieces of paper to the walls of their cabin. She shouldn't have given the map to Aidan. Of course he would recognize the level of talent as Fox had gotten it from his father, not his mother. Raven considered herself an artist, but she couldn't draw. Her medium was clay. Not pencils or paint.

"Think you can navigate us to the cabin with it?" she asked, getting off the subject of Fox.

"Yeah." He glanced at her. "You don't have to come with me. With this map, I'm good."

"I'm coming." She'd like nothing better than to get back into the car and drive away. But she couldn't. Maybe it was the sixth sense that was raising the hairs on the back of her neck, but she needed to be here. See this through. She motioned for him to start. "Lead the way."

"All right." He looked around the area. "Stay in my footsteps. Whatever you do, don't venture from my tracks."

"You don't need to tell me twice."

Aidan turned and treaded carefully, stopping every few feet to glance at the map and his surroundings before continuing. The trek was slow, but they arrived at the back door of the cabin without mishap. Aidan released a deep breath as he opened the door with the key he'd found where Fox had said it would be. Inside the skull of a wolf sitting on the stoop.

She really needed to have a long talk with Fox.

Aidan opened the door, walked in and held the door for her. The smell hit her first, a mixture of stove oil, tanned fur, and age. The place smelled old and dusty. It looked old, dusty, and…wrecked.

Aidan pulled the gun from his waistband and held it in front of him. He reached a hand behind him and grabbed her, pulling her up against his back. "Stay close."

He turned a full circle in the one room that made up the living space, kitchen, and small dining area. "Earl was never the cleanest sort, but this is beyond anything he would have lived with."

Cushions had been torn off the couch and ripped through with a knife. Drawers in the apartment-sized kitchen were turned over, dumping their contents. Books had been thrown from the bookcases that lined the far log wall. Raven followed Aidan into the two bedrooms off to the left. They'd also been shredded. Mattresses pitched from the bed, their innards pulled out like wild animals had feasted on them.

Aidan stumbled as he stepped on something with his bad leg. He went down on his knee.

She reached out and helped him to his feet. "You okay?"

"Yeah." He bent down, his fingers touching a dark spot. "I think this is blood."

She bent to take a look. A dried reddish-brown spot pooled on the pine floor. She kicked clothes and bedding out of her way and found what looked like a trail of sorts. Aidan motioned for her to be quiet as he once again pushed her behind him and followed the trail that lead to the bathroom. There they found more blood. On the floor, around the sink, and wiped on towels.

"I'm willing to bet someone else got caught in one of Earl's booby traps," Aidan said.

Raven looked at him. "Why would anyone be *here*?"

"By the looks of the place, someone was looking for something. Did Fox say anything about the condition of the cabin?"

"No, but why would he?" Her brows furrowed.

"The night I was injured, he came into the cabin and grabbed blankets. He didn't say anything then, but things were hectic. He might not have noticed."

"How could he have missed this?"

"Whoever went through my SUV went through the cabin too. But why now?"

"You mean, why not go through the place before you showed up?"

"Yeah. Earl's been dead since the middle of July. The cabin's been empty all this time."

"You're forgetting that nobody *knew* Earl was dead until you showed up." Her gaze flew to his as the reality of what she'd just said sank in.

"You think someone in town did this?"

"I don't want to, but it makes sense."

He nodded, his expression solemn. "It does." He walked to the window where the blood trail ended. "Whoever was in here was scared off." He indicated the blood trail and the window left open. "By the looks of this place, I'd say they didn't find what they were looking for."

"Which means, they'll be back."

A chill raced up Aidan's spine. Raven was right. Whoever had done this hadn't left happy. They hadn't found whatever they'd come for.

He tucked the gun back into the waistband of his jeans and walked out of the bathroom. The space was too small and Raven too close. He could smell her. That sweet, beguiling brand of pheromones that reached out and grabbed his heart and caused it to pump faster whenever she was near. He needed some space, and he wasn't going to find it here in Earl's cabin.

He walked into the main room, stepping over things as he paced around the room. "Something's not right."

"Something besides someone breaking into the place and tossing it?" Raven asked, coming up behind him.

She really needed to move away from him. All he'd wanted to do since the last time he had her in his arms was to get her right back there. "I swear the room seems smaller."

"You've grown. You're much bigger than the last time you where here."

"Maybe." He rubbed the back of his neck. But something was different about the place. He couldn't put his finger on it. At least memories weren't slamming at him liked he'd feared. "Where do I start?"

"You could call the village council. Or the troopers."

"I've had enough of troopers. Besides, Earl had so many enemies. Everyone in town probably has a motive." He shook his head. "No point in involving the law. I'll get this cleaned up and then clear out. If you want to torch the place in celebration of the winter solstice, you have my blessing."

"Actually, that's not a bad idea. It would put Earl to bed for good, and then we wouldn't have his place as a reminder."

"Consider it done then." If he could do anything to wipe out the awful things Earl had done in his lifetime, to the woman Aidan had loved, he'd do it. "I also want to make sure the gold claim is deeded over to your family."

"No." Raven shook her head adamantly. "I don't want anything to do with that."

"It rightfully belongs to you and your family. Earl never should have—"

"I don't want to talk about it." She put her hands over her ears.

"That's a bit childish, don't you think?" He quirked his lips.

"I don't care."

She looked adorable. More like the teenage Raven he'd remembered. "All right, I won't talk about it." At least not now. He wouldn't put the subject to Raven. Instead, he'd have a talk with Fiona and Pike.

"Are you going to be okay staying here?" Raven asked looking around the place.

"I guess that would depend on if I can get the wood stove started." He walked over to the black potbelly stove, knelt down, and opened it. "Oh, shit." He slammed the door shut and put an arm out to keep her back.

"What's wrong?"

"There's something dead in there."

"Dead? Like rotting?"

"Too cold to rot. No, just dead."

"What is it?"

"It's...a..." Damn, he didn't want to tell her. "It's a raven." She gasped. "No."

"I'm afraid so, honey."

"But..."

"It must have fallen down the stove pipe."

"It would have been caught in there, starved to death, beating its wings against the cold metal sides." She dropped her head against his chest, and he pulled her in closer. She had an affinity to her namesake.

He tried to reassure her. "I'm sure the fall killed it."

She raised her head and looked up at him. "Do you think so?"

"I'm sure of it." He caressed the side of her face, watching his fingers as they lightly touched her soft skin. She was so beautiful. Exotic almond eyes, honeyed skin that he wanted to run his lips over, mouth too wide and too full, lending her an air of seduction that he couldn't resist. He wanted to kiss those lips, lose himself in her heat and drink from her mouth. He leaned closer, waiting for her to push him away.

She didn't.

He lightly touched his lips to hers. She sighed into him. Had she wanted him to do this too? Had she been tormented by the thought of them together like he had? He deepened the kiss, slanting his head, drawing her in closer to his body, loving the feel of her against him. She was perfect. Perfect size as she fit against him, snuggled in his arms, her hips cradling his erection. He unzipped her coat and spread the edges apart, his hands running up and down her sides as he waited for her to slap them way.

She didn't.

Why was she letting him touch her? One minute she wanted to see the last of him, and the next, she was allowing him to dream. To hope.

This was driving him crazy, and he'd never been far from crazy to begin with.

He lifted his mouth from hers. "What are you doing?"

Her face was flushed, and as the temperature inside the cabin was only a few degrees warmer than the single digits outside, it wasn't from that. Which meant he'd caused the flush to her skin.

"What do you mean?"

"You let me kiss you. Kissed me back. Why?"

She moved out of his arms. "Curiosity, I guess." She shrugged her shoulders as though what they had just done hadn't meant anything.

He turned her around to face him. "Don't give me that crap. Why did you kiss me back?"

"Why does it matter?" Her eyes turned hot.

He let go of her and stepped back, his bad leg getting caught up in an old, torn flannel shirt thrown on the floor. He shook it free and looked at Raven again, his heart pounding. "Because you matter." He shook his head. "Don't fool with me."

She dropped her gaze from his. "You're right. I'm sorry. I shouldn't have let that happen, but..."

"But what?"

She glanced at him. "It's hard. Being with you. Remembering what it used to be like." She turned away.

He grabbed her again, made her face him. "You don't get to say something like that and then turn away from me. You broke my heart, Raven. Don't toy with the pieces."

She sucked in a breath, studied him, her eyes wide, questioning. She reached up and cupped his face. "I wish..." She stopped and bit her lip as if to keep the words from being spoken.

"You wish?" he prompted, very much wanting to know what she had been about to say.

"I wish things could have been different. But they're not."

The pain wasn't any less sharp having heard it from her before. He released her and stepped back. "You'd better go."

She swallowed and looked around the cabin again. "I don't think it's a good idea for you to stay out here." She indicated the mess scattered around them. "Besides, what if the person who did this decides to come back?"

"I hope they do. Then I'll find out what they were looking for."

"Aidan—"

"Don't worry about me, Raven. I've always been able to take care of myself."

Her eyes met his, and he stood his ground.

"What about food?"

"I have groceries in the rental. I'll be fine for a few days." He pulled the gun free. "Give this back to Pike for me."

"You'd better keep it."

He pointed to the full gun cabinet left untouched near the front door. "I have enough firepower to take on a small country." He cocked his head. "Surprising that whoever broke in here didn't help themselves. Which means they were after something specific."

CHAPTER TWELVE

Raven sat at her wheel, a lump of clay on the bat, water in her bucket, Stevie Nicks singing on the CD player. She anchored an elbow on her hip and used her palm to raise the clay, her other hand she steadied, then pressed the clay back down. She repeated the movement until the clay was a large centered mound on her wheel. She breathed in rhythmically as she moved the clay, coaxed it to her will, and became one with the elements pulled from the earth. Wetting her hands, she opened the body of clay. All the while trying to forget what had happened with Aidan that morning. Not that she was successful.

Why had she let him kiss her? Touch her? Why had she wanted more? Almost pushed him into taking more? As if by doing that, the decision wouldn't have been hers. If he took, then she didn't have to face giving of herself. But Aidan hadn't fallen for that. Instead he'd wanted to know why she wasn't pushing him away, demanding he leave her alone. She had obviously confused the hell out of him. Fitting since she was confused as well.

She opened the clay further, pulling the walls up into a thick cylinder, wondering what the piece wanted to be. She loved to sit down at the wheel not knowing what she was going to throw, leaving it up to the clay to decide what it wanted to be. She had a feeling this five pounds wanted to be a large pasta or fruit bowl. Something that would stand alone, not part of a set. The glaze would have to be dramatic, she decided as she pulled the walls up with steady pressure while the wheel continued to spin.

She hadn't liked leaving Aidan at Earl's place by himself. The rundown cabin was a hellhole. Earl had lived like an animal, not caring for the civilized things in life. No utilities, no mail, no modern day conveniences.

Aidan had grown up that way. He knew what he was in for, and she shouldn't worry about him. The best thing would be for him to do what he came here for. Clean up Earl's sorry life and then clear out.

The thought made her sad and the walls on her bowl wobbled. She released the thinning clay, rewetted her hands, and lightly placed one hand on the inside, the other on the outside and slowly coaxed it back on center. The bowl spun around and around, like her thoughts.

What if she told Aidan about Fox? He might decide to stay? *Oh hell, what was she thinking?*

She didn't want Aidan a part of Fox's life. She didn't want the evil kind of influence she knew lived inside of him to touch Fox. He'd admitted to killing Earl. But he *had* been forced to in order to save a woman's life. Wouldn't she have done the same? Maybe? Hopefully she'd never know.

Raven finished shaping the walls of the bowl and then pressed her trademark swirl in the bottom as the wheel continued to spin. She cleaned up the foot of the piece and then stopped the wheel. Grabbing her wire, she ran it under the bowl, disconnecting it from the bat. Then she lifted the bat off her wheel and set the bowl on the shelf to dry. It was nice. Just the kind of piece to sit on a table with a bounty of fruit, bread, or filled with salad or pasta for a large family.

She loved that her art was useable, had function. Someone would fall in love with this bowl, maybe even hand it down from generation to generation. An heirloom.

Raven secured another bat onto the wheel and then grabbed a ball of clay that she had previously wedged, throwing it onto the center. She went through the motions of centering the clay. Her days were filled with throwing piece after piece. At least her best days were. Then there was the cleaning of the pieces in preparation for bisque firing, glazing and firing again. When she opened the kiln—which always seemed to take forever to cool—it was like Christmas, seeing her babies, colorful and shiny and ready for use. Her life was good. She was able to make a living at what she loved. She loved being a mother to Fox. The kid constantly made her proud and was growing up into a fine young man. Though he did have his moments. But then she'd be worried if he didn't. No child was perfect and sometimes those imperfections is what set them apart, made them special.

She stopped, releasing her hands from the clay. Aidan wasn't perfect. Had she set her expectations too high in regards to him? Had she set him up to fail because of the people he came from?

Fox slammed into the studio. "Mom!"

"At the wheel," she replied.

He turned the corner of a shelving unit, which held other pottery pieces, already fired and waiting to be glazed. He smiled at her, his dimple flashing, causing an ache in her heart. He was a handsome boy, tall for his age. Responsible, fun, outgoing, and adventurous. She loved him with everything that was inside her. A catch caught in her throat and she had to clear it in order to speak. "How was your day?"

"Freaking amazing. Grand asked Janette to go out with him and she cut him off at the knees. It was so cool."

"What about Grand? Aren't his feelings hurt?"

"He'll get over it, but the best part is that the reason Janette said no was because she likes someone else. Guess who?" He bounced on his heels. "She likes me. Me!" He did a touchdown dance. "Can she come over and watch a movie tonight?"

"Uh…" He was too young for girls. Just last year, girls were gross and disgusting. When had that changed? "I don't like the idea of you and Janette watching a movie together. You're too young for a—" dare she say date? "—get-together like that."

"It wouldn't be just the two of us. There'd be other guys." He looked at her with those dark beguiling eyes. "What do you say? I'll do the dishes and sweep too."

"Uh…" This was new territory. "How many friends, what movie, and how late?"

There, those all sounded like good and responsible questions a loving, concerned mother would need to know.

"I need to make some calls."

"Get me the info and then I can decide. But chores first. And homework."

"Yes, Mom." He turned to head out of the studio but then stopped. "Did you guys make it to Mr. Harte's cabin okay with my map?"

"Yes, we did, which reminds me. Pull up a stool, Fox. I have some questions for you."

"Can't it wait? If I don't get a hold of Grand before three-thirty he'll make other plans for tonight."

"You're going to invite Grand to this get-together with Janette here? Won't that be awkward?"

"Naw. Grand's already got his sights set on Tina."

She shook her head, trying to clear it. "I still need to know how you knew how to get into Earl's place. And when we got inside the cabin today, someone had been there. Do you know anything about that?"

He sat on the stool, letting his backpack slide to the dusty floor. "How did you know someone had been there?"

"Whoever they were, they'd gone through the place, tossed it. When you went in to get blankets for Aidan, how did it look?"

He shrugged. "Normal. It wasn't clean, but then it never was."

"How many times have you been inside Earl's place?" Fear sunk into her bones. "Why were you ever there? Did he touch you?"

"What? *No.* Gross, Mom. Mr. Harte wasn't like that."

"He was an evil man. One I warned you about, and now I find you've been inside his place. What else? And don't think of lying to me, I'll know."

"Jeez. It's no big deal. You always taught me to make up my mind about people and not listen to other people's opinions. So one day, I came across Mr. Harte when I was exercising the dogs. He wasn't that bad. He invited me back to visit when I wanted to. I dropped in every now and then…just to—you know—check up on him. He didn't have anyone who cared about him."

"Didn't you wonder why?"

"He told me why. He'd said that he was a bully and pushed his son, hoping he would push back. I guess Aidan never pushed back."

Yeah, he did and that push had killed Earl Harte. "Interesting parenting idea."

"You kinda got to see where he came from to understand his thinking. I'm not saying it wasn't whacked. He was nuts on a lot of things, but he treated me fair. I couldn't judge him on anything else. Right?"

How did she argue against her own teachings? She'd brought up her son to do exactly what he'd done. She wanted him opened-minded, fair in his thinking, able to make his own judgments and not rely on the opinions of others. But why had Earl Harte treated her son decent? Had he finally felt guilt for killing Fox senior that this had been his way of making it up? Had he mellowed in his old age? He hadn't been that old. Maybe fifty-five, sixty. But the man had been so pickled in his thinking that there couldn't have been any mellowing.

"Why didn't you tell me?" That was what bothered her the most. "Why keep it a secret?"

"Mr. Harte asked me to. He liked it when I dropped by, and he was afraid you would forbid me from doing it."

He was right. If she had known... There was no point in going down that road. It wouldn't help the hurt she felt now that Fox had kept secrets from her.

He gave her the look that melted her heart. "I'm sorry, Mom, I hated keeping it from you."

"Then why did you?"

"Well...I liked Mr. Harte. I know what everyone has always said about him. And I know that you think he killed Grandpa—"

"He *did* kill Grandpa."

"I don't want to get into that."

"How do we not get into it when the man killed *my* dad? And now I find out that my own son was friends with him?"

He tightened his lips and Raven knew she had shut him up. Fox was real good about talking with her until she got angry and then he buttoned up. She bit back her anger and tried again. "What did Earl say about my father?"

"I don't think this is a good idea."

"I need to know, Fox."

Fox looked off to the side. Raven turned off her wheel. She was too keyed up to make anything worth keeping. She threw a piece of plastic over the clay. It would wait until later.

"He claimed that he never meant for Grandpa to die. That it had been an accident."

It was her turn to bite her lips. Because she knew, without a doubt, Earl had planned to set off those charges when her father was panning in the riverbed. It had been deliberate. It had been premeditated. Murder.

With difficulty she kept a hold of her tongue. If she said anything now, Fox would completely shut down on the subject. Her body shook with the effort it took to keep quiet.

"Is this going to affect my movie night?" Fox asked, his eyes downcast.

She wanted to send him to his room. Lock him up and never let him out of her sight. Look at what had been going on right under her nose! She rubbed her forehead forgetting that her hands where covered in clay slip until the grittiness transferred onto her skin. "Go and make your calls, but we'll talk about this later, Fox."

He stood, gaze cast downward. "Yes, Mom." He left, trailing his backpack behind him.

She picked up a wooden wedge, twisting it between her fingers. And here she had always thought she'd been an observant mother. What else had she missed?

Aidan heaved the mattress back onto the bed. It flopped like a dead fish. Who was he kidding? He couldn't sleep here, not until he had the place cleaned up. He'd disposed of the dead raven in the stove, but there wasn't any wood to burn. Since his father hadn't returned this summer, he hadn't chopped the cords of wood waiting outside. Aidan was in no condition to be stomping around in the trap-infested yard with a walking boot chopping wood. He looked around at the sad bedroom that used to be his. It had been left pretty much the same. A corkboard full of school accomplishments. Art awards that his dad hadn't cared a fart for. Amateur drawings of totems that had been the spark for his graphic novels, hockey sticks stood forgotten in the corner along with his skates. Dried stalks of fireweed he'd hung as a remembrance of the first time he and Raven had made love. They were dry and dusty and broken. He couldn't help but see the comparison.

He rubbed his hands together. It was getting colder. The sun had set and he needed heat.

Raven was right. He wasn't ready to stay here tonight. But how did he get back? He had the keys to the rental, but his right foot was also in a boot. It wasn't a cast—he could take it off. He'd done that in order to shower this morning. But driving was different.

He had two choices, stay and suffer through what would was bound to be a miserable, cold night bundled in dirty blankets, or return to the lodge. The lodge won out. Tomorrow he'd return better prepared.

He grabbed the map Fox had drawn from his coat pocket and smoothed it out. The kid was talented. Raven needed to help him develop it. Aidan knew she would encourage him, which was more than he had ever had as a boy.

Using a small flashlight, he locked up the cabin and navigated the tricky path toward his SUV. There was no breeze. The area was devoid of sound, other than his footsteps crunching in the snow and his breathing. Off to the right he caught a flash of light. Two small pinpoints. He came to a full stop, his heart pounding.

A black wolf stood observing him—just outside of Earl's property—his yellow eyes shining in the moonlight. Aidan swallowed. The wolf was beautiful, dangerous, wild. And he scared the shit out of him. He'd left the guns inside the cabin. The wolf could be on him before he hobbled back to safety. He was midway between the back door of the cabin and the SUV.

Neither of them moved.

Was this Alaska's version of a standoff? One of them had to make a move. Aidan took a step, the wolf watched. He took another step. Other than the wolf's eyes following each move he made, the animal didn't shift. Just watched. It was eerie, unnerving.

And freaking cool.

He began to relax, his heart still beat at an alarming rate, but his shaking had lessened. Somewhat. He reached the SUV and still the wolf stayed. He climbed in—breathing a sigh of relief when he locked himself inside—and started the engine. It coughed, and died. "You got to be kidding." He couldn't make the trip back to the cabin with the wolf out there. Chances were the predator wouldn't spare him a second time. That was asking too much. Staying in the SUV too long and he'd freeze. He cranked over the engine again. It flared to life.

The wolf stood there, watching. A peculiar trickle slid down Aidan's spine. He wasn't scared—wary, yes—but he didn't feel fear anymore. Not that he wanted to get out and pet the wild animal. It was hard to explain, but he felt as though he and the wolf could be…amicable. Now that was weird. He needed to grab his notebook and write this down. Excitement spread through him. Maybe he hadn't lost it. Maybe he could lose himself in his story again. Maybe…

First he needed to get his sorry ass out of here. Or he wouldn't have any maybes. Carefully he unstrapped the Velcro on the boot, releasing his leg from the brace. He tried some pressure on the brake. It hurt, but he could bear it. Sure as hell beat sleeping in the cabin with a wolf prowling around outside. He put the SUV in gear and backed it out of Earl's makeshift driveway. Heading back toward Chatanika, he glanced in the rearview mirror to see the yellow eyes of the wolf.

Watching.

Aidan walked into the kitchen and found Fiona, Coho, Chickadee, Eva, and Lynx around the table eating dinner.

"Sorry, didn't mean to interrupt."

"Nonsense," Coho said. "Have a seat. You must be hungry."

Yes, he was, but he didn't want to sit where he *so* did not belong.

"I'm sure he has things to do," Lynx said with a glare.

Eva elbowed him in the chest. "Don't be rude. Besides I want to find out what Doc Jaskoski said today. Sit, Aidan." She said the words much the way a general in the army would.

Aidan was too afraid of Eva to disobey a direct order so he sat. Fiona rose and grabbed another plate, filling it with generous helpings of caribou steak, red potatoes, green beans, topping it off with two homemade sourdough biscuits. "This looks great. Thank you, Fiona."

"You're very welcome, my boy. Now eat up, you need your strength."

"What'd Doc say?" Eva asked, spearing green beans with her fork. "Is it broken?"

"Hairline fracture, which is why he put me in the boot."

"You're lucky," Eva said. "I've seen nasty accidents like yours where the bone split through the skin."

"Hey." Lynx grimaced. "I'm eating here."

"Buck up," Eva returned. "You married a nurse. There's bound to be blood talk at the table." She turned back to Aidan. "Anything else?"

"Nothing other than praise for you."

Eva smiled, giving her an adorable look that would fool anyone into believing she was as sweet as cotton candy. "Ah, that's nice to hear."

Aidan cut into his steak and took a bite. He hadn't eaten lunch since he had been busy cleaning up Earl's place. Not that he'd gotten far. "This is wonderful, Fiona," he said, chewing a piece while he cut another.

Fiona beamed.

"Yes, Mom, dinner is great." Lynx wasn't going to let Aidan show him up.

"Mr. Harte?" Chickadee asked. "Can I ask you a question?"

"As long as you call me Aidan." He smiled when she blushed. She looked a lot like Raven had at that age, and he couldn't help being charmed by her.

"Fox leant me your graphic novels, which I love by the way. But I have to know, are you bringing Senyea back from the dead?"

He'd been plagued with fan mail since the last novel came out when he had sacrificed her. From pleas, to coercion, to threats. The most serious threat had come from his editor. "You'll have to wait and see."

"No. Please tell me. Don't make me wait. I won't tell anyone, promise."

"To tell you the truth. I don't know. I haven't written it yet." Aidan took another bite and chewed.

She gasped. "What do you mean you don't know? They're your characters."

"I know, but they haven't told me yet." They hadn't even started talking to him until he'd seen that wolf tonight. His fingers itched to grab a pencil.

"Isn't that a little weird?" Chickadee asked.

"Dee," Fiona scolded.

"Look at the source," Lynx said, grunting as he received another elbow to the gut from Eva.

"What happened to your manners?" Eva asked Lynx with a scowl. "Besides, I think this is really cool. Aidan, how do the characters come to you?"

"Uhm…" He really didn't talk about this. He didn't do interviews, do any blogging, or attend writers' conferences. Which had actually played in his favor. Gave him a mystique. Nobody even knew what he looked like. Guess he'd chosen to live off the grid too, just like his father. That was sobering. "Uhm, they just talk to me. I don't know how to explain it."

"It is the way of the storyteller," Coho said, who had been quietly eating. "The Great Spirit speaks, and you are the vessel gifted to tell the tale."

"Well, I haven't read them, yet, but they sound fascinating," Eva said. "Dee, when you're done, can I take a look?" She received a frown from Lynx that she ignored.

"Sure. But talk to Fox, he has them all if you want to start at the beginning." Chickadee looked at Fiona. "Can I be excused? I had plans to Skype with a friend."

Fiona regarded her. "A boy?"

Chickadee bit her lip. "Uh-huh."

"Who?"

"Just a guy, Mom. He lives in Fairbanks. Don't worry, we go to school together and it isn't like we can get into any trouble online."

"Remember that I monitor your computer."

"I'm not about to forget." Chickadee rolled her eyes.

"Load your dishes in the dishwasher then," Fiona said. "I'll be up to check on you later."

Chickadee said goodbye to everyone and flew out of the room.

Aidan figured this was a good time to let the adults know what had been going on at Earl's place. "Someone broke into Earl's cabin, looking for something."

Lynx snorted. "The man's dead and people want to cause him grief. Shows you what kind of life he led. Karma's still trying to catch up."

"I just thought you should know. It doesn't look like they found whatever they were looking for, so they might be back. Wouldn't hurt to get the word out. If the person is here in Chatanika, he'll know we're watching. If someone new is about, we'll hear about it through the network."

"Good idea," Fiona said. "I'll inform Pike. He'll get the word out."

"And have us all packin' too." Lynx snorted.

"What's with you?" Eva asked.

"What do you mean?"

"The snide comments, the insults. Ever since Aidan showed up, you have been ornery as a bear with an empty stomach. I don't like it."

"Then make him leave." Lynx pointed to Aidan,

"No. He has work to do here. Important work. I don't care how much everyone in this town hated Earl Harte, the man was still his father." Eva rose ungracefully from the table, her hand caressing her swollen belly. "If all the stories are true about Harte, Aidan needs our sympathy."

"I don't want it," Aidan interjected, getting a scowl from Eva for his troubles.

"Too bad. To grow up with a father like you had and to become the man I've gotten to know is impressive." She turned to Lynx. "Get over whatever it is you have against him. I like him." With that, she waddled out of the room.

Coho chuckled. "You married yourself a wolverine, Lynx. She's right." Coho wiped her mouth with her napkin and gracefully set it beside her plate. "Make nice, Grandson." With a final look she rose and regally left the room.

Silence followed in her wake. Fiona stood and gathered up Eva's and Coho's plates along with her own.

"Fiona, do you mind if I stay the night?" Aidan asked.

"Your room is still your room." She gave him a warm smile. "I was hoping you would be back." She took the dishes to the dishwasher and then addressed Lynx and Aidan, "Looks as though you two could use some time to talk." She gave both of them a pointed look and left them alone.

Aidan had no expectations where Lynx was concerned. So he concentrated on finishing the food on his plate. He couldn't remember the last time he'd eaten this good.

"Well, shit." Lynx pushed his plate forward and folded his arms, leaning heavily on the table. "I'm going to have to make peace with you."

Aidan glanced up from cutting the last of his steak. "Afraid of the little woman?"

"Yes."

"You're smarter than you look."

"Fuck off."

"Not the best way to make peace." Aidan found he was enjoying himself. He scooped up the last sourdough biscuit and wiped his plate clean with it, soaking up all the leftover juices. "I don't expect you to make peace with me. You have a right to feel what you do."

"Yeah, but Gran and Eva have a point," he grumbled.

Aidan paused with the biscuit halfway to his mouth. "Huh?"

Lynx looked around the kitchen huffing out a heavy sigh before he spoke again. "You were just a kid. What does a kid know? And you were a stupid kid."

Aidan dropped the biscuit to his plate. What was Lynx saying? "Yeah, but you were no scholar, either, if I remember."

"I could still whip your ass."

"Might have a harder time of it now."

Lynx sized him up and scoffed. "You're no competition."

"I might surprise you." After getting his ass kicked most of his life, he now held a black belt in Jujitsu.

Lynx snorted, but the sound seemed less sarcastic than earlier. "Right, that'll be the day."

CHAPTER THIRTEEN

Aidan gave up on sleep, sat up and turned on the bedside lamp. Anticipation skipped in his blood, his breathing choppy, as he tried to hold the strings of his imagination together before he lost them. He reached over to the nightstand and grabbed a notepad that rested next to the phone along with a pen. He couldn't write fast enough. Words and images hit like punches, painful and powerful, left and right, until the small pad was crammed full. With haste, he shot out of bed, rummaged through the room until frustration had him pulling at his hair. He needed paper before his characters stopped talking. He had to catch every word battering around in his head before they went silent again.

Quietly, he snuck out of his room and headed to the main area of the lodge, searching tabletops, opening drawers of end tables, the cabinet that held a TV, until he found the small desk in the corner. Inside the top drawer was a notebook—and bless Fiona—pencils. Now he could draw.

The lodge spun away.

Chatanika was gone in an instant as he entered the world of The Spirit Totems where the souls who embodied the power of the totems fought against death and darkness. Darkness that was ever stealing over the Great Land allowing death the chance to roam like a disease.

In this world, he was the hero. Fighting evil, saving lives—instead of taking them—and he was loved and respected by friends and family. In this magical and dangerous place the wolf joined with the other formidable defenders who embodied the powers of the totem. The bear: the guardian with the power to heal, courageous, introspective with great strength, but also an angry disposition when riled. The eagle: a creature with a divine spirit, wise in the ways of the creator, and a risk-taker. The Orca: bright and playful, intelligent and sly. The beaver: industrious, instinctive, a watcher. And the wolf: perseverant, loyal, intuitive, able to balance the spirit of freedom with a strong sense of family.

Aidan found himself adding in a new character, grinning as the face of a fox took shape. A cunning, clever creature with shape-shifting abilities. He couldn't help but give the character Fox's inquisitive eyes. He drew until the early hours of the morning. Until he came to a plot point where he brought in the raven—a character he had always purposely avoided. He'd even been called to task by fans who knew that the raven was a formidable part of the totem. He'd never been able to bring himself to add her, knowing perfectly well why he hadn't. Now he found himself unable to keep her out. This woman had raven hair down to her hips, almond-shaped eyes, a wide, seductive mouth. She was full of courage, cunning, wisdom, and magic.

Morning dawned dark and sleepy. Visiting with his friends again was a gift he didn't think he'd get back since the troubled events of the summer. It clenched his heart, made him shake. He was afraid to get too excited. He'd truly thought he'd lost this, but as the words and images gushed out of him, he silently rejoiced.

"Whatcha doing?"

Aidan jumped, his pencil flying out of his hand, clattering to the floor. Fox stood behind him, just over his shoulder.

"Where the hell did you come from?" He hoped his heart would return to normal. The kid was sneaky.

"Home. Uncle Pike lets me have leftover meat for my dogs. I came up to fetch it." Fox tilted his head to the side, looking at Aidan's drawings. "Are these—"

"Nothing." Aidan grabbed the pages and stacked them together. He didn't let anyone see his work before it was finished.

Fox's face shuddered with hurt and disappointment. "I didn't mean to pry. But...I just love your stories."

Aidan studied Fox. There was nothing in his expression except curiosity and maybe the fear of rejection. "Uhm..." He was crazy to be thinking this. His editor would kill him if he...

Don't over analyze it, Harte. "Fox, I don't usually do this. Hel—heck." He needed to remember he was talking to a kid here and watch his language. "I don't ever do this, but would you let me know what you think?" He offered the papers, his hand shaking.

"Seriously?" Fox's eyes lit up as he held his breath.

"Yeah, and don't sugarcoat it. If it sucks, I want to know."

"Really?"

"Yep."

Fox took the papers like Aidan was handing him the Holy Grail. He took a seat on the couch. Aidan stood, stretched. How long had he been sitting here? He reached his arms above his head and arched from side to side while trying to forget that he'd just turned over his baby to an eleven-year-old for his opinion. Yeah, he'd lost it.

Fox frowned, his brows knitting together just like his mother's, and flipped the page.

Aidan rubbed his hands over his face. He couldn't watch this. He limped toward the kitchen. A cup of coffee—a pot of coffee—would do him a world of good. Maybe a muffin, if he could rustle one up.

Fiona was already there, yawning as she mixed batter in a bowl. "Morning, Aidan. Want some pancakes?"

Man, did he ever. "Yeah. What are you doing up so early?"

"Nobody sleeps in around this place." She yawned again. "How I wish they would. I saw you writing. Get some work done?"

"Uh-huh." He studied Fiona, dressed in jeans and bright blue kuspuk, a native Athabascan top, loose, comfortable fabric decorated along the edges with colorful threads. Her long dark hair, shot through with silver, was pulled back into a long braid. "Why do you do it?"

She glanced at him, confused.

"Wake up so early every morning? Take in guests?" Work so hard at an age when she should be taking it easy or someone should be taking care of her.

"Someone needs to keep the place running. I was hoping Raven wanted the lodge, but she's into her art. Tern has the shop, and Chatanika isn't for her. That one has restless feet and a wandering spirit."

"What about Lynx?" Aidan took a seat at the table, his heart warmed watching Fiona prepare breakfast.

"The Arctic Refuge is his life. I never could keep that one indoors. I have hopes for Chickadee or Fox wanting to run the lodge after they've seasoned a bit." She poured batter onto a hot griddle.

"Does Fox always run around with so much independence?"

"Ah, that boy has an old spirit. Wise way beyond his years." She gave a far off look. "He's always been that way, even as a toddler. He's never one to leap. He studies, calculates, then pounces." She smiled with pride.

"Was it rough for Raven? Being such a young mother?" And alone. Emotion squeezed his throat at the thought of a young, frightened Raven pregnant and alone.

Fiona picked up a spatula, turned up the edge of the pancake before flipping it over, and then looked at Aidan. "She didn't talk much during that time. She was...sad. Very sad." Fiona gave a heartfelt sigh. "We all were after losing Fox senior. But I know it was more than that." She looked at Aidan. "I always thought it was because she missed you."

Aidan sucked in a breath. Had Raven missed him like he'd missed her? He couldn't believe that, couldn't let his heart wish it were true.

Raven stepped into the kitchen, bringing a burst of cold air with her. She froze when she saw Aidan. "How'd you get here?"

"Drove."

She frowned. "With your leg?" She slowly unwrapped the fuzzy purple and orange scarf from around her neck. "What happened at Earl's?"

"I decided when there was no chopped wood that I didn't want to freeze. So I braved driving."

She looked at the boot.

"I took it off."

"Do you think that was a good idea?" She cocked a brow as she unzipped her coat.

"Beat the hell out of freezing to death."

Raven dismissed him and glanced at Fiona. "Have you seen Fox?"

"He's in the other room," Aidan answered, not ready to be dismissed so easily.

Raven frowned again. He was sure getting tired of that frown.

"He was after leftovers for the dogs," she said.

"I know, he caught me in the other room and offered to do me a favor."

"What kind of favor?" Her eyes narrowed like he had somehow disrupted her day.

"He's looking over some ideas for me."

"Why would you ask him to do that? And what kind of ideas?"

"Plotting suggestions, okay. He isn't doing anything suspicious or dangerous. Relax. Have some pancakes."

Fiona set a stack of plates down on the table as though emphasizing his words. "Take off your jacket, Raven," she said, returning to the griddle. "Breakfast will be ready in a jiffy. And don't tell me you don't have time," she added when Raven opened her mouth to object.

Wisely, Raven did as she was told. But Aidan could tell she wanted to stomp into the other room and see what Fox was up to. Aidan picked up a plate and passed one to Raven. Fiona set a platter full of steaming pancakes in front of them. Stacking his plate high, he slathered the fluffy goodness in butter and drowned them with birch syrup. The tastes blended and soothed.

"Hmm." He made an appreciative sound around a mouthful. "You are the best, Fiona." He would have been stuck with a frozen granola bar for breakfast if he had made it through the night at Earl's place.

"You're a joy to cook for, Aidan." Fiona set a cup of coffee in front of him, laying her hand briefly on his shoulder.

Raven frowned at him again as she forked a pancake onto her plate.

Fox rushed into the room. "No *way*. You brought Senyea back! That is *so* cool."

Aidan's heart tripped. With Raven entering the kitchen, his anxiety over Fox reading his pages had lessened. Now it bloomed like a forest fire.

"Mom, you gotta read these." Fox held the pages out to Raven.

Aidan snatched them out of his hand. "No."

"Uh...sorry," Fox said, his expression falling. "I thought she should see—"

"You can't give anything away." Aidan stared Fox in the eye. "Promise me that you will not tell anyone, and I mean *anyone* what you have read."

"But—"

"Anyone, Fox. Word gets out and the next volume gets scrapped. The publishing world is an unforgiving one, and with the Internet, I can't be too careful. Can I trust you?"

"Yes." Fox straightened and squared his shoulders. "I won't tell a soul. Not even my dogs."

Aidan cracked a smile. If the boy wouldn't tell his dogs, then his secrets were safe.

"But...can I talk to you about them?"

Aidan gave a full grin at that. "I would love your input."

"Did you hear that, Mom? Aidan Harte would love my input."

"I heard." And by her tone, she obviously wasn't pleased. "Get some breakfast, Fox, and then you better feed your dogs."

"Yes, ma'am." Fox grabbed a full plate Fiona had just filled and sat between Aidan and Raven. He lathered his pancakes with butter and birch syrup and dug in like he hadn't eaten in weeks.

"Aidan, can I talk to you?" Raven asked, though the question wasn't really a question.

Aidan stood, rolled up his pages and stuck them in his back pocket, then took his plate, over to the sink. Raven bypassed the living room and headed toward his bedroom. He had a feeling he wasn't going to enjoy this 'talk.' She turned to face him as he entered behind her, shutting the door.

"I want you to stay away from Fox," Raven said.

"Why?" He frowned.

"I don't want him getting attached to you. Soon you will be leaving, and I don't want him hurt."

"Like you were when I left?"

She tightened her mouth and glanced to the side. When she looked at him again, her gaze had hardened. "No. This has nothing to do with me. Fox is an impressionable boy. He's coming very close to hero worshipping you. I don't want him disappointed."

He took the arrow to the heart without a flinch. After all he was nobody's hero. He might write about them. Think of himself as Lucien, his wolf totem's character. But he would never be hero material. "Fine." He folded his arms across his chest.

"Good." Raven walked around him.

"Raven?" he said, keeping his back to her. "Are you going to tell Fox to stay away from me?"

"I think it's for the best." She left, quietly shutting the door behind her.

Aidan sank onto the edge of the bed. He really needed to get out of here. He'd over-stayed his welcome.

Who was he kidding? There'd been no welcome.

He sighed. What had he expected? What had he hoped for? *Family?* What an idiot. He rubbed the back of his neck. Enough of wishing, time for doing, and the first thing he needed to do was clear out of the lodge. He wasn't about to fight Raven. She didn't want him around her son, and he totally understood. Part of him agreed, even though he enjoyed the hell out of the kid.

Aidan gathered up his meager belongings. There wasn't much. He'd stop at the lodge's little store and buy a few bundles of chopped wood. That would warm up Earl's cabin until he could chop some himself.

He straightened up the room, gathered his stuff and with one backward glance, shut the door.

Fox was waiting for him in the front room.

"Hey, Aidan," Fox said with a wide smile, a dimple peeking from his left cheek. "You said you wanted to go for a ride with me and my dogs, remember? Today is Saturday."

Aidan's stomach clenched. He did not want to disappoint this boy. He'd been disappointed all his life. He didn't want to treat the kid this way. "Sorry. But I need to head to Earl's."

Fox's face fell and Aidan felt like the worst kind of bastard. "Sorry, kid. I have to get out of the godforsaken place before I go crazy." That was said in truth. Damn, he really wanted to go for a sled ride with Fox. It had been decades since he had flown over the snow pulled by a team of well-trained dogs.

Why couldn't Fox have been his son? He resembled him. But he was probably seeing what he wanted to see.

"But—"

"See ya, kid." Aidan turned and walked out of the lodge, feeling like an ass. Why hadn't he figured out a way to let Fox down easy? Instead, he'd treated the situation the way Eva would've with her rip-off-the-Band-Aid method.

CHAPTER FOURTEEN

Aidan entered Earl's, determined to finish what he'd come here to do. Hurt and anger fueled him on. He built a fire in the wood stove, and the small place heated up fast. His dad had been good at surviving in some of the worst places.

He tackled the job of cleaning up. Walking outside with Fox's map, he methodically sprung every fucking booby-trap he could find. Anyone could step into one—an animal, lost hiker, hunter, or kid with a dog team out for a sled ride. Earl wasn't going to hurt anyone else in *this* world.

Aidan took a break from tramping around in the cold and made himself a cup of coffee by melting snow with the dented tin percolator over the hot stove. He swallowed a few ibuprofens along with the bitter coffee. His medical boot was getting in the way. So he went into Earl's bedroom and rummaged around until he found a pair of well-worn Timberland hunting boots. He pulled off the Velcro plastic boot the doctor had strapped him in, and changed the bandages. His dad's old Timberland's would do just as good of a job keeping his leg tight and would better protect him from the snow and cold.

When he was finished with the first aid, he went back outside with the ax. His leg was bearable as long as he kept the wounds cleaned and managed the pain with over the counter drugs. Besides what was a little physical pain when his emotional pain would have most putting a bullet in their head? He'd thought about ending it all. Had even tried pulling the trigger a few months back, but something had kept him from actually taking his own life. Probably the cowardice his dad had accused him of.

Chalk up another one for the bastard.

Aidan set up logs and began the backbreaking work of chopping wood. The day had turned sunny, deceiving since the temps were hovering around negative ten. The physical activity soon had him shedding his jacket. The last thing he wanted to do was sweat in conditions like this. Sweat would freeze and chill him to the bone as soon as he stopped working. Then it would take forever to get warm.

He heard a twig break and swung around, scanning the area. The black wolf stood thirty feet off. Watching.

What the hell?

Aidan lowered the ax and met the wolf's eyes. Everything he'd read about wolves said meeting their gaze was a big no no. But the wolf took no offense. In fact, he yawned—the wolf actually *yawned* at him. Aidan looked at it closer, wondering if it wasn't a full-blooded wolf. Maybe the animal was a half-breed. Part wolf, part husky or Malamute.

No. Aidan would bet his life he was looking at a full-blooded Alaskan timber wolf.

Why the hell was it watching him?

The wolf suddenly perked its ears and turned its head to the side. Then it was off like a shot as though spooked. Next, Aidan heard dogs. Fox glided his team into the driveway and dropped the steel brake, stepping on it to anchor the teeth into the snow. The dogs pranced, some turning circles until they found a spot to settle down. None seemed to have picked up the wolf's scent.

Fox slowly walked toward Aidan, his eyes landing on the pile of traps, before seeking out Aidan's. "Can we talk?"

What was this? First Raven and now Fox needing to have words with him. Aidan set the ax in the log. "All right. Let's go in and get something warm to drink." If Raven found out about this meeting, which she undoubtedly would, he'd be called to task. Screw it. He was through hurting the kid. "Are your dogs going to be okay?"

"Yeah." Fox rubbed his hands together. "For a bit, they'll be okay."

"I saw a wolf just before you showed up."

"If a wolf tried to mess with my dogs, Lucien would raise a ruckus."

"Doesn't your mother have a problem with you running your team when wild animals are around?" Aidan was beginning to have a problem with it himself.

"There are always wolves, bears, and moose around these parts. Uncle Lynx has kind of a pet moose—we call him BW—who's caused some mischief. Don't worry, I have a gun in the sled in case I need it. But I've never had a problem. Plus, what Mom doesn't know, doesn't hurt me, right?"

Aidan chuckled. Fox had gumption laced with good common sense. If Aidan had had a son who wanted to run all over the countryside, he didn't know if he'd be as okay with it as Raven seemed to be. "Your mom doesn't know you're here, does she?"

"That's what I kinda wanted to talk to you about."

They entered the cabin.

"What happened?" Fox asked, looking around wide-eyed at the destruction.

And here, Aidan thought, he'd made good progress cleaning up some of the mess. "I take it the place didn't look like this the last time you were in here?"

"No." Fox walked around the area, staying to the path Aidan had cut. "Who would have done this? And why? Earl didn't have anything worth—" A look crossed Fox's face as he cut off what he had been about to say.

"Do you know something?"

"No." Fox turned away.

The kid was lying. What did Fox know about Earl Harte that no one else did?

"How did they get past the booby-traps?" Fox asked.

"I don't think they did. I found evidence of blood inside like someone had tried to doctor themselves up."

"Mr. Harte was never one to mess with."

Aidan put hot water on the stove to boil and prepared cups of hot chocolate. "So, if he wasn't someone to mess with, like you said, what kind of relationship did you have with him?" Aidan had wanted the answer to that question from the moment he'd first met Fox.

"Another reason I wanted to talk to you." Fox rubbed his hands together.

"Did your mother tell you to stay away from me?"

"Um...yeah."

"I got the same lecture this morning." Aidan smiled, hoping to relax the kid.

Anger flashed in Fox's eyes. "It's not fair that she would do that."

"Don't be mad at Raven. She's trying to protect you."

"But she doesn't need to."

"She sees things differently." Always had. Aidan poured hot water into the mugs and stirred the lumpy powder. Then he handed Fox a cup and indicated he take a seat on the chairs Aidan had cleared off earlier. "So, what did you want to talk to me about?"

Fox flushed. He set his cup on the table and tore off his hat, unzipped his jacket.

Aidan took a sip of his hot chocolate and waited.

"When I was about, uhm, seven, I was out with my small sled and my first two dogs that I started with. Back then, Mom made me stay closer to town. I was also told never to head this direction."

"So, of course you did?"

Fox glanced up at him and gave a slight grin. "Yeah. I came across Mr. Harte. He was stuck. Truck off in the ditch and he'd hurt his arm. I helped him out."

"Did he owe you his life too?"

Fox snorted and shook his head. "He scared the crap out of me. But when he found out who my mother was...he changed." Fox paused looking around the cabin at everything but Aidan.

"Changed how?" Aidan frowned.

"I don't know." Fox shrugged. "Not happy, but kinda like he had one up on my family. It's hard to explain."

"No, I get it. He liked knowing things nobody else did so he could use it against them later."

"Right, but he never did anything about me visiting him. I don't think he ever told anyone either." Fox glanced at the floor and then dragged in a deep breath.

"Just come out and say what's bothering you. It's the best way."

Fox swung his gaze toward Aidan. "Are you sure?"

Aidan wanted to chuckle but kept the sound back. Fox seemed nervous enough. "Yeah."

"Okay. Here it goes." He rubbed his hands on his pants, looked Aidan in the eye, and then blurted out, "You're my father." He swallowed. "I'm your son."

Time stopped. The sound of ringing rocked his ears. "W-what did you say?" He had to have heard Fox wrong.

"You said to let it out. Just say it." Now Fox started to shake, his eyes wide, panicked.

"Hold on." God, he needed to breathe. Hell, he needed space. No, damn it, he needed the *truth*. "Who told you I was your father?" Had Raven lied to him?

"Mr. Harte told me."

Aidan fell back in his chair like he'd been hit. It was just the sort of thing his dad would do. "He was probably lying to you. Messing with your head."

"No." Fox swallowed hard. "He showed me a picture of you when you were my age. We looked the same. That's how he figured it out."

Aidan got to his feet. Even with the pain in his leg, he paced the small confines of the wrecked cabin. Questions came at him like knives, each cutting deeper to the bone. "Did you talk to your mom about this?"

"No. Mr. Harte told me that she would deny it. But I did talk to my grandma."

"Fiona?" Aidan whipped around and tried to still his expression when Fox's eyes widened in surprise. "What did she say?"

"She never told me for sure. But she told me all about you. And…uh…bought me your graphic novels."

Aidan stared at Fox, saw the dark eyes, dark hair, and finally the truth in the shape of his mouth, the cut of his cheekbones.

He had a son.

Fire burned in his stomach, his chest. The pain almost brought him to his knees. Raven hadn't told him. She'd lied to him. His own father had known and never told him. Even Fiona hadn't told him. He needed to have words with Raven. But first he had to deal with *his son.*

Holy shit, he was a father.

His heart pounded, and his lungs refused to draw air. He found himself scrambling to sit down before he fell down.

"I hope you don't mind much," Fox said, worrying his bottom lip.

Aidan's gaze jumped to Fox. A lump formed in his throat. This boy, this young man was a part of him. He'd been denied knowing him, raising him, being a part of his life. No more. "I don't mind. I'm stunned…proud and honored. And I'm so sorry I never knew."

"That's okay." He shrugged a shoulder. "I know you had no idea."

"I should have known. If I had, I would have been here for you."

Fox looked down, the toe of his boot playing with a shirt lying on the floor. "What do we do now?"

"I don't know." Aidan rubbed his face. First thing he needed to do was find Raven. "But I'd like to be part of your life. Would you be okay with that?" Fear rushed into him. What if Fox didn't want a relationship with him? Didn't want him as his father? Seriously, what did he have to offer the boy?

"Yeah. I'm okay with that." Fox smiled and Aidan recognized the same dimple in his cheek that he sported.

How had he not seen it before?

Fox stayed until his dogs grew restless. Aidan awkwardly patted him on the back and warned him to be careful. Fox gifted him a full smile, and promised to keep the truth he'd revealed until Aidan had a chance to talk with Raven.

They were sure as hell going to have a talk.

After watching until Fox was out of sight, he entered the cabin. The dank, dark, hellhole he'd grown up in. The same place Earl had met with Fox many times with no plans to ever tell his own son he had a kid. He must have loved knowing that he had a relationship with Fox while Aidan had no clue Fox existed. The fucking bastard. It was just the kind of thing he'd get off on. Aidan clenched his fists. All this time Earl had secretly laughed at him, ridiculed him over and over for not being married, not having a family, not being man enough. And all along Aidan had a son he hadn't been aware of. A son Earl could have easily told him about, but chose not to for whatever sick reason the asshole had come up with.

Aidan punched the wall. His fist crashed through the drywall, his knuckles coming back bloody. How he wished the bastard was alive so he could kill him again.

Aidan jerked on his coat, grabbed his keys, and slammed out of the cabin. He couldn't have it out with his father, but he sure as hell could have it out with Raven.

He'd *asked* her if he was Fox's father and she'd lied to him. *Lied to him.* How could she? She'd known how much he'd longed for a family, and she'd taken that away from him.

He stomped over the cleared path, feeding off the pain stabbing up his leg. It sure as hell beat the pain cutting into his heart.

Right in front of him, between him and the SUV, stood the black wolf. Aidan came to a full stop, breathing hard.

"Scram," he yelled, throwing his arms into the air.

The wolf crouched into attack position. Its front legs spread wide, head low, and growled in response. Its teeth glinting like knifes in the setting sun.

Hair on the back of Aidan's neck stood at attention. Okay, so maybe he wasn't going anywhere, just yet.

"Fuck."

He wanted to leave. Needed to find Raven. Needed to give her a piece of his mind.

Tell me to stay away from my own son. Deny him the right to be a father. He needed...

He needed...

He needed to stay put. At least until he got himself under control. If he went to Raven now, who knew what he'd do.

"Shit." He kicked at the snow.

Last year he'd done the unthinkable. He and Sonya had gotten into a fight. A heated fight. He had lost his temper...and hit her. He'd never regretted doing anything more in his life. He'd watched his father hit his mother, beating her bloody. After his mother drank herself to death, his father had turned to him as a punching bag.

He'd lost his temper, just like his father had, hitting Sonya in a fit of rage. She'd promptly hit him back, knocking him on his ass, and broken off their relationship.

It had scared the shit out of him. He'd called a therapist, gotten into counseling, willing to do anything not to turn into Earl. He wished he could talk with Dr. Foster now.

But he had a fucking wolf barring his escape.

Aidan took another step forward, and the wolf bared his teeth again, its gums black, a sharp contrast to the gleaming white teeth. Its lips twisted as though to say, "Go ahead. Make my day." There was no sound, the growl silent this time, and somehow, this act of aggression scared him worse.

"Fine. Have it your way." Aidan backed up, keeping the wolf in his sights until he reached the cabin and let himself back in.

He yanked off his coat and tossed it onto the mess of the other junk littering the place.

What the hell did he do now?

Aidan stayed away from Raven for two days. It had taken him that long to cool down. His anger had gone a long way in helping him clean up Earl's place. There was nothing like anger to fuel a project. While the place wasn't actually comfortable, it was clean. He'd bagged up Earl's clothes, those worth keeping, burned the others, and set aside what he needed to take to Fairbanks and donate to Good Will. There wasn't much. Even in death, Earl didn't have a lot to share.

The black wolf had continued to hang around, barring any chance of escape. It was the damnedest thing.

God, he hoped he wasn't hallucinating.

It was Monday morning, there was no sign of the wolf, and he was on his way to have it out with Raven. Weird that the wolf disappeared when Aidan had finally leashed the beast raging inside him. There was so much he had to do, and the wolf had literally kept him a prisoner. But he hadn't the heart, or the desire, to shoot the animal.

Besides keeping Aidan from talking to Raven, the wolf had kept him from dropping off Earl's stuff, and gathering supplies. He also needed to contact his editor and agent and let them know how he could be reached. He had no plans to leave Chatanika at the moment. If ever. Not with his son living here. He wasn't going to uproot the kid and take him to Seattle unless Fox wanted to visit on vacation or something.

The things they could do together. Vacations, sports, fishing. The list was endless. He had so much time to make up. Time he'd never get back.

Raven had so much to answer for.

He parked in her driveway and headed toward the front door. The day had dawned, around ten-thirty, to a dismal gray, promising snow. As if they needed more. He knocked on her door, clamping down on his anger as it threatened to rage. He could do this. He could have a discussion with the woman who had lied to him, betrayed him for the last twelve years, without losing his temper. Being angry was one thing. His anger was justified. Losing control of that anger would be something he couldn't allow.

He knocked again, thankful for the frigid, icy air. He peered around. Silence greeted him.

Don't tell me she wasn't home? Not when he had waited this long. *Wait a minute.*

He walked toward the studio attached to the house by an enclosed walkway. Muffled music could be heard from inside the insulated building. He should have figured she'd be in her studio. He found the door and knocked. Waited.

Nothing.

Enough of this.

He tried the knob, and it turned easily in his hand. Heat greeted him, warm, beckoning. Deceptive. Music was next, the soul sounds of Marvin Gaye…and Raven's off-key voice singing along. How dare she sing when his life was tied in knots with her lies? He followed her voice, breathing in the rich, musty smells of clay. Around a metal shelving unit full of drying pottery pieces, he found her sitting at the wheel, wearing worn, mud-covered overalls, her hair secured in a loose knot at the top of her head. Tendrils brushed her serene face. Her hands were working smoothly, rhythmically together, pulling up the walls of a large vessel. A vase, maybe. She stood and carefully lowered her arm inside the narrow opening, her arm disappearing to her elbow, all the while singing along with *I Heard it Through the Grapevine.* Fitting.

"You lied to me."

Raven jerked, her head popping up fast, her arm bumping the sides of the cylinder. The form teetered grossly off center and then collapsed.

"Damn it." Raven plopped onto the wooden seat, shut off the wheel, and mushed the clay into a messy mound of mud. "Don't ever come in here and surprise me like that. Do you have any idea how long that took me to shape?" She narrowed angry eyes at him and flipped muddy slip off her hands. It splattered onto the floor, some landing on his boots and the cuffs of his pants. "What the hell are you doing here, Aidan?"

"You lied to me," he repeated, advancing farther into the room.

She seemed to catch onto his mood. She forgot about the clay mess on her wheel, reached for a towel, and slowly wiped off her hands. "Lied to you about what?" she asked with a slight tremble to her voice. One she tried to conceal with a haughty lift of her chin.

"Fox."

Raven swallowed, her eyes not quite meeting his. "What about Fox?"

Aidan stalked toward her, stopping just within reach. Leaning down, he slapped his palms down on the bench, caged her in with his arms. "Give it up, Raven. I know he's my son." He said each word clearly and distinctively.

Her eyes flickered to his, her pupils wide, her honeyed skin went icy white. She opened her mouth to speak, but he cut her off. "Don't you dare lie to me again."

She shut her mouth and rapidly looked around the room. There was nowhere to go, and she started to tremble. He didn't take pity on her, kept his arms like bars on the sides of her hips, jailing her in on the bench where she sat, his face right next to hers.

"H-how…how did you find out?" she whispered.

He slowly straightened as she admitted the truth. He knew from Fox that he was his father, didn't doubt the truth, but having Raven confirm it was like a punch to his already bruised and battered heart. "Why, Raven?"

She met his gaze, hers unsure. Fear shined for a fleeting moment before hard resolve replaced it. He wanted her scared. She should be quaking in her muddy overalls.

With a slight tremor, she got to her feet. "Why?" She gave a laugh. The sound scornful and disbelieving like he'd asked a stupid question. "Your father killed mine. He wasn't even cold in the ground, and I'm supposed to let everyone know that I was carrying the grandbaby of his killer."

"I had a right to know."

"I had a right to protect my child."

"*Our child.* From me?"

"Yes, from you." She threw down the towel she'd wiped her hands clean with, the muscles working in her jaw, her breasts rising with each rapid breath she took.

He slammed his hands into the front pockets of his jeans. "You *should* have told me," he said, his voice an edge of steel. "He's my son."

"Yes, he is, but I couldn't allow him to grow up with that kind of influence."

Emotions swamped him. It was easier to fight, harder to feel. He grabbed her shoulders, his fingers digging into her skin as he gave her a hard shake. *"I am not my father."*

"How was I to know what kind of man you would turn into? All the evidence pointed that you would follow in Earl's footsteps."

"What evidence?"

"You have a temper, Aidan."

"A lot of people do." He let go of her and stepped back. Anger no longer had a hold on him. Instead sadness swept in, depressing as it suffocated. "Why were you, of all people, so quick to believe the worst of me?"

Raven felt sick to her stomach. She'd convicted him based on his father's sins. But—

"I thought you *knew* me," Aidan said quietly. He looked at her, his eyes wounded, lost. Turning, he walked away from her, softly shutting the studio door behind him.

Slam it, she wanted to yell. He had a right to. He was supposed to be mad. Mad she could deal with. But wounded, lost, hurt. What did she do with that?

Her stomach churned like a pot of boiling water. Why was she feeling guilty? Shameful. She'd been a scared, pregnant teenager. What the hell did any eighteen-year-old kid know, especially when *they* were going to have a kid? She hadn't made the choice not to tell Aidan about Fox lightly. A lot of reasons had gone into the decision.

But were those reasons the right ones?

She rubbed the back of her neck. What if she had been wrong all these years? No, absolutely not. She'd been right about Earl.

Could she have been wrong about Aidan?

Had she blamed him unfairly? Her mother had always thought so, but Lynx and Tern had agreed with her when she'd sent Aidan packing. They hadn't known she'd been pregnant, though.

There was no point in rehashing the past. What did she do now? She needed to talk to Fox, but what if he hated her for keeping the truth from him? What if she lost him? Aidan could take her to court. Fox could choose to live with Aidan. The thought crippled her.

All right, stop it now. Fox wouldn't do that. He wouldn't leave her. To be truthful, he wouldn't leave his dogs.

She needed to smooth things over with Aidan. And she'd better do it now, before Aidan told Fox anything.

Raven shut down the studio and entered her house, slipping out of her overalls into a pair of jeans, and wrote a quick note to Fox in case she wasn't back by the time he got home from school. She struggled into her parka and mukluks, grabbed her keys and left.

The drive over to Earl's was fast. Too fast, she didn't have what she wanted to say organized in her mind by the time she arrived. Her stomach churned, but she was better off confronting this situation head-on rather than waiting. There had been enough waiting. While she'd have happily kept the fact of Fox's parentage quiet until the end of her days, she had to admit she felt relieved having the truth out there. A purging of sorts. In fact, it felt like her stomach was going to purge everything she'd eaten in the last twenty-four hours.

Raven parked her Suburban next to Aidan's rental and climbed out. The sun reflected fiercely on the snow, hurting her eyes. Squinting, she viewed the path Aidan had forged, coming up quick when she spotted blood staining the snow.

Bright red, fresh—frozen—blood.

She looked around at the peaceful, crisp, serenity of the wilderness. There was nothing to suggest she should be on guard.

Except the blood in the snow.

Blood trailed toward the back of the cabin. Had Aidan stepped into another trap? She hurried, but was watchful in case there was a threat she couldn't see or feel.

The door to the cabin stood wide open, sending another shiver through her. Slowly she entered, softly calling Aidan's name.

No answer.

The hair on the back of her neck rose. The blood trail led through the kitchen and into the main room. She followed, finding Aidan face down on the floor.

"Aidan!" She rushed over, dropping to her knees. Blood congealed in an ugly spot on the back of his head. She felt for his pulse, giving a sob of relief when she found it strong and steady. "Aidan?" She shook him. "Come on. Wake up."

He grunted but didn't open his eyes.

"Aidan, you have to wake up." She shook him again, harder. He groaned but still didn't open his eyes.

There was no phone and no way could she get him to Eva by herself. She could leave him and get help, but disregarded that thought as soon as it entered her mind. No way was she going anywhere without him.

Raven rose to her feet and rushed back to the door, shutting and locking out the cold. Aidan hadn't done this to himself. Unless he'd slipped and fallen. But then he would have fallen on snow. There hadn't been anything sharp or solid around the blood she'd seen. Had someone snuck up and hit him?

She grabbed towels, wetting them with the pan of melting snow on top of the stove, and returned to Aidan. Placing the wet cloth on the back of his head brought another groan from him.

"Where the hell did you come from?" he grumbled.

"My place." She almost sobbed in relief. "What happened?"

"Someone hit me." He cocked a brow, his eyes still closed. "Sure it wasn't you?"

"Not this time." She continued to carefully clean the wound, his dark hair making it hard to tell if she was getting all the blood. A huge goose egg had formed, which relieved her. If his head was swelling on the outside, it wasn't swelling on the inside. "Did you get a look at him?"

"No. It could have been a *her*."

He was quiet for a long while, and Raven began to think he might have slipped into unconsciousness again. She gave him another shake.

"Stop doing that. My head hurts bad enough without you tossing me around."

"Keep talking to me then so I know you aren't dead."

"Having me dead would make your situation easier."

"Haven't you figured out that I prefer things complicated." She changed cloths, glad to see the new one coming away cleaner. Good. It didn't look as though the wound was still bleeding. "Eva needs to look at this."

He groaned. "Just kill me now."

She choked on a laugh. "You'll be better for it. You might need stitches."

"Is it still bleeding?"

"No...I don't think so."

"Then I don't need Eva, but I do need to get up off this floor. I'm freezing." He pushed his upper body off the floor. She helped him get to his feet, catching him as he wobbled.

"Steady."

"Hold the room still then." He blinked a few times, took a few steps, leaning heavily on her.

"Do you want the couch or the bedroom?"

"Gotta lie down." He shivered. "With lots of blankets."

"How long do you think you were out?"

"I came here from your place. Got out of the car, walked down the path, and bam...stars."

"How'd you get into the cabin?"

"Crawled. Can we stop with the questions? My head hurts."

He was also cold. Raven worried over his shivering. He was wet from crawling through the snow, and she needed to get him out of his clothes...and warmed up.

They reached his old bedroom, and he went to lie down on the bed. "No." Raven pulled at his arm. "We need to get you out of these wet clothes first."

He gave her a sardonic look. "Not tonight, honey. I have a headache."

"Funny." Relieved if he could joke, he couldn't be hurt that bad, she reached for the zipper on his coat and pulled it down. He didn't make any attempt to help her, just watched her with his dark eyes, lids at half-mast. She pushed the parka off his shoulders and the heat in the room seemed to rise. Must be just her, because Aidan continued to shiver. His shirt was dry, thank goodness, but his jeans were wet from his body melting the snow he'd crawled through. She looked at his fly.

"Can you take your pants off?" She raised her gaze to his.

His hands fumbled on the button, slow and clumsy. He hadn't had gloves on when she'd found him. He'd been in the cold, crawled through the snow, and then laid on the floor with the door open. It was fifteen below.

"Let me see your hands." She reached for them herself. They were red and frozen, his fingertips white.

She reached for his fly and tried to put out of her mind what she was doing.

"Careful," he grunted. "I'd like to keep what's behind there."

Heat bloomed in her cheeks. She didn't need to be reminded what lay behind that zipper. Or how she much liked what he could do with that particular appendage.

Get a grip. The man was frozen and probably concussed. Plus, he was mad as hell at her.

She pulled the jeans down to his ankles. "Why aren't you wearing your medical boot?"

He fell onto the edge of the bed, his hands holding his head. "It got in the way."

She knelt at his feet and worked at loosening the laces on his boots. Once those were off she discarded his socks. His eyelids lowered as he surveyed her every move. Again she felt heat. Her face was right in line with what had been behind the zipper. From the glint in his eyes, he was thinking about that too.

"Not that I don't like your current position, but I'm freezing my ass off here."

She finished yanking off his jeans and flicked her gaze up his body. "Are your boxers wet?"

"You don't want me to lose those," his voice was soft and heavy with warning. "And I haven't wet my shorts in decades."

She swallowed. "Swing your legs over." She tucked him into bed and piled him with blankets. "I'll be right back."

"Grab one of Earl's pistols," Aidan muttered. "I want you armed."

Not a bad idea. She went to the gun cabinet and helped herself to a thirty-eight special over the shotguns, loading the cylinder and tucking the weapon into the pocket of her jeans.

She boiled water for tea. While the water heated, she opened the cast-iron door to the wood stove and stoked the dying coals. Adding in wood, she blew on the coals until the flames caught, licking greedily at the dry timber. She added more until she was satisfied that it would heat on its own for a few hours. She prepped the tea and carefully walked the mug back to Aidan.

He was shivering, his teeth chattering as he shook in the bed, hands folded under his armpits in an attempt to warm them with what body heat he had.

She set the tea on the end table. *Damn*, she'd have to crawl in there with him. Shaking like he was, the blankets and tea weren't going to be enough to warm him. She'd discarded her coat in the other room but now kicked off her mukluks, set the gun on the end table, and edged into the bed with him.

"I don't want you here," Aidan said through chattering teeth.

"I know." Scooting over to him, she took his hands and pulled them under her shirt, catching her breath when the frigidness of them branded her skin.

He moaned and drawn by her heat, snuggled closer. She pulled the covers over them, and her body curved into his with a sigh. The rightness of lying next to him, her arms around him, brought tears to her eyes.

This was the man she'd loved. The man who'd haunted her all these years. The man she'd lied to.

They lay like that for a long time. The only sounds that of their breathing. She waited for his to become rhythmic, hoping he'd fall asleep, but then he probably shouldn't sleep since he'd taken a good hit to the head. Should she talk to him, keep him awake? What did she say?

How about what she'd rushed over here to say? But then she didn't want to bring up Fox right now with Aidan hurting. It would only add more hurt. Except she needed to get him to agree not to reveal the truth to Fox. Not yet. She didn't want her child hating her for her lies too.

There were other things she could bring up. Like that hard bulge pressing into her hip. No, she definitely needed to keep that quiet. Right. Like Aidan wasn't aware of his—

Okay, really not going to go there. She took a deeper breath, hoping to settle her nerves. At least she hoped it was nerves tightening her belly. She had a sneaky suspicion it was something altogether different.

Making love with Aidan had never made her nervous. Not even that first time. It had been a rush of hormones, colliding together in a frenzy of lust. The second time they'd slowed, savored, explored.

She swallowed, gulping back a batch of tears. How she'd missed that euphoric summer when everything had seemed bright and promising. Anything had been possible. Dreams had been reachable. Love had been simple. Then death had darkened everything.

Love was anything but simple now. Case in point, the evidence of Aidan's desire growing thicker and harder causing her inner muscles to clench, to weep. To want.

She turned her face up to tell him to move back and found him watching her, his eyes full of hurt and shaded with need. Her heart ached. How did she tell him to back off when her arms wanted to pull him closer, cradle his head against her breast? They'd been destined for each other. Soul mates. He was her sun, she his raven.

He must have read the conflict in her eyes, for his lips tightened, and a hard glint entered his. One that had real nerves fluttering frantically in her belly. Suddenly he flipped her onto her back and pressed her into the mattress with the weight of his hard, muscled body.

His mouth smothered her gasp.

CHAPTER FIFTEEN

No way in hell was she rejecting him again.

Aidan swept his tongue into Raven's mouth while his hands held her down. He was angry, wanted to hurt, demand she give herself to him. She fucking owed him. Years of not knowing he was a father. Years of not being a part of his son's life. Not being a part of hers.

He'd seen the want, the desire she'd tried to hide, and the denial she'd been ready to utter. He'd just have to keep that mouth of hers busy. It was time for her body to speak. Maybe that way he'd finally get the truth out of her.

He forced a knee between her legs, claiming room for his hips as he pressed and ground against her. Hard couldn't begin to describe his condition. Hard, hurting, and unable to stop himself from thrusting against her soft warmth. She moaned, her arms wrapping around his back, pulling him closer.

Why wasn't she fighting him? He was in the mood to fight, to force, to take. Hurt her like he hurt.

He tore her shirt up and over her head, recaptured her mouth to silence any objections, and stripped off her bra. His need drove him to feast like an animal. He bit, sucked, nipped, taking her breasts into his hands, roughly squeezing, grazing the nipples until they hardened like rocks. Capturing them one at a time in his hot mouth, he sucked hard, flattening the nipple to the roof of his mouth, nipping the end until she squirmed and gasped in his hold. Reaching behind him, he grabbed a handful of his shirt and snatched it off, feeding off the pain pounding in his head. He needed to feel her breasts tight against his chest, his flesh pounding into hers, as her heat warmed him to the core.

He'd been cold for so very long.

"Wait," she gulped as his hands wrenched off her jeans, yanked at her underwear until the silk tore free from her body. "Aidan, wait."

There would be no more waiting.

He recaptured her mouth, speared her with his tongue as he spread her legs wider. Twelve years of lies and betrayal had been long enough. He kicked off his shorts, positioned himself at her opening, grasped her hips in his hands, and drove into her heat with a hard, unforgiving thrust, taking him in to the hilt.

She cried out, her body arching in his embrace.

The sound snapped his mind out of the storm he seemed lost in. Each ragged breath he dragged into his lungs was swift and sharp.

"Raven," he gasped. *What the hell had he done?* Oh, God, he'd let the beast rage. "Raven? Oh God, Raven, I'm sorry."

Tears leaked from the corners of her shut eyelids. Feeling the lowest of creatures, Aidan inched out of her wet, tight sheath.

Her legs came up and clamped around his hips, keeping him in place. "It's okay," she whispered, opening her eyes. Eyes that reflected pain and sorrow. "It's just that I-I haven't done this in a while."

He groaned her name, trying once more to pull out of her, but she kept him locked inside. He wasn't going to last if she didn't let him go. As it was he teetered on a sharp edge, barely keeping a leash on the beast.

"I'm sorry. I didn't want to hurt you. No, that's a lie. Part of me does want to hurt you." He dropped his forehead to rest against hers, not wanting to see the shame added to the pain in her eyes. "But not like this. Never like this."

"Aidan," she said softly, her fingers brushing the hair back from the his face. "Look at me."

He raised his head and steeled himself to meet the condemnation in her eyes, but what he saw made him catch his breath.

"I want you, this. I just wasn't…prepared." She arched her hips, and he slid deeper inside her. The sensation, the friction, was the most unbelievable pleasure, causing him to clench his teeth. "I'm ready now." She lowered her eyes and licked her lips, causing the blood to leave his brain. "But if you need more time…"

She wasn't shoving him away? With what he'd done, how he'd pushed, how he'd taken? His eyes never left hers as he slowly slid into her, his heart pounding as she gasped and bit her lip, her eyes shuttering closed in pleasure. That look had haunted him all these years. Showed up in his dreams, catching him unaware when his mind wandered.

A mad, twisted desire had started this, now wonder joined the mix, along with a need so great his body quaked with it. His hands trembled as they reverently caressed her breasts. Breasts so much softer and fuller than before. Lovely, beautiful, womanly. To touch her like this again after all these years had him choking on emotion. They had missed out on so much. He'd barely learned what she'd liked when they were eighteen. What had caused her to lean into his touch, gasp when he licked, moan and claw when he stroked deep inside her. He knew her, but he didn't. There was so much that he wanted to learn about the woman she was now.

His chest rose and fell like bellows as he slowly stroked inside her, savoring each inch of penetration as her inner muscles clenched around his hardness, gripping him in a snare he never wanted to be released from. He'd come home. She was the one. Had always been the one. He settled deeper inside her and held her there, never wanting the moment to end. His eyes met hers, and he saw the emotions churning inside him reflected there. Slowly he leaned down and lightly kissed her lips, caressing the side of her face with his fingers, all the while continuing to stroke in and out. In and out.

Her hands trembled as they, in turn, traced the features of his face, his chest, the tight muscles of his abs. Her eyes searching his. "Make me fly," she said, humbling him. "One more time, Aidan. Make me fly."

Tears clogged his throat, and he had to swallow rapidly in order not to disgrace himself. He traced his hand down her side, until the heat of his palm covered her tattoo of the raven. His raven. Always his.

"Yes," she hissed, her nails digging into the sun on his hip. Both images perfectly aligned, her raven carrying his sun, cradling him within her wings. She arched her hips, taking him deeper, meeting his thrusts as they quickened, hardened. Aidan reached out and grabbed her other hand, tightly lacing his fingers with hers, as he rocked into her again and again until she cried out and took flight.

He followed, carried on her wings.

The problem with flying, Raven decided, was that at some point you had to land. She'd never been good at smooth landings. More like crash landings. It didn't take long for reality to raise its ugly head and demand to know what the hell she'd done.

The room was cast in shadows as the sun readied for its early bedtime. She hated the long, dark winters, the short hours the sun showed itself.

Raven lay on her side within Aidan's protective embrace, his arm wrapped around her back as her head rested on his chest, her leg draped over his. What she would give to have nothing between them. To be able to lay with him like this every night, wake in his arms, soar in his arms.

Obviously she had no willpower around him. Hard to keep her barriers in place when she was the one widening the cracks between the mortar. She really needed to get dressed and get going, but lying next to Aidan felt so...so...right.

Boy was she in an avalanche's worth of trouble. She couldn't fall in love with him again. A rush of heat swept over her followed by a bone chilling realization. Had she ever stopped loving him?

Oh, God, she had to get away.

"Done beating yourself up, yet?" Aidan asked in his husky, sexy, sated voice.

How she used to treasure talking with him after making love. Listening to that voice, which seemed to caress her all over again as they made plans, spoke of dreams.

"I need to go." But she didn't move. His hand stroked up and down her arm in a lazy pattern. If only they could take another flight. But that would make matters worse. She needed to stay grounded.

"I know." He didn't move either, just continued caressing her arm. "Fox will be getting home from school soon."

Oh, God. Fox. The ticking clock felt like it had a bomb attached, and she was out of time. Her son was the reason she'd rushed over here. She still didn't know exactly what she wanted to say to Aidan. There was one thing she had to get him to agree to before she left. "I need you to keep quiet about being Fox's father until I can talk to him."

Aidan's hand stopped its downward path and he slowly turned on his side to face her. "Raven, Fox already knows."

What? "You told him? Oh, no." She pushed out of his arms, and grabbed for her clothes. "How could you do that? How did he react? *When did you tell him?*" Questions fired like bullets while she yanked on her clothes.

Aidan gingerly sat up in bed, his hand holding his head. It clearly still pained him, but she couldn't think about that now. All that mattered was Fox.

"Raven, I didn't tell him."

She popped her head through the top of her t-shirt, tugging it down over her hips, and met his gaze. "How else would he know?"

Aidan closed his eyes for a moment, and when he opened them she felt his unease. "I think you'd better sit down."

His tone, combined with the look on his face, had her slowing her movements as she slipped into her jeans and buttoned them. Raven sat on the edge of the bed, knowing she wasn't going to like hearing whatever Aidan was about to tell her.

"Fox was the one who told *me* I was his father."

Just like that, the bomb detonated inside her. She couldn't speak as the static in her head drowned out all other noise.

"Raven?" Aidan called her name, but it sounded as if it came from a far off place.

Her vision blurred as the static turned to a shrill, and then a loud banging, as white lights flashed in tiny sparks before her eyes.

Her world tipped.

"Raven." Aidan had her by the shoulders and was shaking her.

Breathe, damn it. She couldn't fall apart now, not when she had so much to—somehow—put back together. "I'm okay," she lied. Would she ever be okay again?

"Are you sure? You're pale as snow." Aidan gazed at her with such concern, it made her want to lean on him, rest her heavy head on his broad shoulders.

"Did Fox tell you—" She had to pause in order to swallow the sick feeling in her stomach rising up into her throat. "Did he tell you how he knew?" Her boy, her baby, hadn't come to her with this? Hadn't asked *her* if Aidan was his father? Instead, he'd gone to the source. Which really didn't surprise her. Hurt her, yes, but didn't surprise her. Fox had always been one to tackle problems head on, rather than take the time Raven needed to sort out the best course of action.

Aidan enclosed her hands in his, anguish dwelling in the dark depths of his eyes. "Earl told him…when he was seven."

Time stopped. The room spun and went deadly quiet except for the sound of her agonized breathing.

Fox had known since he'd been seven?

"How the hell did Earl know?" she cried out. Her worst nightmare unveiled and it had happened *four years ago*.

"He guessed. Apparently, Fox is the spitting image of me when I was a boy."

"I gotta get out of here." She jumped off the bed and slipped her bare feet into her mukluks. "I have to talk to Fox."

"Raven, wait. We'll talk to him together." Aidan threw back the covers, his gorgeous nude body causing her to catch her breath for a moment. The reality of what they'd just done stabbed before she could get a hold of herself. Everything was spinning out of control.

"No." Fox was *her* son. *She* needed to talk to him. *Alone.* Raven tore out of the bedroom, ignoring Aidan swearing behind her.

"Damn it, Raven." Aidan grabbed her arm and swung her around as she reached for her coat. He hadn't stopped to dress, standing there in all his glorious nakedness. "You aren't keeping me out of this." His eyes burned with intent. "He's my son too."

She didn't want to share Fox. How did she deal with this? She needed more time.

Aidan gripped her shoulders. "Quit fighting it, Raven. You're caught in a snare with no way out."

Oh God, he was right. She was trapped like an animal left to struggle until someone came along and ended it. Suddenly everything was all too much. Her shoulders sagged, and her legs gave out as a sob escaped her.

Aidan helped her to a chair and lowered her onto the torn cushion. "Let me get dressed. Stay right there."

Raven wiped at the tears trailing down her cheeks, taking rapid breaths, hoping to get herself under control before he returned. With what seemed like mere seconds, Aidan was back fully dressed and slipping into his coat. She watched his movements, noticing the beauty in which he moved. Maybe if she focused on him everything else would fade away.

What was she doing? She wasn't some weak female. Where was her backbone? Her life had taken a hit, unquestionably, but she'd taken hits before. Granted this one involved her son, and all that she presumed to know about him, but she was his mother. She'd raised him. She could handle this.

What other choice did she have?

"Ready?" Aidan asked.

Raven nodded, stood, and walked out of Earl Harte's cabin with Aidan at her side, his hand on her elbow as though loaning her strength or staying close in case she crumbled. He guided her to her Suburban and opened the passenger door.

"Get in."

She didn't move. "If you have to come, you'll drive yourself."

"You're in no condition to drive." He tightened his jaw in a no-nonsense action.

"Like you are?" She indicated his head, seeing the lingering pain in his eyes. "You've been bashed in the head. I bet it's pounding like a jackhammer."

"Yeah, and the longer we stand out here and argue about something you are going to lose, the more it pounds." He picked her up and tossed her onto the seat as though she weighed nothing. "Put on your seatbelt." He slammed the door and walked around the front of the vehicle.

The surprise of his actions left her speechless until he got in the driver's seat and held out his hand for the keys. "How are you going to get back?" She wasn't driving him back out here. He had another thing coming if he thought he could stay at her place just because they'd had sex.

"Let me worry about that. Now, hand over the keys."

She stared into his eyes and realized she was being an idiot. Her fear and hurt had transferred itself into anger as a way of surviving. The pain of knowing Fox had been aware of his paternity all this time, and had never talked with her about it, broke her heart. She reached into her coat pocket, pulled out the keys, and dropped them into his hand.

"Thank you," he said graciously, and started the engine.

She didn't need him being polite and gentlemanly. Where had his mad gone? An afternoon rolling around in bed couldn't have snuffed out the anger she knew he still harbored over her lies.

This was getting her nowhere. She needed to concentrate on what she was going to say to Fox, not her situation with Aidan. Nothing mattered right now except her son.

CHAPTER SIXTEEN

Aidan glanced over at Raven. She sat like a block of ice, gazing out her window as he drove them to her house. She wasn't seeing the frozen landscape—at least what little could be seen in the darkness. The news about Fox had hit her like a sucker punch to the gut. He doubted she'd caught her breath yet.

Much the way she'd stolen his this afternoon.

He was still angry, yet torn with the need to hold her, tell her everything would be okay, that together they could fix this. But how did he do that when she didn't want his help and he didn't know if he could forgive her lies? She didn't want him in her life even after the incredible lovemaking they'd experienced this afternoon.

He tightened his jaw and then tried to relax the muscles as the action caused his head to pound harder. After they talked to Fox, he needed to find Pike. See if he'd noticed any suspicious characters around town. Someone had upped the ante this afternoon when they'd taken a swing at his head.

Aidan parked the suburban in Raven's driveway and turned off the engine. He glanced at her and realized that at some point in their journey, she'd pulled it together. No longer did she look as though she'd collapse if another snag presented itself. He couldn't help wonder, and envy, how she'd done it.

She turned to him, her eyes brimming with hurt, which had his gut clenching. "Since you're insisting on being here, we need to agree on a plan of action," she said.

Damn, but she was formidable. He never would have guessed that the teenager she'd been would have grown into such a capable, confident, independent woman. "Okay, how do you want to play it?"

She seemed taken aback at his easy agreement. Hell, she'd been a parent for almost twelve years. He'd only been one for a few days.

"Well…I'm not quite sure." She worried her bottom lip.

"Raven." He reached for her hand, surprised at how cold it was. "Regardless of his secrets, Fox loves you."

She glanced down at their clasped hands, and he thought she blinked back tears. "Thanks for that."

He tilted her face up and gazed into eyes swimming with tears. He couldn't help himself from leaning over and lightly kissing her lips. "I'll follow your lead, okay?"

She gave him a jerky nod. "Okay." Taking a deep breath, she opened her door and stepped out.

They entered the cabin through an arctic entry where they shed their coats and hung them on hooks. From there they crossed into a great open room with the kitchen off to the left, and a living and dining room area with a cathedral ceiling, all covered with tongue and groove pine. A dramatic wall of windows with a pair of French doors leading to a large deck overlooked the frozen Chatanika River and glacial-topped mountain range beyond.

"Fox?" Raven hollered when they found the room empty.

"Up here," he answered from above.

Aidan glanced up to see a loft over the kitchen area. Fox leaned over the railing and froze when he caught sight of both his parents.

"Uh…hi," he said, obviously knowing the gig was up.

"Could you come down here, please," Raven said.

"Sure. Just give me a minute to save my game." He disappeared from the railing.

Aidan glanced at Raven, caught her taking another deep breath. She met his eyes for a moment and then walked into the kitchen, reached into a cabinet for a bottle of Tylenol, and shook out a few pills. Next, she filled a glass of water and returned to where he'd stayed standing. "Take these."

He took them, speechless that with all the turmoil she was going through, she remembered his head bashing and thought to help relieve the pain drumming his skull. He swallowed the pills and downed the water, handing the empty glass back to her, where she set it on the kitchen counter just as Fox came down the stairs.

"Am I in trouble?" Fox asked, stopping midway, his hand tightening on the log railing.

Aidan couldn't help twitching his lips. Nothing got by this kid. *His kid.*

"No." Raven motioned to the sofa. "Have a seat, Fox."

"Sounds like I'm in trouble." He finished the trek down the stairs and sat down on a leather loveseat that had seen some use. Not so much that it was in need of being replaced, but comfortable, broken in. Raven's house reflected the same. This was a home where you could kick off your shoes and be at ease. Except that now, none of them felt at ease. The tension in the room was rising faster than snowpack levels during a blizzard.

Raven took a seat on the opposite sofa, and Aidan joined her. She glanced at him when he sat but didn't say anything, though Aidan knew she wished he wasn't there. Another deep breath and she began. "I know you're aware that Aidan is your father."

Fox paled. "Mom—"

Raven held up her hand. "Let me speak first. Okay?"

Fox nodded, swallowing, his eyes huge in his young face.

"I'm sorry, Fox." Her voice broke, and she stopped for a moment before continuing. "Keeping your father from you was not to punish you. I love you. You're the most important person in my life. I should have told you a long time ago that Aidan was your father. But things were...*are*...complicated."

"That didn't make it right," Fox said, his initial surprise gone, and years of resentment hardening his face.

"I know." She sighed. "Someday, I hope you'll understand why I did what I did and be able to forgive me."

Fox glanced at Aidan and then back to Raven. "You kept me from my father, how do I forgive that?"

Raven sucked in her breath, and Aidan found himself coming to her defense even though he felt the same anger that Fox did over the choices Raven had made. "Fox, a lot of things happened when your mother found out she was pregnant."

He snorted. "Yeah, but what kept her from telling me about you when you showed up? Or admitting to you that I was your son?" He turned back to Raven. "Were you ever going to tell me the truth?"

She clasped her fingers together, the knuckles white. "Honestly? I don't know," she said softly.

"This is messed up." Fox curled his lip into a sneer and fell back against the back of the loveseat.

"I was young, Fox. Scared." Raven glanced between the two of them. "Still scared."

"You're scared of him?" Fox asked with a raise of his brow.

"Yes." Raven leaned forward, anchored her arms on her knees. "Fox, I'm scared of losing you. I kept your parentage a secret for reasons that I truly believed, at the time—" she flicked a glance at Aidan "—were in your best interest. I did it to protect you. It was a different time, there were circumstances I couldn't control, and I was very young." She took a deep breath. "Why didn't you tell me you knew? Why didn't you come and talk to me? I thought we could always talk about everything."

It was Fox's turn to look down. "He made me promise."

"Earl?" Raven asked.

Fox nodded then rushed to say, "I wanted so bad to know who my father was, and Mr. Harte was the only one talking."

"What…what kind of relationship did you have with him?" Raven asked.

Fox shrugged his shoulder, not meeting her gaze, rather he seemed fascinated with the invisible pattern his finger drew on the leather of the couch. "Mr. Harte liked to talk and show me stuff."

"What kind of stuff?"

He glanced up at her tone. "It's not what you're thinking. He was lonely."

The hell he was, Aidan thought. Earl had an agenda. He liked being alone, chose to live his life as far from civilization as he could comfortably get. He hadn't been lonely. He'd either been using Fox, or maybe he enjoyed the kid's company. Could the old man have mellowed as he'd gotten older and liked the idea of being a grandfather? The thought was hard to swallow, but it was easier to take than knowing Earl had befriended Fox, and kept his relationship from Aidan for the pure evil enjoyment of it. The bastard was probably laughing his ass off from whatever Hell he'd ended up in.

"What kind of…things…did you do with him?" Raven asked.

"Mr. Harte talked, mostly. But he showed me how to do things." He looked down as though he didn't want to admit what kind of things.

"Weapons?" Aidan prompted, his guts twisted.

"Uh…yeah." Fox quickly tried to explain, "He thought it was best that I knew how to protect myself."

"What kind of weapons, Fox?" Raven asked, her voice trembling.

"Uhm, target shooting, traps, how to blow up stuff."

"You were playing with *explosives?*" Raven jumped to her feet. "I have always told you to stay away from that monster. You knew that he killed my dad, your grandfather, by setting off a bomb!"

"Raven." Aidan rose and placed a hand on Raven's shoulder, hoping to lend her support and also calm her down. Fox wasn't reacting to Raven's anger in a positive way. His lips had tightened, and his breathing came in hard pants.

Turning, she shrugged off Aidan's hand. "This is why I didn't want Fox to know about you. I didn't want him anywhere around that sadistic bastard."

"He wasn't like that!" Fox yelled, getting to his feet too. "I liked him. He treated me decent. He told me that Grandpa Fox's death had been an accident, but nobody would believe him. They just blamed him. And you would have kept me away from him." Fox pointed an accusing finger at Raven. "Just like you kept me away from my father!" He turned and ran out of the cabin.

"Fox!" Raven rushed to follow. "Fox, come back here."

Aidan grabbed her arm. "Let him go."

Raven turned on him. "Don't tell me how to handle my son."

Aidan felt like she'd slapped him. He released her and took a step back. *"Our son."* He left her standing there, knowing if he didn't get away he'd do or say something he couldn't recover from. In the arctic entry, he grabbed his coat and noticed Fox's smaller one still hanging on the hook. He grabbed it and slammed the door on his way out. Hearing the sound of the door crashing in its frame soothed the snarling beast inside him.

He found Fox with his dogs. It was where Aidan had always gone as a boy, until Earl had killed Nugget. Fox was on his knees, his face buried in the thick fur of Lucien's neck, the Husky taking the kid's weight and grief like a champ. There was a reason a dog was considered man's best friend. No other being on earth loved unconditionally like a dog.

"Hey," Aidan said as he approached, giving Fox time to wipe his tears, pretending that he didn't notice his son had been crying, though the thought of the troubles wracking Fox, caused pain to tighten his belly. "You forgot this." He handed Fox his coat. "It's more than chilly out here." By his calculations, and the white plumes of air his words produced, it had dropped to twenty below.

"Thanks," Fox muttered, standing, taking the coat and shrugging it on. He didn't meet Aidan's eyes.

Aidan inched closer, petting Lucien behind the ears, who continued to lend support. "You should cut your mom a break."

That had Fox raising his head and meeting Aidan's eyes head on. "Are you serious? She lied to me."

He almost laughed at the repeat of his own words to Raven earlier that day. Had that been only this morning? "Yes, she did. So, she isn't perfect."

"Yeah, but her lie was a whopper."

Aidan couldn't help the laugh. "I agree, but technically, so was yours."

"Huh?"

"Think about how she's feeling right now. She just found out that you knew I was your father, since you were seven, and that you had a relationship with a man she hated and feared." Aidan gave that a moment to sink in. "Tell me something. How would you classify your relationship with your mother?"

"What do you mean?"

"Do you fight, butt heads, or is she one you can talk to, the kind of mom who listens, always there for you?"

Fox twisted his lips. "The last part," he said reluctantly.

"So, you have a good relationship then."

He shrugged. "Yeah."

"Listen, Fox, I'm not excusing her for what she did. Hell, I'm still upset about all this too. But it wouldn't hurt to try and see things from her point of view."

"I guess so," he muttered.

Aidan snorted. "That's some pretty damn good advice I just gave you. I should take it myself."

Fox gave him a half smile. "Yeah, but it's easier to be mad."

That sobered him fast. He didn't want Fox struggling with temper like he did. "Not in the long run." Aidan sighed and looked around. The dogs had lost interest in them, some settling down inside their houses, while a few were curled up on straw in front of the openings. Lucien yawned, stretched his legs out in front of him and laid his head on his paws. "People say and do things when they are mad that are sometimes impossible to come back from."

Damn, this father-son stuff was tough. He rubbed a hand through his hair, wincing when he connected with the bump on the back of his head. "I know you're hurting. That's where most anger comes from. Your mom's hurting too."

"Are you…hurting?"

He found himself having to swallow before answering. "Yeah."

"Are you going to leave? Go back to Seattle?"

"I'm not going anywhere." He cracked a smile. "I just found out I have a son. I'd like to get to know him."

A full smile spilt across Fox's face.

Aidan reached out and ruffled the boy's hair. Suddenly Fox threw himself into his arms and hugged him. Emotion swamped Aidan. He reached around and hugged his son back in return. They separated before Aidan lost his hold on the tears threatening to drown his eyes.

They stood there both trying to man up.

Aidan cleared his throat, knowing he had to address one more thing before he left.

"Fox." Aidan waited until Fox looked up at him. "No matter what Earl told you, he was responsible for killing Raven's dad. She's justified in her feelings. He might have treated you good, but he wasn't a good man." Fox furrowed his brow, and Aidan knew he wanted to argue. "Just think about what I said, okay. And when you've calmed down, talk to your mom. I know she's sick over all of this. Can you do that?"

Fox's chest swelled. "Yes, I can do that."

Aidan smiled. "You are one fine young man, and you owe that to your mother."

His lips twitched again. "Yeah, I suppose."

"I'll see you later then?"

Fox nodded. Aidan made to leave but turned back when Fox called his name. He met his son's apprehensive gaze.

"Would it be okay if I called you dad?"

Aidan felt like he'd just taken an electrical jolt to the heart. He stood perfectly still and prayed his voice didn't fail him. "I'd love that."

"Great." Fox beamed. "See you later…Dad."

Now his voice completely failed him as his throat clogged with tears. He nodded and ruffled Fox's hair again.

What a mess she'd made of everything. Raven sank into the couch cushions, cradled her head in her hands, and swallowed a sob. Tears would have to wait until later. There was still clean-up to do. Who the hell was she kidding? There was no way to clean up the mess she'd made of her life. Pregnant at eighteen, unwed, single parent, she'd lied to her child, lied to her child's father. And for what? Fox had found out who his father was anyway, from her enemy. The last person on the planet she wanted speaking to her son, let alone revealing secrets. Another sob escaped her. What was she going to do now?

How did she make this right?

The front door opened and closed. Raven jumped to her feet, wiping at the tears that had stolen down her cheeks. "Fox?"

"Yeah." Fox shuffled into the room, looking so much older than his eleven, almost twelve, years.

"Honey—"

"Mom, stop. I can't talk about this now."

"But—"

"I've been angry for a long time, just kept it buried. Now it's all bubbling to the surface." He glanced away from her again as though it was hard looking at her. "Aidan—my dad—said that it's better to wait to talk until I'm not so mad." He nodded his head. "I think he's right."

"But—"

"I'm going to bed." Fox turned and headed down the hall to his bedroom, quietly closing the door behind him.

Raven sank to her knees, her body racked with silent sobs. She'd lost so much. She couldn't lose her son. He was everything to her. Every decision she'd made in the last twelve years had been for his benefit. She wrapped her arms around her middle and leaned against the side of the couch, muffling her sobs.

Nothing in her life mattered but Fox. If she lost him...

She wiped her eyes. Fox was acting more mature than she was at the moment. She'd created this problem. She could have told Fox who his father was when he was a child. She could have told Aidan that he had a child.

It was a waste of time thinking of what she could have done. She had her reasons. Real, big, scary reasons. And she knew if she had to choose to do it all over again, she'd do the same thing. Her biggest mistake was underestimating Earl Harte.

She wouldn't make that mistake with Aidan.

CHAPTER SEVENTEEN

Aidan wrangled his emotions and had them corralled by the time he'd walked to the lodge from Raven's place. He'd had a moment of confusion when he realized he didn't have a ride back to Earl's. He hoped he could catch a ride from someone at the lodge or spend the night in the room Fiona had been loaning him. Lynx would probably jump at the chance, just to keep Aidan from hanging around the place. Besides, he needed to have a talk with Pike.

He opened the door to the restaurant, the heat hitting him in the face, a severe contrast to the freezing cold outside. He unzipped and removed his coat as he made his way to the bar.

"Hey, Pike," Aidan greeted the man behind the counter, who was currently filling a beer mug. He hitched onto a stool.

Pike studied him a moment, narrowing his eyes. "What else happened?"

Was he so readable? Aidan hoped Pike wasn't seeing the emotional turmoil he'd been through this afternoon. "Someone tried to bash my head in."

Pike scoffed. "Guess they didn't know how hard-headed you are. Want a beer?"

"No, but a cup of coffee would be good." He wasn't much of a drinker. The few times he'd gotten drunk, his actions had scared him when he'd sobered up. Besides, he remembered all too clearly how chained to alcohol his mother had been.

Pike poured him a cup of coffee. "Did you get a look at who hit you?"

"Nope. Knocked me clean out. I woke up in the snow. It was hell getting inside the cabin."

Pike slowly lowered the coffee pot back onto the burner. "Whoever is causing you trouble means business. You could have died out there."

"Believe me, I know." He probably owed Raven his life for showing up when she had. Great. Did she own part of his soul too? Who was he kidding, she'd always owned part of his soul.

"Want me to call Eva and have her check you out?"

"Hell no."

Pike gave a graveled laugh. "You're smarter than I gave you credit for." He leaned his arms over the bar and lowered his voice. "I've been keeping an eye out for suspicious characters, like you suggested. As you know, most Alaskans aren't the norm, but a few have stuck out more than others."

"A few? How many are we talking?"

"Well, there's this woman who checked in last week—during the week—then she came back this week. Again, during the week. We get most of our visitors on the weekend in the wintertime. Snowmobiling, snowshoeing, ice fishing. You know how it is. But this woman is alone."

"She say why she's here?"

"Some story about finding herself. Getting back to nature. That kind of shit."

"Getting back to nature is all the rage now days." Aidan took a sip of his coffee. Starbucks it wasn't. He reached for the sugar and added enough to rot his teeth.

Pike grimaced. "Don't I know it. But we usually get those types in summer. Who wants to get back to nature when nature, more than likely, will kill you this time of year? Besides, there's something familiar about her. I could be wrong, but I think she strips or used to strip for the Lonely Lady."

"Since when have you been a patron of the Lonely Lady?"

"Don't judge me, you young whippersnapper. Winter gets cold."

Aidan bit the inside of his cheek. "No judging." He regarded the 'nature girl.' Strippers and nature kind of went together, but there was nothing natural about her.

"So, who else have you noticed?"

"A young couple came in today. They seemed anxious. The girl, especially, skittish. They're sitting over there in the corner." Pike nodded in their direction. "Sure like to know what they're whispering about."

Aidan turned and regarded the man and woman bent over the table, their heads together in deep discussion.

Holy shit.

Aidan was off his stool and striding over to their table, ignoring Pike's protests. "Lana? Peter? What the hell are you doing here?"

"Aidan!" Lana jumped up, the action reinforcing her cheerleader good looks. She threw her arms around his neck, and squeezed. "I've been trying so *hard* to find you." Tears flooded her eyes, and tracked down her cheeks, when she let go of him. "I'm so glad you're all right and that you're here."

"What's wrong?" he asked. "And how did you ever find your way to Chatanika?"

"Better have a seat, Aidan," Peter said, taking a stand next to Lana, rubbing her back. "We'll explain everything." A grin cut through his somber expression. "Damn, but it's good to see you."

Aidan offered his hand for a shake. Peter took it and also added in a man hug, with a slap to his back, his dark Russian heritage sharpening the features of his face as he suddenly looked more the man than the teenage boy of last summer.

"How about introducing me to your friends?" Pike asked.

"Pike Maiski, meet Peter Savonski, and my cousin, Lana Harte." They nodded to each other. Peter and Lana retook their seats. Aidan and Pike pulled up chairs and joined them.

Lana looked at Pike and then to Aidan. She'd gotten her tears under control but had a skittish look about her like a rabbit about to be mowed down by a semi. "Aidan, Peter and I need to talk to you." She flicked a worried glance toward Pike. "Alone."

Aidan glanced at Pike who had an I'm-not-going-anywhere look written all over him. "Lana, we've had some trouble here. I doubt you showing up is a coincidence." He reached over and covered her hand with his. "Pike's the head of the village council. If something is going on, he needs to be aware of it."

"He isn't a trooper, is he?" She nibbled her bottom lip.

"Hell no," Pike answered, folding his arms over his chest. "We take care of our own around here."

"Lana, I've known Pike all my life." Aidan regarded the man in question. "I've always known him to be fair." More than fair. He hadn't jumped to conclusions when his own brother had ended up dead, like Raven had. "Aidan—" Lana leaned over the table "—this is *family* business."

"Tell you what," Pike said. "I'll make us a new pot of coffee." Pike gave Aidan a look that said, he'd give them their privacy for now, but he expected every detail.

Lana sighed with relief as Pike walked away.

"Okay, want to tell me what has both of you traveling all the way to Chatanika?"

"Dad sent me a letter," Lana said.

Roland Harte was currently on the lam, wanted by the troopers for questioning in his part of the summer's murderous outcome at fish camp. And the part he might have played in the deaths of Sonya and Peter's parents fifteen years ago.

Aidan glanced at Peter. "Have you informed Sonya and Garrett about this?"

Peter tightened his jaw. "No. I advised Lana that we should, but she made me promise not to."

His little cousin must have Peter tied tight around her little finger to get him to agree to that, since he had a vested interest in bringing Roland to justice. Peter and Lana had started a sweet romance last summer, but Aidan didn't know it had continued once the season ended. In fact, how had it? Lana was attending the University of Minnesota. He wasn't sure where Peter had decided to go to college but doubted it was somewhere in the lower forty-eight.

"How did the two of you end up here?" he asked.

Peter began the explanations as Lana seemed too upset. "Lana called me when she received the letter from Roland. I'm at currently at UAF—"

"You're attending college in Fairbanks?"

"Yeah." He smiled. "Decided at the last minute when Sonya and Garrett got married. Needed some distance from the newlyweds, you understand."

"She married him, huh?"

"Uh…yeah. You okay with that?" Peter looked apprehensive.

"As long as the fish cop makes her happy," Aidan admitted, realizing it was actually true.

"Well, anyway," Peter said. "When Lana called, all upset because she couldn't get a hold of you, we kinda came up with a plan. She flew into Fairbanks, and I picked her up, and then we came here."

"What did you think you were going to do when you got here?" Aidan looked from one to the other. "What was in this letter?"

"Dad's really upset about Uncle Earl dying," Lana started. "He said he was coming here."

Aidan remembered all too clearly the bitter, hateful words Roland had yelled at him after Aidan had killed his only brother. Roland and Earl were not only brothers but cohorts. There was nothing the two of them had liked better than causing mischief and mayhem. It was still hard to swallow that they'd added murder to the mix.

"What does that have to do with you two ending up in Chatanika?"

"Dad's after something. Something Uncle Earl had. And I'm afraid of what he's going to do to you." Lana reached into her purse and pulled out the letter, handing it to Aidan. "He's already in so much trouble. We have to stop him before he does something worse."

Aidan gingerly touched the bump on the back of his head. Had Roland knocked him senseless and left him to die this afternoon? Had he been the one to toss his rental and blow through Earl's place? Aidan took the letter. "What's he looking for?"

"I haven't a clue. But whatever it is, I think he's willing to do anything to get it." Lana pointed at the letter Aidan held. "Read it. See if you can make any sense of it."

Aidan unfolded the well-worn paper. Lana had been over this more than a few times. He read the letter twice. The hairs on the back of his neck rose. Roland was definitely on his last fish fry. He studied both Lana and Peter. "Huh. Well, looks like Uncle Roland wants me dead."

"Uh, yeah," Peter said. "That part about you being gutted and your innards strung out for the wolves was a good indication."

"Aidan, you're the closest thing I have to a brother. I don't want anything to happen to you." Lana's eyes once again filled with tears. Aidan reached over and squeezed her hand.

"What do you think he meant about claiming the windfall that is now rightly his?" Peter asked. "Was Earl rich?"

"No." Aidan frowned. "I haven't found any evidence of bank accounts, tax records, investments. Earl lived under the radar. After he'd served in Vietnam, Uncle Sam wasn't going to get another piece of him. Hell, I had to apply for my own social security card when I left home. It explains why someone has been searching Earl's place, though. There must be something hidden in the cabin."

He took a deep breath, and narrowed his eyes. "I've spent the last few days going through everything, and I haven't found anything of interest." He reexamined the letter. "What kind of windfall would Earl have? Money never seemed important to him. Just causing trouble. "

"Maybe it isn't money," Peter said. "We *are* in gold country."

Gold. Earl had killed for gold. Fox senior had paid with his life. It wasn't a stretch to believe he'd horded whatever he'd found. But where would he hide something like that?

Another thing kept bugging him. If his uncle was serious about his demise, it didn't make sense for Roland to hit him on the head and leave without making sure he was dead.

One thing you could count on about Earl and Roland Harte: when it came to threats, they kept their word.

CHAPTER EIGHTEEN

"All right, sis." Tern breezed into Raven's place, tossing her fur-trimmed black suede coat over the back of the couch. "What's so important that I had to leave town and travel to the boonies?"

"I slept with Aidan," Raven blurted out, looking around the cabin for Fox even though she knew he was at school.

"Well, then." Tern took a seat and crossed her legs, her fingers one-by-one pulling off her black leather gloves. "When?"

"Yesterday." In the middle of the night, after she'd sobbed until she was bone dry, she'd decided to buck up and take control of her life—before others took control for her. She needed to arm herself and rebuild her fortress, so to speak. Time to go on the offensive. Which meant coming clean to her family before they found out the truth from someone else. That someone else being Aidan, or worse, Fox. Tern was the best one to start with. She wasn't only Raven's sister, but her best friend. And she was as honest and forthcoming as bitter coffee.

"Just yesterday? I'm surprised you held out that long." Tern smoothed out her gloves, placing them on her crossed knee.

Raven scowled. "Not helping." She took a deep breath. "There's more."

"Hit me with it. I hope it's worth my while, since I'm paying Sue overtime to watch the shop."

Raven quickly filled Tern in with everything she'd been keeping secret all these years, plus Fox's secret.

"Give me a minute." Tern reached into her purse, pulled out her phone, and made a call. "Sue, I'm going to be gone the rest of the day. Sorry, it can't be helped. All right, fine. You can have Saturday off." She flipped her phone closed. "Hope you're happy. I had a hot date that I'll have to reschedule now."

"You wanted it to be worth your while."

"You sure as hell didn't disappoint." She pursed her dark red-painted lips. "First, forgive me, but I have to get this out of my system. I told you so! *I knew Fox was Aidan's son.* All those lies about some guy you met in a bar. Right. You were never the type to fall into bed with someone. Unless it *was* Aidan Harte."

"Really not helping."

She scoffed. "Helping? How am I going to help you out of this mess?"

"Tern!"

"All right, let me think." She rose and like a runway model walked the area in front of the windows, her stiletto boots clicking with each step over the hardwood. Turning on her heel, she regarded Raven with a raised brow. "How was the sex?"

"*What?*"

She made a 'give me' motion with her fingers. "It's been twelve years. Did the sex measure up to what you remembered?"

"How is that going to help?"

"Probably won't. But I want to know." She raised her chin, and Raven knew there wouldn't be anything more forthcoming until she answered.

"It was…" She swallowed. "Great, it was great, okay." Making love with Aidan again had been so much better than great. And thinking of having sex with Aidan was not going to help her situation. Only muddle it further.

"Great, huh?" Tern tapped her chin with the tip of her finger, calculating. "Bet that's an understatement."

A blush fired in Raven's cheeks.

Tern smiled. "Okay, so you had awesome sex with Aidan—" She stopped and narrowed her eyes. "It was awesome, *protected* sex, wasn't it?"

Raven's blush melted as realization dawned. "Oh, God."

Tern fell back into her chair. "Have you learned *nothing* from your past mistakes?"

"Fox wasn't a mistake," Raven was quick to reply. He might not have been planned, but she couldn't imagine life without him. From the first minute she'd found out she was pregnant, she'd wanted her child, never considered adoption or the other. However the situation turned out, Fox had been conceived in love, and she loved him more than her life.

Tern waved her hand. "Of course he isn't a mistake. That wasn't what I meant." She leaned forward. "Raven is there a chance you could have gotten pregnant again?"

"Uh…I don't know." She felt sick.

"I'd do the math." Tern reached into her purse and pulled out a small box. "Here, there's this great invention called a condom."

Raven raised her hands as though in defense against the small square box. "I don't need them. I'm not having sex with him again."

"Aidan still in the area?"

"Yeah."

Tern tossed her the box. "Better keep them on you." When Raven went to object again, Tern held up her hand. "Do you want to waste time discussing your track record when it comes to that man?"

"No," she mumbled, taking the box, and putting it in the pocket of her overalls, if for no other reason than to shut her sister up. There was no way she and Aidan were going to sleep together again. Besides, he hated her.

"Okay," Tern continued. "I wouldn't worry too much about Fox. The little scamp loves you. But he's got a Y chromosome so he'll need to milk it for a while."

"What about *his* secret?"

"You're going to have to forgive him. Your secret was worse. Besides, you're the adult, and he's just a kid. Do you blame him for wanting any information he could find about his father?"

"No," she whispered.

"Didn't those parenting books you devoured teach you not to lie?"

"I only lied to protect him."

"Doubt he sees it that way." Tern shook her head. "If you want to make this right, you'll have to admit you were wrong. And there's no standing in the way of Fox having a relationship with Aidan. You try to roadblock that and you'll lose him."

"I know." All these years she'd kept quiet to keep the Hartes from influencing her son. A lot of good that had done. She had to trust she'd raised Fox in such a manner that he knew right from wrong. Probably more than she did.

"So, now that Fox is taken care of, what are you going to do about Aidan?"

"Not sleep with him again," she blurted out.

Tern rolled her eyes. "I'm not wasting my time with that one. What are you going to do if he demands custody?"

Raven sucked in a breath. "I don't know. I'm scared, Tern. I can't lose my son."

"Do you really think Aidan would take Fox away from you?" Tern sobered as the reality of that thought seemed to hit her hard too.

"I don't know. Right now, he hates me."

Tern retook the seat opposite where Raven was curled up on the couch. "It's not like you to avoid a problem. Well, that is, I never thought so before. But you've avoided this problem for twelve years."

Raven glanced guiltily away, toward the windows framing the view of the river, iced over now, much like her heart. No, that wasn't true—there were cracks showing in the hard encasement. Like a spring thaw. Spring in Alaska was no simple affair. There was no gradual melting. Break up was the term, and it was apt. That was how her heart felt, like at any moment it was going to rupture open.

"I can't talk to Aidan right now."

"You're right, you can't." Tern studied her. "You definitely have to clean yourself up first."

Raven looked down at her old overalls and ratty t-shirt. "What's wrong with what I'm wearing? It's what I always wear when I'm working."

"Be truthful. Not *just* when you're working." Tern rolled her eyes. "Besides, you aren't working today." She gestured at Raven's outfit. "If you were, you'd add mud to that getup. I'd suggest— *highly suggest*—you clean up and wear something that knocks his socks off."

"I told you, I'm not sleeping with him again."

Tern shook her head and tsked. "You wear something that is going to scramble his brain, whether you plan on having sex with him or not. If he isn't thinking straight, your chances of getting what you're after rise in your favor. I can't believe I have to explain this stuff to you." She sighed. "Now, how are you going to break the news to the rest of the family?"

Breaking the news to the rest of the family was no simple affair. Tern had dragged her to the lodge where she'd gathered everyone, declaring an emergency family meeting. She had them sitting at the kitchen table, except Fiona who was putting the kettle on to boil. Her mother had taken one look at Raven and already knew what was up.

"What's this all about?" Pike grumbled. "The lunch crowd is going to start any minute."

"Brie's managing the restaurant," Fiona said, her voice always seemed to soothe Pike into compliance. "She'll handle everything until you get back."

"All right, Raven," Tern said. "The floor's yours."

Great. At least Fox wasn't here for this. He was still in school. So was Chickadee, which meant she'd have to go through this again later with her baby sister. What a great role model she'd turned out to be. Raven ran her sweaty hands down the front of her overalls, hooking her thumbs in the bibs, and wondered where to start.

"Some of us are getting old here," Grandma Coho said, beading another strip of leather.

"Uhm...well, you see..." Raven bit her lip. Sweat broke out over her body as all eyes turned to stare at her. "Okay...it's like this..."

"Aidan is Fox's father," Tern blurted out. She gave Raven a shrug. "Sorry, sis, but none of us have all day."

Lynx gave a snort and fell back into his chair. "I had a feeling this was coming. How'd Aidan take the news? You *have* told him?" He shared a look with Eva who raised a brow.

"Uh…yeah." Had everyone guessed Aidan was Fox's father? Had she been a fool all these years? Okay, she didn't need the answer to that right now. She worried the end of her braid with her fingers. "You can imagine Aidan wasn't happy. That is, he was happy about Fox, but not happy with…me."

"Well, I should say not," Gran piped up, her beading forgotten. She pointed her needle at Raven, her eyes squinting over her bifocals. "All these years you've lied to him, child. You've lied to us. I know you were brought up better than that."

"Coho," Fiona said. "She doesn't need a lecture right now." Fiona gave Raven an encouraging smile, then returned to the stove, shutting off the burner as the kettle whistled.

Raven glanced at Pike. He had yet to say anything. He'd tightened his lips, and the look of disappointment on his face caused her breath to catch. It twisted her gut, and she suddenly felt like she'd disappointed her father. Pike had stepped in as the patriarch of the family, and with his resemblance to her dad, sometimes it felt as though she was talking to him when she spoke to Pike. Like now. Her dad wouldn't have been proud of the way she'd handled this situation either. But then if her father had lived, she would have made other choices when she'd found out she was carrying Aidan's baby. Life would have turned out completely different.

A hush fell over the room as they all waited to see what Pike would say. He shared a look with Fiona before resting his elbows on the table and steepled his fingers. "I take it Fox is aware of who his father is?"

Raven nodded, the emotion backing up her throat preventing her from telling them Fox had been aware for four years. It would probably be best if she never told them that bit of news.

"That explains why the scamp has been stomping around here like a pup with a wounded paw." He glanced briefly at Fiona, giving her a nod of thanks as she set a mug of tea in front of him. "That settles it then," he said softly.

"Settles what?" Raven asked.

"Aidan's one of us now." Pike blew on his tea and took a sip as though the problem was resolved.

"What? No." She frowned.

"He's Fox's father. That makes him part of the family." Pike's tone clearly stated there would be no argument.

"Pike," Lynx said slowly, mimicking Pike's posture. "Making him a member of the family when there are still unanswered questions about Dad is a bit premature."

"I'm content with the answers Aidan gave twelve years ago." Pike looked at each of them in turn. "All of you need to let it go." His gaze settled on Raven. "For Fox's sake."

Pike set his tea aside and stood. "I need to get back." He turned to Fiona. "Walk with me?"

They left the room together, and Raven knew the two of them would be discussing her and her problems. She felt like a kid who'd just been caught in a compromising position. Well, she had, and she didn't have the excuse of young age to fall back on this time.

"I'll say this for all of you," Eva said having kept quiet throughout the meeting. "Never a dull moment being a part of this family."

Raven entered the restaurant not knowing what she was going to say to Pike, but knowing she needed to speak to him. Somehow she needed to erase his disappointment in her.

As she strode toward the bar, she noticed Aidan at a table with a very young, very beautiful woman, their heads nestling together as they talked. A feeling totally unlike anything she had ever felt before seeped into her body. The woman leaned her head against Aidan's shoulder, and he gave her a hug. Raven wanted to yank the woman out of his arms by her shiny blond roots. She walked up to their table.

"Aidan?"

He jerked back at the sound of her voice. "Raven." He sounded surprised, or was it guilt at being caught with another woman just twenty-four hours after he'd slept with her? He rose to his feet.

"I...uh...I would like you to meet my cousin." He indicated the girl, who looked up at Raven, blinking back tears from her large blue eyes. "Lana, this is Raven. The woman I told you about."

Told what about?

Lana dabbed her eyes with a napkin and gave Raven a timid smile. "It's nice to meet you."

Raven pulled out one of the chairs and sat. She didn't care that she hadn't been invited. "You have a cousin?" Why hadn't she heard of this cousin before? And why was she here?

Aidan retook his seat. "Roland is her father. Lana traveled here with her boyfriend, hoping to stop Roland from causing...some mischief."

"Mischief?" Goodness gracious. Were any of his relatives law abiding? She studied Lana, wondering if her sweet innocence was an act. Aidan must have picked up on her mood, because he leaned closer to Lana as though to shield the little blonde from her.

"Lana, why don't you go and find Peter." Aidan glared at Raven. "I need a moment with Raven."

"Okay, but you won't leave the lodge, will you?" Lana looked up at Aidan all teary-eyed again.

"I won't go anywhere. Same goes for you and Peter. All right?"

"Yes." Lana took a deep breath and tried to smile. She turned to Raven. "It was nice to meet you."

Raven nodded and watched the petite beauty walk out of the restaurant and into the main part of the lodge. She turned back to Aidan. "What's going on?"

"Lana is really fragile right now. I'd appreciate it if you wouldn't scare her to death."

"What are you talking about? I was perfectly pleasant."

"You were not. My skin is still burning from the scorching look you gave us."

"Whatever," she scoffed. "Want to tell me why she's here?"

"Not really," he said, under his breath.

"Excuse me?"

"I'm tired of being judged by you." He leaned across the table, his eyes hard, direct. "Things are going to change between you and me, starting now. First, I'm Fox's father, and nothing you can do will keep me away from him. I suggest you don't even try. Second, you need to quit blaming me for what my father did to yours."

She sucked in her breath and opened her mouth to object. "Aidan—"

"I'm not finished. Third, until I say different I don't want you and Fox out at Earl's place."

That she hadn't expected, and it took the heat out of her anger. "Why?"

His jaw hardened. "You don't want to hear why. For your and Fox's safety, I don't want you there."

Not that she wanted to return to Earl's, but to be told she couldn't, didn't set well.

"Now," he continued, "about yesterday." He rested elbows on the table, his brows settling heavy over his eyes. "You made love with me. We didn't use protection. Whether or not you can love me again, doesn't matter. You are *not* pushing me out of your life this time."

It took her a moment to catch her breath. "That sounds like an ultimatum."

"Call it whatever you want, but you're stuck with me."

"Nice to see you two getting along." Pike came up, plunking down a cup of coffee in front of her. "Might want to take your 'discussion' somewhere more private. You're garnering attention."

Raven glanced around the dining room. Sure enough they had become the entertainment. Chatanika was a small town, barely a town, more like a village. Whatever had been said this afternoon between her and Aidan would be shared with the whole population. Great.

"Thanks for the heads up," Aidan said.

Pike put a hand on Aidan's shoulder and looked at Raven. "You tell him?"

Raven paled.

"Tell me what?"

Pike cocked a brow.

Raven studied the table and drew circles with her finger on the surface. "I hadn't gotten around to it yet."

Pike harrumphed. "Lot of things you seem to take your time with getting around to."

His disappointment weighed heavy on her shoulders. "A meeting was called," she said to Aidan. "I informed everyone that you were Fox's father."

Pike slapped Aidan on the back. "Welcome to the family, son."

Aidan looked up at Pike, speechless. He swiveled his gaze toward Raven.

"You're Fox's father. Apparently, that makes you one of us."

Aidan swallowed, glanced between the two of them, and suddenly stumbled to his feet. "I have to go."

She watched him rush out of the restaurant. What was that all about?

"Don't just sit there." Pike reached down and hauled her to her feet. "Go after the boy."

"Why?"

Pike grabbed her coat and shoved her toward the door. "You aren't that dense." He shook his head. "Actually, with Aidan you've always been minus a fat load of brain cells. That man has always longed for a loving family. Now get out there, and fix this mess you've made." He opened the door and pushed her out into the cold. Aidan was standing next to his rental, staring off toward the sunset.

Raven struggled into her coat. Where did she start? "Aidan—"

"What does that look like to you?" Aidan pointed toward the direction of Earl's cabin.

A plume of gray and black smoke rose above the trees, staining the sunset in purple bruises.

Fire.

Aidan nodded as though he'd heard her dreaded thought and wrenched open the door to his vehicle.

Without thinking, Raven ran around to the passenger side and jumped in.

"You aren't coming with me."

"I'm not letting you go alone."

"Things have changed. I don't want you anywhere near me."

She tried to deflect that barb. "You're wasting time. There won't be anything left if you don't get this thing moving."

He cursed and started the Tahoe, fishtailing out of the parking lot. "You're the most stubborn person I know."

"Back at ya. Now what the hell is going on?"

He tightened his lips into a thin line of defiance. It wasn't going to work.

"Why is your cousin here? And don't tell me she came for a vacation. She's the beach bunny type."

"You don't know a thing about her."

"Then tell me. And why do you seem to care so much about Earl's place burning? You offered to let the village burn it for the winter solstice."

The Tahoe went into a skid, and Aidan let up on the gas, turning the wheel in the opposite direction, safely keeping the vehicle on the road and screaming toward the smoke, which was blacker and thicker the closer they got.

"There's something inside that cabin someone is willing to kill for."

"Then why burn it down?"

He gave her a sharp look. "He must have found it."

"He? You know what it is, don't you? What does it have to do with Lana?"

He let out an impatient sound. "Uncle Roland's in town. Lana received a letter from him stating his intentions."

"What *are* his intentions?" A trickle of dread snaked through her.

"Murder and theft," he bit out.

"Whose murder?" she whispered, already suspecting the answer. The flexing of his jaw answered her question. "Why does he want you dead?"

"I killed his brother, remember? Roland believes in a biblical form of justice."

"But...you were protecting someone."

"He doesn't see it that way."

"Then what the hell are we doing racing toward Earl's? You should be leaving town."

"Because I won't run from him, and he's after the gold."

"What gold?"

"Your father's."

"*What?*"

He sighed and finally gave into her questions. "It's the only thing that makes sense. Somewhere Earl had to have hidden gold in that cabin. In the letter to Lana, Roland spoke of a windfall he was going to collect. Earl didn't have anything...unless he'd hidden it. And the only thing I could think of that he would have hidden was gold. Gold he killed your father for."

Raven sat still in the seat as they raced over the snow-packed back road. Shadows reached like demon fingers across the landscape as the sun gave up the fight. They rounded the corner, and there was the cabin, squatting un-charred but backlit by glowing flames. Smoke billowed and spread out from behind the cabin like death's blanket smothering the birch and spruce trees.

Aidan jerked the Tahoe into park and swung open the door. "Stay here."

"Like hell I will." She opened her door.

"Damn it, Raven, I don't have time to argue."

"Then give it up, I'm coming with you." She slammed her door, emphasizing her words.

Aidan swore a string of profanity, his face a mask of frustration and anger. "Stay behind me then." He reached under the seat and pulled out a handgun. They ventured toward the cabin, Aidan scanning the area for danger. Raven kept her eyes wide open, watching his back, wishing she was also armed. Something besides the smoke didn't feel right. Fire was always a threat in Alaska. Build-up of creosote in a chimney, a fire left unattended—the list was endless of how fires got out of hand, killed, and destroyed. She and Aidan crunched down the path, the sound of their feet and the hiss and crackle of flames the only noise. The pungent smell of smoke, much like a pleasant campfire, scented the area.

Rounding the corner toward the back of the cabin, Aidan suddenly stopped. "Well, shit."

Raven plowed into the back of him. He reached out a hand to steady her, and she finally saw what he had. The lean-to that sheltered the stacks of chopped firewood simmered, reduced to flying ash and snapping coals. Flames had greedily eaten away at the wood and structure, leaving nothing to heat the cabin.

"That took me days to chop."

"Your uncle really doesn't want you staying out here." Raven moved to stand beside him. "Crafty bastard."

"Something's off." He eyed the dense trees. Fat snowflakes started to whisper in the air. "This doesn't feel right."

The flames were dying down as they ate up the fuel, smoke and glowing embers the only evidence of the lean-to and wood pile. There was no threat that the fire would spread. The only thing around the burn pile was snow. The forecasted storm started to dump its heavy load from the gray sky. Soon there would be no sign of the fire left.

"Roland wants me dead," Aidan continued. "Why not just kill me. Why mess with me?"

"Are you sure he doesn't want to toy with you first?"

"No. He's out for blood." Aidan rubbed the back of his neck, still scanning the area. "The law is looking for him. He doesn't have time for games." He turned to the cabin. "Come on. Let's get you back to the lodge and out of the cold."

"You're not planning to come back here?" She knew the answer by the line of his squared shoulders.

"A few bundles of wood from the store will get me by for the night until I can figure out something else."

"You can't stay out here alone."

"Are you offering to stay with me?" He cocked a brow.

She ignored the double meaning of his words. "You can stay at the lodge."

"And endanger the people there? I don't think so."

"You promised your cousin you wouldn't leave the lodge." She tried again. The idea of him staying out here alone and unprotected while some nutcase wanted him dead made claws of fear sink into her bones.

"Careful, you're beginning to sound like you care about me."

She did care. And she was starting to realize how much. "Aidan…"

His attention was caught by a snap of a twig. Suddenly a black wolf came charging toward them, growling with its teeth bared. Aidan pushed her away as the wolf came right at them, knocking them to the ground as the distinct crack of a rifle echoed in the dark. Then the wolf was gone, bounding off into the dense trees.

"*Move*," Aidan hollered, grabbing her arm and hauling her toward the side of the cabin. Another shot rang out as they hurried. They crouched next to the log walls. "Are you hit?"

"Was that a *wolf?*"

"Yes. Are you hit?"

"No, you?"

"The shots are coming from the back of the cabin. We need to get to the Tahoe." They were both breathing hard. The wind picked up, swirling the snow as it fell. "I want you to run for it, while I cover you." He cocked the gun. "Ready?"

She nodded.

"Go." He pushed her away from him and peppered rounds over what was left of the wood pile.

Raven ran and jumped into the passenger side of the vehicle, keeping her head down as shots rang back and forth over the area. She noticed the keys Aidan had left in the ignition. Without a second thought, she shimmied over the console into the driver's seat and started the engine, engaging the gears. She glanced up just as a bullet shot through the windshield, missing her by mere inches. Then Aidan was there, vaulting into the seat next to her. She had the Tahoe in motion before he said, "*Go, go, go!*"

Another shot hit the side of the vehicle and then blessedly there were no more. Regardless, she didn't slow her speed, careening around icy corners, plowing through snow drifts as though the hounds of hell were nipping at her heels.

"You can slow down now," Aidan said, his voice breathless.

She glanced at him, knowing he'd see the fear and panic in her eyes.

"Back off the gas, sweetheart, or we're going to end up dead."

"He was shooting at us." She stated the obvious, letting off the gas.

"I know." Aidan grimaced as she hit a rut in the road.

"What's wrong?"

"Nothing." He tightened his mouth.

"*Did he hit you?*" she screeched.

"I'll be fine." He grabbed the dashboard as the Tahoe slid around the corner. "As long as you don't end us in the ditch."

"Oh, God. You *are* hit. Where?"

"Upper arm. It's fine. Just a graze."

She noticed how he was holding his right arm close to his chest and stepped on the gas. Knowing he was shot wreaked havoc with her emotions, and her driving skills. Adrenaline pumped through her veins like amphetamines. "Where did that wolf come from?"

Aidan smiled. "He's been hanging around the place. I think he's looking out for me."

"If he hadn't…"

"I know." Aidan swallowed.

"Whoever Grandma Harte was, she raised some nasty boys." Raven shuddered. Aidan didn't seem anything like them, but she'd seen his dark side in the past and it had scared her to death.

CHAPTER NINETEEN

Aidan finally relaxed when the lodge came into view. Raven jerked the Tahoe to a stop in the parking lot. He hoped no one would pay any attention to the bullet-riddled rental. She rushed over to help him out of the SUV, but he was already on his feet, meeting her at the front of the vehicle.

"Give me the keys," he said. "I'll head to Fairbanks. There's no need to involve your family in this."

"Don't be an idiot." She stubbornly pocketed the keys. "You heard Pike. You're one of us now." She took his good arm and pulled. He stayed rooted in his spot.

"Raven—"

"So help me, don't give me this crap. Move."

He looked at her in surprise. "Are you going to ground me if I don't?"

"You don't want to find out."

He gave her a slow smile. "Actually, I think I might."

"Aren't you a funny man? Come on." She opened the door and dragged him right through the lodge into the family kitchen, ignoring the looks they received from guests lounging around the main room. "Sit." She pulled out a chair and waited for him to take a seat.

"This isn't necessary," he said, still standing.

"That's enough." She poked him in the chest with her finger. "I'm not buying the tough guy act. You can pretend all you want, but you need me right now."

He grabbed her hand before she drilled a hole in his chest. "I've always needed you, Raven" he whispered, his heart pumping hard.

Something soft flickered in her eyes before she blinked. She pulled her hand free and reached for the phone.

He fell into the chair with a groan as she called Eva. When she finished, she refused to meet his gaze, instead busied herself by grabbing the first aid kit from the cabinet, setting it on the table, taking out peroxide, bandages, and scissors. A cold sweat beaded on his forehead as he took in the items.

"Do you want a stiff drink before we take your coat off?"

He shook his head. What he needed was to know what her look had meant. "We should move out of the kitchen for this. Is my room still free?"

"No. The lodge is full. A snow machining group came in for the weekend." She reached over to help him struggle out of his coat, all business. She worked the parka easily free of his left arm and then started on the right. Blood had soaked into the dark fabric, making it wet and sticky. "Are you sure the bullet just grazed you?" she asked, her voice catching.

Aidan closed his eyes for a moment of strength as they worked the material down his arm. The arm had been a dull throb, now without the coat, the wound started to pulse with pain. "Not totally."

"You're going to need a new parka."

"I didn't get my money's worth out of this one. Think Tiny Tom will give me a discount as a repeat customer?" he asked, trying to lighten the mood. It didn't work as she saw the wound.

"Oh, Aidan." She cut at the fabric of his shirt with the scissors, revealing the extent of the damage. "Why don't you rethink that drink?" She swallowed.

Aidan glanced at his arm. Blood slowly bubbled out of the ragged edges of torn flesh. He turned away. "Damn, I shouldn't have looked." He clenched his jaw.

"Where the hell is Eva?"

He heard tears in her voice. She went to work on the buttons of his shirt, and he watched her face. Her eyes were focused on her movements as her fingers carefully slid open each button, but he caught the tightening of her mouth, her ragged breathing. Realization warmed his insides. She was scared. Scared *for him*.

"Hey." He caught her hands. "I'm going to be fine." He smoothed back the loose strands of dark hair that had escaped her braid, and cupped her jaw. "Everything's going to be fine."

Her lower lip trembled, and a tear blinked to run unfettered down her cheek. "You could have died out there today."

His heart thumped so hard in his chest, he felt something break free. Gently he kissed her lips, tasting the salt of her tears. Tears for him. Her lips quivered under his, and then she was clutching the sides of his face, her mouth pressing harder against his. He groaned and pulled her down to sit on his lap.

"Well," Eva snickered, bustling into the room, a smile splitting her face as Raven jumped out of his arms, a blush firing in her cheeks. "Glad to know the bullet didn't slow you down." She took in Aidan's condition, a frown replacing the grin. "I hope patching you up isn't going to become a full time job."

Lynx and Pike followed in Eva's wake. Raven backed up out of the way, moving to lean against the counter. Her eyes hooded as though what had just happened between them, had shaken her up more than the events of the day.

"What's this I hear about you getting shot?" Pike asked, all bite and bluster. He already had his forty-five holstered on his hip. "Raven, you okay?"

"F-fine." Her eyes narrowed over the firepower. "Lynx, you too?"

Lynx caressed the rifle resting barrel-up on his shoulder. "Fill us in, so we can get the son of a bitch."

"No one is going out there," Aidan said. His tone brooked no arguments. Not that anyone seemed to hear it.

"Son, we take care of our own around here," Pike said. "Someone running around with murder on his mind will get more than they bargained for."

"You don't understand Roland." Aidan winced as Eva poked around his wound. "You won't find him. The law's been looking for him for months, and he's eluded them. This is my problem, and I won't have anyone else getting injured." Slivers of dread needled down his spine at the idea of any of them hurt because of him.

"We'll get together a search party and flush out the bastard," Lynx said, a glint of adventure in his eyes.

Aidan found it hard to swallow. No one had ever stuck up for him before. Having Lynx and Pike willing to take up his fight caused a tightening in his chest.

"Aidan!" Lana ran into the kitchen, Peter on her heels. "I heard you were hurt." She gasped when she saw him. "What happened?"

"Nothing." Aidan pointed at the door. "I'd appreciate it if you would stay with Peter and wait for me."

"It was Dad, wasn't it? Oh, God." Tears filled her eyes, and she cried, "You promised me you wouldn't leave the lodge."

"Peter, get her out of here," he growled through clenched teeth as Eva poked at his wound. Why the hell was there so many people crowding around him? Emotions battered him from all sides. He wished all he had to concentrate on was shutting down the pain from his injury.

"Come on, Lana." Peter wrapped his arms around her and pulled her to the door. He addressed Aidan, "We need to talk when you're through."

Aidan shook his head. "There are too many people in my damn business." He stared at Pike and Lynx. "Put away the weapons. It's snowing too hard out there. Any tracks Roland would have left are covered up by now. The man was in Special Ops in Vietnam. You won't find him unless he wants you to." Eva poured disinfectant on the wound, and he jumped in pain. "Shit, Eva. You could have warned me."

"Wouldn't hurt any less if I did." She reached into her bag of tricks and prepared a syringe.

"What's that for?" Aidan paled.

"You need stitches. Doesn't bother me if you don't want the area deadened, but you'd probably prefer it."

Sweat broke out on his forehead. "Shoot me up."

Eva gave him a sadistic smile. The woman enjoyed her profession a little too much.

Raven leaned back against the counter, spent now that the adrenaline had drained out of her. Pike and Lynx plotted, while

Eva stitched the gunshot wound on Aidan's bicep. All she could think about was that Aidan could have died out there today. They both could have. She didn't want him dead. She didn't even want him gone anymore.

Suddenly he glanced up, and their eyes met. He raised his brows in concern. She tried to smile and reassure him that she was fine, but the effort fell flat. It would be so much easier if he wasn't concerned for her. He was the one who'd gotten shot. He should be worried about himself.

"There," Eva proclaimed. "A shot of antibiotics and that ought to do it." Eva finished wrapping a bandage around the doctored wound and then went for another needle. "You were damn lucky. A few inches to the right—"

"Thanks, Eva," Aidan interrupted.

"No thanks needed. Having you around is honing my skills." She flashed a toothy grin and shot him with the hypodermic. "I'd hate to get rusty." She gathered up her supplies and meticulously put them back into her bag. With that done, she lowered onto a seat and rubbed her belly. "Lynx, you and Pike will wait to do anything until the weather improves. I don't need any more patients under my care this close to term."

Lynx knelt next to Eva's chair and wrapped an arm around her. "Are you feeling okay? The baby?"

She leaned into his shoulder. "We're fine, but we don't need to be worrying about the two of you going off half-cocked." She caught Raven's eye, a twinkle in hers.

Raven smiled, relieved. They needed to get the men focused on something else. "Pike, do you know if there are any shirts here that would fit Aidan? He'll also need another coat until we can get to town. Fox and Chickadee will be home from school soon, and I don't want them to see the results of what happened today."

"Good thinking," Pike said. "I'll find some clothes." He made to leave.

"Stow the weapons too." Raven indicated Lynx's rifle. Lynx reluctantly handed it over to Pike with a pout. "After the kids are taken care of, we can sit down and make a plan."

Eva nodded and patted Lynx's arm. "Would you help me find a place to lie down and rest for a while."

Lynx gathered his pixie wife up into his arms. "I knew you were overdoing it." He carried her out of the kitchen leaving Raven and Aidan alone.

Raven felt the burn of Aidan's gaze as she slowly put away the first aid kit and cleaned the kitchen. Pike returned with a flannel shirt and parka. Aidan thanked him, and he left.

"Where's Fiona?" Aidan asked, carefully sliding his injured arm into the borrowed shirt.

"Fairbanks. Gran had an appointment."

"Is she okay?"

Raven grinned. "Once a month, Gran meets with a group of friends who are concerned over protecting the habitat of the mosquito."

"Excuse me?" His brows shot up in disbelief.

"They get together and drink Bloody Marys in sympathy of the mosquitoes' plight."

Aidan laughed, though it didn't break the tension that weaved through the room like the electric currents of the Northern Lights.

"You can't stay out at Earl's anymore," Raven said. "You don't have any firewood, and—"

"I'm not arguing with you."

"—you'll stay at my place," she finished.

"What?" He paused in buttoning his shirt.

"You heard me." She folded her arms across her chest.

"No." He shook his head, his mouth tightening into a hard line. "I won't put you and Fox in harm's way."

"Your uncle is a coward. He'll wait until you're alone."

A reluctant grin crossed his face. "I'd love to see Roland's face hearing you call him a coward." Then he sobered. "You don't want me staying with you."

She looked at him from under her lashes. "You don't know what I want."

His hot eyes flicked to hers, and he made to get out of his chair just as a wide-eyed Fox barreled into the room.

"Dad?"

Raven's heart tripped. *Dad?*

"What happened to your Tahoe?"

"Uh…big rock hit the windshield."

"Then how'd you get a bullet hole in the rear fender?"

Aidan shared a look with Raven, and then turned back to Fox. "You're too smart for your own good."

Fox pulled up a chair. "What happened."

Raven joined them at the table. "Fox—"

"No more secrets, Mom." He tightened his lips, his eyes those of an adult and not a boy.

Raven shared another look with Aidan. "Okay, no more secrets. Aidan, you want to start?"

Aidan blanched. "Me?"

"Welcome to parenthood." She couldn't help the smirk. Parenting wasn't for wimps.

Aidan cleared his throat and hesitantly started the afternoon events with seeing the smoke from the woodpile. He kept glancing at Raven to see if he was doing okay. The man was as nervous as an arctic hare staring down a pack of ravenous wolves.

She had to give it to him. He downplayed the shooting and focused on the moves that had brought them to safety, even going so far as to compliment her on her NASCAR driving skills. She gave him a nod of approval.

Aidan wiped the sweat from his brow.

"So, you'll be okay?" Fox asked, glancing at Aidan's arm.

"I'll be fine. Eva will make sure of it."

Fox planted his elbows on the table. "Okay, so what's the plan?"

The plan sucked.

Aidan fell back in his chair. How did he get these people out of his life? Being a loner wasn't so bad. Why had he always wished for a large, caring family? They were noisy, opinionated, and they were going to get themselves killed.

All because of him.

He wouldn't have it.

They'd crowded into the kitchen, the whole clan, except Chickadee who'd been sent away with a frustrated Fox, and Gran, who was tipsy from her mosquitoes' plight party. Peter and Lana had been invited to join in the scheming.

"We need to call Garrett," Peter repeated.

"No troopers," Aidan said. Besides, he'd had more than enough of Garrett last summer.

"You were shot at," Peter stressed, holding Lana's hand. "When do *you* think we should bring in the troopers?"

"I'm the law here," Lynx injected. "We'll catch him and then we'll turn him over to the troopers in Fairbanks."

Lana smothered a sob.

"You okay?" Aidan asked, concerned that this was too much for his young cousin.

"I know he needs to be caught." Lana put a hand to her brow. "It's just hard thinking of my dad being hunted down. But we can't let him hurt anyone else."

"Is there any information you can give us that would help apprehend him safely?" Lynx asked, his tone a bit softer than before.

"Uhm...I don't know." She bit her bottom lip. "They called him a ghost in Vietnam."

"We'll have to flush him out then," Pike said. "I'll gather some guys and we'll come in from the top of the hill behind Earl's." He pointed to a map Lynx had laid out on the table earlier.

"He's got to be bunked down in one of the old mining cabins." Lynx indicated the nest of cabins abandoned in the late 1950s when the Fairbanks Gold Mining Company left the area after stripping seventy million dollars worth of gold from the surrounding hills and rivers. "We can access this point with snowmobiles, and then hike in on snowshoes. If we spilt up, and some come down the ridge, and the rest can come up the hill, we'll trap him. There's plenty of cover with the dense spruce. He'll never see us coming."

"He'll have booby traps in place to warn him of intruders," Aidan cautioned. They were crazy if they thought they could flush Roland out. The more planning that went on, the worse Aidan felt. Someone was going to get hurt. He didn't need that on his conscience too. "Roland is mean and methodical. He won't care if he hurts someone. Any booby traps he's laid—and don't doubt that he's set them—will be nasty, designed to hurt and maim."

"I don't want to patch up a whole bunch of hotheads," Eva said, with a frown, her arms folded and resting on top of her swollen belly.

Aidan's arm throbbed. All he wanted to do was crawl away to somewhere quiet and lick his wounds. Raven sat to his left. She hadn't added anything to the plan. In fact, Aidan couldn't remember the last time she'd said a word. Today had been hard on her too. Physically she wasn't hurt, but what kind of emotional damage had been done? Hadn't he given her enough grief?

She must have felt him watching as she looked up, her eyes wide pools of fear. His heart clenched. Once again he was bringing pain and heartache her way.

"That's enough for tonight," he interrupted. "It's late. Roland will expect something come morning after today's shooting. Let's surprise him and not do anything for the next twenty-four hours."

"You sure that's a good idea?" Lynx furrowed his brows. "That will give him a day to plan, or leave town."

"He isn't going anywhere until he does what he came here to do."

Lana gasped. "You mean he isn't leaving until you're—"

Aidan reached over and covered her hand with his. "I told you, nothing's going to happen to me."

"You mean nothing more, right?" Raven added, looking as worried as Lana.

"Aidan's got the right of it," Pike said. "We'll reconvene tomorrow. Lynx and I'll gather some reinforcements. We'll meet back here at sunrise."

The group broke up. Lana gave Aidan a hug with a whispered, "I love you," and then followed Peter out of the room. Raven stayed behind.

"How's the arm?" she asked.

He opened and closed his fist. It throbbed, but he was thankful that was all he was dealing with at the moment. Things could have turned out much worse. "I'll be fine."

"We should get you some anti-inflammatories and then to bed."

"About that." He rubbed the back of his head. "Staying out at your place isn't a good idea. In fact, I should head to Fairbanks and get a motel room."

"Don't be stupid. You aren't going anywhere." Her eyes hardened. "I want you where I know you're okay. And I don't want to hear any more arguments about it." She stood. "Now, it's been a long day, and I'm tired. So if you don't mind, I'll find Fox and meet you out front." She left him sitting in the kitchen.

Well, he'd sure been told. A smile teased the corner of his mouth. He liked this bossy side of Raven. Wonder if she'd ever show that side of herself in the bedroom?

That was not a thought he needed to be having at the moment. Not when he'd be sleeping under her roof.

CHAPTER TWENTY

They entered Raven's home to the smells of a moose roast simmering in the Crockpot. The whole cabin was warm and inviting, so different than living out at Earl's or his own sparse, silent apartment in Seattle.

Raven hung up her coat and entered the kitchen, opened a cabinet and pulled out a bottle of pain pills, laying them along with a glass of water on the table. "Sit down before you fall down."

Since his knees felt like willow branches, he had no problem doing what he was told and took a chair at the dining room table. Fox gave him a worried look, so Aidan put on a brave front. No sense in worrying the kid.

"Fox, will you stoke the fire and then set the table?" Raven asked, pulling the makings for a salad out of the refrigerator.

"On it, Mom." He scampered over to the wood stove and stirred the banked coals, added wood, and lightly blew on the coals until the flames greedily ate at the dry timber. A grin spread over his face, and a dimple peeked as he set the table. The boy was enjoying having his parents sharing a meal instead of fighting.

At the lodge, the feelings Aidan had struggled with over everyone wanting a say over how they were going to protect him, hadn't eaten at his heart the way this little family dinner was beginning to. This was his family. His son. And his woman. The simple affair caused emotions to tighten his throat.

What would it be like to sit down at the end of every day with Raven and Fox? The sweetness of the dream was just within his reach, almost tangible. If he shut his eyes, it felt as though he could hold it in his grasp.

Whatever it took, whatever he had to do, he would keep them safe.

They ate dinner. Fox carrying on most of the conversation, leaving him free to steal glances across the table at Raven, who was more focused on stirring the food on her plate than eating any of it. The longer dinner went the more pleased Fox seemed to become. The talk was mostly about school, friends, a girl named Janette.

After dinner was cleaned up and put away, Fox suggested a movie. Raven agreed, as soon as his homework and chores were finished. He grumbled, but went upstairs to do as she'd said.

"He's a great kid." Aidan approached Raven in the kitchen where she was trying to rub off the surface of the counter. She'd already washed everything down once. She stopped her frantic cleaning and looked up at him, her eyes wide and dark.

"You've done a wonderful job raising him, Raven." He set aside the scrubber and took her hands in his. "Thank you."

"Uh...you're welcome," she softly returned.

He smoothed the hair away from her face, tracing the fine bones of her cheeks, before cupping her cheek and lightly placing a kiss on her full trembling lips.

"Oops," Fox said, sliding to a flailing stop on socks that wanted to skate over the kitchen tile. A blush bloomed on his face along with a smile that spilt from ear to ear. He looked down and rushed through the kitchen. "Don't mind me. Carry on with…whatever. I'm gonna feed the dogs."

"Let me help," Aidan offered.

"No!" Fox's blush deepened. "I mean, you need to be careful with your arm." He put his hands out in the form of stop signs. "Stay here. With Mom." He was out of the room in a flash.

"Well…" Aidan smiled. "I think we just made his night."

"Uh…yeah. I'd better go talk to him." She made to leave and he pulled her back against him.

"Let him go. Stay here…with me," he repeated Fox's words.

"This isn't right. There is still so much that we need to figure out. I don't want to get his hopes up."

"What about mine?" He held his breath.

"I'm sorry." She disentangled herself from him and went after Fox.

Raven let herself outside into the bitterly cold night. Fox's dogs were yipping excitedly over their dinner. Fox made sure he gave each one needed attention before moving to the next one. He sure was a great kid. What had she been thinking to insist Aidan stay with them? She should have thought about the message she was sending Fox. Or what her actions were telling Aidan. For that matter, what were they telling *her*?

What did she really want?

Dinner had given her a glimpse of what she could have. What she could give Fox.

What would it be like to share her life with both of them? But could she find it in her heart to share Fox? He'd been hers for so long. Her little man. Looking at him now though, he wasn't her little man anymore. He was growing up fast. And not just physically.

"Hey, Fox." She joined him and the dogs. He looked up, the joy on his face dimming.

"We're not having a 'talk,' are we?" He frowned.

Yep, the boy was growing up way too fast.

"'Fraid so."

"Dang it, Mom, have you ever heard the saying, 'go with the flow?'"

She snorted. "Yeah."

"Well, then you ought to apply it with Dad." He absently rubbed the fur behind Senyea's ears. "I know you want to tell me that kiss I interrupted didn't mean anything, but we both know it did. I'll promise to not see too much in it, if you don't overanalyze everything. 'Kay?"

"Whatever happened to having adult/child conversations with you?"

"One of us has to act the adult when the other doesn't."

"Hey."

Fox looked at the snow-covered ground for a moment. "Sorry. It's just..." He straightened his hat. "I'm frustrated, I guess. I know you love him. I just don't understand why you won't admit it."

The kid was too observant. "It's complicated."

"So's math, but I'm making an effort."

She laughed. How did she argue with him? Did she even want to? "Come on. Let's go watch that movie you wanted to."

"So, I'm not going to get the 'talk'?" He narrowed his eyes.

"Nope."

"Why not?"

"What? Disappointed? You want to have it now?"

"No. But why did you change your mind?"

"Maybe I want to try that 'go with the flow' thing you were talking about."

He studied her for a moment. "You're as confused as I am, aren't you?"

"More so, I'm afraid."

Aidan paced in front of the view in Raven's living room. It was late. Fox and Raven had been in bed for hours. He'd given up tossing on the pull-out sofa and donned his jeans, leaving his shirt draped over the back of the couch.

More was keeping him awake than the thought of Raven a few feet down the hall. There needed to be a new plan, one that didn't include members of the Maiski clan. This was Harte business, and a Harte would be the one who'd finish it.

One way or another.

"You're going to wear a path in my wood floors." Raven's low voice drifted over the darkened living room.

He stopped and turned, his heart thudding hard in his chest at the outline of her in the dim room. The snow glowed out the window, reflecting the moonlight and the Northern Lights dancing across the midnight sky, but they weren't strong enough to strip the shadows that hovered between them. "Did I wake you?"

"No." She glided farther into the room, just on the fringes of the magical moonlight. He made out her soft shape wrapped in a robe, her bare feet. "I couldn't sleep. I'm afraid of what you're planning."

"What makes you think I'm planning something?"

"You're a man, aren't you? Actions first, consequences later."

He wondered what her consequences would be if he closed the space between them? "I don't want anyone hurt because of me."

"So you'll go alone?"

He nodded. She'd find out eventually.

"You are many things, Aidan, but I never figured you for stupid."

The stupid comment stung, but didn't deter him. "If I can get Roland alone, I might be able to reason with him."

"Since when are any of the Hartes reasonable?"

That stung deeper than the stupid remark. "You think I'm being unreasonable?"

"Yes."

"You'd rather more of your family get hurt or killed because of mine?"

The silver moonlight reflected off her pale face, pain shown like slivers of ice in her eyes. Instead of retreating, she took another step forward. "I don't want you hurt or killed either."

"Don't do this," he growled, fisting his hands in order to keep from reaching for her. "Don't come in here looking all soft and welcoming unless you want me to take you up on the invitation."

"How's the arm?" she asked changing the subject.

"Feeling less pain than my heart," he ground out.

She swallowed. "Do you want me to leave?"

"What do you want, Raven?"

"I'm not sure." She bit her lip. "Can we just...go with the flow?"

He gave a short, disbelieving laugh. "Go with the flow?"

"Uhm...yeah."

"Last time we did that, you ended up pregnant."

"Well, we could go with the flow...protectively." Her blush bloomed like sweet, pink rosehips in the faint moonlight. He couldn't help finding her irresistible.

"Are you asking me to share your bed, Raven Maiski?"

The roses in her cheeks deepened. "I'd rather you quit with the questions and sweep me up in your arms."

"Not this time. I don't want you to have any regrets."

"I've never regretted making love with you."

"Don't." He swallowed. "I won't survive if you tell me to leave again."

"I don't think I'd survive it either," she whispered.

One long step and he hauled her into his arms, ignoring the pain the action caused his wound as he stretched his stitches. He pressed his face into her neck, breathing in her scent like a drowning man. The exotic mix of berries, ferns, and Mother Earth on her freshly washed skin brought a burning ache to his center. Tangling his hand in her hair, he pulled her head back, holding her still as he took in her beautiful face, the sharp cheekbones of her ancestry, the dark almond eyes lowered seductively, and the slightly parted full lips. Her pulse fluttering in her throat was the only movement she made as she waited wrapped in the tight circle of his arms.

Slowly, ever so slowly, he leaned down and gently brushed her lips with his. A rough, impatient sound escaped her, stealing his breath. Was she as desperate for him as he was for her? He deepened the kiss, pushing through the seal of her lips to stroke the inside of her mouth. Tightening his arms around her, he pressed her body flush against the hard, throbbing length of his.

A raw sound of pleasure mixed with pain broke from him. "God, Raven, how have I lived without you in my arms?"

Her chest rose and fell, and her pulse beat like hummingbird's wings. "There's been no one in my arms since you left."

Her declaration stunned him. "No one?" *She'd been with no other man except him?*

"Only you. There's only been you." She bit her lips as though she was scared of revealing so much.

"Raven." He cupped her face in his hands and laid his forehead against hers, swallowing the lump of emotion threatening to strangle him. "I've never stopped loving you," he whispered. "Lord knows I tried." He pressed his lips against hers, overwhelmed with the feelings coursing through his system.

She broke the kiss and reached for his hands that still held her face. Then she led him down the hall and into her bedroom, shutting and locking the door behind them. The room also had a wall of windows that looked out to the frozen river, illuminating the bed in magical moonlight.

Could he be dreaming? She stood before the large queen size, roughly carved, log bed, looking magical herself with her long black hair shimmering with shots of silver and midnight. She slowly opened her robe, letting it fall to her shoulders, and then dropping to puddle at her feet. She wore a silky, flimsy piece of cloth that his trembling hands would tear off her if he wasn't careful.

She reached out her hand, palm up, and he stepped closer taking her hand in his and lacing their fingers together.

"I don't want to rush," he said, his tone reverent. "We've never made love without having to hurry. For that matter, we've never made love in a bed. The other day didn't count."

"Oh, it counted. If anything, it released the pressure of the last twelve years."

"Speak for yourself." He smiled. "I'm feeling enough pressure to fuel a trip to the moon."

Suddenly, she frowned. "What about your arm? Are you in a lot of pain?"

"The only pain I'm in will be relieved once I'm inside you."

"Well, then," she smiled a sexy grin, "I hate to see you hurting." She scooted onto the bed, and Aidan placed a knee on the mattress next to her hip and followed her down.

This was the way it should be, the way it should have been from the very beginning. They'd lost so much time. He swore to himself, then and there, that he would spend the rest of his life making up for the lost time.

Raven held her breath as Aidan loomed over her much like the black wolf that had surprised them earlier that day, saving their lives. Aidan was so big, so strong, so intense, and the gleam in his eyes had her swallowing hard. She felt like he would devour her until he owned her soul. He already owned her heart. She'd given it too him twelve years ago and had never gotten it back. No wonder life seemed so pale and washed out without him in it. She'd barely been living. Going through the motions. Doing all that was required of her, but not taking care of herself. Not seeing to her needs. The man above her certainly seemed intent on seeing to each and every one of her needs.

She gasped as his rough hands slowly inched up the silk of her nightgown. Erotic shivers followed in the wake as fabric lightly dragged over her sensitive skin. This was so different than anything they'd done before. There was no time limit other than morning, which was many hours off. Hopefully that would be enough time to explore each other. She doubted it. Each moment they'd been together, had been stolen. Needs and desire were rushed in order to satisfy, leaving them anything but completely satisfied. She hummed as his hands cupped her bare breasts.

"Yes." She moaned. He molded, then lightly stroked around her nipples, inching ever closer to the taut peaks begging for him to lick, nibble, suck.

"So beautiful," he said, with a groan, taking a nipple into his mouth.

She arched her back, her hands going to his jean-clad behind, and pulling him closer to the junction of her thighs. She burned for him, needed him inside her assuaging the ache that had overtaken everything. She pulled at his jeans, trying to get them off. His hands reached out and grabbed hers.

"No, sweetheart," he said breathlessly. "The minute my pants are off, I'll be inside you."

"And that would be a bad thing?"

Aidan chuckled and dragged her nightgown up and over her head, leaving her wearing only her underwear. "Not yet." His eyes scanned down her body, his fingers looping into the thin elastic of her panties. "I have much more that I want to do to you." He stripped her last barrier down her legs and tossed them away. His smile promised all sorts of wicked things.

She moaned in anticipation. Then his mouth went to work, licking flames of pleasure up and down her body. He worshiped her with his tongue, her breasts, her stomach, and then he spread her thighs, and devoted his attention toward driving her insane. He entered her with his fingers, her hips arching off the bed, his tongue continuing to make her whimper as her body clawed toward the building climax.

Her fingers entwined in his dark hair as he pleasured her with his mouth. His tongue circled, flicked and then he sucked her clitoris into his mouth. She bucked as her body separated from her soul, his name a hoarse cry on her lips as she soared toward the shivery moon.

Slowly she drifted back to earth, back to Aidan. His hands caressed her, sliding long, lavish strokes over her sensitive skin.

"You okay?" he asked, nuzzling the underside of her breast.

"Uh-hmm," she hummed. "I'm fine. *Very fine.*"

He chuckled, the vibrations causing shivers to erupt on her skin. Would she ever get enough of this man?

"We have a slight problem," he said, palming her breast as he kissed her nipple.

"What problem?" How could there be a problem, when everything finally felt so right.

"Your 'go with the flow protectively' is in jeopardy. I know we already let the dog off the leash last time. But we shouldn't take the chance. I don't have any way of protecting you."

She felt the heat of a blush infuse her whole body. How could she be a mother of an eleven, almost twelve year old, and still blush like a school girl? "I have some," she whispered.

Aidan lifted his head and met her eyes, cocking an eyebrow. "You bought condoms?"

"Uh…no. Tern made me take them."

He ducked his head, trying to hide a smile. "Where are they?"

She pointed to the clothes she'd tossed onto the back of a chair. "Front pocket of my overalls."

He was up and off the bed in a flash, rummaging through her pocket and coming up with the square box Tern had thrown at her earlier. Had that only been this morning? Then he was back, a triumphant smile on his face. "We are going to have to do something very special for your sister. And later, much later, I want to hear how she came about giving you these."

Raven's blush deepened, but she ignored it. Instead, she rose to her knees, taking the box from him. She opened it, trying to look sophisticated, and failing as she struggled to free one of the foil wrappers. She flipped it around her fingers, and glanced at him, uncertain. "I don't know how these work," she whispered. "I know what they do, but not the mechanics of getting them on."

His grin got wider. "We'll just have to practice until you get it right."

She lost the blush and shared his smile. Everything between them had always been easy, comfortable. Aidan had not only been her first love, he'd been her best friend. She pushed him back onto the bed, being careful not to bump his injured arm. "My turn."

He answered with a groan of eagerness.

It was her turn to drive him insane and she went about it like the artist she was. She skimmed her fingers over his sensitive skin, and kneaded those parts that weren't, until he growled for her to hurry. If anything she slowed. Savored the control, the feelings she brought out in him, until she had him panting, begging.

He hissed as she scorched her nails over his stomach. Purposely, she fumbled around the zipper of his jeans, until he swore and pushed her hands away, tearing off his jeans.

"Now," he growled, taking her hips in his hands.

"Condom, remember?"

"Shit." He threw his head back against the pillow, closed his eyes and exhaled out of his flared nostrils. "Give me a minute."

Now why should she give him a minute, when he hadn't spared her any?

She was turned on more than she ever thought she would be by taking control. She opened the foil wrapper and took out the flimsy, thin condom, and then looked at Aidan's thick, pulsing erection.

How the hell was *this* supposed to cover *that*?

Being ever so careful, Raven placed the condom on the tip of Aidan's penis. He jerked, and his hands fisted. "Raven," he said in a ragged breath. "I need some time."

"Time's up." She fumbled in her attempts to roll the slick condom down his hot, throbbing shaft.

Aidan swore again, and pushed her hands out of the way. In one expert move, he sheathed himself, flipped her over onto her back and entered her.

Her breath escaped in a whoosh as her body tried to adjust to his hard penetration.

"I'm sorry," he said, thrusting into her. "Next time. We'll. Practice." Then he was lost in her body, grabbing her hips as he plunged into her, their joined bodies automatically lining up their tattoos.

Raven melted around him, relishing that she'd made the man she craved lose control. Next time she was taking top position. Just knowing that there would be a next time had her inner muscles contracting. Aidan moaned, and his thrusts increased. The veins on his neck protruded, the muscles in his shoulders and arms flexed. And then he was grinding against her as he climaxed, her name a guttural prayer on his lips.

She took off in flight right after him.

They'd used up Tern's box of condoms before they were sated with each other. Raven's body still twitched from the electrical overload of so much pleasure. If she put her mind to it, she swore she could levitate. Aidan lay next to her, sprawled out on the bed, breathing heavy.

"You okay?" she asked.

"I think you've killed me."

She leaned up on her elbow and twirled a finger around his taut nipple. He was beautiful in the moonlight cascading through her windows. His dark hair on her pillow, his naked body taking up most of her bed, felt so right.

"I've ascended onto another plane of existence." He turned to look at her, wonder in his eyes. His hand came up to cover her fingers, splaying their clasped hands over his heart. "There's no other explanation for the level of happiness I feel right now."

Tears tickled behind her eyes and she had to duck her head to hide them. She kissed his knuckles where their hands were joined. "I have something for you." She reached over to the night table, and opened the drawer, taking out the leather choker she'd kept all these years, not able to throw it away even in her angriest moments. "You'll need this to help navigate your way."

She held up the leather braid, a hand-carved face of a timber wolf dangling as a talisman.

Reverently, he reached for the wolf his own mother had carved him as a boy, before the alcohol had taken its toll. "I never thought I'd see this again." He looked at her. "You kept it?"

She shrugged, emotions making it hard to speak. He'd given the necklace to her that last summer as a sort of promise ring. "I couldn't throw it away. The wolf is your totem, your protector." Sitting up, she opened the clasp. "You need to have it with you." She reached around his neck—he lifted his head to help her—and she secured the leather, smoothing the wolf in place to hang in the hollow of his collarbone. "Perfect, like it's home."

He caught her fingers, bringing them to his lips for a kiss. "Thank you."

Tears threaten again, so she snuggled down into his arms. He wrapped his good arm around her, bringing her in close to his heart. They stayed that way for a while and then Raven whispered, "Don't go alone."

He stilled. "Was this what tonight had been all about?" She stiffened, and he immediately responded, "Forget I said that. Please." Remorse was heavy in his voice.

"There's still a lot we need to learn about and forgive each other for, isn't there?"

He kissed her forehead, pulling her tighter against him. "Promise me, you'll give us time."

"I promise, as long as you promise not to get yourself killed."

He chuckled. "I promise. I suddenly have too much to live for."

She snuggled down into his arms, his body a warm, comforting blanket that soothed her into a deep, restful sleep.

When she woke, he was gone.

CHAPTER TWENTY-ONE

"Fox!" Raven yanked on her overalls and t-shirt, struggling into socks as she raced for the kitchen. "Fox, we overslept. Hurry!" She had to get him to school and then find Aidan. She searched the main room. No sign. No clothes lay about. He'd even put the sofa bed back together.

"Fox!" Where the heck was he? The cabin was silent, dead silent. She reached for the door of the fridge to pull out Fox's lunch and saw the note in Aidan's handwriting stuck under a salmon magnet.

Raven,

I took Fox to school after we fed the dogs. I couldn't make myself wake you, as you were sleeping so beautifully.

I love you,

Aidan

She glanced at the clock and growled. It was just after nine. If Aidan had planned on coming back after taking Fox to school, he would have been here by now. The blasted man had gone off to confront his uncle. She'd bet her life on it.

Damn it. Why were men so stupid and irrational? He'd promised her, just mere hours ago, that he wouldn't get himself killed. Fear coiled in like death whispers.

She didn't think. Just grabbed her dad's forty-five, loaded it, and headed for Earl's.

Aidan parked the rental a mile up the road and hoofed the rest of the way to Earl's cabin. He was going to settle this for good. He would protect his son, his woman, and her family. All the while trying not to give up his life in the process. After all, he'd promised. A grin flashed as he remembered the staggering love making he and Raven had shared last night. He didn't know when he had felt this happy, this hopeful. Dr. Foster had been correct. He'd needed to return to Chatanika, return to his past, make things right. Everything had been so wrong for so long.

Now he had to neutralize Roland, which seemed child's play compared to winning back Raven's heart.

He snuck up on the cabin, scanning the wilderness, listening for anything suspicious.

A ptarmigan cooed to his lover hidden in the underbrush. The sun still had a few hours until it would peak over the horizon. It was freezing, and the ice fog seeping up from the river valley was thick and ominous.

The cabin squatted in the shadows of the hill behind it. There was no sign of activity. No smoke coming from the chimney, no lights glowing through the curtain-covered windows. If someone was inside, he wouldn't be able to tell. But then Roland wouldn't know he was out here either. A level playing field.

He'd rather have an advantage.

Slipping to the cabin, he stayed next to the logs as he made his way to the back door. The soft powder of snowfall from the day before cushioned his footsteps. For once he didn't crunch through a frozen layer of ice-crusted snow.

He stumbled, almost triggering the thin fishing wire pulled taut across the path to the cabin. The meager light bouncing off the snow had caught the wire just right, glimmering iridescent for a second, before blending with the surrounding area. Aidan followed the wire with his eyes until he saw the cans hanging in the spruce branches. One brush of the twine and the cans would have pealed together like bells. Aidan carefully stepped over it, making sure there wasn't a backup poor man's doorbell.

He reached the back door and suddenly, his feet slipped out from under him. He fell hard and heavy, grunting as he hit, his injured arm taking the brunt of it. The crafty son of a bitch had iced the area by the back door. Aidan struggled to his feet, slipping again when he reached the stairs. Water had been poured over them too. His shoulder throbbed, and he felt wetness seep down his arm. He'd torn his stitches. Eva was going to make him pay for that.

He'd expected the alarm at the back door. It was set up much the way the other one had been. Only this time the cans were positioned to fall if the wire was brushed, clanging on their way down, most likely knocking the intruder out in the process. Aidan carefully disarmed the cans and then cut the wire strung across the door with his knife. He pocketed the knife in his jeans and pulled the magnum out of his waistband. Slowly, he turned the knob and slid the door open a crack without a sound. Deciding to grease the dirty, rusty hinges with WD40 a few days ago had been a stroke of genius. When nothing came at him, he inched the door opened far enough to peek inside.

The kitchen was empty, but he heard scraping from the other room. Silently, he entered the cold cabin, quietly closing the door behind him. He waited, barely breathing, but the sound didn't change from the other room, so he slinked farther into the space. When he reached the corner, he gave a quick glance into the living room.

There was Uncle Roland crouched down, pulling up the floorboards.

The last few months had not treated him well. He'd lost weight, but then being on the run from the law would do that to a person. He'd grayed more, too, and his skin had a yellow cast to it, like he'd upped his cigarette intake. If anything he looked meaner and leaner, with long, wiry muscles that gleamed menacingly in the dim lantern lighting.

"Find anything?" Aidan asked, enjoying Roland's jolt at being caught unawares.

His beady eyes swung to Aidan, scoffing at the gun he held in his hand. "Gonna kill me like you did your daddy?"

"Am I going to need to?"

Roland cackled. "Looks as though murdering a man has finally given you a backbone." He rose slowly to his feet, a plank of wood—bent nails sticking out of one end—gripped in his hand. "So, how do you want to play this?"

"I'm going to turn you over to the law."

He scoffed and rolled his black eyes. "Like that's gonna happen. I've forgotten your sense of humor."

"I'm not laughing." Aidan moved a few steps to the left, blocking Roland's path to the rifle he'd left out of reach, leaning against the cold wood stove. But there was still Earl's gun cabinet, fully stocked, at Roland's back. Aidan doubted the old man would be fast enough to arm himself from the cabinet before Aidan was on him, but he wouldn't put it past him. "Put down the wood. You're coming with me."

"The only way I'm going anywhere with you is if I'm dead." He cocked a brow. "You willing to kill me too?"

"Lana's here."

A spasm of pain crossed Roland's weathered features.

"She's real scared, Roland. For some reason she still loves you after all the crap you've put her through."

"Well…she's too tender-hearted. Too much like her mother. Nothing I can do about that."

"You don't care that your actions are causing her more pain?"

"She's plenty aware of what has to happen here. Not my fault if she doesn't like it. Besides, the blame lies at your feet. None of this would be happening if you hadn't gunned down my brother in cold blood."

"He didn't give me a choice," Aidan ground out, his grip tightening on the butt of the gun. "He would have killed Sonya." He knew Roland was pushing his buttons but couldn't seem to stop the anger and shame oozing like crude oil through his veins.

"You're telling me there wasn't something else you could've done?" His gleaming eyes met Aidan's. "There wasn't a part of you that wanted him dead?"

Guilt fed the anger and shame. He'd wanted Earl dead most of his life. Had wished it were Earl who had been killed in the car accident when he was a child rather than his mother.

"I knew it," Roland purred. "I've seen it on your face. You wanted him dead. Sonya was just an excuse."

Had he shot Earl because deep down that was the outcome he'd preferred?

The gun wavered in his hand, and before he could tighten his grip, Roland swung the wooden plank, hitting him square on his upper arm, right where he'd been shot. Pain flared like gas poured on a bonfire. Cursing, he dropped the gun and cradled his arm. The gun spun across the floor, falling into the hole Roland had created. Roland swung at Aidan again, the plank coming down on the side of Aidan's neck, the twisted nails in the wood cutting into his flesh. He stumbled to his knees.

Roland sneered, walking around Aidan. "I'd hope to see some fight in you. But this—" he gestured with the wooden plank at Aidan kneeling at his feet "—it's a good thing my poor brother isn't around to see the pathetic coward his own son has become."

"If I was a pathetic coward, Earl would be alive now."

Fury and grief mixed in Roland's muddy eyes. "You son of a bitch." He swung his leg out to kick Aidan in the kidneys. Aidan shifted just as Roland was off balance, grabbed his leg, and in one move had Roland on the floor, while he jumped back on his feet.

"Shit." Roland spat out of the side of his mouth, glaring up at Aidan. "Forgot about those fancy moves of yours."

"Might as well give it up, old man. You're only going to get hurt."

"Fuck that." Roland slashed out with a switchblade that he had hidden in the pocket of his cargo pants, cutting through the skin of Aidan's calf. The cut was deep enough to make Aidan lurch back, and gave Roland time to regain his footing.

They circled each other, Roland with the knife, Aidan with his fists. The guns lay forgotten as if they both wanted this to end personally.

"You should have killed me when you had the chance." Aidan swung out with his fist, connecting with Roland's steel jaw. His head jerked back, blood and spittle spraying from his cut lip.

"Yeah, really regretting that, right now." He flexed his jaw, his eyes full of death and hate. "You'd've been dead if it wasn't for that damned wolf leaping out of nowhere." He wiped the blood trailing down his chin, then parried quick with the knife, cutting into Aidan's borrowed coat, slicing through the fabric and into the flesh of his chest. Down feathers floated into the air.

"What about hitting me over the head?" Aidan swung right then left. Roland exchanged him swing for swing. Both were bleeding, their punches sliding on open skin more than connecting.

"If I'd had knocked you on your noggin, I'd've happily slit your throat." He lunged, blocking Aidan's right chop, and slicing left with the knife over Aidan's throat. Aidan caught his wrist just before the sharp blade would have connected with his jugular, and twisted his arm trying to get him to release the knife.

Aidan struggled to keep Roland in his grasp. "You didn't hit me over the head a few days ago?"

"Like I said, if I'd done that you wouldn't be here now. You got more than one man after ya?" Roland head-butted him, breaking the hold Aidan had on his arm.

Stars flickered in front of his eyes, and bells rang in his ears. Then he was flat on his back, Roland on top of him, the knife once again at his throat.

"Oh, this was too easy." Roland shook his head as though disappointed. "I haven't even broken a sweat."

Aidan swallowed, feeling the sharp blade cut into the skin of his neck.

"You know, I've watched you," Roland said. "I take it you finally figured out that you have a bastard son of your own." He scoffed. "I'm doing the kid a favor by killing you. All you've brought to people is pain and death. First your mother, your father. Sonya and her family, and look what ya did to that poor Maiski girl. Murdered her father too."

"I didn't murder Raven's father." His vision turned red.

"That's not how Earl told it. You bought the explosives."

"I didn't know what they were going to be used for."

"Ri-i-i-ght." He snorted. "Just like you had no idea when you set the charges who they were meant for."

Aidan growled and bucked Roland off, slamming the old man's hand down on the hard floor again and again until the knife went skidding under the couch. Then he punched him. Left. Right. "I did *not* kill him!"

Rage overtook him and he kept beating Roland even though the old man was no longer blocking his punches or fighting back. His hands were slick with blood as he battered his uncle.

A gunshot rang out.

He glanced up from Roland's bloody mug to find Raven lowering the forty-five she'd just shot into the ceiling. Her face was white with shock as she took in the sight before her.

Raven.

Bloodlust demanded that he end it. Finish Roland with his hands. Raven's pale, frightened face as she stared at him in sickening horror, had him reining in the beast.

He rose slowly to his feet, dread shaking the very ground he stood on. He stepped over Roland's prone body and moved toward Raven, coming up short when she slowly shook her head, her eyes wide and haunted in her colorless face.

Her gaze narrowed as though she was trying to see the real him. "Who are *you?*"

"Raven—"

"*You* bought the explosives? *You* set the charges?"

Oh God, how long had she been standing there? He vaguely remembered hearing bells when Roland head-butted him. Raven must have tripped the wire of Roland's poor man's door bell.

She pointed with the gun—he knew she wasn't aware she still held in her hand—to Roland on the floor. "Is he dead? Did you kill him too?" she whispered the last part.

His heart stopped at the look of condemnation in her eyes. *Did you kill him too?* echoed through the cavity of his chest, stopping his heart. Aidan looked down at Roland. Oh God, had he killed him? He knelt and felt for a pulse. It was there, steady and strong, like the crafty and resilient wolverine that he was. A groan escaped Roland, but he didn't open his eyes, just lay there a bloody and bruised mess.

"He's alive," Aidan said.

"You would have killed him if I hadn't stopped you. You would have beaten him to death with your own hands." Horror reflected in her face over the reality of her statement.

Aidan had to look away from the fear and revulsion in her eyes. He'd been caught up in a rage so destructive that he knew she was right. "He was trying to kill me, Raven. I had to defend myself."

"He's an old man, twice your age." She gestured to Roland again, in support of her argument. "You had him on the floor. He wasn't fighting you."

Where had she been a few minutes earlier? "This isn't just *his* blood I'm wearing. Don't feel sorry for Roland."

"This is why I never told you about Fox. This Harte rage." She shook her head and tears filled her voice. "Why did I think we could ever work it out? My dad was right."

"Raven—" Aidan reached out a hand—a hand coated with Roland's blood.

She stepped away from him, her gaze glued on his bloody hands. "No. I can't. I can't do this." She shook her head as though to convince herself.

"Raven, I love you. I love Fox. Please—"

"Stay away from Fox." He felt the slap of her resolve in her hard voice. She'd retreated from him farther in more than just distance. "How could I be with the man who was responsible for killing my father? What was I thinking?"

"Please, Raven. You have to listen to me. I didn't kill your father. I love you. You promised to give us time," he pleaded, his heart tearing along the newly mended seams. "Don't do this."

"Our time was never meant to be. Whether you actually caused Dad's death doesn't matter, you put into motion the things that did." She glanced at Roland's body and then at Aidan, her eyes sad, yet full of resolve. "Stay away from us." She turned and walked out of the cabin. The silence was like a death peal, killing any hope of a future he might have had with her and Fox.

"Well." Roland groaned. "That was fun." He slurred the words out the opposite side of his spilt lip. "Guess there are worse things than death, aren't there, boy?" He slowly got to his feet, wincing at the action.

Numb, Aidan turned to look at him. Roland's right eye was already swollen shut, but there was a twinkle of wicked glee in his left. "How long have you been conscious?" Aidan asked.

"Like you had the chops to knock me out. After that little scene, you'd probably welcome death if I offered it, wouldn't ya? Think I prefer you living with this outcome. At least for now."

Roland reached for the rifle leaning against the wood stove and tipped the barrel of the gun Aidan's direction before pulling it back to rest on his shoulder. "See ya around, sucker. Oh, and I'll be back for the gold. I figure it'll be safe. Not like you have a need for it since your reason for living just dropped you like the pile of shit you are." He cackled and then spat blood from his mouth onto the floor at Aidan's feet. "Pathetic bastard."

As Roland left, Aidan sank onto the cold, hard floor littered with blood splatters and snowy white feathers from his slashed coat. The emotional turmoil twisting loose inside him far outweighed any of his physical aches.

He wished Roland had put a bullet in him.

CHAPTER TWENTY-TWO

"There he is!"

Aidan heard voices come at him as though from the end of a long mine shaft. He sat huddled on the floor. Tired. So tired. Someone was pulling at him, checking his pulse.

How could he have a pulse when his heart had been ripped out of his chest?

"He's conscious. But not responding."

What the hell was Lynx doing out here?

"Shit, there's blood all over him, all over this dump. What the hell happened here?"

That sounded like Pike. Nice of the guys to show up. But then they didn't know. Soon they would. Raven would be sure to tell them. Guess, he wouldn't be one of the gang after all.

"Come on, Aidan. Talk to me." Lynx shook him. "Tell me what went down here."

Slowly, Aidan turned his head. Lynx inhaled when he saw his face. "She promised me, Lynx. Promised that she'd give us time."

"Who promised?" Lynx brows furrowed. "Raven?"

He nodded. His head became too heavy so he let it sag back to his chest.

Lynx shook him again. "Where are you hurt?"

"Hurt?" He laughed with no humor. "I'm in too much pain to hurt."

"Who did this to you, son?" Pike asked, kneeling down next to him. "Was it Roland? Is he dead?"

"Nope." Aidan shook his head. "Left."

"He *walked* out of here?" Lynx's voice was disbelieving as he took in the destruction.

"Yep. The bastard wouldn't kill me, neither. Not after Raven was here."

"We'd better get him to Eva," Pike said. "He's not making any sense."

They pulled him to his feet.

"No. Leave me here. I belong here."

"He's like ice," Pike said. "If we hadn't gone looking for him…"

"Let's get him back to the lodge. We'll figure everything out there."

Aidan's footing gave out, so they wrapped his arms around their necks and carried—dragged—him out of the cabin to Lynx's waiting pickup.

He must have dozed. The next thing Aidan knew he awoke to a nightmare. He really didn't see how this day could have gotten any worse. As near as he could tell he was laid out in the guest room he'd used previously, and Garrett Hunt was standing over him, his piercing blue eyes narrowed in his fish cop face.

"Fuck." Aidan shut his eyes hoping the man was a figment of his imagination. He peeked. Nope, still there.

Garrett's hard mouth tilted at the corners. "Couldn't have said it better myself." He cocked his head. "Trouble likes you, doesn't it?"

So did heartache it seemed. "What the hell are you doing here?" His sluggish mind connected the dots. "Peter?"

Garrett nodded.

"Where is he?"

"Hiding in the kitchen with the women."

The ache in chest, thumped. *Women?* "Sonya's here?"

Garrett nodded again and folded his arms across his muscled chest. "Want to fill me in on what happened this morning?"

"Not really."

"You understand that wasn't a question?"

"Yeah, yeah. I remember the drill." Aidan moved to sit up. Hell, he hurt. He had to give it up to Roland. The old man could sure land a punch.

"Do you need to do this now?" Eva asked, moving around Garrett.

Garrett's imposing frame had blocked Aidan from seeing Eva enter the room. But now that she was here, Aidan started to sweat.

Eva's pinched pixie face leaned over him from the other side of the bed. "Glad to see you're back with us."

"Go away," he mumbled. Great. Damn fish cop on one side and the demon nurse on the other. Next time they ran into each other Roland was going to answer for this too.

"Did you hear that? He told me to go away." Eva's voice was more concerned than outraged.

"He's been like that since we found him," Lynx spoke from the shadows, sitting in the rocking chair in the corner. "Damn fool had to be the hero and go off on his own. Do you think he was hit on the head? That would explain a lot."

Eva probed carefully around Aidan's neck and head with gentle fingers.

"I can answer for myself," Aidan said, moving away from Eva. Any minute now her soothing hands were going to dig in and make him hurt.

"Start talking then." Garrett leaned against the dresser, crossing his legs at the ankles. He looked relaxed as though he had all damn day to interrogate.

Aidan glanced between Eva—pulling a pair of scissors out of her black bag of torment—and Lynx who slowly rocked back and forth in the chair.

There was no way he was going to get out of reliving this morning's nightmare.

He addressed Garrett and tried to ignore Eva cutting another bloody, torn piece of clothing off of him. "How much do you already know?"

"Peter filled me in on everything up to the events of today."

"I went to find Roland. I didn't want anyone else getting hurt over Harte business."

Garrett tightened his jaw, obviously remembering the nightmare the Hartes had put him and Sonya through last summer. "I take it you found him."

"He was at Earl's, tearing the place apart looking for gold. I surprised him." And then Raven had surprised them both.

"Blast it, Aidan, you tore my stitches." Eva shook her head in disgust. "You have any idea how careful I was to keep the stitching even and neat so you wouldn't end up with a nasty scar?" She didn't seem to need an answer as she continued to swear under her breath, grabbing gauze and disinfectant.

He flinched when she went to work cleaning and repairing the wound.

"What happened?" Garrett asked, the corner of his mouth lifted in amusement as Eva worked on him. Lynx continued to rock silently in the corner, watching.

"The usual. Insults, punches, and then Roland pulled a knife."

"Weren't you armed?"

"We both were. Turned out we preferred to end it personally."

"What broke it up?" Lynx asked, quietly from his chair.

"Raven."

"Your sister, Raven?" Garrett clarified with Lynx, putting names and faces to all the players. Then he addressed Aidan. "Peter said you and her have history. A son together?"

He nodded. No way was he going into all this with Garrett. The man could arrest him for all he cared. He was not baring his soul, laying his dreams out for the damn fish cop to trample over again.

Garrett nodded as though understanding the past was off limits.

"What happened when Raven showed up?" Lynx asked, stopping the motions of the rocking chair.

Eva poked and pinched as she re-stitched his wound, but it wasn't as uncomfortable as answering Lynx's questions were going to be.

Aidan met Lynx's stare. "She overheard Roland egging me on. He brought up your dad's death." He paused to swallow. "Lynx, I was the one who bought the explosives for the bomb that caused the rockslide that killed your dad." Eva gasped, her movements stilled. Aidan gave that a moment to sink in before he continued, "I was also the one who planted the charges. But you've got to believe me, I had no idea what Earl was up to until it was too late. I'd bought explosives for him many times. If I'd known…"

Silence lay heavy like wet snow over the room. Eva got up and laid a hand on Lynx's shoulder, giving him emotional support. Garrett watched and cataloged like the cop he was.

"How did Raven take it?" Lynx finally broke the quiet.

"Not well. She's real angry and hurt. I don't blame her." He glanced down at his hands, bloody and bruised. Hands that would have beaten Roland to death if Raven hadn't fired that gun. "I had Roland on the ground and was...was going at him heavy with my fists. She told me to stay away from her and Fox." His voice ended on a hush. The reality that he'd lost everything in one flash of temper had him closing his eyes and wishing again that Roland had ended it all.

"Where's Roland now?" Garrett asked, obviously not willing to leave him in peace until he had all the facts. Besides, catching Roland was the reason Garrett would have traveled through the night to get here from the Peninsula. He wasn't here out of concern for Aidan.

"Took off. He figured leaving me alive, after I'd lost everything, was better than killing me."

"Did he find the gold?"

"No." Aidan opened his eyes and rolled his head toward Garrett. There was pity in the fish cop's eyes. "I doubt there's any gold. If there ever was, why hadn't Earl spent it? Chalk up another lie for the bastard."

"Are you done?" Eva asked Garrett. "I need to see to his other cuts and bruises." For once her voice was soft, compassionate. And it made him hurt worse.

"Do you need my help?" Lynx asked.

"No. I should be fine."

"Garrett, why don't I get you a cup of coffee?" Lynx stood and crossed the room.

"Thanks. That would be much appreciated. Aidan, I'll talk with you again later."

"Can't fucking wait." Then he shut his eyes and focused his energy on surviving Eva's ministrations.

"I'm going to give you a shot that will help you with the pain and allow you to sleep." She gently inserted the needle in his arm.

Fucking hallelujah.

Raven stared at her pottery wheel. It was silent, still, as was the room. She usually played a selection of oldies when she worked, using the soothing lyrics to help inspire her. But after what she'd witnessed this morning, inspiration seemed out of reach. Tears flooded her eyes. She wanted to throw up again.

Why hadn't he told her he'd bought the explosives? That he'd planted the dynamite that killed her father? Tears clogged her throat and blinded her.

Would they ever stop?

She'd done nothing but bawl since she'd left Aidan. It was a miracle she'd made it home without ending upside down in a snow bank.

Pain continued to burn a hole deep inside her chest. A hole that would never be filled, she realized with another wave of tears.

This was ridiculous. Sitting here gushing wasn't helping. She should return to the house and do the laundry. At least that would be productive. She wiped her hands on her towel and threw it onto the wheel.

Raven left the studio and wandered into the cabin. Again, silence greeted her. She missed Fox and his constant chatter, but she'd leaped when his friend Grand had offered an invitation for a sleepover. Fox would take one look at her and demand answers to questions she wasn't ready for.

A knock sounded, and her door opened. She froze and then fought disappointment when it was Lynx who entered. With everything that she'd witnessed, how could she still hope that it was Aidan coming home?

"Hey," Lynx said, coming into the kitchen after hanging up his coat. He glanced around. "Is Fox here?"

"No, he's spending the night with Grand."

"Good. We need to talk." He walked into the living room where he stood gazing out the window. "Have a seat," he ordered.

This was her house. If anyone was going to give orders it would be her. She folded her arms across her chest and stood her ground. "What's this about?"

"Do you love Aidan?"

She hadn't seen that coming. She took a seat.

He turned and nailed her with his 'take no crap' look. "Do you?"

"How is that any of your business?"

"Don't give me that shit. You're my sister, he was my best friend. What did you say to him today?"

"Why?" Dread and fear suddenly surged inside her. "Is he okay?"

"No, he isn't. Eva's going over him now. You never should have left him like that, Raven. If Pike and I hadn't gone looking for him, he'd probably be dead now."

"What happened?"

"You ripped out his heart and left him to bleed all over the goddamned floor. How could you do that? Haven't you blamed him enough?"

"What a minute." She caught her breath at the unprovoked attack and got to her feet.

"No, you wait. You sent him away twelve years ago when you knew, *you knew*, you were carrying his child. You kept Fox from him all these years. Blamed him for killing Dad, when you knew Earl had always used him like a pawn." He swore under his breath. "I even fell for it. I believed, too, and blamed him for things he didn't do. But what you did today was unforgivable."

"You didn't see him. He would have killed Roland with his bare hands." The killing rage in Aidan's eyes as he beat his uncle had replayed over and over in her mind all day. She'd seen the hate, the violence, the bloodlust the Hartes were famous for. She shied away from it all this time, not wanting those influences to touch Fox.

"I would have done the same thing in his place. He was protecting you. Fox. Us. Roland had promised to kill Aidan. Would you rather that he was dead instead of fighting for his life?"

"That wasn't fighting for his life. That was taking one."

"Have you ever been in a fight? Hand to hand combat? You're pumped with adrenaline. Drowning in testosterone. It's kill or be killed." Lynx took a breath and physically tried to calm down. "You're so afraid to lose the people you love that you would rather push Aidan away than risk losing him. You're frozen in the past, Raven. Dad's gone. Deal with it. And Aidan will be gone soon if you don't do something."

Raven took everything he said like a hit. Invisible punches landed in sensitive places. Places she didn't want to go, didn't want to acknowledge.

"I know Dad's death hit you hard, but—"

"You weren't at the hospital, Lynx. You didn't see Dad as he gasped for breath, his lung crushed. Bleeding to death internally. He...he made me promise," she finished weakly.

"What?" He walked up to her and firmly took her shoulders in his hands, his eyes boring into hers. "What did he make you promise?"

"That I...that I'd stay away from Aidan."

Chapter Twenty-Three

Raven entered the lodge by the back door of the kitchen. She shouldn't be here, but she couldn't concentrate on anything without knowing that Aidan was all right, regardless of what Lynx had said.

The kitchen was empty, which she was grateful for. She didn't want to talk to anyone. Hurrying through the great room without making eye contact with the guests milling about, she continued down the hall to the room Aidan had been using. Quietly, she opened the door and peeked in.

The room was dark. A beam of light from the hallway sliced a path to the bed where Aidan lay under the covers. He didn't move, so she let herself in, softly closing the door behind her. It took a moment for her eyes to adjust to the deep shadows. A faint beam of moonlight grazed through the snow-laden clouds, highlighting the bed from the window. She walked toward where Aidan laid, his chest bare, blankets folded down over his stomach. White bandages on his upper arm, neck, and chest glowed neon against his dark skin. His face wasn't relaxed in sleep, in fact, it didn't seem as though he slept at all, more as if he were past the point of exhaustion, beaten.

And she'd had a part in that.

It wasn't only Roland who had gotten in a few jabs. While hers hadn't left a physical mark, she'd done Aidan a fair amount of emotional damage.

She pulled the blankets up to his chin. His breathing was even and steady. Eva must have given him something to help him sleep. He had the appearance of someone heavily sedated. Raven sat on the edge of the bed, holding her breath when he moved his head toward her. She released a breath when he failed to shift again.

Silently, she sat, watching him. Her heart aching as it wanted to cradle him to her breast, curl up next to him and feel his warm body align with hers.

Was she doing the right thing?

She'd promised her dying father that she'd have nothing more to do with Aidan. But just twenty-four hours ago, she'd been in bed with him. He'd been inside of her. They'd each been a part of the other, sharing their bodies, their souls, giving the other new promises. She'd been ready to betray her dad's dying wish in order to grant Aidan's wishes and her own.

She wiped tears she wasn't aware she'd been crying from her cheeks.

"Raven."

She gasped as Aidan softly spoke her name. His eyes were closed, and it took her stumbling heart a moment to realize that he was still out cold. Could he be dreaming of her after she'd said such awful things to him?

There was so much to think about, and she was so very tired of thinking. Before she gave in and lay down next to him, she stood to leave. Not able to help herself, she smoothed back the lock of hair lying over his forehead. He needed a haircut. He just plain needed taking care of. Since he'd returned to Chatanika, he'd been caught in a trap, hit on the head, left to die in the cold, shot, and beaten.

And then she'd taken her turn.

Guilt weighed heavy on her shoulders as she opened the door and stole out of the room.

A woman with a scowl on her face was leaning across the hall obviously waiting for her. "So you're the one?"

"Excuse me?" Raven asked.

"The one Aidan never spoke of."

"Who are you?"

"Sonya."

Her eyes widened with surprise. This was the woman Aidan had asked to marry? Raven suddenly felt very plain in her overalls and old t-shirt. Her hair was pulled back into her customary braid, and she didn't have on a stitch of make-up. Sonya, meanwhile, radiated beauty with her sharp classic features, smoky eyes, and rich hair styled loose around her shoulders. The jeans and plum sweater highlighted her dark eyes and smooth pale skin…and showed off her pregnant belly.

"I saw you enter his room. How's he doing?"

"Sleeping." Who was the father of this woman's baby?

Sonya cocked her head to the side. "Let's grab a cup of hot chocolate."

It wasn't an invitation, more of a demand. Raven had the feeling Sonya got what she wanted. Curious though about the other woman and her hold over Aidan, Raven followed her into the family kitchen.

"Your mother said to make myself at home. Lovely woman, your mother." Sonya looked at Raven as though she didn't think the trait had been passed on to her daughter. "Hope you don't mind."

"No." She doubted it would change Sonya's actions even if she did.

Sonya took down a pan from the pot rack, while Raven retrieved the milk from the fridge.

"Garrett filled me in on what happened this afternoon."

"Garrett?" Raven felt completely out of the loop. *Who were all these people?*

"My husband. Peter called us last night, and we headed up from Soldotna." She raised a brow. "Peter's my brother."

All that mattered to Raven was that this gorgeous woman was married. Which meant the child she carried probably wasn't Aidan's. Thank heavens. Jealously had already taken root, and Raven was finding it hard not to hate her.

Sonya narrowed her eyes, haphazardly adding sugar and cocoa to the heating milk. "Garrett told me you broke up with Aidan today, and that you share a child."

"You know, Sonya, not to be rude, but this is none of your business."

A slight smile tipped the corners of Sonya's mouth, but she quickly squelched it. "I care for Aidan and what happens to him."

"*So* why did *you* break up with him?"

A full smile did cross her lips this time. "Want to hand me a couple mugs?"

Raven reached into the cupboard and pulled down a few cups that she had made years ago.

"Oh, these are beautiful." Sonya took them and filled each to the rim with the hot chocolate. "You have any cookies we could add?" She shook her head in disbelief. "All I want to do is eat these days."

Raven grabbed a plate and added the dried blueberry shortbread cookies that her mother was famous for and followed Sonya to the table.

Sonya helped herself to a cookie and bit into it with a moan. She polished off the cookie, washed it down with a sip of hot chocolate and then went for another. "So," she said around a mouthful, "what were we talking about?"

"Why you broke up with Aidan." Raven cautiously sipped her chocolate. It was sweet and delicious.

"We wanted different things. Why do you think I never heard of you before? Aidan writes about those closest to him in his graphic novels. I'm Senyea. I don't know of a character that matches your description."

Aidan wrote about this woman? "How long have you known Aidan?"

"Heavens. Forever. We've fished next door to each other every summer since he was a kid."

Meaning Sonya probably knew Aidan as well as, if not better than, Raven did. And Sonya had known him the last twelve years. Jealously sprang to the forefront again.

"So, why did you break up with him?" Sonya asked.

No way was she going to confide in this woman. She didn't even know if she liked her. Actually, Raven didn't like her at all. She was too beautiful, too tall, and knew Aidan too well. Raven wanted her gone.

"Let me guess." Sonya raised an eyebrow. "Temper?"

Shock rendered Raven speechless.

"Ahh." Sonya lifted her cup for another sip. "We had that problem too. He'd told me he was seeing a counselor and working on his issues. Did he stop?"

How the hell would she know? Aidan hadn't said one word about seeing a counselor.

"Seems to me, you two have a lot to talk about." Sonya reached for another cookie. "Especially considering you have a child together. Where is he anyway? I'd like to meet him."

No. This woman wasn't getting to know her son. Raven felt jealous enough. If Fox found out that Sonya was Senyea, he'd worship her. She needed to get a copy of Aidan's graphic novels and see for herself what they were about.

And how much of a role Sonya or Senyea played in Aidan's life.

Aidan woke feeling like he'd been hit by a snowplow, dragged fifty miles, and dumped into a snow bank. Whatever had been in Eva's syringe had packed a wallop. He had no idea how long he'd been out, just wished it had been longer as he remembered vividly all that had transpired between him and Raven. The room was dark with darker shadows outside the window. He couldn't tell if it was day or night and didn't care. Time lay before him long and lonely. He heard rustling off to his right—*Raven*—and turned his head.

"You're awake?" an achingly familiar voice asked from the direction of the rocking chair.

"Sonya?" he croaked.

"Yeah, it's me. Okay, if I turn on a light?"

He nodded and then realized she couldn't see him. He wasn't sure if he was up to seeing her. She'd been another woman who'd broken his heart. "Yeah."

The light on the bedside table clicked on, and he turned his head, shutting his eyes as the light sliced through his head.

"Crap, Aidan, you look like shit. How do you feel?"

"Like I look." He blinked his eyes until they adjusted to the change in light, though he still had to narrow his gaze in order to see her. She looked…good, better. Happy. She'd never looked this good when she'd been with him, which meant Garrett was probably responsible for that glow in her cheeks, twinkle in her warm brown eyes. Her rich, dark hair was loose and soft around her shoulders, the strong bones in her face softened, more rounder. That was the word. She looked softer…more womanly. His eyes widened. "You're pregnant?"

She blushed and caressed her swollen belly. "Uh, yeah. About five months along."

He did the math. "Looks as if you caught more than fish last summer. Knocked up by a fish cop? You're going to have a tough time living that down."

"Don't I know it." She grimaced and then smiled secretly, as though she really didn't mind. "So…tell me about Raven?"

He shut his eyes as pain vibrated through him at the sound of her name.

"She's the one, isn't she?" she asked softly. "The one you wanted me to be. Want to talk about it?"

"I can't. Not with you."

"Who better than me?" She stood and moved to sit on the edge of the bed. "Aidan, I've known you a long time, but being here, talking with the Maiskis, I finally feel like I understand you." She brushed the hair away from his forehead. "Let me help."

"With what? I have more *help* from your family than I want."

"What about Raven?"

He looked away into the darkened room. "There's nothing to help. She can't get past my family. And I don't blame her. I've been trying to change my DNA all my life."

"You really love her, don't you?"

He sat up in the bed, relishing the soreness of his joints and the ache of the cuts Eva had stitched back together. He wished it were enough to dull the slicing pain of Raven's rejection. But it didn't even come close. "It doesn't matter what I feel. Whatever was between us is over."

"What about your son?"

He froze in the process of getting out of the bed and turned to her. "Drop it or you're going to piss me off."

She gave him a small smile. "Better than feeling sorry for yourself."

"Were you always this bitchy?"

She laughed. "And here I've been taking it easy on you."

"Butt out, Sonya." He stood, his legs wobbly like a gangly newborn moose. He found his clothes, freshly washed—bless Fiona—folded on the top of the dresser and struggled into them.

"Answer me this, Aidan. When I called it quits between us, you fought hard to get me back. Why aren't you fighting for Raven?"

He stared at her as he buttoned up his shirt. She stared right back. There was no intimidating Sonya. The woman could oxidize rust off a ship's hull with that look. "Why'd you come? I understand why Garrett's here. He wants his man. But you—" he indicated her pregnant state "—making Roland pay for his part in last summer's crimes isn't a major concern for you now, is it? So, why are you here?"

She stood and moved around the bed to stand in front of him. "I'm worried about you. I want you to be happy."

"Don't tell me that you've turned into one of those women. The kind who finds love and then wants the same for everyone else?"

The side of her mouth crooked up. "Seems that way. Hormones." She shrugged. "Seriously, Aidan. I want the best for you."

He had to turn away from the emotion in her eyes as it caused his heart to ache. "I gotta go."

"Aidan." The tone of her voice had him turning around, his hand on the doorknob. "I think with all that you've been through you believe you're unlovable, and I just want you to know that you aren't."

Aidan gave her one last look and then turned and left the room.

Unlovable.

Damn, the woman had nailed it. That was how he'd felt all his life. His mother had loved her next drink more than she had him. Earl never loved him, as he was a constant disappointment. Then there were Raven and Sonya. He'd never been good enough.

Would he be good enough for Fox?

The thought had him pausing on his way to the restaurant to see Pike. What kind of expectations did Fox have? Whatever they were, he was bound to let him down too. Maybe he should do what Raven wanted and leave them alone. After all, he'd let down everyone he had ever cared about.

He entered the sparse restaurant and glanced around. The nature-seeking woman was sitting at a table with coffee and a map. She looked too old and used to be after anything other than comfort. A few other patrons he didn't recognize were saddled up to the bar. The mosquito clock said nine. He was assuming it was nine in the evening and the dinner crowd was dwindling down. It was hard to tell with the sun rising later every day. Pike, Garrett, Lynx, and Peter were sharing a bowl of chips and salsa at a corner table. He pulled a chair from another table over and sat down.

"We thought you were going to sleep all night," Garrett said.

"Had a lovely conversation with Sonya," Aidan couldn't help saying. Garrett Hunt always brought out the worst in him.

Garrett's gaze darkened for a minute, but he failed to take the bait. "While you were resting, we gathered a search party and looked for Roland."

"I take it you didn't find him," Aidan spoke the obvious. "He won't be found unless he wants to be."

"We were hoping with the shape you were in that he might not be in top form himself." Lynx smiled. "Guess you didn't slow him down any."

Aidan let the dig slide. "Wherever he's holed up, it can't be far. He has to be close enough to keep tabs on Earl's place."

"Come morning, we'll head up into the hills," Pike said.

"I have a better idea." Aidan leaned his elbows onto the table top. "Let's find the gold, if there is any, and then burn the fucking cabin to the ground. That will take care of Roland. Either he'll leave, empty-handed, or it will bring him running."

The four men shared a look. Lynx was the first to speak. "Can't believe I didn't think of that," he mumbled.

"So we're decided?" Aidan stared at each of them. "Let's meet out there at daylight. Bring whatever tools you think we need to bust the place wide open."

"All right," Peter said all grins. "I've never been treasure-hunting before."

"I'd prefer it if you stayed here to protect the women in case Roland gets fired up over what we're doing."

"Hey." Peter scowled. "I'm not staying behind with the girls."

"I agree with Aidan. Roland could show up here looking for revenge," Garrett added, meeting Aidan's gaze with a knowing nod. Neither man wanted the kid in harm's way. Besides, anything happened to Peter and Sonya would kill them both.

"This sucks," Peter grumbled. "I'm not a babysitter."

"Don't let Sonya hear you talk like that," Garrett said.

Peter sat up straight, looking around the restaurant.

"Besides, she hears what we are up to, and she'll want to be a part of it," Garrett said. "It'll be up to you to watch out for her and Lana."

"Raven too," Aidan added. "She'll probably be in her studio, but anyone trying to get to her will have to pass by the lodge."

"Do I get a gun?" Peter mumbled, knowing he was being patronized.

Pike quirked his lips. "There's a shotgun under the bar if you need it."

"Woohoo."

CHAPTER TWENTY-FOUR

"What did you do?" Fox barreled into the studio, where Raven was attempting to work. She had orders piling up and couldn't center a ball of clay to save her life.

"Hello to you too," she greeted, dreading the conversation to come. He'd obviously been to the lodge and seen Aidan. She wished he'd come home first so that she could have explained things to him. "How was Grand's?"

"How could you tell Dad to stay away?"

"Fox—"

"You're ruining everything!" He threw his overnight bag onto the dusty floor.

"Now listen."

"No." He backed away, his eyes narrowed, furious. "It's my choice if I want Dad in my life. Not yours."

"Fox!" she hollered after him as he scurried out of the room and slammed the door on his way back outside. "Shit." She slammed the ball of clay down onto the wheel, and ran after him. He was outside hitching up his dogs to the sled. "Where do you think you're going?"

"Somewhere I can think."

"You're not running off mad."

"Yes I am. Dad told me when I feel like this to distance myself until I can calm down. And that's what I'm doing. I can't be around you right now."

Raven wrapped her arms around her as the pain of his words hit her like shards of broken pottery. She'd run out of the cabin without her coat and the icy air stole her breath. Physically, she couldn't keep him from leaving. The kid was as tall as she was. She wanted to put him in time out like she had when he was younger. But then he was essentially doing that to himself. Except, rather than sitting on a stool in the kitchen, he'd be racing over frozen tundra. "Be careful. Please."

He didn't respond, just methodically harnessed his excited dogs until he had the team in place. He commanded them to mush and didn't look back.

Raven ran back into the cabin and grabbed her coat. There would be no working in the studio today, not with her emotions all over the place, and her creativity in the toilet. A walk up to the lodge would do her good. Clear her head.

She'd rerun everything in her mind last night when she couldn't sleep. Every time she closed her eyes, she'd pictured making love with Aidan and how sweet and special being with him had been. The contrast to the man who'd shared her bed and the one who'd wailed on his uncle were so different it was hard to reconcile they were the same person.

Raven entered the lodge, hung up her coat, and found Fiona and Gran in the kitchen making a mess of sandwiches. "Something going on?"

"Lunches for the men," Coho said, spreading mayo on homemade bread. "They're treasure-hunting today."

"What?"

Fiona pulled out cheese and deli meet from the fridge. "They're planning on tearing Earl's place apart, hoping to find what Aidan's uncle has been after, and then burn down the place."

"Whose idea was this?"

Gran gave her a meaningful look. "Who do you think?"

Aidan.

"But that was his home. Don't you think it's a bit drastic?"

"Honey," Fiona said. "That poor boy has no fond memories of the place. It will do him good to burn it to the ground."

But then he wouldn't have a place to stay and he would leave. Wasn't that what she wanted? The thought banged around inside her bruised heart like a steel ball in a pinball machine. "When are they leaving?"

"Soon as the sun comes up." Fiona glanced at the clock. "Couple of hours. Pike had to run down his chainsaw he loaned out to Lynx who in turned loaned it to Bree."

"Where's Chickadee?"

"Her room," Fiona said. "She's supposed to be working on a term paper."

"Doubt that's what she's doing," Gran added, slapping on slices of cheese to the assembly line of sandwiches on the counter. "Letting that girl have a computer in her room is a mistake. She's twittering, or tweeting, something like that, with boys."

Fiona sighed and rolled her eyes behind Gran's back. "If you're going to see her, check to make sure she's working on her paper?"

"Sure." Raven gave Gran and her mother one last look before leaving the kitchen. She felt out of the loop. Why hadn't they asked her to help? But then she'd given up her claim to Aidan and therefore the opportunity to go treasure hunting. She walked down the hall, her heart thumping as she passed Aidan's closed door, and continued around the corner to the block of family rooms. She knocked on Chickadee's bedroom.

"Just a minute," Chickadee hollered. Raven heard a bunch of rustling before Chickadee opened the door, her face flushed. "Oh." She glowered. "It's you."

"I'm happy to see you too." What was up with her? They'd always had a great relationship. Not sisterly, since there were so many years between them, but more like favorite aunt and niece. "Can I come in?"

"Suit yourself." Chickadee turned and made her way to her bed, climbing up on the spread and tucking her pajama-clad legs under her. She wore a soft tank under an unzipped hoodie and had left her dark, thick hair to flow down her back. The girl was growing up into a beautiful young woman. When had that happened?

"What's the matter?" Raven asked. When was the last time she'd talked with Chickadee? With all that had been happening with Aidan, she'd forgotten about her little sister.

"Nothing." Chickadee glanced off to the side as though she was bored with Raven.

"School okay?"

"Fine."

"How's it going with that boy in Fairbanks?"

"What do you want, Raven?"

"Uh…" She physically took a step back from the insolence coming off Chickadee in waves. "What is with you? Why are you treating me like this?"

"Oh, I don't know. Maybe it's because I don't know who the hell you are anymore?"

"Excuse me?"

"Yeah, you should excuse yourself." She huffed and folded her arms over her chest, a scowl on her face. "I can't believe what you're doing to Fox and Aidan."

Oh, boy. Raven fell into the plush purple chair next to the desk. "Dee—"

"Don't 'Dee' me. I was three when Dad died. I'd give anything to know him. Fox is just getting to know the father you kept from him all these years and then I overheard Aidan this morning telling him *you* think it's best if they don't see each other for a while. Why did you do it?"

Raven took the verbal arrows one by one. "It's complicated, Dee."

"No, it isn't. You're just making it that way. I don't get you at all."

Silence added a chill to the room that had Raven wishing she hadn't hung up her coat. She held back the ever-present tears and glanced around the room. Dragonflies she'd helped Chickadee paint years ago still flittering on the walls, alongside posters of Hoodie Allen and Taylor Swift.

"Listen, Dee. I've done a lot of things in my life that I'm not proud of, but I'm trying to do the best thing for everyone here."

Chickadee flipped her long curtain of hair back over her shoulder. "Everyone? Seriously?" She had sarcasm down to an art form. Chickadee glanced at her nails and picked at her cuticles. "What did you come here for anyway?"

Not to feel better about herself that was for sure. "I wanted to borrow Aidan's graphic novels that Fox lent you."

"Why?" Chickadee glanced up, her scowl deepening.

"I don't know." Raven shrugged. "I thought it might help me understand Aidan better, I guess."

"Whatever." Chickadee got up from the bed and went to her desk, grabbing the pile of glossy, colorful novels stacked there. "Knock yourself out."

Aidan kissed Fiona and Coho on the cheek. "Thanks for making us lunches. That was very sweet of you."

"Naw," Coho said. "Just our way of being a part of the treasure hunting since you won't let us come with. Now go find that gold. Oh, and I'd like a nugget this size, if you don't mind." She held up her thumb and finger about two inches apart.

Fiona rolled her eyes at Coho. "Be careful, Aidan. Lynx, I want you to watch out for him. You too, Garrett. He's been through a lot and I don't want him to over do or be hurt any worse than he already is."

"Yes, Mom," Lynx said. "Can we go now?"

Yes, can we? The day had already been excruciating. Fox had come to the lodge early and interrupted the treasure planning party, wanting to come along. For Fox's safety, and to adhere to Raven's wishes, Aidan had tried to put some distance between them. It had backfired.

Pike entered the kitchen door from the cold outdoors. "What's the hold up? Truck's running. It's not like the sun's going to stay up all day."

Lynx grabbed the cooler full of food, and followed Pike out the door. Aidan and a very quiet Garrett followed. Aidan never thought he'd be doing anything with the fish cop. Funny how things changed. Maybe he should do what Sonya suggested and fight for Raven and Fox? He had a legal right to fight for Fox, not that he'd take him away from his mother, but he was the kid's father and he wanted the chance to be there for him.

They drove in silence to Earl's. Well, at least Garrett and he were quiet. Lynx couldn't seem to shut up. He was like a kid on his first fishing trip. Any minute now he was going to start bouncing in his seat.

They passed Aidan's rental where he'd left it about a mile up the road from Earl's yesterday. The SUV was covered in a thick layer of frost, looking too frozen to start. It had reached minus forty below last night and his rental hadn't been plugged in to an electrical outlet that would keep the engine from freezing. Chances were he was without a vehicle until he could get it jumped or towed. He didn't want to be at the Maiski's mercy anymore.

They parked and exited Pike's crew cab pickup, grabbing the tools and the cooler they'd brought from the lodge. Garrett carried a pickax with a pistol on his hip, Lynx the chainsaw and a crowbar, Pike a rifle and his forty-five, while Aidan got stuck with the purse-like cooler due to his injuries.

"This is where you grew up?" Garrett asked with a lift of his brows. "And I thought your fish camp setup was bad."

"Earl liked living simply."

"This isn't simple, it's brutal." He scoffed. "Explains a lot about you, I guess."

How did he argue that?

Pike started down the lane, and Aidan called out to him, "Let me go first. Roland had set booby traps yesterday. I know what to look for."

"Crafty bastard," Pike muttered under his breath as Aidan passed him to lead the crew to the back of the cabin.

"Keep your eyes open," Aidan instructed the group as they slowly walked down the path.

Aidan didn't find any trip wires or signs of mischief. They entered the cold-soaked cabin and found Roland in the living room.

Dead on the floor, a knife sticking out of his chest.

"Well…this I didn't expect," Pike said, holstering his forty-five.

Aidan looked at Garrett. "I didn't do it."

Garrett huffed out a heavy sigh. "You complicate the hell out of my life, you know that?"

What did he say? Sorry? "Try seeing it from my point of view." Ah, hell, how was he going to tell Lana? They were both fatherless now. He took a step toward Roland.

"Don't move," Garrett said. "This just became a crime scene."

"What about the gold?" Lynx dropped the heavy chainsaw to the floor.

"That will have to wait until the troopers clear the place."

"How long will that take?" Pike asked.

"A while." Garrett took off his gloves and pulled a cell phone out of his pocket. "I'll make the call."

"Good luck," Aidan said, remembering his panicked attempts to get cell service when he'd been caught in the bear trap. "You won't get reception until you're closer to town."

"What's that piece of paper sticking out of his breast pocket?" Lynx asked.

Garrett pocketed the useless phone. Putting his gloves back on, he reached for the note. His jaw hardened as he read.

"What does it say?" Aidan asked, the chill in the cabin going from freezing to frigid.

Garrett's troubled gaze met Aidan's worried one. "It's Fox."

CHAPTER TWENTY-FIVE

"What about Fox?" Raven demanded, her voice high-pitched and panicked.

Everyone jumped like someone had shattered glass, and as one they quickly turned to block the view of Roland's cold dead body.

"Raven, what are you doing here?" Aidan moved through the group to stand in front of her. Her eyes were wide, dark pools of fear.

"Fox is missing. Something's happened to him."

"How do you know he's missing?" Garrett asked, in his clipped cop voice. "When did you last see him?"

"Couple of hours ago. We had a fight and he took off with his dogs. The dogs and sled returned without him, and Lucien wasn't with them either." She glanced at the men lined up like a wall of warriors. "What's going on?"

"Who is Lucien?" Garrett asked.

"Fox's lead dog! *Now what the hell is going on?*"

"Raven, let's go outside and talk about this." Aidan took her elbow to lead her from the cabin.

She tore her arm from his grip. "Someone better start talking." She stared at Pike who turned to gaze at the wall. Lynx was next, but he seemed to find the floor fascinating. "That's it. Move." She barreled through the line of men, coming up short when she saw Roland's dead body. She turned and stared at Aidan.

"Don't look at me like that." He tightened his jaw as the pain of her silent accusation cut through him.

"Raven," Lynx said, putting an arm around her shoulders. "You need to calm down."

"Calm down!" She shrugged off his arm and pointed to Roland. "Fox is missing and there's a dead body on the floor."

Aidan glanced at Garrett. "What's in the letter?" Raven was right. Fox missing, and a dead body, were too much a coincidence for one morning, even for Alaska.

"What letter?" Raven asked.

Garrett's warning look had dread icing the blood in his veins. Aidan grabbed Raven's hand and held tight. "Tell us."

"Whoever killed Roland has Fox," Garrett said, his voice even and grim. "He wants the gold in trade...for Fox."

"*Oh God.*" Raven bent over at the waist.

Aidan grabbed her and pulled her shaking body into his arms. "What else?"

"We have until dark. We're supposed to pack the gold into your SUV with the keys in the ignition. If we comply, he'll leave the information on where we can find Fox. Any sign of cops or anyone waiting around and..."

Raven cried out, burying her face in Aidan's chest. He wrapped his arms tight around her, swallowing the sickness creeping up his throat.

"That's it, let's rip this fucking hellhole apart," Lynx said, picking up his chainsaw.

Pike laid out a hand. "We need a plan before we start tearing into this place."

Garrett nodded. "Pike, we need to head back to the lodge and call the troopers."

"No cops." Aidan jerked. "He said no cops. I'm not putting Fox at risk so that you can do things by the book."

"I'm advising you against it."

"Too damn bad."

"Who the hell is this guy anyway?" Lynx asked.

"Good question." Pike pointed to Roland. "Did the crafty bastard have a sidekick?"

"Earl was his sidekick," Aidan answered.

"Then who else knew about the gold?" Garrett asked.

Everyone went silent. Raven dragged herself out of Aidan's arms.

"Aidan, who else knew about the gold?" Garrett asked again.

"I don't know. I had no idea Earl had any gold. If there really is any," Aidan said, quietly as the realization of what could happen to Fox if they didn't find him and if there wasn't any gold.

Raven gasped on a sob.

"All right, this is what we're going to do." Garrett took charge. "Pike, head back to the lodge, get together a search party, and find some two-way radios."

"I'm going after Fox," Aidan said.

"Me too," Raven said.

"The last thing we need is everyone running off and getting lost with the temps as cold as they are," Garrett said. "We don't even know where they are."

"Pike, bring a tracker with that search party," Aidan said.

"Bree's dad is the best tracker I know. Fox is a smart kid, and he'll know how to leave us a sign. I'll head back now."

"Just in case, we'd better see if we can jumpstart my SUV out there. If we don't find Fox before…" Aidan cleared his throat. "I don't want him in jeopardy because the SUV is cold-soaked."

"Pike, plan for that," Garrett said. "I'd rather keep Lana in the dark about her father, but inform Peter and Sonya, she'll know what to do. I'll need my camera to take pictures of the crime scene." Pike nodded and left.

"I'm going after Fox," Aidan repeated.

"You don't even know where to start looking," Garrett said.

"Roland was killed here. The note was left here. It makes sense that Fox was also taken from here. There has to be a trail."

"Yeah, I get that, but we could lose you out there too."

"I know these woods. I grew up here. There's only so many places someone could be hiding a boy."

"Roland hid out with no one able to find him." Garrett glanced down at Roland's dead body. "Until now."

Aidan marched to the gun cabinet and picked out Earl's rifle and scope, handing Raven the thirty-eight special. "I'm going after Fox." He reached into the bottom drawer and pulled out a couple of two-way radios and added batteries. "I'll be on channel twelve." He tossed the other radio to Garrett who caught it with a frown.

"I'll go with you," Lynx said. "Hand me the rifle."

"No, you stay here with Garrett and find the gold in case we don't find…"

"I don't like this," Garrett said, nostrils flaring.

"He's my son." Aidan stared down Garrett. "What would you do if he were yours?"

Garrett heaved a sigh. "All right, but keep in contact with us and let us know where you are. And don't do anything heroic and get yourself killed. I don't want to explain another body to the local law enforcement."

Raven followed Aidan out of the cabin, her heart heavy with fear and worry. She'd made so many mistakes, and Fox was paying the price.

Aidan looked her up and down, his mouth tightening. "You should stay here."

"Don't waste your breath. I'm going with you." She dropped her gaze and zipped up her parka. It was too hard to meet his eyes. If she'd only told the truth about Fox from the beginning. If she'd followed her heart and allowed herself to trust Aidan. Hell, if she'd just grounded Fox this morning, he'd be home safe right now. There were so many things she could have done better. Should have.

"Put these on." Aidan reached up and grabbed a pair of snowshoes hanging on the outside of the cabin.

"How do you know they walked out of here?" she asked, strapping the snowshoes to her mukluks while he did the same with another pair.

"There were no other tire tracks when we pulled up." He scanned the area. "Roland's been coming and going from somewhere. I'm willing to bet whoever killed Roland either followed him here on foot or came with him." Aidan pointed north. "I think we should head that direction."

She reached out and grabbed his arm, pulling him to a stop. "Aidan, there's a black wolf that direction."

"I know. I think we should follow him."

"Are you crazy?"

"Undoubtedly," he muttered. "Trust me," he said louder, following the wolf, who'd loped ahead, almost out of sight. Aidan stopped, bending down and fingering tracks in the snow with his glove-covered hand. "What size shoe does Fox wear?"

"Ten. I've always said he's got big paws to grow into." Her throat closed off with emotion. "Why?"

"I've got two sets of footprints. One looks like it could be Fox's, but the other is considerably smaller. This has to be the way they went."

They set off through the heavy forest of tall spruce mixed with birch that grew on the northeast side of the hill. Neither talked as they climbed through the sharp cold, over deep snow drifts, consumed with fear over Fox. Suddenly, Aidan stopped.

"What is it?" Raven demanded.

He knelt, and took off his glove, touching something dark in the snow.

"What is it?" she asked again, her voice higher pitched with worry.

Aidan stood and turned to face her. "I don't want you to overreact."

"Don't tell me not to overreact when you aren't telling me *anything*."

He grabbed her shoulders. "There's blood on the trail."

"Oh, God." Her knees buckled, and he gave her a hard shake.

"Raven, you've got to keep it together, or you're no help to Fox or me. Understand?"

She swallowed back moans of anguish rushing to be let out, and nodded.

"We don't know whose blood it is. Knowing Fox, he's creating a lot of problems for the person who took him." Aidan looked deep into her eyes, his beseeching. "You with me?"

"I'm fine." She nodded for emphasis even though she was anything but fine. "Let's hurry."

"Good." He grabbed her hand either to make sure she would stay on her feet or to help give her emotional support, for whatever reason she held tight to his gloved hand. When she saw the frozen droplets of blood, she tried to keep in the whimper, but it escaped her tightly sealed lips. Aidan squeezed her hand and continued to pull her along behind him.

From the corner of her eye, she caught another set of tracks. "Are those wolf prints?"

"Try not to think about it." Aidan kept trudging through the snow, but he adjusted his hold on the rifle.

"Wolves are tracking them too, aren't they?"

When he didn't answer, she pulled out the thirty-eight special and held it ready in her free hand.

The trees thinned as they crested a small rise. Aidan stumbled to a stop. "Oh, hell."

There, a few feet from them in a slight depression, lay Lucien. Raven rushed and fell to her knees, leaning over his prone body. Her hand trembled as she reached out to touch him. A sob erupted as she felt the stiffness of the animal. "*Who is this monster? Why kill a dog?*"

"Probably because he came after them," Aidan said, anger and pain in his voice. "He must have tried to protect Fox."

It went unsaid that whoever would kill a dog wouldn't have any problem killing a kid.

"Raven." Aidan laid his hands on her shoulders.

"I want the bastard dead." She pushed his comforting hands aside and jumped to her feet. "How dare he kill Lucien? How dare he take my son?" Anger ate through her system like acid. Worry and fear stepped back as a vicious rage moved to the forefront.

They shared an understanding look. Aidan took point again, moving ahead of Lucien's body. They left him where he was.

They'd be back later to give the loyal companion a proper burial. They climbed upward through frozen, brittle branches that tore at their coats, scratched exposed flesh. Aidan grabbed Raven when she stumbled and fell, holding onto her arm as they hiked up the steep mountainside.

They crested the hill, to find a blinding open meadow...full of snowmobile tracks.

"Shit." Breathing hard, Aidan shaded his eyes from the reflection of the sun recoiling off the brilliant blanket of snow. He stomped off right, studying the tracks. He came back and headed left, circled around and stopped. "They left on a snow machine. The trail meshes with the other tracks of snow machines. Son of a bitch."

The pit of dread in Raven's stomach opened deeper. How were they going to find Fox now? There had to be miles of crisscrossing snowmobile tracks throughout the meadow, scarring the snow-packed valley.

"We need a snow machine." Aidan huffed out a frustrated breath.

"Wait." Raven rubbed her forehead in thought. "This valley isn't for day trippers. They wouldn't come out this far if they had to head back to Fairbanks before dark." She lowered her hand and met his hard gaze.

"That means whoever took Fox is staying at the lodge or lives in the area." Aidan pulled out the two-way radio. "I'll call Garrett and have him take a closer look at the guests."

Not able to stand around and wait while Aidan radioed the trooper, Raven snow-shoed around the area where they'd lost Fox's trail. The snow was harder, packed down with the weight of snow machines running over it. Something colorful reflected the light and she moved closer to see what it was.

A Jolly Rancher sat on one of the thin track impressions. "Aidan!" She was never going to complain about Fox's dentist bill again.

"I can't get anyone on the radio. The mountains must be getting in the way." He trudged over to her, coming to a dead stop when he recognized what she was pointing at. Aidan's face spilt into a grin. "Damn, but Fox is one clever kid. And he has great taste in candy." Aidan grabbed her hand.

They increased their pace, half running-jogging over the open packed trails. They'd found six more Jolly Ranchers before Aidan came to a sharp stop, his arm reaching out to catch Raven.

"What?" she asked, her breath coming in thick steam. "Why are we stopping?"

"I hear something. Listen." He cocked his head to the side.

Then she heard it. The revving of a snowmobile.

The ground sloped down and then up again. They were closer to the tree line as islands of birch and spruce rose above the ocean of snow. At the base of one of these islands was a snowmobile stuck with a lone rider gunning the engine, trying to get the big machine out of the snow bank. Disappointment slammed into Raven like a fist of nails when she didn't see Fox. Her eyes scanned the open areas, searching deeper into the encroaching forests.

No Fox.

They reached the rider as he lifted his fur-covered head—*her* fur-covered head.

"Great," Raven mumbled. A lot of help this woman was going to be. They didn't have time to save her sorry ass.

"Follow my lead," Aidan said, under his breath. "Having trouble?" he asked the woman in a welcoming voice.

"Oh my goodness, am I glad you came along." She smiled, though it didn't reach her jade eyes. "I'm in a pickle as you can see."

"Yes, I can." Aidan nodded. "How'd you end up buried in a bank?" He indicated the wide expanse of snow.

"You know how it is. Going too fast, made a sharp turn. That kind of thing."

"You're lucky you didn't hurt yourself." Aidan handed the rifle to Raven, his eyes meeting hers and sending a message. One that was hard to believe. "Let's see if I can get this beast free for you. I'm Aidan, by the way and this is Raven."

Raven nodded her head in greeting, one hand holding the rifle, the other holding the thirty-eight special hidden in her coat pocket.

"My name's Genie. It is so nice to meet you both. I just don't know what I'd have done if you two hadn't happened along." Genie batted her eyes up at Aidan, playing the damsel in distress to the hilt. The woman had man-eater written all over her.

Aidan began digging snow away from the skis of the machine, freeing the front as he continued the conversation. "What are you doing out here by yourself anyway? It's not smart to be alone. You could get into trouble."

"Oh, you know how it is. I came up to get away from everyone. Find some peace. Get back to nature. That sort of thing."

"Hey, aren't you staying at the lodge? I think I've seen you around." Aidan gifted Genie with a smile that said, 'We should hook up for a drink when we're done with this.'

Raven shifted her weight back and forth on her feet. Aidan sent her a warning glance. *What the hell?*

Genie cocked her hip and leaned in closer to Aidan. "Yeah, I am," she said with a husky sexy voice that wasn't lost on Raven. "Great place, the lodge. Nice big beds."

Oh, please. "Can we speed this up?" Raven demanded.

"Sure thing, babe." Aidan lifted the skis of the machine clear of the snow bank. "There that ought to do it." He moved toward Genie in a non-threatening way. Quick as a snake he grabbed her by the arms and twisted them behind her back. "Now, Genie, why don't you tells us what you did with Fox."

She let out a scream as she struggled in Aidan's iron grasp.

It took Raven a moment for the words and the actions to sink in. *This woman took her son?* "You bitch!" Raven flew at her, the rifle she held in her hands pointing between the woman's eyes. "Where the hell is my son?"

"Raven, back off. She can't tell us anything if she's dead."

Her finger itched to pull the trigger. "Where. Is. Fox?"

"How the hell should I know?" Her eyes went wide and Raven would have believed her if it wasn't for the judgment in Aidan's glare.

Raven leaned into Genie. "You're going to be dead if you don't start telling me what I want to know."

"You two are *crazy*, you know that?" Her voice wobbled. "I have no idea what you're talking about."

"Yes, you do," Aidan said. "You've been hanging around the lodge. This snowmobile is one of the lodge's rentals. You probably know who all the players are by now. It's no coincidence that you're out here stuck in the snow at the same time we're searching for our son. Our very clever son, who left us a trail of Jolly Ranchers which led us right to you."

"That brat," Genie spat out the side of her mouth. The mask of innocence fell from her face leaving a hard, bitter shell in its place. Raven couldn't help herself, and sucker-punched Genie in the stomach with the butt of the rifle..

The woman doubled-over. "Ouch. Shit."

Aidan gave Raven a pointed look, that said, *Cool it*. Like hell she would. She wanted this woman dead. It was all she could do not to hit her again, and again. Raven tore off Genie's hat and tossed it in the snow. "Think about how my gun will feel slamming into your skull without that pelt of fur to cushion it."

Genie paled, and then tightened her lips into an ugly sneer. Her lips were scarred with thin lines from too many years of puckering around the butt of a cigarette. "I have no idea where that brat ran off to. He left me here to die after he crashed my snowmobile."

"Why don't you tell us what happened?" Aidan asked.

"Let go of me first."

"Fine." Aidan suddenly released her. Genie fell into the snow on her ass. "Raven, she moves, shoot her. Start with her feet."

Genie gulped.

"Start talking. Raven has an itchy finger."

"You don't know the half of it," Raven said in a deadly voice.

"Hand me my rifle, sweetheart."

Raven passed the rifle to Aidan after freeing her pistol from her pocket and training it on Genie. "I'm waiting."

"I had Roland right where I wanted him until that damn kid showed up."

"What's your connection to Roland?"

She gave a harsh cackle. "You should be asking me what my 'connection' is to your daddy."

"All right, how did you know Earl?"

"I knew everything about Earl. All his secrets. Nothing loosened his tongue like a good fucking."

"Who the hell are you?" Aidan asked.

She laughed and spread her hands wide on top of the snow. "I'm your Genie in the bottle, baby. I grant your every wish."

"You're a *whore*?" Raven asked, caught up in this crazy turn.

"Oh, please. Whore? I'm so much more than that. I'm a celebrated 'entertainer' for the Lonely Lady. I've been Earl's consort for over twenty years. And Roland's whenever he's in town," she added with a nonchalant shrug.

Aidan grabbed Genie by the arm and pulled her up and out of the snow. "I don't give a shit who you are. Why did you take Fox?"

"I want the gold. Since Earl is dead—thank you for that by the way—I figure I'm the closest thing to his wife so the gold belongs to me."

"This is twisted," Raven said.

"You don't know twisted, honey, until you've slept with a Harte." She glanced between Raven and Aidan and laughed. "But then I guess you do, don't you?"

Aidan gave Genie a hard shake. "Where's Fox?"

"How the hell should I know? He left me here." She gestured wide to the trees. "Ran off and left me to die."

"*You* kidnapped him." Raven advanced. "*You* killed his dog."

"Had to. The mutt was after us, plus getting rid of the dog put your kid in line. Guess you spared the rod with that one, didn't you?"

"You bitch." Raven slapped her across the face and pointed the gun at Genie, her finger pressing the trigger.

"Raven," Aidan said, his voice low, calming. "Fox first. You can take care of her later."

Raven forced herself to relax her grip and lowered the gun a few inches. "Last chance. Where is my son?"

"I told you." Genie's tone was shrill, her hand holding her cheek. "He went off that way, into the trees."

"Aidan, do we have anything to tie her up with?" Raven asked, advancing closer to Genie.

"Hey," Genie complained.

"It's either that, or I put a bullet in your head."

Quick as a cat, Genie grabbed the gun from Raven and pointed it at her. "I don't think so. Throw the rifle over there or this bitch gets it."

"Shoot her, Aidan."

But Aidan complied with Genie's demand, dropping the rifle to the snow.

"*You* shut up." Genie waved the gun at Raven. "I'm sick of your mouth. This whole plan has gone to shit because of you. I've been watching. I know what kind of woman you are. And they call *me* names."

"You're the one who hit me over the head," Aidan said, as the puzzle pieces seemed to fit together. "You ransacked the cabin and my rental?"

"Looks as though Fox's smart genes came from his daddy. Bingo. I've been trying to get you out of that shithole this whole time. But then she'd show up and either nurses you back or pisses you off into staying."

"You set the fire to the woodpile."

"Wasn't that brilliant?" Genie chuckled. "Can't live in a place with no heat. Not in Alaska. That should have given me plenty of time to search Earl's place."

"But Roland showed up," Aidan said, obviously trying to get the anger and attention off of Raven and onto him.

"There he was bragging to me that any day now he was going to be flush and how Mexico looked real good this time of year.

No mention of me going with him. And I had been satisfying his every fantasy. Even some he didn't know he had."

"Let me guess. You were adding drugs in with the sex?"

Genie scoffed. "Yep, you're definitely the brains of the family. The bastard caught on to what I was doing."

"Is that why you killed him?"

"It was easy. Killing a man like Roland should have been harder. For you it would have been, you did put a bullet in your own father. Roland was sure pissed about that." A sick smile crossed her hard lips. "Men don't think women have the balls to do what needs to be done. I shimmied up to him, playing all nice promising him all kinds of sexual favors if he'd let me partner up with him. The idiot actually laughed at me. You should have seen his face when I stuck him with my knife. He'll never stick me again. Get it? Stick me again?" She giggled, and the sound of a little girl coming out of the hardened prostitute sent a chill up Raven's spine.

"Yeah, I got it," Aidan said. "So what's your plan now?"

"Well, I gotta get rid of you two. Your brat should be done for soon, if he hasn't frozen to death before now."

A sound of distress escaped Raven, even though she'd tried not to bring attention to herself while Aidan kept Genie busy with her vent-fest. Now Genie focused more on her, the gun level with Raven's heart.

"I figure, with the three of you gone, no one will have the slightest idea that a woman was behind all this. They should have the gold packed into your rental shortly, and then I'll just drive off with it. Smart of me to get you men bending over for me for a change."

"There's something you haven't counted on."

"Oh, you mean the snowmobile getting stuck? Yeah, that was a bad turn. I got a bit hasty in my excitement and took that bend too fast. But then you came along and unstuck the damn thing for me."

"No, I'm talking about that."

"What?"

"You'll never make it back to the cabin. The wolves will get to you first." Aidan indicated the black wolf standing twenty feet off, his gums silently pulled back to reveal shiny, sharp teeth.

Genie screamed, panicked, swung the gun around and shot at the wolf. The wolf was off, with a leap, into the forest, unharmed. Aidan tackled Genie, but not before she got off another wild shot.

White hot pain seared for a second, stealing Raven's breath, and then she felt nothing as the snow reached up to cradle her in its slumbering embrace.

CHAPTER TWENTY-SIX

"*Raven!*" Aidan tore the gun out of Genie's hand, cold-cocked the whore, and rushed over to Raven's prone body. "Raven? Come on, baby, open your eyes for me." He felt around her chest, struggled with the zipper of her parka, until he could part her coat and see for himself what kind of injury she had.

Nothing.

No blood, no wound. What the hell? Had she fainted? Raven wasn't the kind of woman who fainted. "Raven?" He shook her, and she moaned.

Her eyes fluttered and then opened, only to quickly shut again. She reached up a gloved hand and pressed it to the side of her head. Blood coated the light-colored fur of her glove.

"Oh, God." Aidan tore off his gloves and gently removed her hat, then brushed back her long dark hair—soaking up blood—away from the wound, praying under his breath. There, above her left ear, blood bubbled where the bullet had torn through her flesh. Blood poured from the wound, not letting him see how badly she'd been shot. He took snow and washed the area, holding her hair up and out of the way. It wasn't long before Raven started to complain. The words were the sweetest sound he'd ever heard.

"Fuck, that hurts. I'm going to kill that bitch." She winced, but didn't move as he washed and packed the wound, the coldness of the snow slowing the bleeding and hopefully numbing the pain.

"How many fingers am I holding up?" he asked, hoping that the injury hadn't caused a concussion. He held up two fingers.

"Four. Now let me at her." Raven struggled to sit up, weaving back and forth.

"Easy. Easy now." Aidan frowned. "Let me make sure you're all right."

"We don't have time for this. We need to know where Fox is."

Aidan zipped her parka, watching as her eyes dilated when she blinked. He needed to get her to help, but first they needed to find Fox.

Aidan gently wrapped Raven's scarf around her head, tearing the felted wool with his teeth to tie a knot, keeping it in place and then repositioned the hood of her parka. "Hopefully that will hold until we can get you to Eva. Are you doing okay?"

She went to nod and then thought better of it. "Yeah. I'm fine."

He knew she was lying. Her skin was as pale as the snow she sat on.

Genie groaned. He turned to see her slowly sitting up, holding her hand to her head where Aidan had knocked her out.

"Sit here for a minute." Aidan got up and walked back to Genie.

"Hey," she protested, and then snapped her mouth shut when she got a clear look at his murderous face.

He reached into his pocket and flicked open his knife, cutting the strings free from the hood of his parka. Grabbing Genie by the arms, he dragged her kicking and screaming to a crowd of trees.

"You can't leave me here," Genie cried, when Aidan pulled her toward a stand of spindly birch. "I'll freeze to death."

"One can hope." Aidan yanked Genie's hands around the trunk of a tree.

"Okay, you win. I'll take you to where your brat is." She glanced fearfully around, her wide-eyed gaze frozen on the black wolf who'd returned as sentry and stood along the tree line. "Just don't leave me here."

"I'm through playing your games. Where is my son?" Aidan demanded, his voice menacing, as he tied the nylon string around her hands.

"Untie me and I'll take you to him." Genie's eyes drooped, pleaded. But Aidan was immune. This bitch had shot the woman he loved and kidnapped his son. She could rot out here for all he cared.

"Ouch. You don't have to be barbaric," Genie complained when he tightened the thin strings around her wrists, under her gloves. She glanced again at the wolf who had continued to stand like a totem within the cover of trees. "Seriously, you can't leave me here."

"Yes, I can."

"You need me."

"The only woman I need in my life is Raven."

"She's right, Aidan," Raven said. "Leave me. Take her and the snowmobile, it will be faster. Find Fox and bring him home." Her voice cracked on the word 'home.'

No way in hell would he leave Raven here, out in the open, hurt like she was.

"I'll head back to the cabin," Raven said. "Don't worry, I'll be fine. Just go and get Fox."

Aidan glanced around him. Genie had a calculating gleam in her eyes, while Raven's were full of fear and pain.

The wolf howled behind him and suddenly he knew.

"No. She stays. We go." He finished tying off the strings, pulling on them once to make sure they'd hold.

"What? No." Genie struggled, twisted and turned, trying to free herself. "You can't leave me here alone."

"Yes, I can. Just like you left my son alone." Aidan hoped she didn't get free, because he planned for her to be prosecuted to the full extent of the law.

"Aidan, what are you doing?" Raven asked, watching wide-eyed as he finished with Genie and returned to her.

"I'm not leaving you." He bent down and took her cold face within the heat of his hands, staring deep into her frightened eyes. "Trust me. Please."

She studied him, wetted her lips. "Okay."

He kissed her, quick and hard, his heart swelling with emotion he couldn't name. "Thank you."

He helped Raven to her feet, assisting her over to the snowmobile. It was hard enough mounting the machine with the snowshoes strapped to her feet, not to mention her head injury. Aidan sent a prayer to the heavens that they'd get their son back and both Fox and Raven would be safe. When Raven was situated, he got on the snowmobile.

"You'll never find the brat without my help!" Genie screeched.

Raven shivered at Genie's words as she wrapped her arms around Aidan's waist. Aidan started the machine, trying to block out Genie's threats.

He *did* know what he was doing, right?

You're following a wild timber wolf hoping the animal is going to lead to you to your son, like Lassie. What do you think?

The wolf waited until he was close to the tree line and then leapt into the forest. Aidan followed at a slower rate as he ventured the snow machine into the trees, fresh tracks gridded the tight trail. This had to be the way Genie had gone. Aidan didn't know how he knew it, but deep down on some cellular level he recognized the wolf as his spirit brother. Maybe his mother hadn't been so wasted on booze when she'd told him the legends of the wolf and him being born under the sign. Maybe he'd been outside too long and the cold had stunted his brain function. Either way, he was going with his gut.

The wolf ran ahead of them, staying just within sight. When Aidan had to slow down the machine, as the trail narrowed, the wolf slowed, increasing its gait as the trail widened. They were climbing and Aidan suddenly realized where they were headed.

The bitch.

Raven gasped behind him. He felt more than heard her quick intake of air as she, too, comprehended where they were going.

The old mine shaft the Fairbanks Exploration Company had closed down back in the sixties.

The trees thinned and then cleared as the mountain rose like a monster above them. Rusting steel mining dinosaurs dotted the landscape and he slowed the machine to avoid hitting something hidden under the thick blanket of snow. The wolf stood, his sides heaving, on a small rise above the timber-framed mouth of the mine. It was still chain-linked off but that didn't keep kids from coming up here in the summer, scaring each other with dares or finding places to make out. He and Raven should know. They'd used this place a few times for stolen moments themselves.

He slowed the machine to a stop and killed the engine.

Raven climbed off the back, unsteady on her feet. "Tell me, I get to go back and kill that bitch."

"As soon as we get Fox to safety, you can do whatever you like to Genie in the Bottle. Why don't you stay here, while I find Fox?"

"No."

He knew by the clench of her jaw there was no arguing with her, regardless of the pain shining in her shadowed eyes.

They struggled up to the foreboding entrance of the mine. Footprints were cut deep in the snow since neither Genie nor Fox had worn snowshoes. Aidan yanked back the chain-link fencing, held it open for Raven, and crawled through behind her. "Fox!" he hollered into the deep, dark cavern, his voice echoing back at him.

No answer.

"Fox!" Raven screamed his name.

Still no answer.

"*No.*" Aidan grabbed for Raven, but missed as she barreled past him into the darkness. "Raven, stop."

"Fox!" she continued to holler, ignoring Aidan's warning.

He hurried behind her, reaching out into the sinister abyss until he felt the fabric of her parka. His fingers clenched around the material, dragging her to a stop. "Raven, slow down. Think. You're going to get hurt or worse, if you don't slow down."

Her breathing was ragged. Her body twitched with the effort it took not to rush. He understood what she was feeling. He wanted to tear this fucking place apart stone by stone until they found Fox and then he wanted to torture the bitch who had put him here too.

He reached into his pocket, took out the mini flashlight on his key ring, and flicked it on. A black mouth of stone braced with ridges of rough-cut, rotting logs flashed in front of them. Even knowing what the scene would be didn't help the clenching of his heart, knowing his son was somewhere in the labyrinth of tunnels, scared and cold. "Fox!"

"There." Raven pointed to the left. "I thought I heard something."

He grabbed her arm. "Hold onto me." They trekked left, being careful of the loose mix of dead leaves, gravel, and rock that made up the debris littering the floor of the mine. "Fox!"

Then he heard it. A muffled sound. He hurried, keeping a firm hold on Raven. They turned a corner and Aidan's flashlight shone on Fox, his hands and feet tied with rope, a gag around his mouth. He was lying on his side, huddled in a ball, his face tucked into his knees. Raven rushed to him, her cries bouncing off the stone walls.

Aidan felt for Fox's pulse, releasing a breath he didn't know he'd been holding when he found it steady, a bit fast, but strong. Raven released the gag over his mouth and pulled Fox into her arms, tears streaming down her face.

"Mom, Dad?" Fox asked, his voice jagged with emotion, his body racked with shivers. "Are you really here?"

"Yes, yes, we're here." Raven tightened her arms around him, and buried her face in his neck. "You're safe."

"Mom," Fox croaked. "C-can't…breathe."

Raven pulled back, laughter adding to her tears.

"How? How'd you f-find me?" Fox asked. "I-I didn't think anyone w-would ever find me."

Aidan cleared his throat in order to get words past the fear and love thickening his throat. "Let's get you out of here, son, and then we'll answer all your questions." He handed the mini flashlight to Raven. "Hold this on the ropes so I can cut him loose."

Raven took the flashlight with a shaky hand and held it for Aidan as he flicked open his pocketknife and sliced through the ropes binding their son's hands and feet.

"Can you walk?" Aidan asked, helping Fox into a sitting position.

"D-don't know. Can't feel my toes." Fox laid his head back on Raven's shoulder as she steadied him from behind. "I'm r-really tired."

Aidan and Raven shared a look.

"No going to sleep, son." Aidan grabbed Fox's face, looked into his eyes. Fear shot through him at the dazed, glassy-eyed reflection in his son's pupils, the blue tint of his lips. Aidan glanced at Raven, and saw the same cloudy expression in her eyes. He needed to get them to the hospital. "Stay with me." He spoke to them both, praying under his breath to any God who would listen.

He unzipped his coat and lifted Fox into his arms, cradling his son tightly to his chest, hoping his body heat would help quell Fox's shivers. "Raven, can you walk out of here?"

"Is M-mom hurt?" Fox asked, voice shaky, worried.

"I'm fine." She looked at Aidan and blinked, as though the action was as close as she could come to a nod. He couldn't even imagine how she was holding it together.

"Grab my coat. I need to feel you behind me."

She fisted her hand in his jacket and held the small flashlight on the carved rock ahead of them. Aidan led them out of the mine as fast as he dared. The dim light of the setting sun glimmering on the snow was a welcome relief as they exited.

Raven stumbled in the snow, falling to her knees, her head bowed.

"Raven?" Seeing her hunched over, he knew he was losing her too.

"I'm okay." She grabbed his pants and pulled herself up. "Just tripped."

He slowed the trek to the snowmobile, his body shaking with the need to hurry. Fox's eyelids were shuttering closed and Raven was using everything she had to keep up with him. Hell, he didn't know how she'd made it this far.

"Stay with me, guys." He sat Fox on the snowmobile, holding him steady as he mounted the machine, wrapping the edges of his parka around Fox. It was going to be a tough ride back to the lodge with the machine loaded down with the three of them. Raven got on and leaned onto Aidan's back, her arms wrapping loosely around his waist. "Hold onto me tighter, sweetheart." He felt her try, but she was spent. He started the machine and headed down the hill. At least they were close to the lodge and the trails were packed from other snow machines. Halfway to the lodge, Aidan felt his son give into sleep. It felt like forever until the lodge came into view. He pulled the machine right up to the front door, hollering for help.

Sonya and Fiona were the first to appear, followed closely by Peter and Lana.

Lana.

Had she been told of her father's death? He couldn't worry about that now. Not with Fox and Raven in danger.

"We need to get them to the hospital."

"Oh, good heavens," Fiona exclaimed. "Eva!"

Eva waddled out the front door, holding the underneath of her swollen belly. "What the hell happened?"

"Fox is in the second stage of hypothermia, and…and Raven…" He had to take another breath. "Raven's been shot." His heart stuttered over all that he could lose.

Fiona gasped, her hand covering her mouth as tears sprang to her eyes.

Eva rushed over to them. Aidan was afraid to move off the snow machine. Raven and Fox were both awfully quiet and he was sandwiched between the two of them. Any jostling he did could shake them both to the icy ground.

"Fiona, get me some hot water bottles and blankets," Eva began barking orders. "Lana, give her a hand. Sonya, find us a vehicle to take them to Fairbanks. Peter, get those men back here. Let them know we have Fox and what the situation is."

"Yes, ma'am." Peter hurried after the women.

Eva checked the pulse at Fox's neck. He was still unconscious, and his shivering had stopped.

"Where was Raven shot?" Eva softly asked.

Raven stirred behind him, the movement a blast of hope to his heart. It had been so long since he'd felt anything more than her weight pressing heavily onto his back.

"It's just a graze. We need to get Fox to the hospital." Raven moved to stand. Eva rushed to help as Raven stumbled off the snow machine. "Help me get these damn snowshoes off or I'm going to kill myself."

"I've got keys to someone's Durango," Sonya said, coming back out of the lodge with her coat on. "I'll get it started and warmed up." She hurried to the electric-blue SUV parked in the lot.

Aidan climbed off the snowmobile, lifted Fox into his arms, and walked over to the Durango where Eva had opened the door to the backseat. He gently laid Fox on the seat, taking off his coat and wrapping it around his son. His lips were bright blue, his breathing fast and shallow. Fiona appeared behind Aidan and handed him the hot water bottles. He tucked them around Fox, up and under his coat, covering him with the thick blankets that Fiona had also provided. Eva scooted in next to Fox.

Raven stood swaying on her feet. "Eva, tell me he's going to be okay."

"He's going to be fine. Now let's get this sorry-ass group to the hospital."

Aidan made a quick grab for Raven as her head lolled on her shoulders. He caught her up in his arms just before she would have hit the ground.

CHAPTER TWENTY-SEVEN

Aidan paced the putty-colored corridors of the ER. Eva had called ahead on her cell and had the staff prep for their arrival. But things were still taking too long. He'd already been questioned by the troopers as the doctors had to report on Raven's gunshot. There had been no word on Fox. They'd kicked him out of the room since he was in the way and Raven had been sent up for a CAT scan as she hadn't regained consciousness by the time they'd arrived.

Fiona and Sonya had followed in another car and were quietly talking in the corner of the waiting room with Eva. Every now and then he felt their worried eyes on him. Life had never played him a winning hand. How could he expect that now would be any different?

He should never have come back.

But then if he hadn't come back he wouldn't know about Fox, wouldn't have gotten to know what a great kid his own flesh and blood was. And the wondrous stolen hours with Raven, how could he wish those had never happened? Yes, things hadn't gone as planned, but when did they? Who's to say what would have happened if he hadn't been here when Roland and Genie set into motion their play for the gold? What if Fox had stumbled onto one of them like he had today and Aidan hadn't been here to help find him? Fox might not have made it.

One thing Aidan had come to realize, he wasn't giving up on his family. He loved Raven, always had. And he loved Fox. He was staying. He was going to be there for both of them. Even if Raven decided she didn't want him around, he still had a right to be Fox's father. Do fatherly stuff. He'd make right the wrongs of the past by being the man he knew he could be, the kind of father to Fox that he wished he'd had.

The doors to the ER whooshed open, bringing with it a blast of frigid air and Garrett Hunt.

"What's the status?" Garrett asked, hands on hips, in full cop mode.

"They're treating Fox for hypothermia. He's got frostbite on his fingers and toes. We don't know how bad it is yet. He curled up into a ball for warmth, which protected his face. Raven is still unconscious. They just took her up for a CAT scan."

"We got Genie. She's being booked for kidnapping, two counts of attempted murder, and the murder of your uncle."

"How'd the hell did you find her?"

"When you radioed in we could hear you but you couldn't hear us. We followed where you said you'd picked up Fox's trail and found Genie tied to a tree. Pretty smart leaving her there secured with your coat strings."

"Too bad the wolves didn't get to her."

"A meaner pack of wolves will get her in prison. She isn't going anywhere for a long time. But we didn't find any sign of the gold."

"I never thought there was any. How's Lana?"

"Peter's with her. She's upset but resigned. She knew what kind of man her father was. I'm sure it came as no surprise that he'd meet a bad end."

Aidan nodded. "Roland?"

"At the morgue on ice. Troopers are all over everything in Chatanika."

"Yeah, they sent some of their buddies here. I've already talked to them."

Sonya walked up to them. "Hey, guys. Do you know where Lynx is?"

"He should've beaten me here." Garrett checked his watch. "Why, what's going on?"

Sonya worried her bottom lip. "Eva's in labor."

Aidan and Garrett swiveled to stare at Eva. She was sitting in a chair bent at the waist with both arms wrapped around her belly, her face a mask of agony.

"Has she tried his cell?" Garrett asked, his tone rising from calm, cool, collected lawman to the nervous soon-to-be-in-the-same-situation-expectant-father.

"Yeah. Goes right to voicemail."

"When is she due?" Aidan asked.

"Two weeks. She's called her doctor and he's on the way, but she wants Lynx."

"I'll go and find him," Garrett said, turning to leave just as the doors whooshed opened again.

Lynx was wheeled into the ER on a gurney flanked by two EMTs. A bloody bandage was wrapped around Lynx's head and dried blood was all over his face.

"What the hell happened to you?" Garrett asked.

"Got hit by a damn moose," Lynx muttered. "Hey, babe." Lynx looked up at Eva who'd wobbled her way across the foyer when she'd seen him enter. "I'm sorry, babe, but the truck didn't make it."

"Lynx Maiski, don't you dare think of upstaging me."

"Huh?"

"I'm in labor, you idiot." Her words ended on a worried screech. "What do you mean 'you hit a moose'?"

"No, babe. The moose *hit* me."

Eva glanced at the EMT's. "How hard did he hit his head?"

"Uh...well, he took the windshield out with it." The EMT stepped back from the little dynamo when she glared at him and then started dolling out information. "He's got a possible concussion. Definitely in need of stitches....broken nose, possible broken leg."

"Shit." Eva pursed her lips. "Anything else?"

"Uh...he's going to need to see a dentist."

Lynx smiled and showed the hole where his two front teeth should have been.

"You look like a damn redneck." Suddenly she bent over and gave a long dreadful moan.

Lynx's eyes widened. "What's wrong with you?"

"I told *you*," Eva said through clenched teeth, "I'm in *labor*."

"You serious? Now?"

"Yes, now." She slapped him. "Shit this hurts."

"Babe." Lynx reached for her. "Honey, what can I do?"

"Find me some drugs."

"I thought you wanted to do this natural."

Eva gave him a look that had the power to skin him alive.

"Right. You want drugs, drugs you will have." He looked at the EMT guy. "Can you hook us up?"

An observant nurse at the ER station was already bringing a wheelchair. Eva thanked her and gratefully took a seat. She arrowed a look toward Aidan. "Fill me in as soon as you know something." Then both Lynx and Eva entered the ER, one on a gurney, the other in a wheelchair, clutching each other's hand.

"I wouldn't go near that woman until she's delivered that baby," Garrett said under his breath.

Sonya elbowed him in the ribs. "Are you going to be like this when I go into labor?"

"You gotta admit she's over the top."

"You have no idea what we women go through bringing children into the world." Sonya turned on her heel and marched back to her chair.

The ER doors breezed open again. Aidan and Garrett turned to see Tern fly into the room, her long black coat slapping around her slayer black boots. "What in the *hell* has been happening in Chatanika?"

Raven lay with her eyes closed. Her head pounded like a drum on the warpath. Bang. Bang. Bang. The smell of disinfectant assaulted her nose, and her mouth felt as dry as one of her greenware pots. Where was she? Part of her didn't care. That part wanted to sink back into the dark abyss waiting to embrace her. She was afraid to open her eyes. Laying here in the dark, even with the drum gig, seemed preferable to opening her eyes to what might lay ahead. Then she remembered.

"Fox," she said, the sound coming out weak and hoarse.

Someone squeezed her hand. "He's going to be fine. He's demanding to see you as soon as you wake. But let's give that some time. Seeing you right now would probably scare him to death."

Aidan. She sighed. Aidan was holding her hand and her son was okay. Then Aidan's words registered. "What do I look like?"

"Like hell." A straw was suddenly at her lips. "Here, drink some water."

She sucked water up the straw, quenching her thirst, until he took the straw from her.

"Small sips. You don't want to throw up."

He took her hand again and she felt him kiss her fingers.

"Where's Fox?" She struggled to open her eyes, but the dim lighting in the room blinded, slicing shards of ice through her already pounding skull.

"He's just down the hall. They're keeping both of you overnight for observation."

"What happened?"

"A lot has happened since you checked out. Why don't you tell me the last thing you remember?"

"Fox tied up in the mine. Long ride back to the lodge." A ride she didn't think she'd survive.

"Fox has a minimal case of frostbite on his fingers and toes. Something he'll have to compensate for when he's outside. You on the other hand, have a serious concussion. How *did* you remain conscious when we were looking for Fox? The doctors said there was no way you could have achieved what you did with a head injury like yours. I wouldn't have found Fox without you."

She struggled again, trying to open her eyes. She wanted to see Aidan's face, but darkness beckoned on the fringes reaching out with its numbing arms. Her lids fluttered, she saw his blurry outline sitting next to her bed, leaning forward over their clasped hands. "You would have found him," she whispered.

He changed the subject. "By the way, congratulations, you're an aunt. Eva had her baby early this morning. They're following in Coho's footsteps and naming her Meadow Lark."

"A little girl." She smiled, losing the battle on keeping her eyes open. "Is everyone all right?" she asked softly.

"Mom and baby are doing great. Lynx is still recovering. I'll tell you more about him later. Right now I want you to rest."

Raven relaxed. Fox was safe. Her family was safe. She let the darkness cradle her in its drug-induced grip.

Aidan watched Raven sink into sleep and breathed a thankful prayer. Her CAT scan had come back with swelling on the brain, and the doctors couldn't tell him if she'd be all right or not. The longer Raven stayed unconscious the more dangerous her condition. She'd stirred a few times during the long vigil he'd divided between her room and Fox's, but hadn't totally awakened...until now.

Pike quietly entered the room. "How goes it?"

"She woke, we talked. She knows who she is and seems to remember everything."

The gruff old man had to swallow hard before he spoke. "Good. I've come to sit with her for a spell while you get something to eat. I smuggled in some of Fox's Fabulous French Fries. He's waiting for you."

Aidan stood, his muscles complaining. How long had he sat in this spot? "Thanks, Pike." He reached the door and then turned back as a thought struck him. "Who's watching the lodge?"

"Shut her down for the day. The whole family's up here. I needed to be here with the rest of you."

It was Aidan's turn to swallow past the emotion thickening his throat. He hadn't missed the inflection Pike had added to his statement. Aidan nodded his appreciation and quietly left the room. He walked a few doors down and entered.

In contrast to Raven's dim, quiet room, Fox's was full of color and noise. Balloons hung in a helium bouquet in the corner, delivered by Tern before she went to open the shop. The TV was set to the Cartoon Network where Batman was currently getting the best of the Joker. Fox sat crossed-legged on the bed, a stack of pillows propped behind him, while he dipped fries in ketchup. Besides the rope marks and bruising on his wrists and ankles, you'd never know he'd undergone the ordeal of the last twenty-four hours.

Fiona reclined in a corner chair talking with a woman dressed in a designer suit and snow boots and a man, wearing blue jeans and a flannel shirt, holding a television camera.

Fox tore his gaze away from the couple when he noticed Aidan. "Dad!" He smiled, his teeth showing bits of potatoes as he continued to cram fries into his mouth. "How's Mom? Can I see her yet?"

"Not yet. But she woke for a bit and it looks like she's going to be fine." He shared a reassuring glance with Fiona who discreetly dabbed at the corner of her eyes. "What's going on here?" He addressed the question to the two strangers.

"They want to do a story on us," Fox said. "On TV. Isn't that cool?"

"What kind of story?" Aidan frowned.

The woman in the smart navy suit was the one to answer him, offering him her hand to shake. "My name is Brooke Malone. I'm a correspondent for KTVF Channel 11. We'd like to do a follow up on the—" she glanced at Fox and lowered her voice "—the unfortunate incidents of yesterday."

"She means Mr. Harte's murder, my kidnapping, Mom's shooting, all done by the famed Lonely Lady stripper, Genie in the Bottle," Fox said around a mouthful of fries.

Aidan tried not to smile. "Hmm."

"It's a hero piece, Dad. Isn't that perfect?"

"Hero piece?"

Brooke Malone stepped forward, gesturing with her hands. "We want to tell about what you did, rescuing your family under such hostile conditions. You're the hero of the hour and we'd like to do a special interest report on it."

"Uh…" A rush of emotion stole Aidan's breath. *Hero? Him?* He wrote about heroes. He'd never been the hero in anything.

"Isn't that cool, Dad."

"Uh…yeah." He needed some air. "If you'd excuse me for a moment, I gotta…go." Before he melted like a snowman under a spring sun, Aidan rushed out of the room, down the hall, until he found the stairwell. He pushed the metal door open and fell back against the cool surface. What the hell was wrong with him? He was acting like a sissy girl all because someone thought he was a hero. He was no hero. He hadn't done any more than any other man would have done for the people he loved. So why were tears flooding his eyes?

He pushed away from the door and sat on the stair riser before his legs gave out. What a mess he was. A blubbering, sniveling mess.

The door cracked open and Fiona peeked her head around the corner. "I thought I saw you duck in here." Rather than leave him in peace, she entered the stairwell and sat next to him.

He quickly wiped his eyes on the sleeve of his shirt. "Fox okay? Raven?"

"I'm more worried about you right now. It's difficult seeing yourself in a different light, isn't it?"

He nodded as emotion, he couldn't seem to turn off, flooded him.

She gently smoothed back the hair that had fallen over his forehead. "I always knew this man was in you. I'm glad you are finally meeting him." She leaned over and kissed his cheek. "That son of yours wants to be on TV."

Panic stirred in with the other crap he was trying to stamp back in its place, making breathing next to impossible.

"You can't disappoint him."

That was the crux of the problem. Dealing with people seeing him as he'd always wanted to be seen scared the shit out of him. What if he failed them now?

"Come on. Go and splash water on your face, maybe take a quick trip out in the cold. You'll look refreshed rather than spent." Fiona smiled at him with love shining from her eyes. "Either that, or I have some makeup in my bag we could try."

He choked out a laugh, got himself under control. "Thanks, Fiona."

"No. Thank you." She smoothed back his hair again, looking deeply into his eyes until she touched his soul. "I love you, Aidan, just as much as if you were one of my own."

Tears tightened his chest. He couldn't keep himself from reaching out and wrapping his arms tight around her. She smelled like blueberries.

Fiona rubbed his back and held him for a moment, then patted his shoulder. "Go. Get yourself cleaned up. I'll hold off the reporters until then."

He released her and stood, helping Fiona to her feet. "Thanks, again. And just so you know, I've always loved you and Fox senior."

"I know you do, Aidan. I've always known."

Dealing with reporters was hell, but the news segment was taped and due to air that evening. Fox was over the moon, he'd spent the rest of the afternoon calling all his friends. The doctors had released him, but decided to keep Raven one more night. Aidan was relieved when she awoke again to see that the dark film of pain had released its hold on her and the deep, warm brown of her eyes was showing through.

Aidan hung back in the corner, leaning against the wall of Raven's room, enjoying Fox's impatient wait for the news program to begin, regaling Raven with the story how they had interviewed them earlier. Fiona and Pike had returned to the lodge. He hadn't seen any sign of Garrett and Sonya. He figured they were helping Peter with Lana until he could be there with her. They'd had a short conversation on the phone and she'd promised not to leave until he'd returned to Chatanika.

There was a knock on the door and Eva wheeled in Lynx who held their new baby girl as though she were made of glass. "Heard you were up for visitors," Eva said.

"What happened to you?" Raven asked Lynx, her expression one of disbelief. "Eva, what are you doing wheeling him around? You just had a baby?"

"Yeah, you don't *need* to tell me that." Eva grimaced. "Just goes to prove again, who the stronger sex is."

"I'm never living this down, am I?" Lynx murmured, shaking his head.

"Not in this lifetime." Eva took a seat near the bed and asked Raven, "So how are you feeling?"

"Better. What about you?"

"You should have seen her," Lynx said, pride in his voice, "giving the nurses and doctors orders as she pretty much single-handedly delivered little Lark. Do you want to hold her?"

"Oh can I?" Raven held out her arms as Eva transported the baby into them. Raven's face lit up and she cooed to the sleepy, pink infant in that womanly, motherly way. "She's beautiful."

"We think so," Eva said.

"The most beautiful baby girl in the whole world," Lynx said.

Raven glanced at her brother. "Want to fill me in on why *you* are in the wheelchair?"

"A moose hit me."

Eva rolled her eyes. "Come on, Lynx. You hit the moose. I'm not buying that a kamikaze moose lay in wait until you rounded the corner and then broadsided you."

"But that's what happened. It came barreling out of the trees, hit me on the passenger side and pushed me off the road. The tree I hit killed the truck. The moose snorted as it walked away." He let out a frustrated breath. "Just you wait until you see the truck. Then you'll believe me."

"Okay, hon. Whatever you say."

Lynx tried to convince Eva again with another play-by-play, but Aidan lost interest. He couldn't take his eyes off Raven. She looked so natural holding the baby. How had she looked cradling their son in her arms? Did she ever wish she'd had more children?

She must have felt his eyes on her for she glanced up and their gazes caught. Heat began to smolder between them and just when he thought he'd implode, she turned back as Tern entered the room, carrying a vase of flowers.

He should have bought Raven flowers.

Tern set the vase down and jockeyed for position to hold the baby next, oohing and ahhing. The hospital room had gone from small to cramped.

"Hey, guys," Fox interrupted the chatter. "Look, there's me and Dad." He turned off the mute button on the remote and increased the volume.

Aidan flicked his gaze to the television. Brooke Malone introduced the segment, standing to the side of Fox in his hospital bed with Aidan sitting on the edge looking scared shitless. The walk Fiona had suggested hadn't done the trick. He looked flushed, his eyes bloodshot, his skin waxy. Maybe he should have let her have at him with the makeup?

Brooke's words blended together creating a static in his head as the interview was replayed on the screen. Luckily it was a short segment, and the camera faded to Brooke standing outside the hospital.

"Something like a Greek tragedy unfolded in the otherwise quiet town of Chatanika this evening. Acclaimed graphic novelist of the best-selling Spirit Totem series, Aidan Harte, is being hailed a hero tonight. Just like one of the heroes right out of his own novels, Mr. Harte saved the lives of his son and the mother of his child, while also apprehending alleged kidnapper and murderer Alba Flake.

"What makes this story even more sensational is that Mr. Harte reportedly gunned down his father, Earl Harte, last July, while defending two hostages. The deceased, Earl Harte's brother Roland, was wanted for questioning in three deaths, and according to sources, both men were intimate acquaintances of Alba Flake, street name 'Genie in the Bottle', who is currently being held without bail on charges of murder, attempted murder, and kidnapping."

I know this reporter will sleep better knowing that the heroic Aidan Harte is living nearby."

Aidan sucked in his breath. The news reporter had certainly done her homework.

The room, which had been full of love and well-wishes, went silent.

Then Tern laughed. "Your editor's going to love this when it hits the Internet. Think of all the free press."

Ah, hell. Aidan wanted to sink into the institutional gray walls. Just his luck, the networks were bound to pick the story up and broadcast his horrific family history.

"You'll probably become even more popular." Eva nodded.

"Yeah," Lynx added. "Your family connections will finally be worth something. Bet they'll add an extra zero to your next contract."

He risked a glance in Raven's direction. She was focused on the baby, but he knew she felt his gaze on her. The room turned silent again, until Fox who seemed clueless to the undercurrents said, "I'm hungry. Can we head to the cafeteria? I'm in the mood for Jello."

"Sure," Aidan said. "It's been a long time since I've had Jello."

CHAPTER TWENTY-EIGHT

Raven fell back against the pillows. Eva, Lynx, and little Lark had returned to their wing of the hospital. Aidan had taken Fox home, but Tern was still visiting. She'd had enough visitors. All she wanted was quiet and peace. Quiet so deep, she didn't have to think. Her head still pounded and if she stood for too long the room spun. She'd be released tomorrow. Then what?

"Want to tell me what the hell that had been about?" Tern asked, waiting two seconds after the door had shut on Fox and Aidan.

"What was what about?"

"Come on. Don't milk the concussion." She planted her hands on hips covered in designer jeans. "You didn't say one word after that interview."

"What was I supposed to say?"

"Let me tell you something. You're going to lose the only man you've ever loved if you don't get over whatever this 'thing' is."

Pain sliced behind her eyes and she had to shut them. "Can we do this later?"

"How much longer are you going to drag this out? It's been twelve years." Raven felt the bed give and opened her eyes enough to see Tern perched on the edge. "Is this still about Dad?"

Raven gave a heavy sigh. "When Dad was dying, he made me promise to stay away from Aidan."

Tern sucked in her breath. "Oh, honey. Dad didn't know what kind of man Aidan would grow into." She covered Raven's clasped hands with one of her own. "Dad knew who killed him. He was only trying to protect you. Do you really think he would make you promise something like that now?"

"I don't know," Raven whispered. It was too much effort keeping her eyes open. "I just don't know what to do anymore."

"You've got to listen to your heart. Lord knows, listening to your head has seriously fucked up your life."

Aidan entered the restaurant of the lodge looking for Lana. He found her at a corner table with Sonya, Garrett, and Peter lending her support. It was late, and he'd seen Fox tucked into bed, camping in Chickadee's room where she wasn't letting him out of her sight.

She stood when she saw him and rushed over to give him a hug. "Hey, how is everyone?" she asked.

"Fine. They're going to be fine." He looked into her clear blue eyes. "How are you doing?"

"Okay." She gave him a smile that didn't quite reach her eyes. "Really. I'm all right."

They took a seat at the table. Sonya sat next to him, Lana on his other side, Peter next to her, and Garrett right across the table staring him down.

"CSI has released the cabin. Your cabin," Garrett said. "You're free to move back there whenever you want."

"Are you planning on staying?" Sonya asked.

"I'll have to make some adjustments to the cabin, but yeah, I'm staying."

"I'm staying too." Lana worried the edge of a napkin, looking shyly up at Aidan. "Would you mind if I lived closer?"

"No, that would be great. I'd love having you near, but you don't want to stay at the cabin, do you?" Not in the place that her father had been murdered.

"Oh, no." She shuddered. "Peter and I have been talking and I've decided to transfer from the University of Minnesota to UAF." She looked at Peter with more than puppy love. "So, I'll be living in Fairbanks."

With Peter or on campus, Aidan wanted to ask, but didn't feel it was his place. But then maybe it was. He was her family, her only male relative. He cleared his throat. "Uh, where in Fairbanks are you going to be living?"

Peter blushed but Lana smiled. This time it reached her eyes. "I hope to find a place on campus. If not, I'll get an apartment." She paused a moment. "Alone."

"He gives you any trouble, you talk to me." Aidan eyed Peter, who was pulling at the collar of his t-shirt.

Sonya laughed and patted Aidan on the shoulder. "Glad to know someone will be watching out for the two of them. Thanks, Aidan." Her face was soft and caring as she regarded him. Probably those pregnancy hormones.

"Just how long do you two plan to stay?" he asked, the question directed at Garrett. While Aidan didn't find the fish cop as offensive anymore, he was still damned obnoxious.

"We're leaving in the morning."

"We have anything to drink to that?"

Garrett threw his head back and laughed. "You know, given enough distance, I might get to like you."

"Hell, I hope not." Aidan had a tough time keeping the grin off his face.

Raven had been home from the hospital for two days. Other than the day Tern had brought her home, with the excuse that she had to check things out in Chatanika since everything had gone to hell, she hadn't seen Aidan. He'd given her a nod, asked if she needed anything and then when she said she didn't, he'd left. Eva and Lynx had returned with little Lark. With the newborn baby in residence, not much attention was given to Raven, which was just the way she needed it. She had a lot to think about.

On the third day, Raven got out of bed, showered, stared too long in the mirror at the ugly stitches and shaved section of hair above her ear. Her hair grew down to the middle of her back, how was she going to work with the shaven path? For now, she carefully pulled a brush through the long mass and left it to hang. At least that covered most of the area. She'd have to make an appointment with a beautician to see what kind of hairstyle worked with bullet wounds.

Fox had taken his dog team out for a much needed run, promising he wouldn't go far and Tern was helping Fiona and Pike at the lodge.

She couldn't put this meeting off any longer. She shouldn't have put it off this long. But that blasted man had stayed away from her. Why? Why had he stayed away?

Because you acted like that was what you wanted, dimwit.

Dimwit was one word to describe her. Bitch was another.

There were a lot of names Raven called herself before she finally parked her Suburban next to Aidan's rental. Smoke curled cheerfully from the stovepipe into the overcast sky. Snow had been cleared, creating a safe, direct path from the road to the back door of the cabin. While the cabin didn't look inviting, it didn't scare the pants off her either. She noticed some improvements Aidan had made on the way to the back door. Tin had been replaced on the roof, a new lean-to for wood had been built and stacked with logs waiting to be chopped.

Her hand shook as she raised it to knock on the door. It seemed like forever before it swung open.

Aidan stood there wearing blue jeans and a gray SeaHawks sweatshirt. His hair was too long, unruly and utterly adorable. His eyes widened in surprise. "Raven, what are you doing here?"

"Well, since you weren't going to come and see me, it was up to me to come and see you."

"I didn't think you wanted to see me."

"You were wrong." She shivered. "Can I come in?"

"Yes, of course."

He stepped aside and she entered the small area, brushing against him as she moved into the bigger room. She didn't miss his sharp intake of breath.

"How are you feeling?" he asked as he took her coat, turning and hanging it on a hook that hadn't been there before.

"Fine. I still have headaches, but the doctor said that was normal for now." She glanced around the room. Blankets covered the old couch and draped over the two chairs, with a rug covering the floor where Roland had laid dead. A small desk had been set up in the corner and was covered in drawings. Some of the drawings were tacked to the wall. She knew what those drawings meant now and how talented a storyteller Aidan was. The last few days, she'd pored over his graphic novels. It was like seeing through a window at the last twelve years of his life. And a little into his soul.

"Would you like a cup of coffee?" he asked, shoving his hands in the front pocket of his jeans.

"No, thank you." She stared at him now. He hadn't shaved in days, but he seemed comfortable, decided she thought. As though he'd come to a realization. "You're staying?"

"Yeah." His jaw tightened and he straightened his shoulders as if ready to take a blow. "Fox is my son. I need to be here. He needs me in his life, and I need him in mine."

Raven nodded. "You're right." His brows lowered in obvious confusion. "Fox does need you." She took a deep breath and let her heart finally speak. "I need you too."

"Say again?" he whispered as though he couldn't believe what she had said.

Raven laid her hands on his chest. His heart pounded wildly under her palms giving her strength. "I'm so sorry, Aidan, for lying to you, for the things I said to you the other day, for making you leave twelve years ago."

"Raven—"

"No, let me finish. I've never understood that kind of rage until Fox had been taken. I would have killed Genie, relished getting my hands around her throat." Just the thought of what that bitch had put her son through had anger rising in Raven like the river after a heavy winter. It took a lot to dam it back.

"I judged you based on the sins of your father. You aren't him, could never be him. I see that now, and I'm so sorry that I didn't see it sooner. I need you. I need you to stay. I need you to promise never to leave me again no matter what I say. I love you,

Aidan Harte. I always have." Her voice broke as emotion welled inside her.

Aidan yanked her against him and buried his face in the crook of her neck. "No take backs." He pulled away and held her shoulders in his tight grip. "You can't take it back this time."

"Never. I lied to you twelve years ago. I never wanted you to leave, and when I told you to and you did I was so angry. I thought you would return, but you never did." Tears ran unchecked down her face, and she didn't care. There were tears in his eyes too. Either that or she was crying enough for the both of them.

"You made me promise never to return."

"I know." She sobbed. "There's so much I need to ask forgiveness for. Please forgive me."

He kissed her, letting his lips speak for him. After a very long while, he lifted his head and gazed lovingly down into her eyes. "Will I ever understand you?"

"No. Not completely. All you have to remember is how much I love you."

He pulled her back into his arms and held her tight against him. "God, Raven. I love you. Marry me. Finally, be my family."

"Yes," she cried. "Tomorrow, if we can."

The door slammed. "What happened!" Fox hollered. "Mom, why are you crying? Dad? Did someone else die?"

Aidan and Raven jumped apart, both wiping tears from their eyes.

"No. No one died." Raven laughed through her tears. "What do you think about your parents getting married?"

"It's about time you two got hitched." Fox beamed, rushing forward to give them hugs.

They stayed together, a tight unit, until Fox squirmed. "Can't breathe," he said.

"How'd your team do today," Aidan paused, "without Lucien?"

"They were confused. It took them a while to get the hang of it, but we had a quiet moment for Lucien and then Senyea took lead."

"She would be the one." Aidan chuckled and ruffled Fox's hair. "What do you say we look for a new dog to balance out the team?"

"Hey," Raven said. "We should discuss things like this, *as parents*, before we let the kid in on it."

Aidan sauntered up to her, trailing his fingers over her cheek. "What do you say we work on making another kid, maybe a sister for Fox?"

"Ohh." Raven melted into Aidan's arms, the tears back in full faucet mode.

"TMI," Fox said, closing his eyes. "Is there going to be a lot of that kind of talk going on? Because that's going to take some serious getting used to." He shuddered. "Besides, there's something I have to show you."

They moved apart, but still held hands.

"What do you have to show us?" Aidan asked.

"Gold."

"What are you talking about?"

Fox moved over toward the side of the stove.

"Careful, that's...hot," Raven warned unnecessarily as Fox turned a bolt on one of the cast iron feet.

There was a loud click as the sidewall behind the stove moved slightly. Fox pried open the door, which when closed fit seamlessly into the wall. He reached in and pulled out a small canvas bag the size of a cantaloupe. With two hands, he carried the heavy sack to Aidan.

"No." Aidan shook his head. "Whatever is in that isn't mine." He looked at Raven. "It had to have been your dad's, which makes it yours."

Fox set it on the floor between them and opened the drawstring bag. Yellow gold nuggets glittered in the light. Raven caught her breath and reverently reached for one, pulling out a nugget two inches long, weighing at least four ounces.

"There's a fortune in this bag," she whispered.

"Yeah, and there's at least a hundred more bags stacked in the wall," Fox revealed.

"How did you know about this?" Aidan asked.

Fox smiled a clever smile. "Haven't you figured it out by now? Kids know everything."

Raven chuckled and shared a look with Aidan. "Our kid certainly does."

Aidan moved to the opening in the wall, whistling when he saw the truth of Fox's statement. The wall was only a foot wide, which fooled the eye into thinking it was a normal stud wall, but it ran the length of at least eight feet. And all of those feet were stacked waist-high with bags identical to the one Fox had opened. There had to be millions of dollars' worth of gold hidden away in this ransacked cabin. "No wonder Genie was willing to kill for this."

"What had Earl planned on doing with all this gold?" Raven echoed his thoughts, having come up behind him, seeing the evidence for herself.

"Who knows what the old man was thinking." Aidan shook his head. "We need to hide this back up and plan on moving it under the cover of darkness. If anyone found out about this..."

"We've already dealt with that," Raven said.

"Dad's right," Fox said. "The gold needs to be moved. Genie's not going to stay quiet in prison. She knows it's here. Earl paid her in nuggets for her…services."

How did Fox know this stuff? Aidan picked up the bag, surprised over the weight, and put it back in the hiding place and then shut the door.

"Wait." Raven held up the nugget she still held.

Aidan took it from her and put it in his pocket. "I have plans for this one." He got caught up gazing into Raven's warm, inviting eyes until Fox cleared his throat.

"We gotta get back in time for dinner."

Raven glanced at her watch. "Oh, we'd better hurry. Aidan, do you mind driving? I'm still a little shaky behind the wheel."

"Uh, sure." Guess he was invited to dinner. Having all his dreams come true was going to take a little getting used to.

"I'll meet you there," Fox said. "I need to get the dogs back."

"Be careful," Raven said.

"Yes, Mom."

"Listen to your mother," Aidan couldn't help adding with a silly grin.

Fox's grin was even sillier. "Yes, Dad." And then he scampered out of the cabin, the dogs excited barks sounding as soon as they saw him.

Aidan wrapped his arms around Raven. "How much time do we have before dinner?"

Raven gave a totally feminine sound that thrilled him to his soul. She tucked her hand in the waistband of his pants and pulled him toward the bedroom. "We'll have to be quick."

"Woman, 'quick' isn't going to be my problem."

They arrived at the lodge late, but totally satisfied. Raven made him pack an overnight bag because he was moving in with her that night. They could get the rest of his stuff later. At some point, he'd have to return to Seattle and sell his condo, along with packing and moving his stuff to Alaska. Maybe Fox and Raven would like to take a trip to Washington over Christmas vacation?

They entered the kitchen where the whole family was seated, including Peter and Lana, Eva and Lynx and little Lark. The table had been stretched to accommodate the many seats and was stacked with food. A golden-browned turkey waited to be carved, along with mash potatoes and gravy and all the fixings for a bountiful Thanksgiving Dinner.

Today was Thanksgiving?

"What took you guys so long?" Fox asked from his seat, next to two waiting chairs.

Raven blushed bright red. "Car trouble." Which the disbelieving group didn't buy.

"Actually we were bringing a gift for Coho," Aidan said, reaching into his front pocket.

"Me?" Coho asked.

Aidan held up the two inch long gold nugget. The group hushed. "I believe this was the size you requested."

"Oh my goodness gracious." Coho took the nugget into her hands, her eyes wide. "Unbelievable."

"You found the gold?" Lynx asked, a note of betrayal in his voice. "I wanted to help."

"We didn't find it," Aidan said. "Fox knew were it was all along."

"Well, why didn't you say something?" Lynx asked.

"Nobody asked me." Fox shrugged. "Can we eat now? I'm starved."

Pike stood, waited for Aidan and Raven to take their seats and then he began. "This year our table truly runneth over. There is much to be thankful for. A new member of the family and old members finally returned back to us." He indicated little Meadow Lark cradled in Eva's arms, and nodded at Aidan, who had to lower his gaze to his plate to hide the emotion shining there. "And to new friends." Pike gestured to Peter and Lana, then cleared his throat and shuffled his feet as though nervous. He reached down and offered his hand to Fiona, which she took. "Also, Fiona, has finally consented to be my wife."

A shocked silence vibrated through the room followed quickly by loud cheers and a few, about damn times. Food was forgotten as congratulations were passed around, though Fox did help himself to a roll during all the ruckus.

As the noise echoed around them, Raven leaned in close to Aidan, touching the wolf totem he hadn't removed since she had given it back to him. She picked up the carved wolf, caressing it with her fingers. "You know the wolf symbolizes family."

"Yes." Words were suddenly difficult for him to utter. This woman was his mate, these people his pack. Aidan leaned over and gently kissed his Raven. "Wolves also mate for life."

Raven smiled and shook her head. "Spirit wolves mate forever."

A PREVIEW OF

DEATH CACHE

Tiffinie Helmer

By Special Invitation Only

1st Annual Extreme Geocaching Competition

June 7th – 14th

Time & Place: 8:00 a.m. N64° 49.098', W147° 55.0349'

Lodging: Rustic cabins on a pristine glacial-fed lake.

What to bring: Pack for survival in Alaska's Extreme Backcountry.

Do you dare to be the best?

CHAPTER ONE

"Well, hell. I've slept with everyone here." Tern Maiski's gaze swept the airplane hangar. All four of her exes stood next to the Cessna, chatting it up, and outfitted like they were headed on the same geocaching trek she was.

"Except you refused to put out for me when I wanted to experiment in college." Nadia Hanson, best friend extraordinaire, came to a stop next to her, giving a slow whistle at the impressive line-up of testosterone. "Damn, girl. Remind me again why you let these guys go."

All eyes turned their direction. The men stood in a row like a reception line from hell.

Tern tightened her hold on the strap of her backpack. She had no problem meeting each of the men's stares. Except Gage Fallon's. The bastard had walked out on her without a word six months ago. Not an email or lousy text message to explain the hard dumping he'd given her. "I should tuck tail and run right now," Tern murmured.

"And let these guys prove that they're better at geocaching than you? You're the one who introduced them to it," Nadia pointed out, knowing it would put her back up.

Sure enough, Tern straightened her shoulders and sauntered forward with a walk that was part take-no-prisoners and part promise-to-rock-your-world.

She greeted Addison 'Mac' MacFearson, fifty-two, with a hug and a kiss on his leathered cheek. He was a rugged Alaskan Bush guide with a 'No Crybabies Allowed' attitude, and she hadn't seen him in a few months. He released her from the bear hug and cocked a knowing smile. "You're in for a trial here, sweet cakes."

Lucky Leroy Morgan, world famous mountain climber, stood next to Mac and winked, his come-hither smile tempting Tern to sidle a little closer.

Man, he'd been fun.

"I thought you were in Africa," she said, staying just out of reach. A lot of good that did, as he took a step forward and grabbed her into a swinging clench.

"I was, until this little adventure presented itself. Damn, but it's good to see you." He followed the swing with a dip and planted a searing kiss on her lips. When he'd righted her, she was dizzy, flushed, and half tempted to follow up on that kiss. But she knew better.

Lucky Leroy was a gambler, not only with his money but his life. He'd climbed Everest and Denali twice—the second time in the dead of winter. There wasn't anything he wasn't willing to try at least once. It hadn't taken her long to know that he was the kind of man she couldn't trust with the grocery money, let alone with her heart. He sure as hell had been a lot of fun, though. Even though she'd ended their relationship, he still looked her up whenever he was in the hemisphere.

"I stopped by the shop last night, but they said you were in Chatanika visiting your family," Lucky said. "Seems lately every time I look you up, you're busy."

"Thought I was waiting around pining for you?"

His hand covered his heart and his bedroom eyes warmed. "A guy can hope."

She introduced him to Nadia, and those eyes heated further in appreciation for her best friend. Another reason she'd cut Lucky loose. The man had a weakness for the ladies, and she didn't share. Period.

Robert Coate was next. He solemnly nodded his head. "Tern," he greeted. His gaze still had the power to nick her heart when she looked directly at him. She'd broken his and the guilt of it weighed heavily on her shoulders.

A business owner of a sporting goods store just down the street from her own shop, The Arctic Tern, Robert had made the most sense in her husband search. He also understood the Native Alaskan in her as he was part Athabascan himself. He was involved in the community, regularly attended church, loved dogs, and was a single parent in need of a mother for his beautiful six-year-old daughter, Chloe, who Tern adored. He was about as close to Mr. Good Enough as she'd found. But no matter how ideal he seemed, she couldn't get past their lack of physical chemistry. And to be honest, she didn't want to be known as Mrs. Tern Coate.

"Hi, Robert. How are you doing?"

"Fine." He straightened his shoulders and hooded his eyes, trying to hide what he still felt for her. It was like this every time they ran into each other since their breakup last fall. Though Tern had tried to let him down easy, easy hadn't worked, and she'd been forced to be brutal in order to make it clear that she was no longer interested in anything more than friendship. Since then they had stuck to 'fine' and 'okay', still feeling around for a more comfortable footing.

And then there was Gage.

Tern's heart hurt just knowing he breathed the same air. It had the added benefit of pissing her off too. She had no business caring about a guy who wasn't man enough to pick up a phone.

From the moment he'd walked into her shop—looking for a gift for his mother—they had ignited. She'd glanced up from her cash register ready with her welcoming spiel, but the words had died on her tongue as everything in her body shivered with awareness. He'd felt the same. Or so she'd thought. She'd sold him a gift for his mother, had dinner with him that night, and made breakfast for him the next morning. They'd been inseparable after that. She'd fallen in love so hard and so fast that when he'd taken off with no word, she'd been devastated.

It still bothered the hell out of her that she didn't know what had gone wrong. One night they couldn't get enough of each other and the next day Gage had vanished from her universe. She'd even gone so far as to contact his employer when days had passed and she couldn't reach him, thinking he'd fallen prey to foul play. But the Director of the Geophysical Institute at the UAF, where Gage taught and studied Space Physics and Aeronomy, had assured her Gage was fine. Fine? She'd been going out of her mind with worry and the bastard was *fine?*

While she refused to look at Gage as she greeted the other men and introduced them to Nadia, she'd felt his eyes burn through her. An answering heat rippled under her skin. She did her best to ignore it and failed.

When she finally turned to face him, heat exploded inside her, and it was all she could do not to lick him like an ice cream cone, all six feet and three inches of him. He'd changed in the long months since she'd seen him. He was leaner, with an edgy danger to him that somehow made him even more attractive. That shouldn't cause her blood to race and her heart to thump harder.

His green eyes were colder, his dark hair longer, and it looked as though he hadn't laughed in a long, long time. The biting remark hanging on her tongue died.

"Tern," he said, in that same husky, deep baritone that had her insides clenching. "Seems you know all the players. Are you the one who sent the invite?"

Like she was a masochist. "No. I'm just as surprised to see you as you are to see me." She met his gaze and tried not to flinch. He didn't look happy to see her at all. She'd bet he wouldn't be here if he'd known she'd been invited on this excursion. It hurt knowing he hadn't missed her the tiniest bit.

Deadbeat. He wasn't worth her heartache.

Nadia bumped into her, and she grabbed a deep breath to introduce her to Gage, but Nadia greeted Gage with a hug. Then Tern remembered. They were both employed by the University. Nadia had been the one to suggest Gage check out her shop when he needed to do his Christmas shopping.

Tern didn't like seeing Nadia in Gage's arms. He smiled at her friend, his eyes crinkling up at the corners as they caught up with each other. Why couldn't he have greeted her like that? She turned away before she gave in and kicked Gage in the shins or fell into a blubbering puddle at his feet.

Through the door of the hangar sat her white Jeep, beckoning like a rocketship. She even took a few steps toward it, before realizing what she was doing and stopped. She couldn't back out now. Not with Gage's eyes boring into her back. If she walked off, he would know how much he'd hurt her. But then, how did she spend a whole week with him in the wilderness and refrain from killing him, or worse, sleeping with him again?

A sandy-haired man, who looked as though he preferred spending more time in the air than on the ground, entered the hangar. "Folks, my name is Hugh, and I'll be ready to take off in about five minutes," their pilot announced. "We'll be taking the DeHavilland Beaver tied up next to the dock. If you'll carry your bags down there, I'll get them loaded, while you take your seats."

"Do we know where we're going?" Robert asked, grabbing his pack and following the pilot.

"Everything will be made clear to you once we're in the air." The pilot shrugged. "Those are the instructions I've been given. Can't have one of you with an advantage."

How about disadvantage?

Tern sure as hell felt like she was at a disadvantage starting out. It didn't seem like anyone else was carrying the emotional baggage with them that she was.

She caught Gage watching her from across the hangar and suddenly felt like a rabbit being hunted by a wolf. Her nipples tightened as something that felt like excitement shivered over her.

"Ready to take off?" Nadia broke through Tern's connection to Gage.

"Nope."

"Ah, come on, Tern." Nadia flashed a smile and gave her newly darkened hair a toss. She'd recently exchanged her natural cinnamon for Tern's raven coloring. Tern was still getting used to the change. "It'll be fun. Once we get there and the games begin, you'll forget all about Gage Fallon."

Right. And they'd see stars in the arctic sky tonight too.

They climbed aboard and took their seats in the floatplane. Nadia sat in back with Gage, sandwiching Tern with Lucky on one side and Robert on the other. Mac sat up front with Hugh.

Fortunately, once they took off on the man-made Chena Marina and were soaring northwest into the brilliant blue sky, the noise in the plane was too loud to carry on a conversation without headphones and mics. Mac and Hugh were the only ones outfitted, which suited Tern just fine. There was too much back and forth going on inside her head to pay attention to anyone else.

Why had she let Nadia talk her into getting on this plane? There was no way that this trip could end well, other than winning and being named the best geocacher in the state. Regardless if she'd seemed a coward, she should have run from the hangar and left this crew on their own. The plane bumped along in a pocket of turbulence as though nodding in agreement.

She'd introduced all these people to the high-tech sport of geocaching, a treasure hunt where the participants used GPS to find hidden caches full of rewards that ranged from simple trinkets, to further instructions, and sometimes money. Damned if these people would prove that they were now better at the techie sport than she was.

After about an hour, the floatplane dipped, beginning its decent. She caught a view out the windows and anticipation replaced the foreboding that bubbled in her thoughts. A glacier-fed lake glistened like an expensive jewel below them, a color man would never be able to duplicate. Iced mountain tops, perfectly frosted by Mother Nature, crowded around the lake as though hoping to pick up any secrets it might whisper of time and space. Spruce ranging in colors of the darkest blue to green to black competed for room among the birch trees. A clearing revealed a nest of small cabins along the south bank of the lake, directly opposite the glacier that receded above the valley.

The DeHavilland skimmed the placid waters of the lake and came to a stop along the sandy bank near the cabins. Hugh powered down the Beaver and silence pressed in.

"Welcome to Nowitna Lake," Hugh said, rolling up his hip waders and climbing out onto the float of the plane. He hopped onto the bank and secured the plane to a birch tree before wading into the water. One by one, they climbed out onto the floats and jumped to shore. Hugh unloaded their packs, tossing them the short distance. It was up to them to catch them or not. Tern seized hers just as it would have smacked her in the face. As it was, she stumbled back a few steps.

Hugh waded to shore, pulled out an envelope from his back pocket, and handed it to Nadia. "Here you go. Instructions are in there on the rules of the game. I'll be back in a week to pick you up." Once that was done, he didn't waste any time in untying the plane, turning it around, and hopping aboard.

They watched, standing in a line, as Hugh took off. Tern wondered if they were all thinking the same thing she was.

Just where the hell were they, and what would they do if he didn't come back?

"Well," Mac said, hitching up his backpack on brick-like shoulders and grabbing his rifle. "The day isn't getting any younger. I suggest we make camp and cook up some grub."

They gathered their gear and headed toward the base camp just a few hundred yards up from the lake. The spot was breathtaking. Grasses so green it hurt Tern's eyes to look at them were intermixed with wildflowers of blue bells, forget-me-nots, brook mint, and cowslips. The air was clean and crisp. Rejuvenating.

Tern breathed in a deep breath and slowly let it out. She'd been locked up too long in her shop this season getting ready for the tourists. It was actually unheard of for her to take time off from work during the summer. It was her money making season, but she had a good crew and she badly needed the break from commitments and responsibilities. The sun beat down with teasing fingers, tempting her into shedding her jacket.

The camp was made up of three small log cabins making up a half moon. Tern and Nadia entered the first cabin, while the men carried their gear into the remaining cabins. The small space housed two cots each. A shelf, hooks for clothes, an end table between the cots, and a wood stove for heating in winter. The bare necessities. It caused a smile to spread over Tern's face, while Nadia frowned.

"This is it?" she asked, scanning the small space as though some modern day amenities would suddenly appear.

"Did you expect maid service?"

"Running water would have been nice."

"There's a pristine lake out front." Tern gestured to the view out the door she'd left propped open for air and light. The little cabin only sported a tiny window, which wasn't able to brighten the dark, rough-honed log interior.

"You're enjoying, this aren't you?"

"God, yes." Tern rolled out her sleeping bag on one of the cots and then laid down on it. "I didn't realize how badly I needed to get out of town until we got here." She turned her head to gaze at Nadia, who fought to untie her sleeping bag. "Thanks for talking me into coming."

"Don't thank me yet," Nadia mumbled. "We still need to find a bathroom."

"I'm sure there's an outhouse in back of the cabins."

"Eww, seriously?" Her mouth dropped open.

Tern laughed at Nadia's staggered expression. "Come on, let's unpack and then get something to eat." She sat up and opened her backpack. As she pulled out her GPS, clothes, toiletries, extra pair of shoes, and pistol, she began to notice some things missing. And her stuff was always more organized than this. "Nadia, do you have everything you packed?"

"Hmm?" Nadia lifted her head from reading the back of one of the many steamy romance novels she was never without. "What?"

"I'm missing my satellite phone, mammoth bag of M&M's, moose jerky…it looks like someone rifled through my pack." Tern frowned.

Nadia dropped the book onto her cot and rummaged through her own backpack. "What the hell? My phone's gone, too, so are my waterproof matches and the goodies I packed."

Lucky knocked on the outside of the cabin. "Hey, the old man's called a meeting."

A shiver of unease settled into her bones. Tern looked at Nadia, and they silently followed Lucky to where the men were standing around a dug out fire pit with sawed-off logs for seats circling the area.

"Your things have been gone through too?" Tern asked.

"Seems to be the case with all of us," Gage said, his jaw hard, eyes narrowed. "My satellite phone is gone, along with the food items I brought."

The same was murmured around the empty fire pit.

"My first aid kit was taken, too, along with the MREs I'd packed," Robert said.

"Didn't the invite say food would be provided?" Lucky asked. "Aren't you guys jumping to conclusions?"

"I think it's damn right suspicious that all our food and emergency supplies were taken," Gage fired back.

"Those of you who brought weapons were left with them," Lucky pointed out.

"I suggest we start a fire," Mac said, calling a halt to the bickering. "The temperature is going to drop fast, once the sun settles over those peaks. Then we'd better do an inventory of what we've been left with. Does anyone have any matches or a lighter?"

"My matches were taken," Nadia said in a small voice and a few of the men shook their heads.

"I've got a lighter." Robert reached into the front pocket of his jeans. "Gave up the smokes months ago, but can't seem to give up carrying the lighter." He looked at Tern as he informed the group of this little personal fact. Another of her complaints about him had been the cigarettes.

Gage broke the uncomfortable silence. "I'll gather some firewood." He headed for the trees.

"Good idea," Mac said. "I suggest we all do the same."

Tern and Nadia walked down to the lake to gather what they could find along the bank.

They returned with enough dry wood to feed a fire throughout the night. Robert started a nice blaze with the dried spruce moss Gage had brought back with the wood he'd gathered. Soon a pleasant snap and crackle was a comforting song to the breeze tickling the coin leaves of the birch trees.

Tern took a seat, reaching her hands out to the flames. She'd put her jacket back on as the temperature had indeed dropped when the sun, while not setting this close to the Arctic Circle, had dipped just below the high peaks of the mountains surrounding them. The breeze wafting off the glacier to the north plunged the temperature twenty degrees cooler than it had been when they'd arrived. They were in for a cold night.

One by one the players of the game took seats on the stumps. Nadia sat next to Tern, Lucky close on Nadia's left. Robert on Tern's right while Mac sat across and Gage remained standing, whittling a piece of diamond willow.

"This is much better," Nadia said, reaching her feet closer to the heat of the fire. "But what are we going to do about food?"

"Nadia, let me see the envelope the pilot gave you," Mac asked.

"Oh, right. I almost forgot about the game, what with all our stuff liberated." Nadia jumped up and rushed to their cabin, returning quickly, and handing the envelope to Mac.

He opened it with a slice of his knife, bending the blade back into its case and slipping it into the scabbard on his belt. He shook out the folded pages, scanned them. "Well, it seems we aren't just to have a race against each other to find the geocaches, but finding them will aid in our survival." He passed the pages around the group.

"What?" Nadia jumped to her feet. "There isn't any food?"

"Doesn't seem like it. We either catch what we eat, or start searching for geocaches and hope they have the supplies these pages promise."

"How the hell is this a competition?" Lucky asked, a scowl on his face.

"It's a test of our survival skills," Mac said, not looking unhappy about the prospect.

"That isn't what we signed up for," Robert added, though he didn't seem adverse to the challenge presented either.

"We knew this was an extreme competition," Mac said. "We all agreed by showing up to this little party."

"I'm here to prove I'm the best geocacher in the state," Lucky said. "That's what I signed up for."

"We already know who the best is." Mac nodded toward Tern.

"Is there any food at all?" Nadia asked. "I'm starved."

"By the looks of the rules, we aren't going to eat until we locate a few geocaches," Mac said. "It's getting late. I suggest we divide up into pairs. No sense in being stupid. There will be protection against the unfriendlies if we stay in numbers. Tern, you pair up with me—"

"What?" Robert scoffed. "No way do the old man and the broad get to pair up."

"Who the hell are you calling a broad?" Tern asked. "Talk like that is going to get you hurt."

"I'd love you to try it, babe." Robert cocked his brow at her in challenge, then turned back to Mac. "And who the fuck put you in charge?" he sneered.

"Age and wisdom, you little shit." Mac stood over Robert, who at least had the survival instincts to back down. "Now—"

"The little shit has a point," Gage interrupted. "No offense, Mac, but you're older and the women are weaker—"

"Hey," Tern spat.

Gage ignored her objection and continued, "We should keep the strength ratio as close to even as we can for protection."

"Draw names," Lucky said. "Luck of the draw."

"I'll get some paper and a pen." Nadia once again rushed back to their cabin. She returned, wrote everyone's name on a piece of paper and tore them into slips. "Gage, can I borrow your hat?"

Gage took off his ball cap and handed it to her, being careful not to get too close to Tern.

Nadia put the names into the cap and one by one drew out a name.

"Robert with—" she reached for a piece of paper "—Mac." She tossed the names into the fire and glanced around waiting for objections, when no one said anything she drew again. "Lucky with, oh, me." She smiled at Lucky, and then faced Tern. "I guess that leaves you and Gage." She mouthed a sorry.

Sorry didn't begin to cover it.

Tern couldn't look at Gage, but felt his irritation from behind her where he'd waited for the return of his hat. Of all the people to be paired up with, Gage was her last choice. Everything had seemed to go wrong since she'd entered the hangar this morning.

"All right then," Mac said. "Let's divide up and see what we can find. Does everyone have a weapon?" He answered their nods with a short one of his own. "Fire three shots with a full second between each shot if you get into trouble." He motioned with the paper that had the geocache coordinates on them. "Leroy, you and Nadia head south over that hill. Tern, since you're more mountain goat than human, you and Gage head north. By these coordinates, looks as though you might have some ice to navigate. Be careful. Robert and I will head west. I suggest we only give ourselves two hours. Find what you can in that time frame, then reconvene back here." He looked at each of them in turn. "Got it?"

"I need a minute." Tern grabbed Nadia's arm and dragged her toward their cabin. "What the hell was that all about?"

"What?" Nadia wrenched her arm free.

"Pairing me up with Gage? You know he's the last man I want to spend time with."

"Sweetie, it was the luck of the draw." Nadia continued ignoring Tern's scoff, "You need to find out what happened between the two of you anyway."

"Nope." Tern folded her arms over her chest as if that would help protect her heart. "If he couldn't tell me then, I don't want to hear it now."

"Yes, you do. It's been eating you up inside." Nadia cocked a hip. "Ever think that maybe this is fate?"

"Fate isn't this sick."

"Oh, I don't know. It paired me up with Lucky." A smile she tried to hide gave her away.

"As if that wasn't who you wanted to be with anyway."

She shrugged. "He's the most fun of the bunch. There's an unfair ratio of men to women, and since they've all had a taste of you, it's up to me to protect myself from being passed around," she said, tongue in cheek.

"You bitch."

Nadia laughed. "Come on, get over it, and let's have some fun. Think of the havoc you can cause Gage. Get back at him for his mistreatment of you."

"Right."

"Hey, you wouldn't mind if Lucky and I hooked up, would you?"

"Uh…" Did she care? There was a part of her that still cared deeply for Lucky, and she wasn't hiking down that trail again. But Nadia and Lucky? He'd break her heart. "Be careful, Nadia. He isn't the kind of man who sticks around."

"My favorite. Use 'em and abuse 'em." Nadia gave a sly smile. "Time for the games to begin."

Tern hopped onto a smooth boulder that had been tumbled and spat out by the glacier. The air coming off the ice chilled her to the bone every time she stopped to catch her breath. As long as she kept moving the cold didn't sink in.

The glacier nestled blue in a valley of black spruce with craggy outcropping. The crystal clearness of the lake lay below, topped by a sky so azure it was almost white. Not even a jet stream marred the translucent sky. It felt as though if she focused just enough, she'd be able to catch a glimpse into Heaven.

The only thing to ruin this moment was the man trailing behind her. Gage cocked the shotgun again.

"How many times do you need to check that thing? It isn't like the bullets are going to disappear."

"I don't like this."

"You could have stayed in camp."

"That's not what I meant. This whole set up. It doesn't feel right. Having no contact with the outside world concerns me. What if someone gets hurt? A week can be a long time to wait for help to arrive. *If* it arrives," he grumbled.

"Afraid of a little adventure?" Tern taunted. They'd only spoken a few words on the hike toward the glacier. Nothing that wasn't absolutely necessary.

"I'm not afraid."

She turned and gave him a long look. He'd been afraid of her.

"I'm not afraid of you either," he said, reading her expression correctly. It irked her that he could still do that.

"Riiight." Like he wouldn't have agreed to this 'little adventure' if he'd known she was going to be along. She dismissed him and started climbing again, her feet sliding to a hard stop when he grabbed her arm and swiveled her to face him.

"I am not afraid of you," he repeated through strong, white teeth.

She studied him, eyes bright green, flashing golden specks from within, his nostrils flaring. She moved in closer and laid her hand on his chest. His heart hammered under her palm, and he swallowed hard.

"You're so afraid of me you can't stand it," she whispered, slinking closer, until their bodies touched from breasts to thighs. His eyes smoldered over and his lips parted.

"Your very bones melt when I get close to you," she continued. "The blood runs hot in your veins, and you want to do wicked things with me. You're scared to death of what I can make you feel." She let that sink in before she stepped back.

His hand fell from her arm as though in defeat.

"Don't worry, Gage, you're safe from me. A man dumps me like you did and there isn't anything more that I want from him." She left him there, hoping his mouth gaped open as he salivated after her. She almost turned back to relish his expression, but knew she'd lose ground if she did. Instead, she consulted her GPS. The geocache had to be around here somewhere.

While the GPS coordinates got them close to the cache, it didn't put them on top of one. The excitement of the hunt replaced the twisted pleasure of messing with Gage.

Served the deadbeat right.

Six months she'd waited for him. And nothing. She was disappointed in herself that she still gave a damn. She should have been able to turn off her feelings like a faucet. But then she'd never been so deep before.

Tern mentally shook herself and concentrated on finding the cache. The light bouncing off the glacier hurt her eyes. So she reached into her front pocket—where she'd stored her sunglasses when they'd been in the darkness of the trees—and put them on. As she did, it cut the rays of the sun and allowed her to see the sharp corner of something square. As far as she knew, Mother Nature hadn't gotten around to perfecting the square.

She hiked up a few more feet and knelt down on the icy crust. The coldness melted into her jeans, but she didn't care. Someone had chipped a small cavity in the ice of the glacier and set a five gallon cooler into it. She dug around the edges and pulled the cooler free. She pivoted the handle, which acted as a lock, and opened the top.

Moose steaks, smoked salmon, many different kinds of cheeses, and a bottle of wine. Hot damn. Her mouth watered. Whoever was running this game was one smart cookie. Encasing the cooler in the ice of the glacier kept the food from spoiling and animals from sniffing it out. She liked the way he thought and couldn't wait to sink her teeth into one of the steaks.

"What did you find?" Gage's tall shadow fell over her.

"The mother lode." She shared a real smile with him this time. When he returned it and held out a hand to help her up, her traitorous heart flipped-flopped. "You're cooking tonight."

"It'd be my pleasure to feed you." He pulled her to her feet and kept pulling until she was pressed up against him. "And you're right. You scare the shit out of me." His hand came up and framed her face, the other anchored behind her back keeping her close. "But I scare you too."

Before she could utter a protest, his lips seared hers. Heat erupted between them and flushed her body with enough warmth to melt the glacier they stood balanced on.

Damn, she'd missed him. The way their bodies naturally curved together, the way her insides liquefied in readiness for him, and the way his body hardened to steel. She'd loved his body. Roped with muscle, strong and flexible, she'd loved lavishing attention on his body for hours. Her fingers itched to touch his skin again, feel his flesh hot against hers as he—

"I'm not the only one who wants to do wicked things," he murmured, his voice husky with arrogance. He nipped the skin below her ear, and licked the sting.

Her fingers curled into fists, and she pushed him. He slipped on the ice and fell on his ass at her feet.

She stood over him, enjoying the view. "The wicked things I want to do involve sharp implements." She brushed her hands over her clothes as though that would erase his touch. "I found the cache. *You* can carry it back to camp."

Trying to look as if she wasn't running away, Tern took her time and carefully watched her footing as she descended the ice. She could hear Gage cussing behind her as he struggled with the cooler and his slippery toehold on the glacier.

Serves him right for putting the moves on her after all this time. Like he had to disprove her earlier statements of fear. There was no way in hell she was afraid of him.

A shiver caught her by surprise.

ABOUT THE AUTHOR

Photo by: Kelli Ann Morgan

Tiffinie Helmer is an award-winning author who is always up for a gripping adventure. Raised in Alaska, she was dragged 'Outside' by her husband, but escapes the lower forty-eight to spend her summers commercial fishing on the Bering Sea.

A wife and mother of four, Tiffinie divides her time between enjoying her family, throwing her acclaimed pottery, and writing of flawed characters in unique and severe situations.

To learn more about Tiffinie and her books, please visit www.tiffiniehelmer.com

ALSO BY TIFFINIE HELMER

NOVELLAS

Bearing All (sequel to Edge)
Impact (prequel to Hooked)
Moosed Up (prequel to Shiver)
Dreamweaver (sequel to Death Cache)
Bait (sequel to Hooked)
Reel Trouble (sequel to Hooked)
Bushwhacked (sequel to Edge)
Fireweed (sequel to Bait)
Icebreaker
Mooseletoe

BUNDLE

Wild Men of Alaska
Wild Women of Alaska

ROMANCE ON THE EDGE NOVELS

Edge
Hooked
Shiver
Death Cache

THE WITCHES OF PORT TOWNSEND SERIES

Which Witch is Which?
Which Witch is Wicked?
Which Witch is Wild?